WELCO
DU

It is a struggle across the
ice caps.

It is a dark and myster
century London and a pub that transforms into Hell itself.

It is a journey through space and a strange asteroid
where giant insect monsters wait to attack.

It is the ninth and final level of the labyrinth . . . and a
final battle with the Masters of the Dungeon.

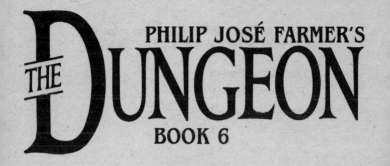

PHILIP JOSÉ FARMER'S
THE DUNGEON
BOOK 6

THE FINAL BATTLE

Richard A. Lupoff

SPECTRA

BANTAM BOOKS
NEW YORK · TORONTO · LONDON · SYDNEY · AUCKLAND

THE FINAL BATTLE
A Bantam Spectra Book / July 1990

Special thanks to Lou Aronica, Betsy Mitchell, Henry Morrison,
David M. Harris, and Alice Alfonsi.

Cover and interior art by Robert Gould.
Book and cover design by Alex Jay / Studio J.
THE DUNGEON is a trademark of Byron Preiss Visual Publications, Inc.

ISBN 0-553-28542-4

Published simultaneously in the United States and Canada

Bantam Books are published by Bantam Books, a division of Bantam
Doubleday Dell Publishing Group, Inc. Its trademark, consisting of the
words "Bantam Books" and the portrayal of a rooster, is Registered in
U.S. Patent and Trademark Office and in other countries. Marca Registrada.
Bantam Books, 666 Fifth Avenue, New York, New York 10103.

PRINTED IN THE UNITED STATES OF AMERICA

OPM   0 9 8 7 6 5 4 3 2 1

FOREWORD

Here at hand is a book which resembles, in many respects, the final book of the Bible, *The Revelation of Saint John the Divine*.

All things are explained; all loose threads are tied together. The mysteries and The Mystery are revealed. The trumpets of the angels announce the falling away of the veils, and we see who are the angels, who are the devils, who are the villains, and who are the heroes and heroines.

I won't disclose who wins this mighty battle. Read for yourself.

This is Volume VI: *The Final Battle* of *The Dungeon* series. It is the last of the epic that began with Volume I: *The Black Tower*. Both were written by Richard Lupoff. Volumes II-V were created by different writers. These were derived from the "spirit" of my own works, not as spinoffs from any one of my series or stands-by-itself stories.

I have been worrying—somewhat—about the immense task Richard Lupoff would have when he wrote this concluding volume. He gave it a magnificent start, started the ball rolling. No, that's not accurate. What he did was to start an avalanche. His first book was the explosion that caused the avalanche. Each succeeding book added to the mass sliding and rumbling down the mountain. And Lupoff had no idea how each writer would develop the plot and introduce new themes, twists, and characters which he did not have to explain.

It was like five weavers working on one tapestry, and four of them given only general directions about the pattern to be woven. When these had done their work, the first weaver became the last one. It was his goal to finish the pattern and to make sense of the work of the other four. He had to make a pattern which would, in a sense, magically reshape the other patterns so that the result was one self-consistent work.

On the whole, this goal was achieved.

Only a writer would know how much Lupoff had to sweat and strain and reach way down into his pocket of imagination and ingenuity to find explanations for things which he had not dreamed of when he wrote the initial volume.

He had to dive deep to bring up the pearl of great price.

You not only have this pearl at hand. You have a book (considering this volume as part of one six-volumed book) which is a sort of encyclopaedia—or compendium—of most of the traditional themes of science fiction and fantasy. In addition, there are new themes. But the traditional ones are recut to make novel facets.

Old or traditional themes, such as time travel, parallel worlds, alternate universes, shape-changing, and so on have never died out or become obsolete. They are being reworked and will always be reworked. Human ingenuity finds new uses or applications and new explanations for the traditional themes.

This set of six volumes (a sexology?) has all of them or almost all of them. In fact, if I had written the final volume, I might have slyly inserted a Magical Kitchen Sink. Or a Chirality or Superstring Kitchen Sink in order to make it scientific-sounding.

Doing this is one of my weaknesses. I can't help it if I am sometimes facetious.

One of the inventions I admire in this series is Esmond the Unborn. There may be a literary precedent for Esmond, but I don't know of it; although there is a reference to an Uni the Unborn in a genealogy in the Icelandic saga, *The Story of Burnt Njal*. But this is just a name with no explanation about the epithet. (How would you like to go through life with this name?) I doubt if this was the source for the character of Esmond.

You have here a work the range of which exceeds that of the poet John Milton (1608–1674). His great epic works were about Heaven and Hell and the conflict between good and evil. These were *Paradise Lost* and *Paradise Regained*. This series, *The Dungeon*, not only covers the above subjects and locales, it goes beyond them into other dimensions.

The language, of course, is not Miltonic. If it were, you probably wouldn't be reading this series. (My apologies to those who would read both.) But its scope certainly is Miltonic, and it, too, is about the battle between good and evil. The good guys, however, reflect reality. They have certain touches of evil; they're not perfect. But the hero, for instance, while battling Nature and hostile beings and forces, is also battling inside himself to overcome his prejudices and irrational attitudes.

In this respect, Clive Folliot is human, unlike Milton's Satan. Being a fallen angel, Satan has no self-doubts or any consciousness of being wrong. His only doubts are whether or not he is going to win the battle against Heaven. Our hero, Folliot, has his doubts about winning over the forces of evil, of, in a real sense, the hosts of Hell. But, since this is a science fiction story, Hell is something different in origin and nature from Milton's Hell. And it does not spawn beings of the same origin, though their nature is the same.

In fact, without a program, you can't distinguish the angels from the devils. You have to wait for the final act.

But isn't this true of our own world, of the Earth we know? Haven't we mistaken angels for devils and vice versa? And, though people can't change their shapes in this real world, don't they do the equivalent? Put on different masks, play different roles, depending upon their environment and the people they deal with?

We're all shape-changers, if you define "shape" as "role" or as "behavior adaptation."

Another unexpected concept is the introduction of a character whom we thought existed only in fiction but who is portrayed here as existing in reality. I was surprised by this, though I suppose I should not have been. After all, I've done something like this in a similar fashion. And Lupoff, mindful that this series is in my "spirit," out-Farmered Farmer.

I won't reveal just who this character is, but it'll be familiar. Even those who haven't read about it will know it from the movies. I was delighted with its sudden entrance.

We have here a work which exemplifies the classical Quest story. It resonates with *The Odyssey*, the tale of Jason and the Golden Fleece, the search for the Holy Grail, the fairy tale of the little tailor, the saga of Sigurd, the slayer of the dragon Fafnir, of the great seductresses Lilith and Ayesha, of Castor and Pollux, of the journey underground by the hero, and, indeed, of the hero-cycle which Joseph Campbell and Robert Graves have depicted.

That is all to the good because it plucks at the strings of our unconscious mind, that part of the collective unconscious which contains these primal stories. But the music brought forth from the plucking has notes which would be strange to the ears of the ancients. They knew nothing of time travel, of voyages to the distant stars, of the fearfully destructive weapons in this story, of other dimensions, of computers, of superstrings.

They did know about shape-changing. This concept must have been popular among the Old Stone Age people long before literature was invented. In fact, it was universal among the preliterates encountered in modern times. Such stories must have existed since humans began to speak.

I also suppose you could say that the concept of other dimensions was foreshadowed in the ideas of Heaven and Hell, of the underground afterlives of the ancient Egyptian and Greek religions, of the Tir na nOg, the other world of Irish myth. But these did not have a scientific or pseudo-scientific rationale. They belonged strictly to the supernatural.

The hero, Clive Folliot, is a man of whom I approve as a Ulysses or Parzival. He starts off with a quest for his lost brother and ends up being something he had not dreamed of when he began his long painful search. In fact, he could not have imagined such a quest because he did not know, could not have known, that such things could exist. Nor had he ever read about them in the wildest novel that had ever come his way.

Wildness of imagination is, I believe, one of my traits. The book at hand, the entire series, certainly reflects that aspect of my character and so displays the "spirit" of my writings.

Herein is a wild book in the best sense of the word. Like all wild things, its actions cannot be predicted. It is full of wonders and surprises.

Philip José Farmer

· CHAPTER 1 ·
The Ninth Level

For a moment he was too dazzled by whiteness to notice anything else. Not the cold, not the wind, not the clouds that swirled and dived overhead like living things. All of these he would notice—but not yet.

Clive Folliot clasped his hands to his eyes.

It was as if he had been struck by a solid mass of light, a pure essence of undifferentiated color so overwhelming that it forced its way past the irises of his eyes and filled his whole skull. His brain reeled before the dazzling onslaught. He grew dizzy, felt himself stagger, folded onto his knees.

Instinctively, he dropped one hand, resting his knuckles on the hard surface to give himself a sense of balance, to assure himself that he would not fall prone. If he permitted himself to do that, he feared, he might slide, tumble, roll into nothingness.

His sense of direction had been snatched away from him.

He had no inkling of east or west, of up or down. He felt as if he might plunge into the earth itself, or into the sky.

He forced the fingers of his other hand apart. Between them the whiteness still smote at him, but he was able now to control it somewhat. And his eyes were adjusting. Recovered from the initial shock of unbearable lightness, they were beginning to provide him with a fuzzy image of the world into which he had fallen.

Whiteness in all directions. Whiteness above and below. And now he began to notice other things. Now he noticed the cold, and now he noticed the wind that stung his cheeks and hands, and now he threw back his head and squinted at the sky above him. Shards and fragments of cloud still swirled overhead, chasing one another like ferocious beasts in cannibalistic pursuit.

Was this the ninth level of the Dungeon? A wilderness of windswept, frigid whiteness? His mind returned to his first entry into the Dungeon, that strange world (or series of worlds—he could never be certain even of that) where he had wandered for he knew not how long.

His first entry into the Dungeon had occurred in the Sudd, that mystery-laden swamp north of the Equatorian lake country where he had sought the answer to his brother Neville's disappearance. Neville, who had set out to find the headwater of the White Nile and vanished from the continent of Africa and the face of the Earth.

Traveling with Quartermaster Sergeant Horace Hamilton Smythe and the ancient and wizened Sidi Bombay, Clive had found himself tumbling through a rock like a great shining diamond with a heart of pulsing ruby, into a world of blackness and mystery. The Sudd had been a place of prostrating heat, and the Dungeon . . .

The first level of the Dungeon, the World of Q'oorna, had been a world of blackness. Black earth, black vegetation, black landscapes through which black rivers wound beneath eternally black skies. Overhead the enigmatic spiral of brilliant stars.

Clive had made his way through eight levels of the Dungeon, and now he found himself in what seemed to be the ninth. The ninth: this world of blinding whiteness and numbing cold.

The wind keened in his ears, but somehow through that keening he heard another sound, a sound like the buzzing of an engine. He was able to scan the sky, by this time, without recoiling in pain from the sheer burning brilliance of its whiteness. He turned slowly on his heel, scanning the sky until he caught a glint.

It came again.

He was able to identify it with the source of the buzzing.

And now he was able to see it as a black speck against the grayish whiteness. A speck that grew and took shape.

It resembled a cross, and for a moment he feared that he was going mad, was experiencing a religious hallucination, but then as it grew larger he was able to make out a tail structure, and a whirring disk at its front end that he knew was an aerial screw. A propeller, his great-great-granddaughter Annabelle had called it.

It was an aeroplane, its configuration and painted markings identifying it as the same Nakajima 97 in which Annie had escaped the Japanese encampment at New Kwajalein Atoll back on level— He couldn't even remember which level of the Dungeon they had been on when they had encountered the Imperial Japanese marine detachment.

The Nakajima waggled its wings.

Clive waved his hand in response.

The aeroplane dipped lower. He could see Annie in its cockpit, her hands on the Nakajima's controls. He waved both arms frantically. Annie raised one hand and returned the greeting. Clive could actually make out her features, see her smiling at him.

And then the Nakajima disappeared.

There was little or no sound—possibly the faintest of *pops* that was drowned out by the keening polar wind. There was a wink of colored light, a lurid purple that faded to lavender and then disappeared.

And the Nakajima was gone. There remained a small, glowing spot in the sky, as if a seaman's distress flare had burned and died. Then that was gone, and there was a tiny fluff of cloud that accelerated, and faded, and then was totally gone with the wind.

Clive blinked and rubbed his eyes. Had the aeroplane been there? He had thought at first that he was experiencing a religious hallucination. Clearly, that was not the case. But had this been a hallucination of another sort? Had his tortured mind and half-blinded eyes conjured up the illusion of the aeroplane?

Or had the Dungeon added still another puzzle—and potentially, still another horror—to its long roll-call of mysteries?

Through the whirling wind a softer sound seemed to whisper, then to grow louder. It was a metallic clicking, a mechanical, almost metronomic clattering.

Clive spun and saw something that looked like a child's spring-driven toy moving across the ice toward him. At first glance it appeared tiny, but as it approached him more closely he realized that it was neither tiny nor toy-like, but was in fact larger than he. The clicking sounds had come from the contact of its metallic feet with the surface of the ice.

"Clive Folliot! Being Clive Folliot!"

The voice was mechanical and uninflected, but Clive recognized it at once and felt his heart leap with joy. "Chang Guafe!"

"It pleases me to see you still functioning, Being Clive!"

"And it pleases me to see you as well, old friend. I feared that I was alone, stranded here on the ninth level of the Dungeon. Chang Guafe, did you see the aeroplane with Annie in it?"

"Is that where we are—the ninth level? No, Being Clive, I saw no aeroplane."

Clive turned slowly, surveying the unbroken vista of whitness. If only Chang Guafe had arrived minutes earlier, even seconds earlier, he could have verified Clive's sighting of the Nakajima. He might have been unable to prevent its subsequent disappearance, but at least he could have told Clive that he was not mad. "The ninth level," Clive muttered. "Where else could we be?"

Chang Guafe lifted his shoulders in a hideous parody of a shrug. When Clive had first encountered the alien cyborg, it had been able to change its shape almost at will, extruding new mechanical parts and reconfiguring its organic components to suit the needs of the moment. The Dungeonmasters, those enigmatic manipulators of the destinies of uncounted victims, had crippled Chang Guafe's ability. But perhaps Chang Guafe had overcome the handicap. A being of the immense will and intelligence of Chang Guafe might overcome almost anything. Almost anything. Almost, almost . . .

"A good question, Being Clive." Chang Guafe nodded his head, artificial sensors reflecting the whiteness. Although the sun was not clearly visible through the cloud cover, it could be seen as a glowing patch of brightness not far above the horizon. "We learned that the Dungeon is of nine levels, and we traveled together through eight of them. It would seem to follow, then, that we have reached the ninth and final level. Is it, then, a featureless wilderness of whiteness? That seems an unsuitable anticlimax to our long adventure."

"But if this is not the ninth level . . ." Clive swung one hand in a circle, taking in their white surroundings with the gesture. "If this is not the ninth level of the Dungeon," he resumed, "then what is it? Where can we be? Why were we brought here, and what can we do about it?"

A violent shiver ran through him, making him realize for the first time how very cold he was. He blew on his hands to warm them, then drew another breath and released it. The exhalation plumed away like a streamer of smoke. He wore only the clothes he had worn on the eighth level of the Dungeon—hardly an adequate costume for his present icy environment.

What ignominy, if he should die here, alone, of exposure to the cold. If he should die here of exposure after all the perils of the Dungeon, the battles with men and with monsters and at one point with the very demons of Hell . . .

But an idea struck him. "Chang, you are the possessor of senses varied and keen beyond the human. Do you think—"

"—that somewhere," Chang Guafe continued Clive's thought, "maybe even somewhere nearby, there is more to this world than featureless whiteness?"

"Exactly! Something, perhaps, hidden by the glare."

"Stand by, Being Clive. I will see what I can see!"

"Have you regained any of your ability to change yourself?"

Chang Guafe uttered a hideous grating sound. The portion of the alien that Clive thought was a mouth curved into what Clive thought was a smile. "You have seen Hell itself, Being Clive, and you know something of the torments of the damned. Compared to the pain of my recovery, my friend, the torments of the damned are the pleasures of a sprat's outing. But yes, Being Clive, I have overcome the affliction placed upon me. And I shall avenge every twinge of pain that my recovery cost! But for now—behold, my friend!"

Before Clive's eyes, Chang Guafe underwent an amazing transformation. He spread his mechanical limbs like a giant spider—like the alien Shriek, Clive realized with a pang of loss—and steadied himself on the ice. Like a telescope extending, Chang Guafe extended his neck up and up until it towered twice the height of a man and then some.

Strange devices were extruded from Chang Guafe's head, feathery filaments like the antennae of African moths, and glittering, multifaceted viewers like the astonishing eyes of a fly or a honeybee. Slowly Chang Guafe rotated his head, turning it in a manner that would have been impossible to any ordinary living creature but that seemed effortless and natural to this being who was as much machine as he was organism.

At last the head completed its rotation and came to a halt. The telescoping neck retracted until the strange configuration of organs and devices that passed for Chang Guafe's face was approximately level with Clive Folliot's eyes.

"You were right, Being Clive." Chang Guafe nodded solemnly. "Beneath our feet the ice extends far downward until it comes to water little warmer than itself. But yonder"—and he raised a limb, using a clawlike extrusion as if it were a pointing finger—"the ice rises as tall as a bungalow. It is as if an iceberg had been captured and held in place within this great ice floe. And within that iceberg—"

"Is what?" Clive could not contain his eagerness.

"I could not tell in detail, but my sensors indicate an irregularity of density."

Clive was crestfallen. "An irregularity of density, Chang Guafe. And what does that mean?" Clive clutched his fists in his armpits, trying to avoid frostbitten fingers. He stamped his feet to keep them from freezing. He could last a while longer here on the ice, but only a while. And then . . .

"I will put it another way," the cyborg grated mechanically. "If the iceberg were a solid block, there would be very little variation in its density. Instead, I detected great variation. It is my inference, then, that since this variation includes zones of greater density than ordinary frozen water, the iceberg contains objects, artifacts, or even creatures frozen within itself."

Chang Guafe drew his legs up beneath his body, raising his torso and head above the ice so that he glared down into Clive Folliot's haggard face.

"The iceberg also contains pockets of far lesser density than ordinary frozen water. Pockets of so little density, I infer that they actually contain air. They may be either caves or rooms."

Caves or rooms! The iceberg might contain a means of contact with humanity, with civilization. Perhaps with the Q'oornans or with the greater masters of the Dungeon, the Chaffri, the Ren, even the most powerful and mysterious of all, those beings known as the Gennine—said by some to be the actual creators of the Dungeon.

If not—well, at least it might provide temporary respite from the chill and the wind that swept the ice floe. It might provide a few more hours of survival for Clive Folliot, hours that he and Chang Guafe could apply to trying to figure out a means of escape from this terrible place. If Clive and Chang Guafe could survive their present chilling dilemma, they might make contact with Annabelle Leigh—Clive's great-great-granddaughter—and with Horace Hamilton Smythe, with Sidi Bombay, with whoever of their beleaguered party still survived.

But Annabelle Leigh had already made contact with them! The sun-glittering aeroplane that she had obtained from the Imperial Marines at New Kwajalein—what had happened to it? Where, now, were the Nakajima and Annie?

"Come along then, Chang Guafe! You point the way, and let's get us to that wonderful iceberg of yours!"

Chang Guafe settled down between twin rows of long, metallic limbs and clattered in a direction that coincided with that of the glowing blob of the sun.

Clive fell in beside the alien cyborg. The pace that the cyborg set was a rapid one, but Clive was able to keep up and was grateful for the exercise that warmed his limbs. He knew that the cold was sapping his reservoirs of strength, and that the same exercise that provided warmth simultaneously served to drive his reserves of energy toward exhaustion. But there was nothing to be gained by remaining behind and passively awaiting the end.

Rage at destiny! Fight to the end! Then, if death must come, he would at least have lived his life to the full, to the last breath of his lungs and the last beat of his heart.

Clive staggered and reached one hand to clutch at Chang Guafe. The cyborg had detected Clive's growing weakness and had offered once to carry him, but Clive had recognized in Chang Guafe's manner the fact that the alien, too, was growing weak. His power was immense, but so also were his needs for energy. And with neither food nor fuel, struggling across the face of this ice floe, both of them were approaching exhaustion.

"Being Clive," Chang Guafe said.

Clive clutched one of Chang Guafe's metal-sheathed limbs near the point where it met his body. He knew that the metal would be devastatingly cold, but his own hands were by now so numb that he was unable to feel it.

"Being Clive," Chang Guafe repeated. "Battle onward! Our goal is within reach!"

Clive raised a hand to shade his eyes. They were walking straight into the blobby sun. The bright, fuzzy circle had hardly moved in all the time they had walked toward it. It seemed neither to be rising nor setting, but merely to be waiting for them, a quarter of the way up the sky, perpetually at late afternoon or early morning, nor had Clive Folliot any way of telling which.

Could he use mental telegraphy to reach his friend George du Maurier or any of his other acquaintances in London, from his sweetheart Annabella Leighton to his editor, Maurice Carstairs of the *London Illustrated Recorder and Dispatch*? He lacked the mental energy and power of concentration needed even to make the attempt.

He could only struggle onward, placing one foot in front of the other, holding his hand against Chang Guafe's metal carapace for guidance, hoping to reach the iceberg. He blinked, and could not be certain whether he saw the sun and the sky and the ice that surrounded him and his alien companion. There was so much whiteness, so much cold and whiteness. Was he seeing it all, or had be become blinded by the glare, a victim of snow-blindness?

He held his free hand before his eyes and was able to distinguish his spread fingers as black silhouettes against the gray-white glare of the ice. At least he was not blind! At least, not yet!

"Courage, Being Clive!"

"You can say that, Chang Guafe! You're as much machine as—"

"This is not mere bravado," the cyborg interrupted. "Look ahead, Being Clive!"

Clive Folliot halted for a moment and raised his eyes from the ice beneath his feet. Towering above him, silhouetted a darker gray-white against the glaring gray-white of the sky, loomed the iceberg.

Together, Clive Folliot and Chang Guafe managed to cover the final few rods of their trek. Clive stood, staring up at the iceberg. From this distance, he could see that it was as tall as a small tenement. If only he could enter its confines and climb the stair to Annabella Leighton's cozy flat!

But that was out of the question.

With a new burst of energy he began edging sideways, circling the iceberg. Within it he could make out vague and shadowy forms.

"Here!" he heard himself shouting hoarsely. "Here, Chang Guafe! A doorway! A doorway! We are saved, Chang Guafe! It is a doorway!"

Without waiting for the alien to catch up to him, Clive staggered through the man-high opening in the iceberg. He found himself standing in a room-shaped vacuity within the ice. It appeared to be featureless, filled with a weirdly shifting gloom, the feeble light filtering in part through the opening through which Clive had entered and in part through the living ice itself.

As far as Clive Folliot could tell, there was nothing in the room save himself. No furnishing, no chair or table or couch, no stove—oh, what he would have given for the warmth of a merrily flaming oven or hearth!—nor closet nor bed nor any other furnishing or sign of habitation.

He circled the walls, peering as best he could into the shadowy world of the living ice until he came to . . . a figure that suggested the human form! He strode forward and pounded his fists on the ice, forgetting all his cold and fatigue, his mind filled suddenly with the excitement of his discovery.

"A man! A man! Come out! Tell us your story! Tell us—" He stopped. How far was it into the ice, to reach this man? And was he indeed alive?

He did not speak, he did not move. Had he been frozen into the ice when a ship was blown off course and its passengers and crew died on the polar cap? Worse yet, had he survived the shipwreck and then been trapped by some horrid happenstance, in the ice, and frozen there alive?

Clive shuddered, half from his own coldness, half from terror at the thought of what might have happened to this mute, anonymous, unmoving stranger who seemed to gaze unblinkingly at Clive from his place deep within the ice, even as Clive gawked at him.

From behind Clive came the clicking and scrabbling sounds that meant Chang Guafe had followed him into the opening.

"Chang Guafe," Clive grunted, "come and see this." He spoke the words without so much as turning away from the terrible sight that held him mesmerized. The longer he stood before the frozen figure, the more details could he make out.

The man—for he seemed clearly to be a man—loomed well above Clive's own height, and Clive was himself a person of goodly size. The frozen one's shoulders were broad, his head tall and hatless, but surmounted by a generous mane of black, unkempt hair. His face was of an unmatched pallor; whether due to a natural lack of pigment or to the cold, Clive could not tell.

The figure wore an outfit of matching jacket and trousers, tattered and threadbare and of a dull black material. His collarless and uncravated shirt was of the same color. So huge was the man that neither the sleeves of his coat nor the cuffs of his trousers reached their normal place, but rode high above wrist and ankle. His shoes were thick-soled and heavy.

"You have made a discovery, Being Folliot," Chang Guafe's voice grated.

"Indeed I have," Clive replied. "Indeed I have!"

"Have you a plan to propose?" the cyborg asked.

"Chang Guafe!" At last Clive turned so as to face the alien. "In all your repertoire of tools and organs, do you think you could find something that will permit us to free this fellow from the ice?"

"Free him?" Chang Guafe asked. He scuttered forward to stand close to the wall of ice, peering into it with an extruded sensor that looked for all the world like a sea-captain's telescope. "Free him?" Chang Guafe asked again. "How do you know he lives, Being Folliot? And if he does live, how do you know that he will do us good rather than ill?"

"I don't know that he lives. I merely suspect it. And as for doing us harm, how can our plight be made worse than it is? As things stand now, we shall both perish. If we free this prisoner, who knows what favors he may perform for us, out of sheer gratitude? I think, Chang Guafe, that this strange pale fellow is our last, best hope. But the way to find out whether he lives, and whether he is benevolent or malign, is to liberate him from his icy prison. The question, Chang Guafe, is, can you do it?"

Chang Guafe emitted the shuddering, grating sound that reminded Clive Folliot of a piece of chalk vibrating shrilly against a polished slate, that he knew passed with Chang Guafe for laughter. "Can I do it, Being Folliot? Of course I can do it!"

"Then in the name of all that is holy, Chang Guafe, do not stand there dithering!"

Clive stepped aside to give the alien better access to the wall of ice that contained the towering human figure. He watched in awe as the alien shifted and strained. He seemed not merely to be rearranging the metal parts that made up the mechanical portions of his body, but in some miniature machine shop contained within a cavity of his body to be fabricating the very parts and mechanisms that he would shortly call into play.

At last, Chang Guafe extended toward the wall an instrument that resembled a rotary saw blade.

The blade spun.

Chang Guafe pressed it against the ice.

An ear-splitting scream rent the air, a scream that came from no throat of human or beast or alien but from the living ice itself as the saw blade marked its path against the wall. Chang Guafe guided the blade first in a vertical path, cutting a line so straight and true that Clive Folliot was unable to distinguish it from the perfection of a plumb bob.

Extending one of his telescoping organs, Chang Guafe drew the line he had scored as high as the top of the frozen man's head, and then a bit higher, as if allowing for good measure. Then he rotated the blade so that it spun in a horizontal plane and continued to cut the ice until it was time to turn the blade once again and draw it downward toward the icy floor of the cave.

In due course Chang Guafe had carved from the living wall a gigantic ice cube in which the frozen form of the giant was embedded like a fly in amber. Chang Guafe hefted the cube out of its niche in the wall and laid it on the floor so that the giant's frozen eyes glared ceaselessly at the roof of the ice cave.

While Clive Folliot gazed in awe, Chang Guafe fabricated from his internal machine-shop a weblike metallic filament that he strung about the gigantic ice cube. There was a humming sound. The filament glowed first rose, then red, then white-orange.

With perceptible speed, the ice block began to melt.

Water dripped from the block of ice, puddling and then refreezing on the icy floor of the cave. Soon a cloud of steam formed around the block, obscuring the figure that lay within. But at the last moment before the immobile giant disappeared, Clive felt a bolt of psychic energy pass through his body.

He had caught the eye of the frozen man—or the frozen man's glance had caught Clive—and the glare of pure malice that passed from the giant to Folliot was the source of that psychic jolt.

· CHAPTER 2 ·
The Frozen Giant

"Stop, Chang Guafe! Stop!"

The cyborg revolved a telescoping eyestalk toward Clive. "Why should I stop, Being Clive? You yourself indicated that this being is our best hope of survival and escape from this place."

"I did, I know. But there's something about it—about him—that is chillingly familiar to me. I feel almost as though I have met this giant before."

"You would leave him, then, frozen here?"

"Yes!"

"But if that seals our own doom, Being Clive? If it means our own death?"

"There are worse things than death, Chang Guafe!"

"And you would abandon all our companions, Annabelle Leigh, Sidi Bombay, Shriek, Horace Hamilton Smythe? Your musical companion, Finnbogg? Your own brother, Neville?"

"They can fend for themselves. They have as great a chance at survival as we, Chang Guafe—or as poor a one! For all we know, they have made good their escape and are happily pursuing their lives at home. Or, for all we know, by now they are dead. In any case, Chang Guafe, I beseech you, stop what you are doing!"

The cyborg raised metal-covered shoulders in a shrug. "As you wish, Being Clive."

The glowing filament dulled to a cool metallic gray. Like an alien Izaak Walton reeling in his trout line, Chang Guafe drew the thread-thin filament back into his metal machinery.

The last of the steam swirling about the block of ice rose like a puff of fairy-smoke. There lay now revealed the form of the frozen giant, covered by a coating of ice little thicker than the glaze of ice left on the trees of a Staffordshire forest after a freezing February rain.

The ice disintegrated into a million glittering crystals and fell from the form it had so long imprisoned as the giant raised first one mighty arm, then the other, then pushed himself upright. For a moment the giant sat like a child on the floor of its playroom, his feet stetched before him, his palms pressed to the icy cave bottom.

Then with a mighty effort he heaved himself to his feet and stood with his head almost brushing the roof of the cave. He cast his glance down at Clive and at Chang Guafe.

"Too late," Chang Guafe grated in an undertone, "too late, Being Clive. Shall I attempt to recapture him?"

Clive shook his head. "We're in it now, Chang Guafe. It's sink or swim. Let's do our best to swim!"

Chang Guafe swiveled a compound eye at Clive Folliot. "Your expressions sometimes puzzle me, Being Clive, but this one I believe I comprehend. Yes, let us see if we can swim."

"Vile insects!" The giant's voice boomed out, sounding to Clive like the bass notes of the pipe organ in St. Paul's Cathedral. "What peace I had ever found, I found here in the quiet and solitude of this ice. And you have stolen from me even that pale solace. Vengeance shall I wreak upon you for the sins committed by your kind from the day of Creation! O, despicable insects! Miserable creatures that you are, not satisfied with the degradation you have visited upon yourselves and the victimization of Heaven's innocents, yet you have chosen to bring into being a new race of blameless things only that they may suffer and weep."

Clive Folliot stared into the giant's face, appalled as much by the chilling familiarity of the monster's speech as by the terrible content of his words.

"I recognize you, Monster! I know who you are!"

"You have the advantage of me in that regard, insect! But I need not know your identity. It suffices that I recognize you as a Man, the spawn of Adam. It was one of your kind who created me, who then spurned me as a god would look upon his own creation and reject it! It was you who created for me a mate and then destroyed her before my own horrified eyes! You, or one such as you, for to me, now, all Mankind is as one. One evil and poisonous to all that is innocent and good, all that ever prayed and hoped for a single moment of innocence and joy and companionship!"

The monster drew a shuddering breath, but before Clive could respond, it resumed its tirade.

"I will crush you beneath my foot as you would crush an ant beneath your own! I will—"

"Wait, Monster!"

The words were spoken in the grating, metallic voice of Chang Guafe. "What of me? I am not a human; my kind never built you. Do you plan to crush me, also? Do you think you can?"

Slowly the giant turned, casting his glare for the first time fully upon Chang Guafe. "You are the one who freed me from the ice, are you not?"

"I am, yes."

The monster stood, to Clive Folliot's eyes lost in contemplation. What heart pulsed in that gigantic breast, what brain worked within the monster's skull to comprehend this strangest of confrontations?

"You are not a Man, you strange thing."

"I am not."

Still the monster peered at Chang Guafe. "I have never before beheld such as you." He reached forward with a pale hand, the arm protruding far beyond the end of his ragged garment. "May I touch you, strange thing?"

How odd, Clive thought, that the monster asked permission of the cyborg before laying its clammy hand upon him!

"Touch me indeed," Chang Guafe grated.

The monster extended a death-white finger and touched Chang Guafe, first upon his metallic carapace, then upon a section of the living flesh that remained exposed.

"You are indeed peculiar. Are you even of this Creation?"

"Your meaning is not clear to me."

"I sense a strangeness in you," the monster replied. "A strangeness more total and profound than the strangeness of the octopus of the deep, the wolf of the northern wood, the flashing parrot of the tropical jungle, the python that falls upon its victim in the basin of the Amazon. I sense in you an alienness, strange thing, that leads me to the inference that you are not of this Earth."

"You are right, Monster. I am not of this Earth."

"There are other worlds, then, inhabited as this one?"

"More than you can count, Monster. More than you can imagine!"

"Then what do you here? And in the company of this Man, this most despicable of all God's creatures?"

"Clive Folliot is not so bad, Monster."

"He is a Man, and that is enough for me! I curse the day that God created Adam, and I curse each and every one of that first sinner's descendants!"

"They are not all so bad."

"You dare to make league with these foulers of the Earth?"

"I am not in partnership with all humankind. But I am in alliance with Clive Folliot and a few—just a few—of his fellows."

The monster swept his glare from Chang Guafe to Clive Folliot.

"I know you," Folliot asserted once more. "I have seen you upon the London stage—you, or an actor, at least, garbed and painted to resemble you."

The monster's face crinkled into a horrifying parody of a smile, and his booming voice gave out with a similarly dreadful version of laughter.

"I—upon the London stage? Am I a vaudevillean, a music-hall clown? Better should I declaim the lines of your Shakespeare. He, at least, was able to peer into the depths of the human heart and portray in his dramas the vices and the tragedies of your despicable breed."

"No, you were not an actor! It was the actors who portrayed you. Portrayed you in the dramatizations of the Widow Shelley's great novel."

The look upon the monster's face was not more sympathetic, but its expression shifted, at least, from one of cold malice to one of contemptuous bemusement. The monster looked at Clive as one would look at a bothersome mosquito in the moment before he crushed it out of existence.

"A novel? A literary romance devoted to me? A new *Robinson Crusoe?*"

"Yes."

"And the name of this fancy?"

"*Frankenstein, or The Modern Prometheus!*"

The monster's expression grew more pensive, its posture less threatening. "Frankenstein." Its voice fell in volume. Its tone was almost musing. "Henry Frankenstein was my creator."

"And your own name?"

"None gave me he. But I suppose he was my father, and as you, Folliot— You say that is your name?"

Clive assented.

"As you received your name from your father, so I am entitled to receive my father's name from him. The modern Prometheus? No, Man, the name is one that I reject. Instead I shall take the name of my maker, my father, and my enemy. I shall be known to the generations of your kind by this name. My name will be one spoken with shuddering and fear. His name and mine, one and the same, shall echo down the corridors of time until it becomes a synonym for terror and destruction."

He drew himself up to his full height, his black-haired head nearly brushing the ice cave's frozen roof.

"I name myself—*Frankenstein!*"

As if the words had been a command issued by and to himself, the monster strode forward. For a moment Clive thought that he was about to be crushed beneath the massive boots of the mighty being, but instead the monster strode past him, past the cyborg Chang Guafe, and, ducking his head to avoid striking it against the ice, clumped from the cave.

Clive and Chang Guafe looked at each other.

"What think you, Being Clive?"

"I don't know, Chang Guafe. He hates me so. Perhaps you should accompany him. But this much I do know. At the end of the Widow Shelley's novel, the monster was left drifting upon a polar ice floe. This is the creature we have freed. We thus know where we are: upon the Earth! Don't you see, Chang Guafe? I entered the Dungeon from the surface of the Earth, and to the surface of the Earth I have returned! How close am I, now, to finding my brother Neville? Such was my original goal, and in the Dungeon I found him, yes, only to lose him again. What mad universe is this, with its clones and simulacra and illusions, its replicants and its imposters? How can one be assured of any truth?" He shook his head despairingly. "And yet, if this be Earth indeed, perhaps I may find Neville again, once and for all time. After all my travail, I feel at last that I may yet achieve the goal upon which I first set my purpose."

He thought for a moment. "But you, Chang Guafe—you are not of this Earth, nor was your mission the same as mine. Perhaps you will choose another path."

"I will not abandon you, Being Clive."

"Thank you, my friend. Thank you." Clive Folliot felt tears stinging his eyes. He wiped them away before they could freeze. "But will the monster accept me?"

"He recognizes in me an essence as alien to humankind as is his own. He seemed to accept me. I think I can persuade him to accept you as well."

"I don't know."

"What is the alternative? Would you remain here until you perish of starvation or of sheer cold? If death is what you wish, Being Clive—that, either the monster or I could provide to you more quickly than the ice. You can be spared the suffering and despair of a slow death." Chang Guafe paused, then asked, "Is that your wish?"

With only the briefest of hesitations, Clive shook his head. "No, Chang Guafe. I have not come through all that I have—we have not endured all that we have together—to give up at this point. A voluntary death—whether at your hands or those of the monster, or in the slow, frigid embrace of the ice—would be abhorrent and cowardly. I must do my best, whether it brings me to triumph or defeat, life or death. I am an English gentleman and an officer of Her Majesty's Imperial Horse Guards. As long as I live and can struggle on, I will do so!"

Chang Guafe's head dipped and rose in his cyborg's

equivalent of an assenting nod. "Come, then, Being Clive. We will do our best together!"

Chang Guafe scuttered through the opening, onto the ice floe outside the cave. As the opening of the cave was too narrow to accommodate both of them at once, Clive permitted the cyborg to precede him.

He halted, then, for a final glimpse around the cave. How long had the monster stood frozen in ice? His mind raced, trying to recapture all it had ever known of Frankenstein's monster. Mrs. Shelley had written her famous romance and published it many years before Clive's birth. By the time he was a growing boy on his father's, Baron Tewkesbury's, rural estates, *Frankenstein, or The Modern Prometheus* was a world-famed tale, printed in countless editions in England and abroad and performed in mime, drama, and even musical form on stages round about the globe.

Both Clive and his elder twin, Neville, had read the book as children, had seen it in several performances on visits to London, and had even been introduced once to the great Mrs. Shelley. The twins were mere stripling lads of fifteen at the time, and she a dignified widow within two years of her death. But even in that single encounter, the young Clive had been struck by the haunted expression in Mrs. Shelley's eyes and the distracted manner of her conversation.

It was as if there were more to *Frankenstein* than fantasy, than the supposed ghost story concocted by the young Mary Wollstonecraft. She was not yet Mrs. Shelley when she wrote the tale, and in truth was little older than the Folliot lads at the time of their meeting in 1849. Could this girl of nineteen truly create the wild tale, or had she received her data from some other source?

Clive shook himself back to the present. He would discuss this with his friend du Maurier if he ever had the opportunity to do so. But for now, he must deal with the mortal potentialities of the real world as it now confronted him. He strode from the cave and stood facing the alien cyborg and the monster.

"We must get off this ice floe," he volunteered.

"How, Being Clive?"

"I think I have a plan. We can walk to the end of the ice—at least, we can attempt that."

"And then?"

"Build a boat, and sail to land."

The monster glared at Clive. "An excellent plan, insect. And of what materials shall we build that boat? Know you of a forest where we can fell trees for timber?"

"I'm afraid not. But I remember a lesson in natural philosophy that I learned at Cambridge. We can build a boat of ice."

"Ice!" Chang Guafe's metallic grate and the monster's booming bass echoed in unison.

"Yes, ice! You can produce a heating filament similar to the one you used to thaw the monster from his frozen tomb, Chang Guafe?"

"Yes, I can do that."

"We can use it to scoop out a concave shell, and launch it from the edge of this ice floe."

"And as we sail to warmer climes and our ice shell melts, Man?" the monster questioned. "What then? Do we swim the rest of the way?"

"I'll admit that there's an element of risk," Clive conceded. "But there's a good chance that we'll drift to some northern island, or even to the mainland or Europe or Asia or the New World. Or we may encounter a sailing ship on the high seas. It's true that we'll be gambling our lives. But not to gamble them means to remain here and die."

"I was frozen here before. I can survive again," the monster boomed.

"Then that is your choice."

There was a pregnant pause. Then the monster said, "No, Folliot. I shall accompany you."

Clive nodded.

"I perceive upon your countenance an expression of skepticism," the monster resumed. "You wonder why I should accompany you, puny human bug, and your peculiar companion. But I tell you this: Even in extremis, when I sought oblivion in the eternal cold and silence of this distant realm, I was not left unmolested by Man. Man—the scourge of Creation! Man it was who created me, and lived to regret that deed—and Man it was who disturbed my rest. Thus do I vow by the very God in whose name your foul species has committed enormities uncounted from the dawn of your so-called civilization to this very cursed day, that Man shall regret once more the deed of awakening me from my frigid slumber."

The sky was no longer its featureless gray-white, nor the sea its unvarying green-black.

They had reached the edge of the ice floe after a march the length of which Clive Folliot could hardly estimate. Weak as he was, wracked by hunger and exposure to the elements, he felt that he could have lasted only a matter of hours, traveled at most a mile or two. But beneath the arctic sky, it seemed to him that he had trekked over an infinity of ice, counted an eternity of hours. He had no way of measuring the miles that they covered, and even his estimate of elapsed time was based on periods of activity and rest, waking and sleep. He was not sure what body of water they had reached, assuming that it was the Arctic Ocean. They might reach the northernmost edge of the great Eurasian land mass, or that of North America, or they might drift into the Atlantic, out of sight of land, and to their doom.

The sun seemed to describe a wobbling course around the horizon, neither rising to the zenith nor falling below the rim of distant ice fields, but instead maintaining a perpetual twilight, now marginally brighter, now almost imperceptibly dimmer, but never giving them the brightness of full daylight nor the full darkness of nightfall.

When they approached the edge, Clive could hear the gentle lapping of water against the ice. His stomach had shrunk by now from lack of food. Clean water was readily available—Chang Guafe was able to melt the ice to provide drinking water for any of the three of them. But there was no food.

Clive did not know the nourishment requirements of the metal-clad cyborg that scuttered and clicked over the face of the ice, nor those of the black-clad monster that plodded tirelessly beside the human and the cyborg. He did know that he was himself growing weaker by the day. How long he could survive on clear water was problematic.

But when they reached the edge of the ice floe and saw the green-black sea spreading unbroken to the horizon, Clive was filled with a mixture of joy and dread unmatched in his long days in the Dungeon. Was he merely exchanging one death for another? Was it going to be a contest between starvation and drowning instead of death from exposure on the ice floe?

He could not permit himself to dwell upon this. Action, movement, that was what he needed. For well or for ill, he would meet his fate struggling to the last. Surrender was not an acceptable option.

They managed to construct their boat of ice as Clive had suggested. The monster stood morosely watching and listening as Clive and Chang Guafe discussed their plans. Chang Guafe was an ideal mechanician, having not only the skills requisite to the task but a complete set of tools either built into his body or subject to his own fabrication.

Clive had not formally studied marine architecture, but he had sailed small craft as a boy and traveled on both sailing ships and the new steamers as a man, and together the two of them were able to plan an ice shell capable of bearing the three companions and surviving on the northern sea.

With Clive's plans scratched onto the smooth surface of the ice, Chang Guafe carved out the rough body of their boat, then melted and cut at the ice until the boat was completed. Chang Guafe was even able to create a sail of a thin sheet of ice, and to manufacture oars for them to use should the sail melt away. He attached a rudder at the rear of the boat and pronounced it ready.

Clive christened the boat *Victoria* in honor of the monarch he hoped still to serve. They climbed in and shoved their cockleshell away from the ice.

Even now, Chang Guafe's amazing toolshop came into play. At Clive's urging, the cyborg found that he could manufacture a crude compass. "I can sense the planet's lines of magnetic force," Chang Guafe protested, "there is no need for this toy."

But Clive had pleaded. "It isn't that I mistrust you,

Chang Guafe. But I will feel more confident if I can look at a compass and tell for myself the direction of our movement."

"As you wish, Being Clive." They set a curving course, sailing in an ever-expanding spiral southeast from their point of departure.

A course due south might have brought them to land sooner than this spiral, but it might also have sailed them to their doom. By sailing in their spiral course they inferred that they would sooner or later reach the northerly coast of a continent.

Sooner or later, Clive thought to himself. *Well, it had better be sooner than later, or our dead bodies will wash ashore rather than our boat making land!*

He knew they were making good progress, for now the sun did dip beneath the horizon, giving them periods of true night, and it did rise well into the sky to give them periods of true daylight. They took watches, turn and turn-about, keeping *Victoria* on her compass course.

Chang Guafe spun a lengthy filament and crafted a fishing lure, sending the line overboard to troll behind *Victoria.* If they could catch fish they could all obtain nourishment from it, consuming its cold raw flesh in the fashion of the exotic Japanese.

The thought of the Japanese sent Clive's mind spanning the time to their arrival in the Dungeon, and his encounter, along with his early companions, with a Japanese Imperial Marine detachment. He and Horace had already been joined by the doglike Finnbogg and by young Annabelle Leigh, and Annabelle had been captured briefly by the Japanese.

She had made good her escape in a flying machine brought to Q'oorna by the same aliens who had abducted the marines, snatching them from an island redoubt in the Pacific Ocean in the midst of a war nearly a century in Clive Folliot's future.

And Clive had seen her, had seen Annabelle, flashing her wings above the polar ice cap.

Or had he? He had seen the Nakajima 97, and had assumed that Annabelle was piloting the aeroplane. But was the pilot Annie? Or had she been taken prisoner again, either by the Imperial Marines or by someone other, who in turn had commandeered the aeroplane? And what had happened to the flying machine when it disappeared above the ice cap?

Clive and Annie, Chang Guafe and Finnbogg, Horace Hamilton Smythe and Sidi Bombay . . . the adventures they had shared, the perils and the triumphs! *And now,* he wondered, *now what was to be their fate? Dear God!* He stole a covert glance at Chang Guafe, and at the stolid, pallid form of the Frankenstein monster.

What was to be their fate?

· CHAPTER 3 ·
"Your Eyes Will Remain Open!"

Clive was awakened by the weight of a massive, corpse-gray hand shaking him by the shoulder.

He blinked into the red, hating eyes of Frankenstein's monster. Although the hideous creation had claimed his maker's name as his own, Clive refused to think of him as Frankenstein. That was the name of a natural philosopher or scientist, a man of noble instincts and lofty aspirations.

According to the Widow Shelley's narrative, Frankenstein had achieved more through his experiments than he had bargained for. Unable to cope with his own creation, he had fallen prey to fear and craven impulse, to the weakness that besets any man, however well intentioned. Frankenstein had been a weak man, perhaps, but not an evil one. His name ought not to be a synonym for horror and destruction.

To Clive, the creature was now and would always be simply the monster.

"Folliot, you are dying," the monster's bass tones rumbled.

"I am not," Clive managed. "I am merely hungry and cold."

They had caught a single fish on the end of Chang Guafe's line. That was, what—two days ago? Three? It had been a small fish, and its flesh had furnished precious little nourishment for Folliot and Chang Guafe and Frankenstein's monster. Chang Guafe had divided the fish, scrupulously doling out the precious food to the others. They had wolfed down the cold flesh, and Clive decided after the fact that though the meager meal had given him a little more strength with which to survive, it had done still more to whip up his flagging appetite and increase the pangs of his hunger.

Their need for water was more easily tended to. Chang Guafe had indicated that he thought he could distill the choppy brine into potable water, but rather than risk that, the companions had loaded blocks of ice into their boat before leaving the floe. Now, when thirst demanded, Chang Guafe could carve off small slivers for the three of them. The slivers of ice, melting slowly in their mouths, slaked the thirst of all three.

"You are dying," the monster intoned over Clive Folliot. "I care but little should you perish, insect. But Chang Guafe values your continued existence. This, for some reason inexplicable to me. And so for his sake I will try to keep you alive."

"I am not dying," Clive repeated angrily. He pushed himself upright and realized, with horror, that the monster had been right. It would be all too easy to permit himself to lapse into a cold- and hunger-induced trance, and to slip thence gently from life into death, hardly taking notice of the transition himself.

The monster seized him by both shoulders and shook him. "Do not die, Folliot!" it roared. It drew back a massive, death-pale hand and slammed it, open-palmed, across Clive's cheek. The blow set his head to ringing. The humiliation of being so treated by this subhuman creation brought the blood flaming into his cheeks.

"Put me down!" he commanded.

"You may sit, but your eyes will remain open and you will move frequently, insect. Or I will give you a thrashing to make that slap seem like a lover's caress." A sneer spread over the monster's face and he released Clive.

Clive collapsed onto the bottom of the boat. He drew himself up to one of the seats that spanned its narrow width and rubbed his cheeks with both hands. A brisk breeze was shoving the boat along, pressing on its sail of ice sheeting. Chang Guafe sat in the stern, one eye fixed on the crude compass he had fabricated, guiding *Victoria* by her rudder of ice.

It had seemed like a good idea. For a time, Clive had

halfway expected them to make land within a few hours of setting sail . . . or if not within a matter of hours, then surely within the first day or two.

But they sailed on, and on, and only dark water stretched in every direction.

Clive fixed his eyes on a point at the distant horizon, a point that seemed to bob up and down before the stationary boat, even though he realized that it was the boat's own bobbing that created the illusion of the moving horizon.

He used that point at the horizon as a focus for his own consciousness, and attempted to place himself in a mental state to communicate with his friend George du Maurier, safely working away as cartoonist and critic for *Punch* magazine in London. He had tried innumerable times since entering the Dungeon to establish mental communication with du Maurier. It was amusing in an ironic fashion that back in London, du Maurier had expressed his belief in the possibility of life on other worlds, direct communication and the establishment of invisible mental bonds by sheer force of will, and other such mystical stuff.

Clive Folliot, by contrast, had scoffed at du Maurier's theories. Sensible materialist that Folliot had been, his experiences of recent times had convinced him that there were worlds within worlds, realities beyond realities, and that the skeptic spoke at his own peril when he scoffed at even the most exotic of beliefs.

Several times he had felt that he was indeed in mental communication with du Maurier—or at least that he was on the verge of establishing such contact. If only he could reach the cartoonist, he could ask du Maurier to pass word to Clive's editor, Maurice Carstairs of the *Illustrated Recorder and Dispatch:* his sweetheart, Miss Annabella Leighton of Plantagenet Court, London; his father, Baron Tewkesbury; his commanding officer, Brigadier Leicester of Her Majesty's Imperial Horse Guards.

At the very least, he might offer them some solace, the knowledge that as yet, at least, he had survived, and might someday, by some means, manage to return to England. And perhaps, just perhaps, they might mount an expedition into the Dungeon to rescue him and his descendant Miss Annabelle Leigh from their predicament.

"Oh, du Maurier," he whispered half-aloud, "my friend, can you hear me? Is there any hope, any connection, any link between us other than in my recollection of you?"

He felt hot tears welling in his eyes, and wiped at them with a hand now white with cold and near frostbite, cracked and peeling with exposure.

Is that you, Folliot?

He started and looked in all directions. Chang Guafe attended impassively to the management of their boat while the black-clad monster glared from his red-rimmed eyes. There was no sign of a speaker.

Du Maurier?

Yes! Clive Folliot, it is I! Where are you? How have you reached me?

I am adrift in the Polar Sea, accompanied by two such as you would never believe!

And you have reached me without physical or mechanical assistance?

By application of my mind alone, du Maurier.

In Clive's mind there was a ghostly suggestion of a laugh.

You were right all along, du Maurier. But, to reach you at last after so many years, so many attempts—

This is not the first time you have reached me, Folliot. Are you unaware of your former successes?

I thought we were close, Folliot. Many times, it seemed that we were close. I could sense your presence, sense the energy of your mind striving to reach my own. I tried each time to respond. Did I succeed? Did you feel the touch of my mind in your own?

More than that, my friend, du Maurier continued. *You have sketched the many sights and the strange beings you have encountered on your adventures, and those pictures have reached me here in London.*

But—I never sent you sketch-paper, du Maurier. How could my pictures reach you?

As mental images, Folliot. Perhaps because I have my-self worked as a sketch artist, I was attuned to your drawings. I have received no words from you. And for all that I tried to send messages back, I had no indication of success.

No. No, my dear friend, I never knew whether I had reached you or not. At times I had vague feelings, undefined inklings of companionship. But I never knew. I could only hope. Only faith in you sustained me, du Maurier.

Faith. How amazing to hear you speak so, my friend. Faith can move mountains, Folliot, can it not?

Clive paused to collect his thoughts, yet striving to maintain the link that had been established between himself and du Maurier.

Du Maurier's silent voice resumed. *What a comfort to me, after all these years, Folliot, to know this. What a comfort it is to a dying man.*

Dying? The word hit Clive like a thunderbolt.

Dying peacefully, Folliot. I am an old man, and I lie now on my deathbed. I wonder if that helped to establish our bond. As my mind prepares to separate itself forever from my flesh, it is able to rove the dimensions and connect itself to yours. Or perhaps it is the work of Dr. Mesmer that had succeeded. I must summon her to my side while still I breathe.

I don't understand, du Maurier. You are not an old man. When I left London—do you remember that last night at your club, du Maurier, after the premiere performance of Cox and Box *—how you entertained Miss Leighton and myself, our encounter with Carstairs of the* Recorder and Dispatch?

Very well, Folliot. Indeed do I remember that night very, very well.

But you were a man of but middle years, du Maurier.

I was fifty.

And that was some months ago. Why do you call yourself old?

Months ago? Months! Again the laughter rang in out perfect silence. *That was 1868, Folliot.*

Yes.

This is 1896. You have been gone for twenty-eight years.

The monster's clammy hand held Clive by the throat; his other hand held him by one leg. Clive felt himself lifted in the air. Before his eyes there was a swirl of darkness, a blur of the creature's death-white face and dead-black garments, of points of starlight glimmering on the polished metal that covered much of Chang Guafe.

"Stop! What are you doing?"

Clive was suspended over black water. Chill air swept his body, his inadequate costume providing little protection from the cold. A thin spray of frigid brine splashed his skin.

"You live, insect?"

The monster threw him into the air as a playful parent would toss a merrily squealing babe. To Clive the sensation was terrifying, and when the monster caught him again he clutched at the thick black cloth of his sleeve.

"I live, I live! Put me in the boat again!"

"I warned you, despicable creature." The monster's eyes glared with hatred, the little light that reflected from them coming from the stars that dotted the black sky above.

"You warned me to live, and I am alive!"

The monster threw him contemptuously back onto his seat. "What say you, Chang Guafe?" He turned his mighty frame to face the impassive cyborg. "Did this bug give any sign of life?"

The cyborg's mechanical voice grated, "No, Frankenstein. He looked as dead as anything I've ever seen. Deader than you," Chang Guafe added sardonically.

The monster laughed, a horrible, nerve-twitching sound.

"You are fools, both of you," Clive accused. "I was in communication with George du Maurier. He is my friend, and he is in England, and I had managed to establish a mental link with him."

"Looked dead to me," the monster grumbled.

"He might have sent an expedition to help us."

Chang Guafe raised his metal-capped countenance in interest. "Sent an expedition from where?"

"England!"

"To where?"

"To find us here upon the ocean."

"You are certain we are no longer in the Dungeon?" Chang Guafe prompted. "Does he know how to reach the Dungeon?"

"I don't know. Perhaps via the Sudd."

"And this expedition, do you expect it to trace your path through the nine levels of the Dungeon and come to your rescue?"

"I told you before that I am convinced we have returned to the Earth. I am thoroughly convinced of this," Clive asserted. "I thought you had accepted my reasoning."

"Tell me once again, Being Clive. You claim that you have spoken with your mind, to the mind of your friend?"

"Yes."

"If this is true, I suppose anything may be true. Still, Being Folliot, upon what evidence do you base the belief that we are upon the Earth?"

"Upon this evidence!" He rose from his place and pointed his finger at the monster. In the faint light of distant stars, he could see his own pale flesh and the paler flesh of the monster. "I realize now that Mrs. Shelley's tale was no mere romance, no fantasy. It was absolute truth, done up in trappings of fiction to make it acceptable to a skeptical world that would otherwise have recoiled in horror from the facts laid before its collective eyes."

"And so?"

"At the end of Mrs. Shelley's tale, the monster—*this* monster!—is seen pursuing his creator across the ice floes of the arctic region. What became of that tortured soul, that fantastic experimenter, we do not know. Perhaps we will find out, perhaps the answer will remain a mystery forever. That is to be seen."

He whirled and pointed once again. "But the monster remained in that polar realm, trapped and frozen in the very ice that caps our globe. There it was that we found him. Ergo, we are not in the ninth level of the Dungeon, but have been returned in some manner to the Earth."

He paused for the beat of a heart. "Or else, we may be led to conclude that the Earth itself is the ninth level of the Dungeon!"

Chang Guafe extended one telescoping, metallic eye-stalk toward the monster, another toward Clive. "Well, Frankenstein—what do you think? What became of your maker? And what do you know of the Dungeon and its contending would-be masters?"

The monster did not answer. Perhaps it would have,

Clive thought, but a whirring, sizzling sound interrupted the conversation and drew the attention of the three upward.

There Clive saw once again a sight that he had first seen on Earth, in the sky above the coast of eastern Africa. On that occasion he had been en route from the island of Zanzibar to the mainland of the mysterious continent, in search of his missing elder twin, ignorant of the very existence of the Dungeon, the black world known as Q'oorna, the levels and layers of reality that lay hidden behind the veil of the Sudd.

Many times he had seen the sign: in the skies above Earth and Q'oorna, on the midnight-blue grip of Horace Hamilton Smythe's silver revolver, in the architecture of vaulting, ancient cities on worlds whose very existence he would never have imagined. And every time he saw that sign, it had foretold terrible events.

Now he saw it above Earth's black arctic sea.

The swirling, hypnotic spiral of stars.

And, as if coming from that spiral of stars, this peculiar, buzzing sound, remindful of a child's Guy Fawkes Day firework. Or, more sinisterly, like the sizzling, sputtering combustion of a fuse, or a powder trail that might lead to a barrel of black powder ready to explode and blow everything within range of its blast to kingdom come!

Clive stood transfixed, vaguely aware of his two inhuman companions doing the same, staring upward, attempting to locate the source of the sizzling sound.

The spiraling stars surrounded a patch of blackness far more profound than that of the ordinary polar sky that surrounded the spiral. And from the center of that blackness there now appeared the tiniest and faintest of embers, an ember that brightened and grew until it became apparent that it was itself a nearly circular figure of light.

The light grew and brightened until Clive realized that the change in its size and brightness was an illusion. It was not growing—it merely *appeared* to be growing.

It was approaching!

It was descending toward their boat!

It was speeding in a downward spiral, like a long railroad train making its way down the long course of a track that wound from the peak of a conical mountain to its base.

Downward the train moved, sizzling and flaring as it advanced.

"I've seen that before! I've seen it in the Dungeon! Chang Guafe, I cannot recall—had you yet joined our party when we encountered that train?"

"I have never seen its like," the cyborg grated.

"It is a railroad unlike any other, Chang Guafe—a railroad that travels between worlds, that picks up passengers from every locus of time and space, that moves between ordinary worlds and the Dungeon!"

"I have seen railroads," the monster boomed.

"But not such as this one!" Clive rejoined. His excitement was unbounded. If they could board this train, there was no telling where they might travel—to other levels of the Dungeon, to ancient Rome or Greece or Egypt, to far Cathay where Horace Hamilton Smythe had once traveled—perhaps to the world of the Finnboggi or even the planet where Chang Guafe had first come into being.

"Here!" Clive shouted. He seized an ice oar and waved it around his head, wishing that he had a flag of bright cloth, or better yet a flaming brand with which to attract the attention of the train and its crew.

But there was no need for that. The train continued to spiral downward, downward, circling all the time over the heads of the three oddly assorted companions.

When the bellies of the cars were a few yards above the surface of the black ocean, the very waters of the Arctic bubbled and steamed, sending clouds of vapor up into the night air to greet the circling cars.

Finally the train settled onto the face of the sea. The heat of its passage through Earth's atmosphere was transferred to the water itself, boiling away unmeasured thousands of gallons and heating the region within the circle of cars so that the ice boat Chang Guafe had carved from the arctic floe, already perilously thin and porous from its days and nights afloat, disintegrated into a hopeless scattering of icy particles that quickly melted away and disappeared.

Clive Folliot began swimming toward the nearest car of the train. Behind him he could hear the monster's clumsy but powerful strokes as it emulated his action.

But the grating voice of Chang Guafe emitted a single, despairing cry followed by a hopeless gurgle.

Clive Folliot turned to see what had become of the alien cyborg, but there was only a final flash of metal as Chang Guafe slipped beneath the surface, followed by a concatenation of bubbles. The black waters closed calmly over the cyborg.

He couldn't swim, Clive thought. *He was built mainly of metal. He was so heavy that he couldn't swim!*

The sides of the train were lined with windows, and the windows were ablaze with lights from within the train. As Clive stroked his way through the once more cooling waters, he peered at the cars of the train. One, he saw, was filled with couches and chairs where comfortable travelers inhaled fumes from long-stemmed pipes. He had encountered users of fumes in the Dungeon, intelligent men and women—and nonhuman creatures—who had found peace and happiness in the smoke-induced realm of the dreamers.

Theirs was a pleasant enough existence, but it was not for Clive. He could not give himself to an existence of idleness, however comfortable. In England and in remote military posts, he had known men who had given themselves to drink, spending their days and nights in the companionship of fellow idlers, accomplishing little. The smoke-eaters of the dungeon were no better than these!

Clive had started his long odyssey in search of his brother. He had encountered others and his sense of responsibility had grown. He could not abandon Annabelle or Horace, Sidi Bombay or Finnbogg or Chang Guafe—for he could not believe that the cyborg was dead, either. Somewhere beneath him, buried by fathoms of icy water, Clive felt that Chang Guafe still lived. He would be heard from again!

And there were other characters here in the Dungeon about whom he was less certain. There was Tomàs, the Portuguese seaman. Annie herself claimed to have found evidence that Tomàs was a distant relative of the Folliots. There was the American Philo B. Goode, and there were Goode's two confederates, Amos Ransome and Lorena

Ransome, who claimed at various times to be brother and sister or husband and wife. There was Baron Samedi.

And there were Clive's brother, Neville, and their father, Baron Tewkesbury . . . or the simulacra of Clive's brother and father. Until he had resolved their true identities, he would never know whether he could leave the Dungeon once and for all, for if they were imposters they could remain in the Dungeon and rot forever, for all Clive cared. But if they were real . . . if they were real, he could not abandon them. No, no matter how cold and unloving Baron Tewkesbury had been to Clive, blaming him for the death of his beloved baroness, and no matter how arrogant and churlish the bullying Neville might have been in their childhood and might be even now, Clive could not abandon them to the endless Gehenna of the Dungeon!

He swam to the next car. The water that the train's energetic arrival had heated to near boiling temperatures was cooling as rapidly as it had warmed, and a killing cold was seeping into his bones. Clive knew that he could not remain in the water for much longer. A matter of minutes, at most, and he would sink to the sea-bed. And, unlike Chang Guafe, he knew that he could not survive there.

He could hear the monster yet, floundering in the water behind him. The creature was a far from skillful swimmer, but Clive was confident that he would safely reach the train and haul himself from the brine.

And as for Chang Guafe, there was nothing he could do now for the alien. If he knew Chang Guafe, he would find a way to survive at the bottom of the sea, make his way back eventually to land, and then go on about his business.

But as for now—

CHAPTER 4

No Roman Orgy

Clive hauled himself up, using the railing that descended along with a short metallic staircase from each car of the train. He peered behind him, over his shoulder, and saw that Frankenstein's monster had somehow turned in the water. He seemed to understand little of what he was doing. He paddled clumsily away.

Even as Clive watched, the monster reached a distant coach. The train had drawn itself into a circle, like the legendary serpent of the Scandinavians that swallowed its own tail. Whatever direction the swimming monster took, he would still return to the train. The monster raised a corpse-gray hand flounderingly from the water and managed to grasp the nearest railing. Using the overwhelming strength of his huge muscles, the monster hauled himself bodily from the sea and clung to the side of the coach.

He fumbled at the car, eventually found the handle that unlocked the door, and disappeared within.

Clive Folliot was prepared to do the same, but even as he set himself to the task he was nearly thrown from his feet, for the train had started to move.

It gained speed with breathtaking rapidity, plowing its circular course upon the face of the arctic sea. Then, with a sudden shift of direction, the engine-car of the train straightened its movement. The following cars were tugged into perfect alignment and the train accelerated wildly, throwing up spectacular walls of foaming, boiling spray that stood taller than an obelisk on either side of the train.

Then the front of the train lifted from the water, and the remainder of the coaches followed suit, tugged from the grip of the sea. The train tilted ever more precipitously upward, until Clive realized that he could not hold on to the railing longer than a few seconds more. He tugged at the coach door to open it, hauled himself into the car, and slammed the door behind him.

He turned to see what kind of world he had entered, and staggered with shock.

This was no Roman orgy nor Red Indian pow-wow, no Himalayan mountain peak nor Mississippi riverboat nor Turkish seraglio. Nor was it a world of exotic landscapes and alien habitants, for Clive knew now that the Earth was only one of a huge, perhaps infinite, number of habitable and inhabited planets.

The room was lined with dark panels, perhaps of dark-stained beechwood or even darker mahogany. The ceiling was a high one, almost lost in shadow, although he could tell that curlicues and pediments served as decoration. Tall windows reached from near the floor to very near the ceiling, but so little light penetrated them, thanks to the heavy drapes with which they were covered, that Clive could not tell whether it was daytime or night beyond the tightly sealed glass.

The room was lined with crammed bookcases. Near the shrouded window stood a massive desk of wood so dark it appeared black. The drawers were mounted with well-polished brasswork. The top of the desk was covered with sheets of paper, most of them written upon in a neat, careful hand, others bearing skillfully executed sketches. Several pens lay scattered on the documents.

The room's only illumination was provided by an oil-lamp, its wick turned low so that the golden flame cast tall, flickering shadows where it was not turned back, as by the metalwork on the heavy desk, in the form of fiery reflections.

Clive turned from the desk. Against the opposite wall, beneath a large dark canvas mounted in an ornate gilt frame, stood a huge four-poster bed. What a difference from the sleeping accommodations Clive had utilized since reaching the Dungeon: a skimpy cot, a pile of fetid rags, a leafy crotch high in a tree—wherever Fate placed him, and whenever opportunity presented itself for rest, there he rested. There had been a few comfortable beds, as well. Most he had occupied alone. Others . . . A memory of pale skin, emerald eyes, and exotic, green-tinted hair arose. Clive blinked the recollection away, his eyes stinging with sudden tears. He drew his awareness back to the present.

An elderly figure lay propped in the bed. Thin wisps of gray-white hair surmounted his nearly bald head. Mutton-chop whiskers of the same pale color marked his cheeks, which were themselves of a papery dryness and pallor. This apparation of death lifted a white-gowned arm and pointed a trembling finger at Clive.

"It is he!" The voice was weak and quavered, but the words were clear enough. The thin face turned to one side, and again the old man said, "It is he!"

Clive followed the direction of the oldster's glance. For the first time he became aware of the second figure in the room, a tall, slender woman shrouded in a gown of midnight blackness from neck to shoe. As Clive studied her he realized that her hair, although drawn severely into a bun behind her neck, was lengthy and rich and of a glossy black that shone in the dim lamplight like the brasswork on the desk. Her figure, although slim, was graceful and in other circumstances might even prove voluptuous.

Her dress, he realized, was not all of black, but was trimmed with panels of a purple that approached magenta in shade.

And her face— Seldom had he looked into so compelling, so exotic, and yet so human a face! Perhaps—and he cast his mind back over the innumerable females he had encountered on Earth and in the Dungeon—perhaps only the breathtakingly beautiful, exotic woman Nrrc'kth could be compared to this woman.

"Calm yourself, Mr. du Maurier. I see him. But—*who* is he?" Her voice was cool, smooth, with a contralto deepness that set something to vibrating at the very core of Clive's being.

"It is Clive Folliot—or his son, for he appears twenty years younger than Folliot ought to be!"

"I am Clive Folliot, yes sir. But you have the advantage of me, sir."

"I am your friend du Maurier. George du Maurier. You must know me, Folliot."

Clive took a few hesitant steps across the room. He half-expected freezing brine to drip from his soaked clothing, but he looked down at himself and realized that he was dry. And instead of the tattered rags he had last worn in Chang Guafe's jerry-built iceboat, he was outfitted in a proper uniform of Her Majesty's Fifth Imperial Horse Guards—crimson tunic, glittering brass accoutrements, dark blue trousers trimmed with cloth-of-gold, polished leather boots.

He peered into the old man's face. Yes, it was George du Maurier. But this was a George du Maurier ravaged by the passage of time, and possibly by other factors of which Clive Folliot knew little if anything. The George du Maurier whom Clive had last seen in London was a vigorous man of fifty, a cartoonist of accomplishment, a musician of at least semi-professional attainments, a student of the occult and the esoteric, and an aspiring novelist.

This creature, this sorry specimen that lay propped against pillows, swaddled and warmed like an infant—this could hardly be his friend du Maurier.

"What year did you say it was, du Maurier?"

"It is of our gracious monarch's happy reign the fifty-seventh year, and of Our Lord, the one thousand eight hundred ninety-sixth."

"1896!"

"Did I not tell you that?"

"When?"

"When last we spoke. You seemed to be sailing in a very strange boat, in the company of two even stranger companions."

"Yes," Clive acknowledged almost inaudibly. His head felt light. "Yes, I remember. But I thought it was a hallucination, a fantasy, a delirium."

"It was none of those, Folliot. It was real."

"And is this real?" His gesture encompassed the room and its occupants. "Is this woman real?"

"On my deathbed, my manners desert me, Folliot. Doctor, may I present Major Clive Folliot, of Her Majesty's Fifth Imperial Horse Guards, and one of my oldest and dearest friends. Folliot, may I present Madame Clarissa Mesmer, great-granddaughter of the famed Doctor Anton Mesmer. And a doctor in her own right, I may add."

"Major." She extended her ungloved hand.

"Madame Mesmer." Clive took the hand in his own and bowed over it. Her skin was soft and smooth, cool at the first instant of contact but revealing a warmth within moments that caused Clive to raise his eyes to her own. "Is it Madame, then? You are a married woman?"

She withdrew her hand. "I have taken the title to discourage gossips—and the unwelcome advances of aggressive males." Clive pulled a breath deep into his lungs. There was a detectable—and exciting—scent in the air around Madame Mesmer.

The woman resumed. "Mr. du Maurier has spoken of you often, Major. In fact, it might be said that I stand beside Mr. du Maurier's deathbed at Mr. du Maurier's own behest, but on your account."

She spoke with an indefinable accent. Clive tried to place it—German? Hungarian? He had heard of Anton Mesmer, and held him in low regard. Mesmer had been a German, studying and working for much of his life in Austria. But there were mysteries in his life, periods unknown to history. Where had he spent those years?

"Always the ladies' man, Folliot." The feeble du Maurier managed a papery laugh. "Cat got your tongue?"

"You both speak of deathbeds," Clive blurted. "Is there no hope for your recovery, du Maurier, nothing at all that can be done?"

The old man pushed himself higher against his pillows. Madame Mesmer reached for his age-raddled arm and assisted him. Du Maurier said, "The leeches have had at me, Folliot. I've enriched half of Harley Street by now, and the other half would come panting to my door if I permitted them, each to poke and prescribe and carry away my treasure, but I've had enough of their kind. Enough and more. I am dying, but I have no fear of death. No! Death is the last of life's great mysteries. Greater than finding the sources of the Nile, greater than exploring the center of the atom, greater even than traveling to Mars or Jupiter or the planets of another star. And I am eager to unravel this final mystery."

He lay back against his pillows, catching his breath, gathering his strength.

"I'd have been gone by now, Folliot, but I wanted to see you once more before I go. And Madame Mesmer has helped me to pass the final barrier to perfect psychic communication. Communication—and more—for are you not here, drawn across the leagues of space and the pages of time and the unfathomable twists of dimension? This is my triumph, Folliot!"

The old may lay back against his pillows, his eyes drooping shut, his nearly toothless jaw sagging.

"Is he—has he?" Clive leaned forward to peer beneath the bed-curtains.

"No. He lives yet." Madame Mesmer had laid her fingers on the old man's wrist, then nodded affirmatively as his pulse made itself clear to her. "He has yet some strength. The end is drawing upon him, but it is not yet imminent."

Clive looked around himself, found a chair, and drew it close to du Maurier's bed. To Madame Mesmer he said, "Will you . . . ?"

She shook her head and walked a short distance away. Clive seated himself. Madame Mesmer had remained sufficiently nearby to continue the conversation.

She looked at Clive, raising her eyebrows inquisitively. "You have really been drawn to this place from far away?"

"From the polar sea, Madame. And I seem to have got an attentive grooming and a complete change of costume into the bargain."

"An interesting epiphenomenon. But of significance—you say that you were drawn here from another year as well."

"I left London in 1868. I have been traveling—to Zanzibar, then to the African mainland at Equatoria, and from there to other places whose locale I cannot even describe."

"And you were gone for how long, Major Folliot?"

"Du Maurier claims, twenty-eight years."

"But you look very young to have been away so long."

"To me it seems a matter of . . . I cannot be certain,

but, I would think, some months. At the most, a very few years. Two or three years. Four at the most."

"Surely not twenty-eight."

"Surely not." -

Madame Mesmer clasped her hands in the small of her back and paced the room like a man. After a while she returned to du Maurier's bedside. She bent solicitously to study the man, then rose again. "He is asleep. His strength has a limit. But the end, although it is rushing upon him, is not here yet."

She turned to face Clive.

"I suppose you wonder at my role in this little drama, Major."

"Indeed!"

"You have heard of my illustrious ancestor, perhaps. The great Franz Anton Mesmer."

"I have heard of the great charlatan, Anton Mesmer. Forgive me, madame, for speaking bluntly. But I believe it more honorable to speak truthfully, even at the price of giving offense to one whom I would not wish to offend, than it would be to dissemble."

Color flared in her graceful cheeks, and the flame of the oil lamp seemed to flare briefly in its reflection. Her eyes were very dark. Perhaps, in the dim illumination of the sickroom, the irises had opened, creating a darker appearance than would normally have been the case.

"My ancestor, Major, was pilloried by the envious and the ignorant. But his theories of animal magnetism and his experiments in its control—in what has come to be known as *Mesmerism*—have never been disputed. Not once. On the contrary, experimenters on every continent have duplicated Anton Mesmer's work, and without exception their results have sustained his beliefs. The time will come when he is recognized as one of the truly great figures of human history!"

"I do not wish to quarrel, Madame. Perhaps you will kindly come to your point."

"My point, Major, is that the discrepancy in time as experienced by Mr. du Maurier and by yourself is subject to several explanations. One is that you did, indeed, live only a few years while Mr. du Maurier lived for twenty-eight. This other reality which you experienced, this . . . *Dungeon*, may exist in lockstep with the Earth. In that case—"

She had resumed her restless pacing again, her hands clasped, as before, in the small of her back. As she passed between him and the oil lamp, Clive could not but notice the flicker of lamplight upon her graceful bosom. He suppressed a sharp intake of breath and concentrated on her words.

"In that case," she repeated, "your 1870, let us say—the *Dungeon's* 1870—exists side by side with the Earth's 1870. You lived but, let us say, two years. You reached the year 1870, at which point you were snatched up by George du Maurier's psychic force and carried twenty-six years into your future. Your future. Our present. The year 1896."

"A pretty fancy," Clive rejoined. He rose from his chair and stood facing her. "Travel through time. Thus might one journey to observe the building of the pyramids, the parting of the Red Sea, the landing upon Mount Ararat, even the Crucifixion of the Savior—"

"—or one might fly in the opposite direction and observe the slow evolution of our descendants, at least according to the theories of Messrs. Darwin and Wallace. The slowing of the Earth's rotation, the dimming of the sun to a dull red globe." She had picked up Clive's narrative in midstride and continued it without missing a beat.

"But you said there were more explanations than one," Clive said, taking up the thread. He had advanced toward the woman and stood now, facing her, noting that her unusual height, in contrast to his own middling dimensions, brought their faces to a level. The warmth which the lamplight imparted to her olive skin and great black eyes made his pulse roar in his ears.

"Suppose," she said, smiling, "that the rate of time is not absolute and universal. Suppose that the stream of time flows more rapidly in one sector of Creation than in another."

"Absurd." Clive frowned.

"But a stream of water may flow very rapidly in one region, where it rolls down a steep declivity or pours from a cliff. Did you never see the great falls in East Africa?"

"I did, Madame."

"So! And yet that same stream might slow its course where it moves slowly across a plain. It might pause to form a lake. It might even, in case of a tidal estuary, hesitate at the edge of the sea, advancing timidly when the tide flows outward, returning to visit when the tide returns."

"A very pretty set of images, Madame. I congratulate you upon your poetic attainments. But what has this to do with the Dungeon, and with du Maurier and with me?"

"I was but drawing a simile, Major Folliot." She smiled at him.

"Time is not water, nor is its flow the flow of a stream. There are no time-rapids, time-falls, time-lakes, or time-tides. Your images are affecting, but ultimately they are false. Totally, absolutely false."

He started to raise his hands toward her shoulders, but a glance from her great eyes and a curl to the corner of her mouth dissuaded him. He turned away and stood with his back to her, clasping his elbows in his palms, gazing contemplatively at the wan figure propped against its pillows.

"Leave aside your theories of time. What matters is this. For as long as I traveled through the Dungeon—and its levels and regions, its denizens and its perils are far beyond the power of word to convey or imagination to picture—I attempted to communicate with George du Maurier."

He took the frail, wrinkled hand that lay on the coverlet and held the fingers sadly in his own.

"Many times I thought—I just thought—that I reached him. There was a feeling, a prickling beneath my scalp, a whispering in my mind, that led me to think that he heard my mental message and was sending one of his own in response."

He whirled to face her again.

"But I was never certain of that. What I received in return for my messages was never more than the vaguest of suggestions of contact. Then, mere hours ago—or at least, so it seemed to me—du Maurier spoke quite clearly. Hah!"

He crossed the room to a stone-faced hearth where the makings of a fire had been arranged but never ignited. He looked around for flint and steel, found instead a tall box of long-stemmed sulfur matches, and without obtaining permission of either du Maurier or Madame Mesmer, set the kindling straws alight. Even as he watched, the flame spread from straws to twigs, from twigs to heavier slivers, and thence to the substantial logs that lay upon a heavy iron grate.

"There is in the Dungeon a wondrous thing, a kind of train that moves not on tracks as does a railroad train, but on whatever course it chooses. It runs upon land, upon water, even in the sky. And its cars are not mere coaches filled with seats and travelers. Each coach represents a different period or locale in time or space. Once before I visited this train, and had a surprising experience in a Roman bath. That was long ago and far away from here."

He looked at Clarissa Mesmer, and saw that she was following his words with fascination and eagerness.

"Today I entered that train again, entered a car wondering where I would find myself, in what era and what nation. The last that I would have guessed would have been George du Maurier's private bedchamber!"

He stood with head bowed, studying the polished tips of his boots. "I could leave here, I suppose."

He crossed the room and drew aside the heavy curtain with one hand, peering through the tall window into the London street. It was indeed night—full dark had fallen upon the city, and the street outside, deserted except by a dank-appearing fog, was illuminated only by the points of gaslamps and a few shade-covered windows in other houses, windows that glowed orange behind their translucent shades.

"I could leave here and find my family's country seat, or return to my Guards unit. I could search for my sweetheart, Miss Leighton—although by now, damn it, she would be old enough to be my mother! *Damn!* Pardon me, Madame Mesmer. I could raise an expedition and return to the Sudd, seek out the point of transition to the Dungeon, and attempt to rescue my fellows."

"Or?" Clarissa Mesmer prompted.

"Or?" Clive Folliot echoed.

"Or what? It is clear that you do not intend to leave here. Not through the doorway like an ordinary visitor. No, Major Folliot. Grant me that much, as a judge of human nature. I do not know your intentions, but they are not to walk from this house into the London night. What, then, are they?"

"As yet, Madame," Clive replied, "I do not know."

▪ CHAPTER 5 ▪
"Death Is the Least Fearsome Thing"

After a while there came a rustling from the bed.

Clive Folliot and Clarissa Mesmer raced to the edge of the four-poster.

"I slept," du Maurier's papery whisper announced. "Each time I close my eyes, I wonder if it will be the last. Do I cross the line that separates life from death? Do I face, at last, the final and greatest of all mysteries? Or do I merely lapse for a time into the realm of dreams, to return after a while and live a bit longer in this material world of ours?"

"You merely slept," Clive Folliot told him. "We are here, old friend. There is nothing you need to fear."

"Fear?" The old man's eyes brightened as he spoke the word. He turned his face and looked at the fire now burning on the hearth. He smiled approvingly. "Of course there is nothing to fear. Death may be many things, but fearsome it is not. Life is fearsome. Life hold threats and anguishes without number, but death is the least fearsome thing there is."

The old man took Clive's hand in his two. "There is nothing to fear beyond the veil—that much I know."

"How did you reach me?" Clive asked. "Did you bring me here, or did I come by some other agency?"

"Give credit to Madame Mesmer," the old man said. "By her methods I was able to concentrate my psychic forces upon reaching you. And, behold, first clear communication, then you are translated from that other time and place—wherever they may be—and here! A marvel, Folliot, a marvel!"

"How much do you know of my adventures in the Dungeon, old friend?"

"Enough. At first, of course, your dispatches reached home. Carstairs was delighted. His rag scored one beat after another. Even your sketches, Folliot, became quite a rage. You'll pardon me if I mention that they're somewhat faulty in technique. But then, you are an amateur, are you not? It would be unfair to demand professional skill of an amateur."

"But those were all sent before we entered the Sudd," Clive demurred. "Once Smythe and Sidi Bombay and I were in the swamp, and once we passed through the heart of ruby to enter the Dungeon, I was able to send back no reports."

"That I realize." The old man hoisted himself higher against the piled pillows. Even though the room had not been cold when Clive arrived, there had been a dank quality to the air. The fire he had lighted on the hearth was doing much to alleviate that condition, and du Maurier seemed to draw strength from the flickering flames and the lighter air.

Du Maurier crooked a skeletal finger at Clarissa Mesmer. "Come closer, my dear. You have provided the means for this joyous reunion. You deserve to participate in it."

The tall woman knelt beside du Maurier's bed. The old man held Clive's hand in one of his, took Clarissa's in the other, then drew them together so the three were linked. Clive felt the energy of the three of them flow together. Clearly, Madame Mesmer felt the same exchange. She shot a glance at Clive and their eyes locked and held. Even George du Maurier, sinking slowly toward his death, was temporarily buoyed by the strength he drew from the others.

Clive turned his face toward du Maurier. "Once we had entered the Dungeon, when I was no longer able to send dispatches . . . how much of my mental emanation were you able to receive?"

"In a way, Folliot, I was able to receive everything. The mind is a subtle and complex organ. Madame Mesmer's ancestor gave his life to its study, and only began to scratch the surface. When you tried to send me messages, they penetrated the barriers that separate our world from the Dungeon. But you must realize, Folliot—the events that you experienced, compressed into, let us say, two years—these events were spread for me over a span of twenty-eight years."

He released Clive's and Clarissa's hands and dropped his own to the coverlet. "May I have a cup of tea and brandy, please? Will you ring for a servant, Madame Mesmer?"

Clarissa rose to her feet. As she stood over him, Clive detected the scent of her, a subtle essence. It penetrated to his core.

"Let us avoid the presence of servants, Mr. du Maurier. I know my way about your establishment. I shall fetch tea and brandy myself."

She swept from the room.

Du Maurier gestured to Clive, who bent close to the old man's face.

"Be careful of her, Folliot."

Clive drew back, astonished. "She is your personal aide, is she not? You attribute to her wondrous powers."

"Those she has."

"But then—?"

"It is neither her powers nor her works that I suspect. It is her motives. Her intentions."

"What do you know of her?"

"I summoned her from the Continent."

"And she came."

"Ah—but not directly. After arriving from the Continent, Madame Mesmer first paid a visit in the countryside."

The old man dropped his voice to a whisper. Already he had been speaking so softly that Clive had to lean over the bed, but now du Maurier looked fearfully about, assuring himself that no one overheard their conversation. "Before coming to see me," he explained, "she visited Tewkesbury."

"Tewkesbury!"

"Yes."

"But . . . that is my ancestral home. It was the home of my childhood. It is the Barony of Tewkesbury that my brother, Neville, will inherit if he lives and returns from the Dungeon—and that I will inherit if Neville dies."

"All of that I know, Folliot."

"And in Tewkesbury . . . what did Madame Mesmer do?"

"I know only that she visited Tewkesbury Manor. That, when there, she saw your father the baron, and—"

"Are you certain?" Clive interrupted. "I thought I saw the baron in the Dungeon, but then it appeared that it was not truly he, but an amazing simulacrum of him."

"Arthur Folliot, Baron Tewkesbury, has not been out of England in all the years you were away. If you saw a man who purported to be him, you were surely dealing with an imposter of some kind."

"Then I must go to Tewkesbury! My father, for all his shortcomings, is yet the holder of the title of baron and is head of our family. He is entitled to a report on the search for his heir." Clive hesitated, struck by another thought.

"But if it is really 1896, du Maurier, the baron is twenty-eight years older than when last I saw him. He will be . . ." He permitted himself to lapse into silence.

"Yes." Du Maurier smiled. "He will be an old man, like me. "Growing old has indeed been somewhat of a burden to me, Folliot. Don't be afraid to say it. Don't be afraid to acknowledge it. I assure you, I vastly prefer growing old to the only alternative I know of."

He waited patiently, smiling his indulgence while Clive unraveled the circuitous logic of his statement.

"Not only is Baron Tewkesbury in residence at Tewkesbury Manor, I have reason to believe that he is being attended by your brother, who arrived recently in company of a missionary priest, a Father O'Hara."

"Father O'Hara!"

The words had barely escaped Clive's lips when the door to du Maurier's chamber swung open and Clarissa Mesmer stepped through.

"Silence," du Maurier whispered to Clive. He pushed himself upright once again and reached toward the woman. "You are too kind, Madame," the old man said.

"I would be of what service as I am able, Mr. du Maurier." She carried an ornate silver tray to the massive desk across the room. On the tray were cups and saucers, a steaming silver pot of tea, and a crystal decanter. As she prepared du Maurier's cup, she said, "Mr. Folliot, may I offer you refreshment?"

Clive declined the offer.

Clarissa Mesmer carried a cup of gold-trimmed china to du Maurier's bed. Whatever else had befallen him in twenty-eight years, Clive thought, George du Maurier had surely prospered in things material.

But his friend and mentor's words had put new worries into Clive's mind. New worries, and a new sense of urgency.

He must return to the Dungeon and see about Annie, Horace, Sidi Bombay, and the rest. But what was it that du Maurier had said about Neville Folliot's being back in England? And Father O'Hara!

Obviously, the transition from the mundane world to the Dungeon was one that could be made in either direction. Clive had known that—or at least suspected it—since his early days on Q'oorna. There he had visited a town that bore an astonishing resemblance to a bucolic English village. And there, in the home of the elderly mayor and his wife, he had seen a wedding portrait that showed not only the happy couple but the officiating clergyman as well.

And that clergyman, also younger by many years but unmistakable nevertheless, was Timothy F. X. O'Hara. The same Father O'Hara whom Clive had encountered in the East African village of Bagomoyo!

To this point, O'Hara was the only individual whom Clive had been certain—or almost certain—to be capable of traveling between the Dungeon and the surface of the Earth. Clive didn't even know where the Dungeon was. For a time he had thought of it as a series of spheres similar to the pre-Copernican notion of spheres surrounding the Earth and carrying upon their transparent surfaces the moon, planets, and distant stars.

Only the Dungeon was a series of spheres that lay *beneath* the surface of the Earth. As one penetrated each, one approached closer and closer to the ultimate center of the Dungeon—which might or might not coexist with the geological center of the Earth.

That was a theory that Clive had entertained. But later experience had caused him to doubt its validity. It was comfortingly graspable to the mundane mind. But, alas, the more Clive experienced of the Dungeon, the less was he able to maintain his belief in that notion.

Q'oorna itself had proven, in due course, to be a planet comparable to the Earth. But it was one that existed on the very edge of being, a rogue world whose rotation brought it to face the vast sea of astral objects known to nineteenth century man for half Q'oorna's diurnal cycle. And for the other half, Q'oorna faced an unplumbable blackness wherein only the enigmatic spiral of stars offered any relief at all.

And if Q'oorna was truly a planet at the edge of all being, then what of the other levels of the Dungeon, worlds of jungle and desert, of rolling sea and granite peak? And what of the ultimate level of the Dungeon, the ninth level? Was it truly the Earth itself? Was the whole terrifying geometry of the Dungeon but a loop that returned after its wild coursings to its own point of origin?

Father O'Hara seemed to hold a clue to that riddle!

And now Clive had learned that his brother Neville, in search of whom he had set out upon his adventure, had also returned from the Dungeon. If Neville was back, then what of that other baffling trio, Philo B. Goode and Amos and Lorena Ransome?

Clive leaped from his chair and bolted for the door.

"Mr. Folliot!" Clarissa Mesmer called after him. "Mr. Folliot, where are you going? Mr. Folliot!"

Clive paused in the doorway but a moment. "To Tewkesbury! I must go to Tewkesbury! Farewell, du Maurier! I hope you are not disappointed with the answer you find to death's mystery! And you, Madame Mesmer—it has been a pleasure making your acquaintance!"

The blackness outside was as nothing compared to the blackness Clive Folliot had encountered in the Dungeon, and the loneliness of this deserted London street was as nothing to the loneliness Clive had encountered in the Dungeon.

No, the fog that billowed around him as he stood on the

stone steps of du Maurier's house—and only now did he realize what a large and splendid establishment that house was—seemed like an old friend welcoming him home to England. The ghostly gaslights that lined the kerb and the windows that were illuminated were like welcoming eyes. The cobblestones of the thoroughfare felt comfortable and familiar beneath his boots.

He jammed his military cap onto his head and strode toward the nearest intersection. For the first time he examined his accoutrement, finding it completely in order and trim. He even carried a ceremonial saber in a scabbard depending from his belt, and a purse full of currency at his waist. Did Her Majesty's officers wear the same uniform in 1896 that they had in 1868? Clive smiled at the thought of a man from 1836 appearing for formation in 1868. Were he to reappear like a figure from the past, he would face curiosity, ridicule . . . but that was a small problem compared to the others he faced.

The intersection led to a street vaguely familiar to Clive. He was certain that he had been there before, but the buildings seemed to have changed.

Of course! he realized with a start. In twenty-eight years, stately Georgian buildings would have fallen into disrepair and ruin, greed-driven land speculators would have bought them up to be demolished and replaced by the atrocities considered smart by newer, cleverer generations.

Clive strode along, his heart filled with pangs of recollection. For a moment he thought of making his way to Plantagenet Court, in hopes of catching a glimpse of Annabella Leighton. But he knew that she was no longer there. His descendant Annie had given him the history of her family, and he was aware that Annabella, despairing of his return to give a name to the child he had got upon her, had long since departed for the New World. Why, he might be a grandfather by now!

He picked up his stride. He came to the entry to an underground railroad station and contemplated briefly taking passage on a train to carry him to a major railroad terminus. But he feared to bring himself to do so. It was too much like reentering the Dungeon.

He shuddered and passed by.

He had become disoriented midst the unfamiliar architecture of this modern London, and when he saw a window gleaming across the way and heard the sounds of commerce and social intercourse from within, he headed toward the establishment.

What was the hour? It had already been full dark when he arrived at du Maurier's home, but depending on the time of year—he didn't even know the time of year!—nightfall might come anywhere from five o'clock in the afternoon to eight in the evening. And making allowance for the time he had spent with du Maurier and Madame Mesmer, it still might be anywhere from an early and respectable hour to shortly before dawn.

Surely the quiet and almost wholly deserted streets he had traversed suggested that the hour was indeed very late.

He stood before a lighted window and peered through. The neighborhood, he realized, had altered in nature as he walked, and he was now in a working-class section not very far from the West India Docks.

Another irony, he realized. For it had been from the West India Docks that he had sailed aboard the *Empress Philippa* that early morning in 1868. Where now were the captain and crew of that ship? Where the other passengers, including the mysterious mandarin who had proven to be his onetime batman, Quartermaster Sergeant Horace Hamilton Smythe, and the trio of Philo B. Goode and Amos and Lorena Ransome?

He swung open the door of the lighted establishment and was staggered by the volume and intensity of the light, the noise, and the odors that assailed him. Clearly he had found his way into a lower class dive, and he hesitated, thinking that it might be wisest to beat a hasty retreat and seek elsewhere for passage to the railroad terminus.

But he had no chance to retreat.

Almost before his eyes had had a chance to adjust to the increased illumination, he found himself taken by both elbows and half-invited, half-dragged into the room. Not that the two individuals who had seized him did so by virtue of brute force. No, they were two of the most astonishingly attractive—and forward—women he had ever encountered.

He had seen slave women for sale in Zanzibar; he had encountered African maidens who thought no more of showing themselves as naked as Eve than did an English lady of showing her flashing eyes. But he had never seen women as done up to arouse the animal side of a man as were these two.

One of them had blond hair, a heart-shaped face, long, curving eyelashes, rouged cheeks, and painted lips. Her gown, of a brilliant shade of blue, was cut so low at the bodice that her more than ample breasts were clearly visible to the taller Clive Folliot. Her arms were naked from shoulder to elbow, her long gloves covering them from that point to her fingertips. Her skirt was generous, but the gown was cut so closely to her torso that every curve was clearly visible.

Her counterpart, grasping Clive by the other arm, had hair of a shade of red that clearly Nature had never given her. Her eyebrows were darkened and her eyes ringed with paint so that her viewer's attention was drawn to them and the startling green shade that contrasted with her hair but was matched almost perfectly by her gown. The bosom of this garment was cut low, although not as low as that of her partner. But as she twisted in place, Clive became aware that the back of her garment was cut in a declivity that extended far below her waist.

He gasped and started to back away, but the women drew him forward. The blonde said, "Look 'oo we 'ave 'ere, dearie!"

The redhead said, "This is the prettiest fing I've seen tonight, ain't it?"

They laughed, and before Clive knew what had happened to him he was halfway across the room. A long bar of mahogany wood stood against one wall of the establishment, and a crew of bartenders handed out beverages and took payment for them. In a distant corner of the establishment a small stage bore a trio of females harmonizing wistfully to the accompaniment of a three-piece orchestra. The refrain of the song, and (Clive presumed) its title, was

"Her Hair Was Hanging Down Her Back." Both the lyrics and the singers' delivery were startling to Clive, accustomed as he was to the more sedate practices of a quarter-century earlier.

The two women maneuvered Clive to an empty table, apparently the only such in the establishment.

"Have a drink, sweetie," the blonde urged Clive.

"Get a bottle," the redhead amended. "A bottle and three glasses and we'll have ourselves a party, we will!" She leaned toward him and he smelled the gin on her breath and the perfume in her hair.

"I have to go," Clive pleaded.

"In a bit, dearie."

"Soon's we've 'ad our party, cutes."

The tables surrounding Clive's were packed with burly men and flashy women. A broad-shouldered tough in a striped shirt and seafarer's cap turned and fixed Clive with a curious stare.

"Will ya have a look at the fancy Dan, mates?" he addressed his companions.

"Ain't you in the wrong part of town?" another seaman growled.

"You think you're goin' ter amuse yourself, taking in the lowlife, then beating it back to your swell friends, brigadier?"

Clive shook his head, frowning. "Now, look here, you men, I just wandered in here looking for a railroad station, and I'll be very happy to leave if someone can simply show me the way."

"Just wandered in!" the first seafarer roared.

"Show me the way!" the second one mimicked, following the words with derisive laughter. "We'll show yer the way, fancy Dan, if that's what yer wants!"

The seamen were on their feet and heading, none too steadily, toward Clive. His two female companions, no longer plastering themselves to his scarlet-clad arms, were squealing and scrambling to get away from the imminent battle.

Clive was glad that he hadn't had time to consume any liquor. He leaped to his feet and balanced to meet a potential attack. He thought for a moment of the saber that was part of his accoutrement, but left it in his scabbard. If he could limit the confrontation to a verbal level, he would be relieved. If not, then let it at least remain a battle of bare fists, not the lethal hardware of war.

· CHAPTER 6 ·
"I Am Not at All Surprised!"

The two bruisers came at Clive, fists raised, looks of menace and determination on their faces. Carousers at nearby tables drew back. Clive's two erstwhile friends seemed to fade into the crowd. Even the singers on the stage and the musicians clustered before it grew quiet.

It appeared that fights were not uncommon in this den. If anything, they were looked upon as a frequent source of amusement.

The first tough who had spoken to Clive leaned across the table toward him. Clive, standing to face the man, realized that the bruiser was a full head taller than himself and proportionately more wide. His breath carried a dizzying mixture of tobacco fumes, alcohol, and another essence that Clive could only guess was dope of some sort. The man was of dubious race. His skin was swarthy, his eyes carried an exotic look, his hair was worn long, plaited into a greasy queue that hung down his grimy striped shirt.

The second tough hovered behind his companion, darting menacing looks and gestures around his massive shoulders.

The first tough said, "We don't like your kind aroun' here, mister! Fancies and swells what thinks they's better 'an us. Comes aroun' here lookin' for fast women and cheap thrills!"

Clive was on his own feet, facing the man. "I told you, my good fellow, that I was merely looking for the railroad terminus. These two ladies chose to make my acquaintance, not I theirs."

■ 57 ■

He looked around but the redhead and the blonde had disappeared.

"I'm gonna teach you a lesson, Mister Redcoat!" The ruffian lifted the table that separated himself from Clive and hurled it sideways. It crashed to the floor, sending spectators scrambling for their safety.

The man raised a beefy fist and launched a crude blow at Clive's face. Clive ducked the blow easily, feinting with his own fist to keep the fellow at bay. Behind the big man he could see his smaller companion and hear him calling advice. Still farther away, Clive caught a glimpse of the huge mirror that backed the serving bar, and the bartender standing before it, observing the confrontation.

The big man launched another blow, this time with more care than he had the first, but with equal lack of effect. The blow was a straight jab with his fist, and Clive evaded it with a simple shift of his head.

Enraged, the man attempted a brutal kick. His muscular legs were encased in thick-soled boots, and Clive suspected that if he should ever be knocked down by the man, his ribs would fall rapid prey to that heavy footgear.

But the lessons that Clive had received in personal combat were coming into play. He had fought countless boxing matches with his brother Neville, and while Neville was the more accomplished fighter—and also possessed far stronger instincts to compete and punish, while Clive's predilection was to cooperate and assist—still, the younger twin had picked up many a useful move. He had learned both fencing and further lessons in fisticuffs at the behest of Horace Hamilton Smythe while serving with the Imperial Horse Guards, and his fighting prowess had been perfected, willy-nilly, in his journey through some eight levels of the Dungeon.

As the giant bruiser hurled his massive boot at Clive, Clive stepped aside and slipped behind his assailant and added his own strength to the man's momentum by the simple device of shoving him with both hands, as hard as he could.

The bruiser staggered forward, lost his balance, and tumbled into the crowd.

Jeers rose. "Not so tough tonight, Bruno!" "What's the

matter, man, losin' yer touch?" "Bruno's takin' a lickin' for once!"

And even a few encouraging calls directed at himself. "Nice work, Redcoat!" "The toff's a slick one, i'n 'e?" "Where'd yer learn that, fancy Dan?"

Clive turned to face the giant Bruno, who was struggling to regain his feet. He heard a scuffling behind him, and a voice—a woman's voice, perhaps that of one of his erstwhile companions—called a warning.

He whirled in time to see Bruno's smaller companion charge at him, a heavy-handled dagger in his hand.

Clive was able to sidestep in the nick of time, accelerating his second attacker into his still wobbly first. There was a resounding thump as the two of them crashed to the floor, but Clive realized now that his attackers had further allies. Moans of protest rose from the crowd, but hands remained unraised in Clive's defense as a half-dozen ruffians arrayed themselves in alliance with Bruno and his first confederate.

Clive backed away, trying to avoid being surrounded and sapped or stabbed from behind, as he was sure would be his fate if his enemies managed to circle him. He scrambled through sweating men and perfumed women until he stood with his back to the bar. No fewer than eight men, a phalanx four wide and two deep, confronted him. The giant Bruno had also drawn a dirk, and he and his first confederate stood front and center, crouched and ready to attack.

For the first time Clive considered defending himself with a weapon other than his wits and his bare hands. His ornate saber still hung from his waist, a weapon whose significance to Her Majesty's servants was increasingly ceremonial rather than practical. Even in earlier times, the saber with its curving blade and razor edge was intended for use by the cavalry, by fast-moving horsemen who would slash at an enemy in a fleeting instant of combat. A sharp-pointed rapier, such as Clive had used so long ago in the castle of N'wrbb Crrd'f, would have been more suitable.

Still, the saber was the best weapon available to Clive, and use it he would. He gripped the scabbard in his left hand, ran the fingers of his right through the basket hilt, and drew the blade.

A sound rose from the crowd. It was a collective response to Clive's gesture, a combination of sigh and moan and gasp and a half-articulated exhalation of encouragement.

Then, for a tingling moment, the room lapsed into a silence so nearly perfect that the rhythmic breathing of its many occupants united to form a weird, organic harmony.

"I did not come here to fight," Clive said. "I will still leave peacefully if you will but open a way for me."

He raised the basket-hilt of his saber before his chin, almost as if in salute, then swept its point downward to the horizontal, pointing it toward the exit that gave back onto the street.

As Clive's blade stood quivering at the horizontal, the companion of giant Bruno stuck sideways at it, a twisting, lunging blow designed to sweep the saber from Clive's hand and bring the man's dagger slicing dangerously toward Clive's torso.

With a practiced twist of his own wrist, Clive sent the man's dagger whirling across the room to fall with a clatter near the now-deserted stage. Again a collective response rose from the crowd. Clive could sense that he, who had arrived a stranger and been greeted as an unwelcome interloper in the establishment, was winning their support with his sportsmanship and his skill in the face of bullies.

Someone in the second row of Clive's attackers handed a bottle to an unarmed man in the front row. The man held the bottle by its neck and smashed it across a table. Clive had heard of such a tactic, wondering if it could succeed. More likely the bottle would simply spin across the room, knocked from its wielder's hand by the force of its impact.

But the ruffian showed every sign of the experienced killer. Under his control, the bottle was converted in a moment to a deadly weapon. The thug lunged at Clive, the glittering shard of glass thrusting to impale its victim. Now the sharpened edge of Clive's saber came into play. He slashed at his newest attacker with it, slicing into the man's forearm above the wrist. With a curse and a howl the fellow dropped the bottle and plunged backward into the crowd, blood spraying from his wounded arm.

Now two more attackers came at Clive, one from either side, with Bruno following, crouched low and slashing at Clive's legs with his dagger. Clive landed a boot on the point of Bruno's jaw and the man flew backward, his dagger, too, flying above the massed onlookers to clatter against the far wall of the room.

But even his superior combative skills—in a calm corner of his mind Clive blessed both Horace Hamilton Smythe and his bullying brother Neville for the lessons they had taught him—even Clive's superior skills could not hold out indefinitely against the odds that he faced.

He leaped backward and up, hoisting himself with one hand onto the service bar as he did so. For a moment he stood on the polished wooden surface, spied the naked shoulders and colorful dresses of his two erstwhile female companions milling in the midst of others, then dropped behind the bar.

The tender there hustled Clive toward one end of the narrow space. "This way, sah! This way!" They scurried toward a door of dark-stained wood and polished brass fittings. "We'll get yer out of 'ere in a mo' now, yes we will, sah!"

Clive had a bare instant as the barkeep twisted the doorknob for him, opening the door and shoving Clive through it. Even as he stood in darkness, cavalry saber in hand, Clive blinked, stunned by the face he had beheld.

Was that malleable countenance the one he thought it was? One who had appeared first as a Chinese mandarin on the West India docks, and then again aboard the *Empress Philippa*, as an Arab guard in the heated atmosphere of Zanzibar, as a onetime duelist in the American city of New Orleans?

Was this none other than Quartermaster Sergeant Horace Hamilton Smythe?

Before Clive could clear his mind, before his eyes could adjust to the new darkness that surrounded him, there came the sound of a safety match being scratched into flame, then a tiny pop as a gas fixture was lighted.

The man who had ignited the illuminating gas turned to

face Clive. He wore a frock coat, a frilled white shirt, and a cravat of purple silk. His hair was curled, and rich muttonchop whiskers met to form a luxuriant mustache.

"A drawn saber, Major Folliot? Such melodrama, really." The man extended an elegantly manicured hand, not to be shaken but merely to indicate a brass-studded, leather-covered chair that stood between himself and Clive. "Please, Major. Put up your wog-sticker, you will not need it here. Or, if you did, it would be to meet a challenge for which it would be a wholly inadequate response. Of that, I can assure you."

He paused for a beat, two. Then, "Please, Major. I appeal to you."

Cautiously, looking in all directions to assure himself that no third party was present in the room, Clive returned his saber to its scabbard. Slowly he lowered himself into the indicated seat.

The frock-coated man nodded approvingly. "You do look splendid in your uniform, Major. Red is not a color all men can wear, but against your patrician features it is most flattering."

Clive gazed, astonished, at his host. He had been startled just moments before to recognize the bartender as Horace Hamilton Smythe. But if his encounter with Smythe had been a startlement to him, it was nothing compared to the shock of recognition he now experienced.

"Philo B. Goode!"

"Yes"—the other man bowed graciously—"at your service, sir." A table stood nearby, and Goode drew a chair for himself and sat at the table. "Will you join me, Major Folliot? I think we have a great deal to discuss."

Clive's head swam. Philo Goode! Philo Goode! The mountebank gambler from whose cardsharpery Horace Smythe had saved Clive in the passenger saloon of the *Empress Philippa*. Clive had exposed Goode and his two confederates to the ship's captain, and they had been put ashore in West Africa to fend for themselves.

Later Clive learned from Horace Smythe that Goode and his confederates, Amos and Lorena Ransome, had caught him, Smythe, in a complicated scheme aboard a Mississippi River steamer. The scheme had led to a duel in New Orleans and the snaring of Horace into an even wider conspiracy involving the three others. It was a scheme that involved them in the Dungeon, Clive knew, although in what capacity he had only the fuzziest of ideas.

Now that Clive had been drawn back to London in the year 1896, he had found Horace Hamilton Smythe tending bar in this disreputable establishment, while Philo Goode stood ready to greet him as a long-lost associate in the back office.

It was too much to assimilate in such a brief moment. Clive lowered his face to his hands, rubbed his eyes, then raised his face once again and sat in anticipatory silence.

In the sparsely furnished, officelike room, the only sound for a few moments was the soft hissing of the gas fixture. Sounds from the outer establishment, apparently a combination saloon and small-time music hall, with a possible additional function as a place of assignation, penetrated to the rear chamber.

Clive's precipitous departure from his confrontation with Bruno and his associates had prompted a major uproar in the place. But after a brief period the voice of the bartender could be heard, restoring order with a series of commands given in crisp, authoritarian tones.

The music started up again. Clive heard a piano, cornet, and drumbeat. Then came female voices uncertainly harmonizing upon a tune unfamiliar to Clive, its semi-audible lyrics apparently dealing with a request from a young lady and addressed to her gentleman. "Do, do, my huckleberry, do," Clive heard, without noting a clear specification as to what it was the huckleberry was supposed to do. His imagination supplied a variety of answers.

"You *are* Mr. Philo Goode, of America, are you not, sir?" Clive addressed the frock-coated man.

"That I am, sir."

"And that"—Clive gestured with a jerk of his head—"that was Sergeant Smythe? Sergeant Horace Hamilton Smythe?"

"It is indeed Horace Hamilton Smythe, Major Folliot. As for the title you give him—*sergeant*—I suppose it is one to which he is entitled. But to me he is known in a far more exalted role. One which you yourself might envy."

"And what rank is that?"

"I fear that I am not at liberty to reveal that information to you, Major. There are organizations and entities of immense power and importance whose very existence would startle a man of your modest attainments. Forgive my candor, please."

Clive flushed. "The rank of major is a not inconsiderable one, Mr. Goode, the attaining of which is no inconsiderable feat. Nor is it altogether beyond imagining that I may yet accede to the title of baron, although my elder twin Neville is at present the heir presumptive to the rank and its accompanying lands and perquisites."

"I quite understand that, Major Folliot." Goode leaned part of the way across the ornate table and opened a humidor of polished walnut and brass. He extended the humidor toward Clive. "Máy I offer you a cheroot, Major? I have them imported from Cuba, made to my personal specifications, rum-soaked and carefully seasoned."

Clive shook his head.

"I am sure you will not mind, then." Goode extracted a brown cigar, lighted it, and exhaled a cloud of heavy blue smoke toward the ceiling. "Now, sir," he addressed Clive after removing the cheroot from his mouth, "I should not be surprised at all to learn that you have some questions for me."

"I already asked you the first, Mr. Goode. What is Sergeant Smythe doing in this establishment, tending bar for a saloon's worth of ruffians and harlots?"

"For one thing, Major Folliot, he was saving your neck. As I understand he has a habit of doing."

Again Clive flushed. He had to admit, at least to himself, that he had been saved more than once by Horace Hamilton Smythe. To Philo Goode, however, he said nothing at this point.

"You do understand that you faced a severe battering at the very least, at the hands of my . . . guests." Goode tipped his own head toward the outer room. "A severe battering at the very least," he repeated, "if not a maiming—or even your death."

"I was holding my own quite nicely, thank you very much."

"Indeed you were. I was most impressed by your performance, Major Folliot." Goode rose and strode to a drapery that stretched from ceiling to floor. With a single sweep of his arm, he drew it aside to reveal the inside of the saloon. The long mirror behind the bar was transparent from its rear; any occupant of the office could thus observe activities in the business establishment without himself being noticed.

"You are no longer the soft weakling who set out from London in 1868 to find your brother, Major."

"What do you know of my adventures, Mr. Goode? And what has been your role in them? A cardsharper? A mountebank operating on a Mississippi steamer?"

"Those things, yes," Goode acknowledged. He returned to the table, drew and released another long plume of blue smoke from his cheroot, and tapped ashes from it into a heavy ashtray. "Those things and more, I suppose I ought to say."

"You ought to say, indeed, sir! You are connected with the Dungeon. I saw you on the level which I can only describe as"— he flushed to speak the word—"Hell."

"Well, one has one's duties, Major Folliot. One has one's duties."

"Are you the master of the Dungeon?"

Goode collapsed into his chair, doubled over with laughter. When he had recovered himself, he said, still chuckling, "I—the master of the Dungeon? Well, I suppose a cat can look at a king. A street-urchin can envy a senator. Oh, I am far, far from being master of the Dungeon."

"Are you connected with the Ren? With the Chaffri? With the Gennine?"

"Ah, now you address me with a more realistic question. Yes, I am connected with . . . a group."

"With which? And for what purpose?"

"You will learn everything that you need to know, Major Folliot—when you need to know it."

"I can see that I am going to receive no satisfaction from you, Mr. Goode. It would be tempting to take action against you directly—I know enough of you to know that you are up to no decent end—but for the moment, I will simply take my leave of you. Good day, sir—or should I say, good night!"

Clive rose from his seat and strode back toward the door.

Philo Goode moved more rapidly even than Clive, but rather than blocking his path to the exit, he moved to the mirrored panel that revealed the outer room. "Look before you leap, Major Folliot. Look well!"

Clive stood staring at the glass panel. He saw not a saloon filled with carousers and harlots, but a pit of roaring, dancing flames.

"It is Hell!" Clive exclaimed.

"You would not survive five minutes out there, Major Folliot. In fact, not one minute. But there is another means of egress." He bent and pulled up the corner of an oriental carpet. Beneath it, a trapdoor fitted with a heavy iron ring was revealed.

With a grunt, Philo Goode tugged the trapdoor open. A flight of stone steps led downward into the gloom.

"You want me to go down there? To face I know not what? To face, perhaps, my death?"

"Major Folliot, had I desired your death, I assure you, you would have been thoroughly and irrevocably dead long before now. Take my word for that. Please, go down these steps. They are the only way out of this place—for you."

Clive hesitated. He considered trying to leave the same way he had arrived in this room. Perhaps the vision of the flaming, hellish inferno was an illusion, a trick designed to mislead him. But he did not believe that was so. Still, he carried his saber yet. He could draw it, possibly take Philo Goode prisoner, force him to reveal what he knew, force him to reveal a safe means of egress from this trap.

But Goode *had* revealed a safe means of egress. Or such was his claim. The longer Clive pondered, the more convinced he became that Goode's suggestion was the only reasonable course of action for him to follow.

He rose from his chair, adjusting his tunic, saber, and cap, and stood over the open trapdoor. "If this is a trick, Goode, I warn you, sir—I have survived perils that you would not believe."

"I must differ with you, sir. I know more than you could possibly realize. I would believe everything you could tell me. That is the only reason you are here this night, sir, and the only reason that I offer you the opportunity that now stands at your feet."

"Nonetheless, if this staircase represents still another act of treachery on your part, Goode, I will extract from you a dear price indeed!"

"And I shall pay it gladly, Major Folliot. Now, if you see no further need to delay . . ."

Clive set his polished brown boot upon the first step of dank gray stone.

CHAPTER 7

But the Smallest Hint

The steps led downward into darkness, curving in a spiral that swiftly carried Clive into the unknown. He paused for a moment to glance upward. The open trap had shrunk to a tiny square, had done so far more rapidly than Clive would have expected.

Even as he stood gazing up, the square of light disappeared. Apparently Philo Goode had slammed shut the trapdoor. If he turned back, Clive suspected, and climbed the steps once again, he would find the door unmovable from below.

Not that he had any intention of turning back. He had committed himself to a course of action, and if there was one thing he had learned through his adventures in the Dungeon, it was to press ahead. Always, to press ahead. Peril might lie in his path, doom might await him. But no matter what the odds, there was always a chance of success. There was nothing to be gained by turning back. Surely not now.

Although the steep staircase led through darkness, there was a sufficient emanation of luminosity from the steps themselves to guide his feet. Clive set a steady pace for himself, neither counting steps nor attempting to calculate the passage of time. Eventually he would come to the end of his descent, and then he would find out what lay beneath Philo Goode's establishment.

Something brushed against his face and was gone. He wondered what it could be—a bat, perhaps. Some dark-adjusted creature flying through the blackness here, as much at home in the subterranean gloom as Clive would have been on his father's estate in Tewkesbury.

At length he emerged onto a level patch of flagstones. Here panels of illumination in one wall revealed that the stone flooring ended abruptly. There was a low drop, then a roadbed of sorts.

As if in response to Clive's presence, although he wondered if the timing were coordinated or merely happenstantial, he felt a rush of cold wind and heard a sound that grew from a soft *whooshing* to the scream of fast-driven wind.

He turned to see a lighted car barreling up the roadbed. It appeared to be made of glass or some similar transparent substance, molded over a framework of metal. He could see within the car a passenger compartment bearing a solitary traveler. The car resembled those of the train he had encountered first on the plain of Q'oorna and then again in the arctic waters of Earth.

The car slid to a halt. Clive could hear its engine pulsating like a living heart.

He looked toward the passenger compartment, started violently, then ran at top speed to the car. The passenger swung the door open and called to him. "Clive!"

"Annie!"

Without hesitation he jumped into the car. The young woman stood and Clive swept her into his arms, whirling her in a joyous circle. "Annie, my darling girl! My dear great-great-granddaughter Annie!"

"Put me down, Clive. Grandpa!" She used the term rarely, preferring to remain on a given-name basis. Her time was one of informality, and besides, in real age Clive was but a dozen years older than she, although through the twisted chronology of the Dungeon she was in truth his descendant, born some 144 years later than he.

"The joy I feel!" Clive exclaimed. "At first I feared that you were lost forever on the eighth level of the Dungeon. Lost forever—or worse! And then, when I stood upon the polar ice floe and saw the sun glinting off the wings of the aeroplane in which you escaped from the Japanese . . . There is so much I yearn to ask you, my darling Annie!

But for now, all that matters is that you are unharmed. You have not been . . . ?"

"No, I am well—as you can see, Clive." She curtsied before him. "And don't you look splendid in your scarlet tunic and clean-shaved cheeks!"

Although her attitude was still that of a woman prepared to make her way in the twenty-first century, she had been done up as a proper young lady of the nineteenth. Her hair was arranged in a crown of braids that coiled around her white forehead. Her face was modestly made up. Her gown was of a light color and material, cut modestly across the bosom and tightly at the waist. She was a contrast of one sort against the two harlots who had cozened up to Clive in the drinking den, of another against the severe Madame Mesmer in her high-necked, long-skirted outfit.

"Annie! You must tell me everything, everything that has happened."

"That will take a long time, Clive."

"But first—what is this car? What is this all about? How did you get back to England, to 1896? This is 1896, is it not? I saw du Maurier. I last saw him as a vigorous man of fifty. Now he is old. He says he is dying. He says I have been away for twenty-eight years."

"It is indeed 1896, Clive. Sit now, or you'll be knocked over!" The pulsation of the car's engine had increased in force and frequency, and Clive and Annie indeed had barely time to seat themselves, cozily side by side, before the car slid forward, pressing them against the padded back of their couchlike seat.

The car accelerated until Clive calculated that it was proceeding at a high rate of speed. It moved through a nearly featureless tunnel. Now and then a lighted panel cast a dim glow through the gloom. Now and then Clive caught sight of a branch or side passage curving away from their own. Where these branches led, he had no idea save for the wild conjecture that they were connected to different levels or sectors of the Dungeon.

For that matter, he had no idea where the car was bearing them. They were alone in it, and neither he nor

Annie did anything to control its progress or its course. There were no visible controls to be seen.

"My dear child, Annie—" Clive began.

Before he could continue, Annie said, "Clive, tell me—do you still have Neville's journal?"

Clive patted his tunic, investigating its pockets for the precious volume. "I fear not," he said. "When I was translated to London, I—" He paused to gather his thoughts, then began again. "On the eighth level—you remember that some of us were reduced in size to Lilliputian proportions, others enlarged to Brobdingnagian."

"How could I forget!"

"Fortunately, well before I was transported to the ninth level—or back here to Earth—perhaps they are the same—I had regained my normal stature."

She nodded, encouraging him to continue.

"I found myself on the arctic ice cap, along with Chang Guafe. It was just before I found him that you flew over in the Nakajima."

She made no comment on the aeroplane. Instead she inquired only about Chang Guafe. "And he, Clive?"

"He is there on the sea-bottom, as best I can surmise. What will become of him, I know not."

"And you?"

"The, well, I shall call it the space-train, arrived, and I climbed aboard, and found myself here in London. In 1896. Surrounded not by phantoms but, as far as I can tell, by reality. Including yourself." He paused to catch his breath and to gather his thoughts. He peered through the transparent wall of the car.

To appearances, the car had emerged from its long tunnel and was making its way along a wholly ordinary railway line. The long night was ending; Clive could detect the rosy blush of dawn to the east, behind the car, which sped along the tracks in a westerly direction.

As the car passed an early-rising farmer driving his hay-laden wagon along a dirt track beside the railroad bed, Annie took Clive's wrist. "He cannot see us, Clive. We can see all the world from this car, but we are protected from being seen."

"What is this car?" Clive demanded. "Have you made

league with . . . whoever is behind this? With Philo Goode and his confederates?"

She smiled up at him. "All in good time, Clive. You were telling me what happened to Neville's journal."

"The messages we received were seldom reliable anyway. I question both Neville's motivation in writing them and the authenticity of at least a number of them."

"You met Neville in the Dungeon."

"Yes. Neville—or a simulacrum."

"Did he acknowledge that he truly wrote all the messages in his journal?"

"He denied them all!"

She looked stunned, struck speechless.

Clive continued. "But now—was it truly Neville who denied writing the journal entries? And even if it was, can we believe him?"

Annie frowned. "Maybe we'll be able to find that out, somehow. But for now, where *is* the journal, Clive?"

"As I was explaining to you—when I entered the space-train, I was ragged, unshaven, half-starved, half-drowned, and half-frozen. When I found myself in London—in the bedchamber of my old friend du Maurier—I was nourished, shaven, magnificently togged, and bone dry. I do not understand what happened. I can only attribute it, like so many other mysteries, to the Dungeon."

"And Neville's journal?"

"I have no idea."

"Did you have it on the ice cap, Clive?"

"I don't know. I don't remember having it there, but I had other things to occupy my attention than thinking about my brother's notebook."

"Then it might still be on the ice cap. Or on the train. Or in George du Maurier's home, I suppose."

"Or back on the eighth level, in fact."

"Never mind. Never mind. We must cope with our situation as we find it."

The light from the east had increased, and Clive's observation of the green fields and budding trees that lined the railroad bed told him that it was a spring morning in the English countryside. One of nature's most beautiful creations—an English country spring.

"Where are we headed?" Clive asked.

Annie smiled. "Don't you recognize the landscape?"

Clive studied the vegetation and the lay of the land. "It looks like Gloucestershire."

"Right on the first response!"

"We're going to Tewkesbury!"

"Correct."

"Who is there, and what is your connection with them, Annie"

"Why, your family seat is there, Clive. At Tewkesbury Manor!"

"I know that. I did not ask *what* is there. I asked *who* is there."

"We'll access that data when our cursor reaches the designated address."

Oh, Lord, Clive thought, *she's lapsing into that strange futuristic jargon of hers.* "Annie, please—can't you speak in everyday language? Is the Queen's English inadequate to meet your needs?"

"Sorry, User. Uh, Clive. I forget myself. We'll find out when we get there, okay?"

"Very well. But Annie—so much has happened! Where are the others? Finnbogg and Shriek, Tomàs and Sidi Bombay . . ."

"You didn't mention Horace, Clive."

"I have seen Horace."

"At the North Pole?"

"No. In London. I was with him, although briefly, not more than an hour ago."

Annie's manner grew far more serious than it had been since their reunion in the transparent car. "You must tell me exactly where you saw him. How he looked. What he was doing."

"Well—" Clive hardly knew where to start. While he strove to set his thoughts in order, he peered through the glass wall of the car. Morning was well along by now, the English sky a brilliant shade of blue, dotted with tiny puffs of cloud. The railroad passed through farming country, and happy countrymen followed horse-drawn plows putting in their summer crops.

Before Clive had answered Annie's question, their little

car slowed precipitously. Annie peered ahead of them. "It's a roadblock, Clive! Quick, we'll have to defend ourselves."

She leaped from the seat and shoved the startled Clive Folliot from it. Despite her wide skirt she quickly knelt before the seat and raised its padded cushion to reveal an arsenal of astonishing weapons stowed beneath.

"Here, Clive—you can use one of these!" She handed him a machine that bore a certain resemblance to a carbine. He held it to his shoulder and lowered his face to peer through its sights. To his astonishment, he seemed to be looking through a telescope of some incredible, unfamiliar sort.

Annie took another of the weapons from its place, slammed shut the seat, and turned to take Clive's elbow.

"Annie—I should have thought to ask you—do you still have your Baalbec?"

"It's here, Grandpa!" She tapped a thumb against her bodice, indicating the place beneath her sternum where the versatile device was installed. She ran her other fingers over the skin of her forearm where the controls of the machine had been installed in the strange world of the future whence she came.

"Are we being attacked, Annie? Who is the enemy? Can you use the Baalbec to protect us?"

"Quick, out of here!" She swung open the door through which Clive had previously entered the car and gave him a vigorous shove. He tumbled from the car and onto soft English grass and felt her collide briefly with him as she landed.

There was a flash of brilliant green from a point ahead of their car, and the machine went up in a flash that blinded Clive for a moment. As he recovered his sight he saw bits of bent metal, fragments of shattered glass, odd pieces of wrecked machinery scattered over and around the railroad tracks.

"The next train to pass will be derailed!" he exclaimed.

"No it won't, and that's not our worry anyhow, Clive. Here comes our worry!"

Advancing toward them on the opposite side of the tracks came a squad of beings that bore a distant resem-

THE FINAL BATTLE ■ 75

blance to humans. They were helmeted, and garbed in black uniforms with green insignia and piping on them.

Their metal fittings—Clive assumed they were metal— were all of the same glowing green that was almost impossible to look at. Clive's eyes stung and watered and he had to look away to avoid unbearable pain.

Even so, the soldiers seemed to fade and waver as Clive looked at them. Now and again one of them disappeared altogether, only to reappear as a vague, ghostly image of himself, yards away from the point of his disappearance.

"What—what are they?"

"Chaffri," Annie whispered. "This is as close to them as a true human normally gets. And if you bring yourself to their attention, you're not likely to survive the meeting! Stay down, Clive! Be wary!"

"I cannot see them clearly. Something here is not right."

"They can't see us either. Not any better than we can see them. Probably not that well, even."

The Chaffri had reached the wreckage of the car in which Clive and Annie had been riding. The apparent leader of the squad bent and picked up a piece of twisted metal tubing. He held it close to his face, then opened a pouch in his uniform and dropped it in.

Even as the Chaffri advanced and Clive and Annie watched, the wrecked car seemed to waver and run like a melting ice cube. In minutes it had soaked into the ground—or so it appeared to Clive.

The Chaffri were speaking in a language that bore no resemblance to anything Clive had ever heard before— emphatically including the patois that was common in most regions of the Dungeon. The Chaffri squad had divided in two, and half its members advanced along either side of the track.

Annie was right. The Chaffri gave no evidence of even being able to see the erstwhile passengers. Annie rolled away from the tracks as the Chaffri soldiers advanced, signaling for silence and tugging Clive to get him to move with her, out of the path of the advancing troopers.

But it was too late. The last of the Chaffri stepped squarely on Clive's chest.

To Clive's astonishment, the Chaffri's foot sank into his

body, like a boot sinking into thin mud. The sensation was one of the most vivid and unpleasant that Clive had felt in his lifetime. It wasn't exactly pain—it was more a sense of wrongness, a revulsion and disgust, as if he had been touched by, violated by, something not only ineffably alien but utterly perverted and disgusting.

The Chaffri leaped back, as if his response to contact with Clive was similar to Clive's reaction to him. He began gesticulating and shouting to his fellows. He already held a weapon at the ready and he swept it over the ground at his feet, obviously intending to blast Clive out of existence.

But he was fated for disappointment. Clive had already rolled away, and he and Annie were sprinting toward a nearby field.

Seedlings and earth spurted around Clive's feet. His military instincts asserting themselves, he threw himself to the ground, rolled twice, and sighted back at the Chaffri. The Chaffri's weapon fired again. More accurately, it sizzled, emitting something that looked like a bolt of lightning. Even though no tangible projectile was involved, Clive was convinced that a hit from that bolt of electricity —or whatever it was—would prove no less damaging to its victim than would a lead bullet.

He could see Annie nearby, crouched on the earth. She was moving, but there seemed to be something wrong with her. Perhaps she had taken a hit from one of the Chaffri weapons.

Clive called to her to get lower to the ground, but she gave no indication that she heard his words.

He sighted his weapon at the nearest Chaffri. Its sights almost had a life of their own, drawing his aim onto the target with uncanny sureness. He squeezed the weapon's not-unfamiliar trigger and it made a sound that seemed almost to be a sigh. Its sight dropped away from the Chaffri and Clive lowered the weapon and looked at his target.

The Chaffri wavered and faded in the fashion Clive had previously observed, but this time he did not reappear.

Clive aimed at a second Chaffri trooper. Again his weapon assisted him as if it had a life and a will. He squeezed the trigger, the weapon sighed and dipped like an athlete relaxing at the termination of a contest. The second trooper wavered and threw his arms into the air, his own weapon clattering to earth. As the Chaffri faded into nothingness, his abandoned weapon did the same.

Clive scuttled sideways across the grassy earth. He reached Annie's side, dividing his attention between her and the remaining Chaffri. He was still severely outnumbered, especially as Annie, although showing no visible wound, had been clearly rendered *hors de combat*.

A Chaffri trouper pointed his weapon at Clive and Annie. Clive raised his own weapon and they fired simultaneously. Clive felt the bolt of energy that flew past him, making the very air quiver and drawing Clive like an iron filing suddenly exposed to a magnet. But close as it was, the Chaffri's shot failed to harm Clive or Annie.

Not so the answering shot from Clive's weapon. The third Chaffri followed his two predecessors, wavering in air, fading, and disappearing. At this the apparent commander of the Chaffri detachment shouted an incomprehensible order to his troopers.

The commander ran along the railroad bed. He brought down a booted foot that did not quite reach the level of the earth. His next step terminated a short distance higher in the air. With each successive stride he rose higher and higher, his troopers following him not only along the railbed but into the air, until the Chaffri had all disappeared.

Clive shook his head. He turned to Annie. She had curled into a ball and was quivering visibly. He tried desperately to determine the cause of her distress. "Annie! Can you answer me? What is the matter? How can I help you?"

She turned panic-stricken eyes upon him. "Baalbec. Baalbec. Circuits scrambled. Software—catastrophic error— master reset. Here! Here! Here!"

She jerked away from him spasmodically. Her hands were balled into fists, pounding futilely at the earth. She managed to bring one to her bodice. "Here! Clive! Master system reset! Here! Only hope!"

His face flaming the very scarlet of his tunic, Clive followed Annie's frantic commands, tearing at her cos-

tume, reaching toward her sternum. He felt a blow from
her fist but it was not designed to drive him off, but to
encourage his assistance. He pressed frantic fingertips to
her sternum, at first feeling only soft flesh, but then a
switch.

"Left! Left!" Annie cried. "Master reset to left!"

His own left? he wondered. His mind raced. Clearly
this was no time for calm dialogue. He had to think fast.
No—Annie would think of this operation in terms of her
own perspective. His own left, as he faced her, was equivalent to her right, and vice versa. They were like mirror
images of each other.

His left—her right.

Her left—his right.

"Yes! Quick, Clive! Reset! Master reset! Switch left!"
Her heels were kicking at the earth and her fists beating at
her sides. Her face was turning a horrid shade and her
breathing was coming in desperate, irregular gasps. Clive
thought he could hear her very heart pounding, desperately pounding, as if about to burst. Perhaps it was. The
Baalbec was a device of unknown capabilities as far as
Clive was concerned. He had seen it used as a weapon, as
an aid to navigation, as a device for storing and manipulating information, and on one occasion as a power source for
a flying machine brought to the Dungeon from a South
Seas island in the course of a future war between European and Japanese forces. Where was the Nakajima 97?
There was no time to worry about that now!

What was the Baalbec doing to Annie now?

Clive studied Annie's body for a moment, desperate
that he not make an erroneous—and potentially disastrous—
move. But he must act quickly, for it was obvious that if
he did not do so, Annie would die. His own great-great-
granddaughter, this child-woman who in some odd way
had become the most precious person in the world to him
. . . if he did not act quickly, and correctly, Annie would
surely die.

The lives of others had been in Clive Folliot's hands
before now. Some he had saved, some he had spared,
some he had failed to save, and some he had taken by
means of his own, conscious, deliberate act. Some would

call such conduct a usurpation of a function belonging rightly to God alone. But this was not a power that Clive had sought, and it was not one that he wished. It was one that had been forced upon him—more times than he cared to remember.

Now it was forced upon him again. And this time the person whose destiny he would decide was neither enemy nor stranger nor friend, but his own flesh and blood, his own descendant, his own darling girl Annie. Not a religious man in normal times—in fact a doubter at times of the very existence of the Divine—now Clive closed his eyes and, under his breath, yielded up a brief, silent prayer.

Feeling Annie's flesh soft and warm and yielding beneath his hand, he managed a momentary grip on the switch and swung it to . . . the right!

· CHAPTER 8 ·
Into the Very Den of Peril

Annie quivered and toppled onto the greensward.

Clive drew her bodice back into place, covering her tender bosom. He held her hand, peered into her precious face. Her hand was relaxed, no longer balled into a fist. Her legs lay still on the earth, no longer pounding out their desperate tarantella.

The scarlet coloration was fading from her features. Would it be replaced by a normal rosy shade, or by the pallor of death? Her frantic, ragged gasps had ceased. Would they be replaced by calm, normal breathing, or by stillness?

Clive pressed his ear against her bosom. He heard her heart's beating, her lungs' breathing. Both were steady, unlabored.

Annie would recover!

He had moved the switch on the Baalbec in the proper direction!

Hard on the heels of his prayer of supplication, he sent up a second prayer: this one, of thanks. He slid a hand beneath Annie's shoulders and assisted her to a sitting position.

"Clive—grandfather—what happened to me?"

"You were struck by a bolt from the Chaffri's weapon. I feared for your survival, Annie."

She clung to him. "You must have— It's coming back to me now. You—you saved my life, Clive. The energy from the Chaffri's weapon scrambled my Baalbec. You reset the Baalbec for me, didn't you?"

Blushing, Clive admitted that he had done so.

"Thank you, Clive. Thank you."

"Annie, you told me to switch the device to the left for the master reset."

"Yes."

"What would have happened if I had switched it the right?"

She frowned. "Under normal conditions, nothing. The Baalbec's SD unit is interlocked so it can't be activated by misadventure—say, by an accidental elbow in a crowded elevator or a mistake by some overamorous groper."

"And under abnormal conditions?"

"If the interlock is disabled, you mean?"

"I don't know what an interlock is, but I suppose so. You said that the Chaffri weapon scrambled your device. Would that, ah, disable the interlock?"

"Absolutely!"

"Well, then—what would have happened if I'd set the switch the wrong way?"

"Why, the SD unit would have been activated." She smiled. "I thought I'd made that clear."

"But what is the SD unit, Annie?"

"Self-destruct. It would be too dangerous to let a Baalbec A-9 get into unauthorized hands. So anyone who tries to tamper with it, say, by removing it surgically from my body, or by scrambling the circuits and not hitting the master reset correctly— It just destroys itself."

"And what happens to you, Annie? Are you harmed by this?"

"Oh, I wouldn't be there anymore. If the Baalbec SD's, I'm gone. So is everybody and everything for about a mile in any direction. There's just a big hole in the ground."

She got to her feet, drawing Clive with her. She still had the weapon she had removed from the seat of the now-destroyed car, as Clive had his, also.

"Let's get out of here, Clive."

"Perhaps there will be a train along soon," he suggested.

"We'd do better on the road, I think." She took him by the hand and led him away from the railbed, toward the rural dirt road that paralleled the metal rails.

Before they had walked for an hour the sound of a creaking wagon, its iron-rimmed wheels jouncing when it struck a rut, could be heard. They turned and waited while the wagon hove into sight. It carried a load of vegetables. The driver sat alone on the box, reins in his hands, as two horses plodded docilely along.

Clive and Annie planted themselves in the center of the track and flagged down the slow-moving vehicle. The driver peered at them from beneath the broad brim of his hat. His hands and face showed the calloused roughness of an outdoorsman; his clothing, the dust of the dry dirt road.

The man sat peering down at Clive and at Annie. His face strained with deep thought. At length he spoke. "Young Master Folliot, is't?"

"I am Clive Folliot." Clive peered up into the other's face. "Farmer Cawder? Old Mr. Cawder, are you? Old Jim Cawder?"

"Nay, old Jim be dead these full score years, sir. I be young Jamie."

"Jamie! I remember you! Your dad was one of my father's finest men."

"Aye! A good and loyal fellow was me dad! And I'm as loyal to the Folliots as any Cawder has been for a thousand year! Can I give you and the missus a lift anywhere, Master Folliot"

"She isn't the missus, Jamie. But we'd be most obliged for transportation to Tewkesbury Manor."

"Well, I hope that the young lady don't mind ridin' on a farm wagon, then, sir. But it's all I've got."

"I don't mind, Jamie," Annie said.

They climbed aboard. Jamie whistled up the patient horses and they resumed their slow pace.

All the way to Tewkesbury Manor, Jamie maintained a slow, droning delivery of Gloucestershire activities in recent years. Most of the news concerned marriages, births, and deaths. There was the occasional scandal, the occasional oddity. Farmer Mayhew's wife had given birth to triplets, the first set on record hereabouts. Yes, all were well and the children were now toddling about and speaking a few baby words. Farmer Morgan's cow had given birth to a two-headed calf, which had not fared as well as Missus Mayhew's triplets. Farmer Horder's son Pauly had run off with Farmer Johnson's daughter Alice, setting all the shire abuzz not once but twice, both when they ran off and then again when they came back and Alice returned home looking angry as a hornet and not willing to talk about the matter at all while Pauly looked chagrined but equally unwilling to talk.

Somehow, in the midst of all the gossip, he never commented on Clive's reappearance after so many years, or his surprising youthfulness after so long an absence.

Jamie pulled up his team at the cast-iron gates of Tewkesbury Manor. "If you and the young lady don't mind, Master Folliot. My team are aged and the track from here is steep. If we might drop yourself and the young lady here, sir, I would be ever so grateful, sir."

"Of course." Clive and Annie climbed down from the wagon. "Thank you, Jamie. And good luck to you!"

The wagon creaked away.

"What did you make of that?" Clive asked.

"He saved us a long walk."

"Yes, he did that. But I know that man as a child. I was a few years older than he. His father—ah, what a man! He used to come up to the manor now and then, and Neville and I would run out to see him. He could pick us up, one in each hand. And he always had a piece of fruit for each of us. Gone now, gone and his son a man of middle years, too beaten down by his life and too cowed by the Folliots to notice that I haven't aged in a quarter-century."

"Never mind that, Clive. Let's get a move on. We're practically there."

The gates swung open at the pressure of his hands, and they strode up the long approach to Tewkesbury Manor. The manor was a huge building, dating back almost to the time of the Norman conquest. Clive had played there as a child, running up and down its long corridors, ducking into concealed passageways hidden by tapestries and high-backed wooden chairs.

"Have you been here before, Annie?"

She hesitated before answering, then gave a soft, affirmative response.

"I should like to know the details of that," Clive said.

"Please—there's so much you don't know, Clive. I wouldn't know where to start. Let's just get there."

"I can remember as if it were yesterday," Clive said. "The great hall, the armory, the kitchens where Neville and I were never supposed to go."

"But of course you did." Annie laughed. She seemed relieved to let Clive reminisce. As long as he did so, she did not have to answer his difficult questions.

"We did. There were other places we were forbidden to go, also. Sealed rooms. The subcellar. The inner library."

"You were forbidden to enter the library?"

"The manor has a great library, Annie. Father encouraged us to use it. But that was only the outer library. There was an inner library, as well. The door that opened to it was never left unlocked. Father alone possessed the key. Every Baron Tewkesbury for—well, for so long that the origin of the custom has been lost—every baron has had custody of the key to the sealed library, and the key has been handed down along with the succession to the title."

"Then you never saw the inner library."

"Never."

They had reached the grand entryway of the manor. A liveried footman bowed and reached for the huge iron knocker before Clive could reach for it. The footman pounded the cast-iron implement against its sounding plate, and its boom echoed from the house.

The front door swung open, and Clive ushered Annie in ahead of himself.

"Miss Annabelle." The butler bowed her into the hall. "And Major Clive. A pleasure to see you again, young sir."

Clive looked into the butler's face. The man was ancient, his sparse hair a mere white wisp surrounding his nearly naked scalp, his pink face a sea of wrinkles. "Jenkins?"

"Yes, sir."

"I'm happy to see you again, Jenkins. And Mrs. Jenkins, and the little ones?"

"The missus is still in the kitchen, sir. Most kind of you to ask. With your permission, sir, I shall convey your greetings."

"By all means. And I'll stop by to see her."

"She'll be very happy, sir. And you asked of the youngsters. They're grown now. Young Madeleine is married to a barrister in London. We're very proud of her, sir. I hope you won't think ill of her for rising above her station, sir. And the boy Tom has gone out to Australia to start a sheep station."

"That's wonderful, Jenkins. Wonderful."

"The baron wishes to see you in the library, Mr. Clive. If you feel up to it, sir. If I may venture, you do look a trifle ruffled."

Annie said, "I've other things to do, Clive. I'll see you later." She disappeared through a drape-hung archway. Clive had wondered about her having previously visited the manor; that question was now answered by Jenkins' promptly recognizing her and by her own obvious familiarity with the layout of the house.

Jenkins preceded Clive to the library. His formality was surprising, but Clive didn't question it. More to the point was Jenkins' instant recognition of him—and the fact that the man did not comment on Clive's youth.

The butler had aged normally in the past twenty-eight years, while Clive had aged by a matter of months. Surely Jenkins had noticed the change—rather, Clive thought, the *lack* of change—in the younger man. Why had he not commented? Jamie Cawder, the farmer who'd given Clive and Annie a ride on his wagon, was a dull soul who might simply have failed to take any note. But Jenkins was a bright man with a good mind. That, Clive remembered from his own childhood.

It was inconceivable that Jenkins, having bid farewell to Clive in 1868, would welcome him back to the manor in 1896, a Clive who looked hardly older than he had twenty-eight years earlier, and fail to notice something very strange about the series of events. Perhaps it was professional reserve on Jenkins' part. Or perhaps it was . . . something else.

Jenkins knocked on the door of the library. A voice called from within, and the butler opened the door for Clive, standing aside and closing it behind him as Clive entered the room.

Clive stared thunderstruck at the two men who awaited him.

His father, Arthur Folliot, Baron Tewkesbury, stood beside his high-backed, ornate chair behind his familiar desk. In childhood, Clive had thought the chair a throne, and had fantasized endlessly of his father as a king, himself as a prince who stole moments of sitting on that throne when no one else was in the room.

Baron Tewkesbury had aged indeed in the past twenty-eight years. When Clive last saw him in England, the baron had been a vigorous man of late middle years. In the Dungeon, Clive had encountered his father again—or a simulacrum of the man—and he had been little changed, if any, from his former state of being.

But now the baron had aged shockingly. He was wizened and bent. He had lost all of his hair and most of his teeth, and he stood—rather, swayed—peering at Clive through pale, milky eyes. Holding on to his chair with one hand, he raised the other, pointing a trembling, bony finger at Clive.

"So," he managed in a voice that conveyed bitter hatred despite its quavering weakness, "the traitor returns!"

"I? Father—*traitor?*—how can you call me that? I have never been a traitor to you or to the Folliots. It was you who always scorned me, who blamed me for my mother's death. And after our reconciliation in the Dungeon, I thought that all was peace between us!"

The baron stared at Clive, saying nothing.

"No." Clive held a hand to his brow. "No, it was not you, was it, Father? I remember now. I learned, even before I left the Palace of the Morning Star, that I had expressed my love and fealty to a simulacrum. Not to you."

"Correct," the old man whispered. "You made up like a sniveling bastard with a simulacrum of your father. No, Clive," he repeated, "I was never in the Dungeon."

"But *I* was." The words were spoken by another voice, a voice that broke in shockingly upon Clive's confrontation with his father. Clive turned at the sound of the second voice. So flabbergasted had he been at the sight of his father, and so distressed at the old man's accusations, that he had ignored this other.

The second man looked like an older version of Clive.

His hair was longer, steel-gray throughout, and his heavy mustache was of the same metallic hue. His face was tanned with decades of sunlight and seamed with long years of exertions. His blouse showed a slight paunch, but overall he gave the appearance of a man in excellent physical condition for his years. The uniform he wore somewhat resembled Clive's, but the design was that of a different unit and the insignia of rank indicated that the wearer held the rank of lieutenant general.

"Neville?"

"Indeed."

"But you—you have aged so—"

"I have aged but normally. Like you, I was born in the Year of Our Lord 1834. It is now 1896. Do I not look like a man of two and sixty years?"

"You do. You look remarkably fit for a man of sixty-two. But . . ." Words failed him. Instead, he indicated himself with a gesture of his hands, implying silently the comparison of his relative youth with his brother's apparent age.

"Of course, brother. You were brought here from the year 1871. You are but thirty-seven years old. And your charming descendant, I might mention—"

"You know Annabelle?"

"Were you not present at our first meeting, brother? Or have your encounters with simulacra so confused you that you doubt it was truly I—or truly she! We were both ourselves, authentically and in the flesh." He smiled suggestively. "Oh, I know her very well indeed, brother!"

Clive balled his fists and started to lunge at his brother before drawing himself back. "Only the difference in our ages keeps me from giving you a lesson, Neville! Be careful how you speak of my granddaughter! If not by reason of common decency, then because she is also your own grandniece."

"Why, brother—what did I say to offend you? Miss Leigh is a charming young person. Some of the customs and standards of her generation are different from those of our own, to be sure. Some of them may even be shocking. But I assure you, I hold her in only the most affectionate avuncular regard."

The old man had slumped into his seat, and now he

managed to call the others' attention. "To business, to business, Neville and Clive."

Neville drew a chair for himself; Clive did likewise.

"I am a very old man," Baron Tewkesbury quavered. "I have not long to live, and when I die the title of baron and all its perquisites and obligations shall pass to one of you. To you, Neville, if you survive me."

"I intend to do that, sir."

The baron turned Neville's response aside with a twitch of his head. "To you, Clive, if Neville does not survive me. And if you can purge yourself of your treasonous acts and affiliations."

"But, Father—you continue to accuse me of treason, and I am innocent of the charge!"

"Did you not make league with the Ren in the eighth level of the Dungeon? Is that not treason enough?"

"Father—I entered the Dungeon involuntarily, and only because Neville had disappeared and I was attempting to follow his trail. Everything I did in the Dungeon, on whatever level, has been done out of loyalty to the Folliots— and out of the needs of survival."

Lord Tewkesbury peered at Clive. The room was silent, its atmosphere charged as Lieutenant General Sir Neville Folliot and Sir Arthur Folliot, Baron Tewkesbury, waited for Clive to continue.

"I seem to have blundered into—or been lured into! —the greatest conspiracy in the history of the world. Philo Goode, Amos Ransome, Lorena Ransome . . . my long-faithful batman Horace Hamilton Smythe! He has saved my life repeatedly, Father, in the course of my adventures— only to disappear, then reappear in one exotic guise after another. Is the man a turncoat, or is he himself a victim of some alien force?"

He shook his head. Where to take this bizarre conversation? He would attempt a different tack.

"You, Neville." He rounded on his older brother. "You are sixty-two years of age?"

"I am that."

"And I am not yet forty. Yet we were mere minutes apart in time of birth. The year is 1896. I was snatched here from 1871. I have traveled across landscapes as terrifyingly unearthly as the mind can grasp, I have fought monsters the likes of which . . ."

He studied the faces of his two closest living relatives, his father and his elder twin. The baron seemed to be drifting, in the manner of a man approaching his ninetieth year. But Neville Folliot, immaculately groomed and punctiliously outfitted as a lieutenant general of Her Majesty's Royal Somerset Grenadier Guards, was listening intently. His expression was inscrutable as to his reaction to Clive's words and as to his own intention, but at the very least he was listening closely to Clive.

"Neville, my brother, let me tell you of one of my first encounters upon entering the Dungeon. In the company of my former batman Smythe and his East Indian associate Sidi Bombay—"

"I know Sidi Bombay," Neville interrupted. "I had the pleasure of making his acquaintance in the city of Zanzibar."

"Yes. And quite some reputation you left behind with our consul in Zanzibar, and with the Sultan Seyyid Majid bin Said!"

"Ah, some of the colorful residents of Zanzibar! And of the mainland of East Africa! I fear that I shall not see their likes again. The responsibilities of rank, the weariness of age—they conspire to keep an old veteran like me close to the flagpole. You younger chaps get to play at heroics."

"I refer not to heroics, Neville! Wherever I went, your reputation preceded me! I was branded a blackguard and a scoundrel—by utter strangers, Neville!—thanks to the mischief you had wrought."

"A pity. But it was all so long ago, Clive. Back in the sixties, ah, we were such wild youths, were we not? Colorful and rebellious, ready for any experiment, eager for every new experience. There will never again be an era like the sixties—at least not for us. But we live in a later decade now. The nineties may be better than the sixties, or they may be worse. Opinions must needs differ. But in either case, let us contend with the realities of the present."

"You will have to explain to me what you mean by the realities of the present, Neville. Precisely what realities are those? I know only that George du Maurier claims that he brought me here by the power of his mind and with the aid of Madame Clarissa Mesmer."

"Du Maurier? You have been in communication with du Maurier?"

"I came here from his home."

"What were you doing there?" The look in Neville's eyes was intense, the pupils glowed like coals. The expression on his face was severe.

"He is one of my oldest friends, Neville. The man is on his deathbed. In no way could I withhold from him whatever small comfort my presence can provide."

"But he is allied with our enemies! You fool, Clive! How much did you tell him? How much does he know?"

"What does it matter, Neville? I told you, the man is dying. As for our enemies—your phrase, brother, *our enemies*—you act is if the Folliots were engaged in a feud, like some wild American mountaineers. You—"

"This is far worse than a feud, Clive! *War* would be a more appropriate word for it. But a war that would make the contests of Greeks against Persians, Hebrews against Philistines, Romans against Carthaginians—even our own parents' struggle against the conquerer Napoleon—all pale by comparison. We are engaged in a war of worlds, of realities, of dimensions of being so vast in scope that precedent and comparison are pointless."

"That I doubt not, brother. Not after what I have seen in the Dungeon. But your adjectives convey little meaning to me. Pray, give me some facts."

Neville lowered his brow into his hands. Looking at the top of his brother's steely gray head, Clive was struck by an unexpected pang of compassion and, yes, even of brotherly love. Neville had chivied and bullied him for decades, but his brother he was, and more than a brother, a twin. Even in the Dungeon, Neville's presence had dominated Clive's actions at times—and his absence, at others.

Now, for all that he was a vigorous man and healthy for his years, still Neville was well into his middle life, beginning to approach the long and irreversible decline of old age—while Clive was a far younger man with many more years ahead of him.

Clive reached his fingers hesitantly and touched his brother on the back of his hand.

Neville jerked away from the contact as he would have from the touch of a hand of red-hot iron. He jumped to his feet. "All right, brother. It's facts you wish, and it's facts you shall receive."

Neville crossed to his father, who had slumped in his great thronelike chair and was snoring softly. "Summon Jenkins to help Father to his bed. A nap is a good restorative for him."

Clive called the butler. Neville helped Baron Tewkesbury to his feet, embraced him briefly, and then turned him over to Jenkins. Gently leading the frail baron by the hand, the elderly servant guided his even more aged master from the library.

Neville Folliot turned to face Clive. "Follow me, brother." He raised his hand and displayed the huge, ornate key that Clive knew unlocked the door to the sealed sanctum sanctorum, the mysterious secret library of Tewkesbury Manor.

· CHAPTER 9 ·
The First of the Folliots

Clive stood gaping after his brother. "The—the key! You have the key to the sealed library, Neville?"

"Is that not self-evident?"

"But that key is supposed to be the exclusive domain of Lord Tewkesbury."

"Is it really?"

The sardonic note in Neville's voice grated on Clive, but Clive chose to ignore that and pursue his questioning. "Is that a duplicate? Or did you take the key from Father?"

"Oh, Clive, Clive, little brother . . . what difference does it make? I have the key. The sealed room is open. You've been so full of questions—I'll concede that you are justified in your curiosity—but come along and you shall have some answers."

He disappeared through the doorway. Clive followed.

The sealed library was utterly dark. Clive heard the scrape of a match, saw it flare into sulfurous life. Then the match flame was replaced by the warmer, gentler illumination of a lighted candle. Clive could see the face of his brother Neville sinisterly illuminated from below by the golden light of the candle.

"Please close the door behind you, and make sure that it is bolted, Clive. I do not wish others to enter this room. Ah, thank you, little brother. And beside you there, you will see a comfortable seat. If you please—"

Clive complied, sliding into the comfort of an over-stuffed, leather-covered easy chair. He watched Neville take similar action, having first placed the candlestick on a convenient table. Beyond Neville the room remained in darkness. There was a flow of fresh air, and now and then, when an errant air current set the candle-flame in motion, huge shadows danced against an uncertain background.

"You seem quite familiar with this room, Neville. I take it you have been here often."

"Perhaps not so often, Clive. But I come here from time to time. As my duties require."

"What duties? I see by your shoulders and collar that you have risen in Her Majesty's service. You are no longer restricted to the Grenadier Guards, but have attained the status of a general officer."

"My privilege to serve crown and country, Clive."

"Then you must spend most of your time inspecting units."

"Good staff work, brother, associates carefully selected and properly trained, and a commander may come and go at will. Fortunately, for I fear that I am gone from my command a great deal of the time."

"I doubt it not."

"Still, I am a man of patriotic impulse. I have had several audiences with Her Majesty, Clive. I take great pride in that."

"Your loyalty is not to this sceptered isle, Neville."

"Put it this way, brother. A man may love both his mother and his wife. May love each, truly and loyally. Yet these are different loves and different loyalties."

"Very well, Neville. If Britain is your mother, who is your wife?"

"A greater power than any empire of this little Earth, Clive."

Clive shook his head sadly. "The Ren, Neville, or the Chaffri? Does it even matter? Who are the true masters of the Dungeon? Beings alien, heartless, and cruel. Your loyalties are to them, then? To these abductors, tyrants, murderers? Your loyalty to them shames you, brother. It shames me and all of our blood."

Illuminated only by candlelight, Neville's face was hard to read. Yet Clive thought he saw the flash of anger in his brother's eyes.

"You know not whereof you speak, little brother! You think you have seen the Dungeon, and having seen the

Dungeon you think you have seen all that is terrible and strange in this universe. But listen to me, brother. I tell you that you have seen only the smallest sampling of the Dungeon. You are like a man who spends an hour on the beach at Dar es Salaam and thinks he knows all of Africa. Believe me in this—I know whereof I speak! You have barely sampled the perils and the horrors that the Dungeon contains. And the Dungeon is but a tiny microcosm, the tiniest sample of the perils and the horrors of this universe!"

His eyes reflected the candlelight, brighter and hotter than the flame they gave back. "I know whereof I speak, Clive. In this thing if in nothing else, you must believe me."

"My question, then, that you so adroitly avoided when I started to ask you it."

"What question is that?"

"In the Dungeon—on Q'oorna—I encountered a monstrosity almost beyond description in its horror. It was crossing a bridge of midnight obsidian across the abyss near the City of the Tower."

Neville nodded. "Ah, yes—I remember it well."

"The monster was equipped with tentacles, feelers, claws, mouths, fangs—every appurtenance imaginable, with which to horrify and then dismember its prey."

Behind Neville, in the darkness of this sealed library in the safety of Tewkesbury Manor, still Clive could see the monster, looming and dripping its horrendous exudations. He could almost see Sidi Bombay scrambling up the monster's flank, disappearing into its clusters of waving tentacles like a South Sea islander scrambling up the trunk of a wind-angled coconut palm, disappearing into its waving fronds.

"We fought that monstrosity, fought it to the very limit and end of our resources. Fought it—well, not to victory, but at least to a stalemate, so that at last it tumbled from the bridge and disappeared into the blackness beneath that span, the blackness of the abyss."

"Yes, Clive, yes. But you said you had a question."

"When that monster went tumbling, I was able to catch a glimpse, first of its underside, and then of its crown."

Clive's brow was coated with perspiration and his hands twitched in subconscious reenactment of the titanic battle. "Its underside was a horror all its own. A transparent membrane held sealed a compartment in which miniature replicas of the monster floated. I took these to be its young."

Neville nodded, the movement of his head making his shadow dance menacingly. "You are correct."

"Among those young," Clive continued, "I saw other creatures, victims I assume of the monster, engulfed by the parent and held as food for the horrid spawn."

"Correct again, brother."

"But most horrifying of all, as the monster tumbled from the bridge, I saw revealed upon its peak a giant replica of a human face. Of your face, Neville! And as it fell from view, that face spoke to me. It cursed me. It cursed me, Neville—with your face, and in your voice."

Neville Folliot hid his face in his well-groomed hands. "Your memory serves you truly, Clive. The creature did have my face and it did curse you there on Q'oorna. I can say only that the creature was not I, for all that it looked like me and sounded like me. It had my face, or an image thereof at any rate. It even had my recollections, my mind or part of my mind, for a time. But it was not I, nor I it. I will not apologize, for it was by no will of mine that that event took place. No. I did not and would not do such a thing. As brothers we have had our differences, Clive— any pair of siblings will have their differences—but I would not treat my brother in the manner you describe."

Clive Folliot considered, then said, "I cannot accept an apology not tendered. Therefore let it suffice that I understand your explanation, and will consider the matter closed."

"Good!" A faint smile creased Neville's face. "Now— what else do you wish to ask?"

"Who are the Ren, Neville? How did you become involved with them? Is Father aware of your affiliation?"

"Clive, I will endeavor to satisfy you. But to understand this, you must have prior knowledge. Prior knowledge of the universe around you. When we were younger, I attended Sandhurst and received an education in military science and engineering. That education—plus my service in Her Majesty's campaigns—served to make me a hard-headed, practical man. I can look at a revolver, at a fortification—or at a distant star—and see it and attempt to comprehend it in practical, realistic terms."

He shook his head, then continued. "You attended Cambridge, Clive. Your studies were in the realm of art, literature, music, and philosophy. Remember our debates, when we were home from university for the holidays, Clive? Remember how Father would ask us to report on our learning, and I would discuss campaigns and fortifications and lines of supply—and you would speak of Homer and of Virgil, of Spenser and Marlowe and Michelangelo and Mozart?"

"I remember all too well, Neville."

"I remind you not for purposes of disparagement, but because you may simply not comprehend what I am about to tell you, brother. But try to accept what I say."

"Pray, proceed."

"You know that the Greeks believed that the fixed stars in the sky were suns like our own, only incredibly distant from the Earth. And that they believed that the moving planets were worlds not unlike our own. Hence even the strange fable—"

"That I know better than you, Neville. Lucian's *True History* with its populated Sun and Moon and Venus, its intelligent cabbages and its ship that sailed through the void between worlds."

"Indeed, Clive! Well, I tell you that the *True History* contained more truth than its author may have realized. Not that the sun and moon are populated. But that there are other populated worlds, more than we puny humans can imagine, more than we can count, more than we can even comprehend. The number of stars is so huge as to defy calculation, and among those uncountable stars are scattered uncountable worlds, and on those uncountable worlds there swell uncountable races of men. Of men, and of manlike but unhuman species. And of species so utterly unlike us that the monster you saw with my face would be as familiar as a tabby cat by comparison."

"A tale I am more prepared to accept after my journeys and my travail in the Dungeon than I was before, Neville.

I will posit the truth of all you have said. Where do the Ren and the Chaffri fit in? And, still, what is your connection with them? And what is the Dungeon? What is the *purpose* of the Dungeon, Neville?"

"You would have guessed that the Ren and the Chaffri are but two of the uncounted races scattered through our universe who—at least in a poetic sense, to adopt your mode of discourse, Clive—inhabit the stars. These races are endlessly varied. Some of them are more primitive than the naked bushmen of our Earth's remotest regions. Others are so advanced as to make a Faraday or a Herschel look like children splashing in puddles and wondering at the worms they dislodge from the mud."

"The Ren, then, are such a star-race?"

Neville nodded.

"I am not as surprised to hear that as you might think, brother. In the Dungeon I encountered beings from many worlds. The faithful doglike Finnbogg, the spidery Shriek, and Chang Guafe, strangest of all."

"There are those who are not so strange, too."

"Indeed. The Lady 'Nrrc'kth and her false consort N'wrbb Crrd'f. I might have loved the Lady 'Nrrc'kth. Her beauty was exotic—her skin a white as pale as freshly fallen snow, her long hair and deep eyes the green of a forest rising through that snow. In all my travels I never encountered one to compare with the Lady 'Nrrc'kth."

"And where is she now, brother?"

"Dead," Clive whispered. "Fallen in the course of a peril-ridden descent from one level of the Dungeon to another. For that alone, Neville, I despise the Ren. If they are the masters of the Dungeon, then they are responsible for the Lady 'Nrrc'kth's demise. I will never forgive them for that, Neville!"

"But you approve of the Chaffri?"

"I know little of them, but what little I know indicates that they are no better than the Ren. No better."

Neville held up one hand. "The Ren are not the masters of the Dungeon, Clive! Do not be deceived into thinking that." He emitted a sardonic laugh, the greatest show of emotion on his part since his reunion with his younger twin. "The Ren are but one of the competing powers in the Dungeon. And the Chaffri are another."

Clive made no further comment. There was little new to him in his brother's words. Much of this he had long known—but to hear it from his own brother's mouth brought it home to him more chillingly than even the reality of his own all-too-vivid recollections.

After a while, Neville spoke again. "As for your paramour, what was her name—'Nrrc'kth—do not lose hope. You tell me that she died in the Dungeon, but what if we were to intervene at a moment *prior* to her death? What if a force should enter the event-line between levels of the Dungeon and move her to a point of safety elsewhere in the Dungeon—or out of it?"

"Can that be done? Neville, can it?"

"But, brother, I thought you were pledged to a Miss Leighton."

"Miss Leighton, I have been led to believe, left London in 1868, shortly after my departure for Zanzibar and Africa in search of you. By now she is well established in the city of Boston in the United States. From the things Miss Leigh—Annie—has told me, Annabella has no desire to have anything to do with me."

"But think, little brother—if you could return to a moment before she left London—?"

"I have thought of that, Neville. It is a tempting prospect, an intriguing prospect, but I am finally reluctant to tamper with Annabella's life. To save 'Nrrc'kth—well, to save an innocent woman from her undeserved death, that is a prospect I would wish to pursue. But the case with Miss Annabella Leighton is a different one. Not only would such interference amount to tampering with her own life, it would also interdict the establishment of a whole line of descent, leading from her to Annie Leigh. No." He shook his head. "No, Neville. It tempts me, but I will resist."

Neville rose and carried the now-guttering candle to the far side of the room. He reached to a gas jet affixed high upon the wall, turned the cock to permit the flow of illuminating gas, and raised the candle to set the gas alight.

"Are you ready, then, to proceed, Clive?"

The room was now lighted by the gas jet, and as he

waited for Clive's response, he moved about the room lighting additional fixtures.

"Proceed to what, Neville?"

"To meet the Ren."

"You mean, to return to the Dungeon? Will Annie accompany me? Is she, too, part of this strange conspiracy of yours?"

Neville's face darkened and the corners of his mouth twitched downward, pulling the tips of his mustache so as to add to the power of his angry frown. "I need not tell you that I find your language and your implications offensive, little brother!"

Clive found himself growing equally angry in response to Neville's conduct. He rose to his feet and leaned toward his brother. "I have conducted myself with propriety throughout this affair, Neville! I set out in hopes of rescuing you—"

"Or of finding me dead," the older man interrupted, "so as to assure yourself of succession to the family title and estates upon our father's death!"

Reddening at the aptness of the accusation, Clive resumed. "I suffered shipwreck and suffered a near-fatal dose of spider's venom. I struggled through jungle and swamp, endured tropic heat, and risked attack by lion, crocodile, or snake. All of this occurred before I even entered the Dungeon! While you, Neville, have been in this— this collusive plot—from the outset! To apply the term *conspirator* to you is not merely accurate, brother, it is positively charitable!"

Neville turned his back. The only sound in the room was the soft *shush*ing of the gas jets. When Neville turned back to face Clive, it was as if he had aged another five years in the minute or less that his back had been turned.

"There is some truth in what you say, Clive. I have been involved with the Ren . . . all my adult life, and even since childhood. This was to have been a secret shared only by Father and me. Such has been the case, generation after generation, for as long as there have been Folliots in Tewkesbury. Truth be known, Clive, the record of our affiliation with the Ren extends into the distant past, to the creation of the first Baron Tewkesbury by Richard the Third in 1483."

Neville was pacing now, and Clive found himself following his brother's progress back and forth, back and forth, as an Egyptian cobra follows the piping music of a snake-charmer. "The leaf on our crest, the very word *Folliot* itself, proclaims our alliance and our allegiance to the Plantagenets. Since Richard's death in 1485 the throne of England has been occupied by usurpers. When the Ren triumph in the Dungeon they shall install a Plantagenet on the throne of England! The throne shall be restored to its rightful heir! Clive, that heir shall be a Folliot!"

"Treason!" Clive could contain himself no longer. "You speak high treason, sir! You, who aspire to the title of baron, who have taken Her Majesty's shilling and served in her Grenadier Guards, who have commanded her troops in battle and seen them die in defense of crown and country—you have been a traitor to Queen Victoria all along!"

"Not a traitor, sir! A patriot!"

Clive spun on his heel and headed for the door.

"It's locked, little brother."

"Then I shall break it down or else wrest the key from your possession. I will not remain a minute longer in the presence of such foul perfidy."

"There will be no need for that, Clive. It is true that you have been put through your paces in this affair, all against your will and largely without your knowledge of what you were in."

"Yes—and so you propose what, Neville? I tell you, I desire no part of your treasonous scheme, and if justice have its way, I shall live to see you strangled with a silken cord."

"I have no such expectation, Clive. But you may be right. You may be right. The more we learn of things, even of the past and of the future, the less we are able to call the turn of Fate. But I shall unlock the door and permit you to exit if you will agree to travel with me to the home of the Ren, and confer with them there. Once you have done so, you will be free to choose your course. I will not attempt to force your choice, Clive."

Clive stood silently, studying the strange installation behind his brother, waiting for Neville to continue.

"Will you give me your pledge, Clive? Will you return to Tewkesbury Manor and travel with me to the home of the Ren?"

"There is business I must first transact in London. I but arrived there last night and was leaving du Maurier's home when I was shanghaied by your agents, Neville. There is more I must do in the metropolis."

"You have not given your pledge to return to Tewkesbury Manor, Clive, but I will accept your statement as a tacit pledge. Go, then." He reached past his brother and unlocked the door. "Transact your business, Clive Folliot, and Godspeed to you, and I pray I shall see you again."

Clive stood in the doorway one moment longer, fixing his brother with a glare. "Well may you pray, brother. But first consider well what you pray for."

He found Annabelle in the kitchen, visiting Mrs. Jenkins. Annie had admitted to Clive her former visits to Tewkesbury Manor, and it was clear that on such earlier occasions she had made the acquaintance of the faithful cook and housekeeper, and they had become instant, fast friends. Thus, the egalitarian customs of Annie's home, the American city of San Francisco in the year 1999.

Seeing Mrs. Jenkins stirred profound feelings in Clive. His mother had died at the time of his own birth. He and Neville had been raised by their father with the assistance of a series of nursemaids, governesses, and tutors, one more stern and unyielding than the next. Baron Tewkesbury had reserved his own affection for his firstborn, Neville. Even though the brothers were separated by mere minutes in time of birth, their father had lavished his affection upon the elder of the two, blaming the secondborn for the death of his mother and treating him with cold hostility from the day of his birth.

Mrs. Jenkins had been the closest thing that Clive had ever known to a mother, his dearest companion and strongest ally. Her kitchen was always his place of refuge in times of trouble. She always had a hug available for him, and a sweetmeat. Her apron had absorbed uncounted tears and her hands had soothed away uncounted hurts.

Today she held Clive at arm's length. "How wonderful, Mr. Clive. My little Clive, my little friend. You do look so young, compared to Mr. Neville. Of course, I know that he's the elder." She chuckled at her own witticism. "Miss Annie is a wonderful young lady, Mr. Clive. Do you plan to . . . ?" she winked and tipped her head suggestively.

"I fear not, Mrs. Jenkins. I am as fond of Annie as it is possible to be, but there are reasons—reasons I cannot explain." He turned to face Annie. "I must return to London. There is much that you must explain to me, Annie."

"I know. I'll do my best."

"Are you involved with—"

"Please," she said, cutting him off. "These are things that are best discussed tête-à-tête. You understand that, surely." She rolled her eyes almost imperceptibly toward Mrs. Jenkins.

"Of course, I quite understand," Clive said. "Do you wish to accompany me on my journey to London?"

"Will you return to Tewkesbury?"

"Very soon."

"Then I shall await you here, Clive."

▪ CHAPTER 10 ▪
He Is Long Dead

Jenkins arranged a trap to take Clive to the station at Tewkesbury Village, and from there he rode unimpeded to London. It was a journey that contrasted with his wild progress from London to Tewkesbury with Annabelle Leigh. This time there was no Chaffri attack, and Clive's fellow passengers were a typical assortment of country folk headed for London to transact business of their own.

When Clive reached the great metropolis he headed at once for the offices of the *Illustrated Recorder and Dispatch*. When last Clive Folliot had visited those offices, they were located in a dingy series of cubbyholes. Overaged scriveners, failed would-have-been literary lions, slicksters, and hacks had held court in a dilapidated building that smelled of ancient meals of uncertain origin and of musty clothing and men, the two equally in need of a proper scrubbing and refurbishment.

Now a tall, modern building stood in place of the old *Recorder and Dispatch*, while a modern sign prominently affixed to the front of the establishment proclaimed it still to be the home of that formerly disreputable daily.

Clive had changed from his somewhat tattered uniform to an outfit of civilian garb that he found still awaiting him in his room at Tewkesbury Manor. He smiled to find his card case still handy, and he left the manor with a full purse and a supply of calling cards. The clothing, so long unworn, was a good fit still. But it was a quarter-century out of date, and he found himself encountering stares of curiosity both aboard the railroad coach that carried him from Gloustershire and in the streets of London.

He entered the offices of the *Recorder and Dispatch* and was greeted by an efficient-mannered young lady seated at a walnut table near the building's portal.

She inquired as to whether she might be of assistance to him. Clive took note that her hair appeared to be long and glossy, of a most appealing chestnut shade, although she wore it done up atop her head where it would not interfere with the efficient performance of her work. Her figure, too, appealed to Clive's eye, perhaps the more so because of the demure outfit with which she attempted unsuccessfully to conceal it.

"I am seeking the editor of this paper, Mr. Carstairs, young lady. Is he in?"

"Have you an appointment, sir?"

"No."

"May I inquire your business, then, with Mr. Carstairs? He is very busy, and if you are a tradesman there are other persons here with whom you might transact your business."

"I am a correspondent of this paper, young lady, and Mr. Carstairs is my editor." He took a calling card from his pocket and handed it the young woman.

After peering at the card, she raised her eyes once more to Clive, then dropped them once again. "Major Folliot, Fifth Imperial Horse Guards," she read.

"Perhaps you are familiar with my work—with my dispatches and illustrative sketches."

"No, sir, I fear such is not the case."

"But they have but recently run in this very— But no, I beg pardon." Clive chided himself silently. Of course the young person had not seen his pieces in the *Recorder and Dispatch*. They had appeared before her very birth! "Never mind. If I may see Mr. Carstairs."

"Very well, sir." She signaled a young boy to show Clive to Carstairs' office, first turning over Clive's card to him. Clive followed the lad down a corridor, up a stairway, and into a palatial suite of offices that would have contained the entire staff and much of the production facility of the *Recorder and Dispatch* of an earlier era.

Clive's guide rapped clean-scrubbed knuckles against well-polished mahogany, received an answering summons, and disappeared though the portal. Clive heard a brief, muffled conversation through the door, then it opened and the youngster reappeared. The lad nodded to Clive and held the door for him as he entered the editor's inner sanctum.

A very young man—he could hardly have been five and twenty years of age—looked up from a desk cluttered with sheets of paper. He was well, even wealthily, dressed. His hair was thick, and curled about his head. He squinted at Clive as if weak of vision, fumbled amid his papers for a pair of steel-rimmed spectacles, then frowned and rose tentatively to his feet.

"*Mister*"—he lifted Clive's card in one hand and held it close to his eyes to study it—"or is it *Major* Folliot?"

"Either will do, sir. But may I ask who you are?"

"Carstairs. I am the editor of the *Recorder and Dispatch.* May I inquire, sir, your business with me?"

"Perhaps I have the wrong Carstairs. I am seeking Mr. Maurice Carstairs."

"I am he, sir."

"Impossible. Maurice Carstairs engaged me to furnish the *Recorder and Dispatch* a series of reports on my expedition to Equatoria in search of my lost brother."

"I am very sorry, sir. I have no recollection of any such arrangement, nor do I have any recollection of you. When do you claim this, ah, arrangement was made?"

"It was the month of May, sir. The end of the month of May."

"Of this year, Mister Folliot?"

"It was May of the year 1868, sir."

The bespectacled young man slid precipitously into his seat. "You are aware of the present year, are you not, Mister Folliot? If you ever received such a commission, it would hardly have been from my hand. It was the year 1871 in which I first saw the light of day."

"And the Maurice Carstairs who was the editor of this paper in 1868—where is he, sir?"

"Alas," the young man said, "that Maurice Carstairs was my father. I regret that he is long dead. Long dead and buried, Mister Folliot. I'm afraid that in the years since his death—"

"In what year did Maurice Carstairs die?" Clive interrupted.

"It was 1886. I was fifteen at the time, and had to fight tooth and claw to claim my position as proprietor and editor of this newspaper. But as you can see, sir, I succeeded."

"Oh." That was all Clive could gasp, for the moment. He took a chair, all unbidden, and stared in silence at young Carstairs. Then he said, "Maurice was your father."

"He was, sir."

"The *Recorder and Dispatch* was a far less splendid enterprise in 1868 than it appears today. I fear that the paper and its editor at that time both suffered somewhat in repute."

"I have no illusions regarding my late father's character." The young man smiled whimsically. "But he was a man of real talent and possessed a certain eccentric integrity all his own, Mister Folliot. He taught me a great deal about the newspaper business—pardon my use of the cliché, but I might even say that he taught me everything that I know. It was by the application of his lessons, and upon the foundation that he laid with the *Recorder and Dispatch*, that I was able to bring the paper to its present position of prosperity and respect."

The young man looked down and opened a drawer of his desk. He bent very close to the drawer, squinting into it. At length he looked up at Clive. "If you are indeed the same Major Folliot whom my father employed in 1868, perhaps you will be able to answer a question or two, to verify your identity."

"Are neither my card nor my word sufficient, sir?"

"Ah, there you have the great paradox, sir. If you are truly Major Folliot, your word alone would surely suffice. Your card is a mere fillip of superfluous substantiation. But if you are an imposter, you would easily lie as to your identity, and you could surely furnish yourself with a false calling card. So we are caught between Scylla and Charibdys, Major Folliot. If you are he."

"Very well. What are your questions?"

Carstairs peered into his desk drawer once again. It looked almost as if he were going to climb into it, but at length he sat upright. "First, sir, what is the name of the missionary-priest whom you encountered in the village of Bagomoyo? And, second, who was the East Indian gentleman who joined the party comprising yourself and the traitorous Sergeant Horace Hamilton Smythe shortly before you entered the Sudd?"

Clive leaped to his feet, anger boiling within him. "Your questions are easily enough answered, sir. Those two I shall never forget—although for very different reasons, sir. The priest was the Reverend Father Timothy F. X. O'Hara. And the East Indian was a most remarkable personage who called himself Sidi Bombay."

Carstairs nodded noncommittally.

"But your application of the adjective *traitorous* to Sergeant Smythe is most offensive!" Clive resumed. "If it were possible for me to strike a person wearing spectacles, I might just seek immediate satisfaction for that insult to my companion. Horace Smythe is—was—as noble and gritty a man as ever it was my privilege to serve with in Her Majesty's Guards. And in our adventures in the Dungeon he performed uncounted deeds of heroism. His behavior was inconsistent and at times may have *appeared* disloyal. But he had been victimized by nefarious operatives and was acting under an irresistible compulsion at those times!"

He drew a deep breath, then added, "Sergeant Smythe is an upstanding man, and I will not permit him to be slandered by any ink-fingered panderer of Fleet Street. In fact—"

Clive halted in amazement as young Carstairs, without a change in his expression, disappeared still again beneath the level of his desk. There was a lengthy delay punctuated by soft thumps and ill-suppressed exclamations.

Then the chair was shoved back from behind the desk and Quartermaster Sergeant Horace Hamilton Smythe, smiling brilliantly, rose with his hand extended to Clive.

There was a moment of stunned immobility. Then Clive sprang to his feet, circled the desk, and embraced the other man. "Smythe! Smythe! I knew you could not have gone over to Philo Goode!"

"Of course not, sah. And I trust that you'll forgive my

little charade of a moment past. You see, what I said—what Mr. Carstairs said—was quite true, sah. There are forces at play, sah, to whom the secrets of disguise are as an open book, and to whom the creation of an apparently living, perfect simulacrum is little more than child's play."

"I know that, Smythe, all too well. I have encountered simulacra of both my father and my brother, as well as at least one female member of my family, all to my regret. But tell me, please—were you the publican who rescued me from a mob of ruffians the other night, only to turn me over to the untender mercies of Philo Goode? It was this incident to which I just referred."

"No, sah—that was not I. And what you tell me raises an alarm within me!"

"Then where have you been? If you have not been employed as a publican, have you been engaged in the publishing trade? Is this identity of a younger Maurice Carstairs a fictitious persona which you have assumed?"

"No, sah. Young Mr. Carstairs is a real enough person, and is indeed the editor of this paper. He is a good man, sah! One of our own, sah! I assume his identity from time to time, as necessity dictates. You might say that on occasion I act as Mr. Carstairs' very shadow."

"His shadow, eh? Well, shadow, tell me—what do you mean by the expression, *one of our own*?"

"I'll willingly tell you all that I know, sah. As ever, I am your ally. You will recall my occasional lapses." An expression of discouragement appeared on the man's face. "Such conduct was the product of devices implanted in my brain. In my very brain, sah! But I have managed to overcome their influence. I am myself now, my true self. I hope the Major will believe me!"

"I believe you, Horace."

"The Major has my gratitude. And I will tell you what I meant by *one of our own*, sah. But first, sah, there is another man here at the *Recorder and Dispatch* whom you must meet. A gentleman of color. The first such, I believe, employed by a London daily in a position of authority and respect."

Clive accompanied Smythe to an adjoining office, where

a man of dark skin, with black hair and mustache, labored behind a desk. He looked up as the others entered.

"Major Folliot," Carstairs-Smythe said, "may I introduce our chief editor for overseas reportage, Mr. Pandit Singh."

The Indian rose to his feet. He was costumed in morning coat, wing collar, and cravat. As he stepped from behind his desk he revealed striped trousers, spats, and properly polished boots.

Clive gaped and his jaw fell open. "Sidi Bombay!" Once more he embraced another. Then he said, "I have already seen Miss Annabelle Leigh, my brother Neville, my father, and Philo Goode since my return to London. I suppose the only one left to make a miraculous reappearance is Father O'Hara."

It was as if a pall had fallen on the room. Horace Smythe and Sidi Bombay looked at each other in silence. Clive felt that he had said something dreadfully wrong.

Horace Hamilton Smythe broke the long silence. "P'raps I'd better explain, sah. I promised that I'd elucidate upon the phrase, *one of our own*. I might begin by saying, sah, that Philo Goode is *not* one of our own. He is the very opposite of being one of our own, sah. The very antithesis, sah."

"You mean he is of the Chaffri?"

"I wish that were all I meant, sah. It's far worse than that—although I wasn't aware of how much you know of the Chaffri, sah."

"I know of the Chaffri. And of the Ren. And somewhat, I know of the Gennine, although almost nothing save that they exist and that their home world is a place mentioned only in whispers and dread."

"If the Major will pardon my playing schoolmaster, just what is it that the Major *does* know of the Chaffri and the Ren and the Gennine? Specifically, sah, if the Major doesn't mind."

"Why, that the Q'oornans and others that we encountered in the Dungeon are the pawns, some of them—and the agents, others—of two great warring empires. These are the Chaffri and the Ren. Their homes are on planets far beyond the scope of our astronomical knowledge. And they are engaged in a longtime, deadly struggle. So great is their power, there are some who suspect that they are the basis for the Zoroastrian tradition of the struggle between Ahriman and Ahura Mazda."

Pandit Singh—or Sidi Bombay—nodded. "You know of the beliefs of the Zoroastrians, then?"

"Travelers returning from journeys to Persia and Irak have described that fascinating religion. At Cambridge, it might have been compared to some of the heresies that wracked the early Christian church."

Throughout Clive's peroration, Horace Smythe and Sidi Bombay had exchanged significant glances and nods. Now Smythe said, "That's very apt, sah. And of course, the Dungeon is their chief field of struggle, with uncounted persons and uncounted other creatures snatched up from this world or that, from this era or that, and transported to the Dungeon to serve as pawns in their grand chess game."

"But what of the Gennine, Smythe?"

"The Gennine are most troublesome, sah. They seem to regard the Chaffri and the Ren equally as foes—or as rebellious inferiors. Consequently, sah, the Chaffri and the Ren have been known to make alliance, from time to time, in opposition to the Gennine. Sort of, the enemy of my enemy is my friend."

"There is a maxim in the Arab world," put in the man who was Sidi Bombay, " 'I fight my brother until our cousin appears, then we fight him together until a neighbor appears, then we fight *him* together until a stranger appears, and we *all* fight against the stranger.' "

"What is the point of all this?" Clive asked.

"The point, sah, is that there is a great organization whose purpose is to fight the Chaffri and the Ren—*and* the Gennine. There are agents in place in every era and every region. In the Dungeon and on the Earth and on other planets as well. They are among the Finnboggi, among Shriek's people, among Chang Guafe's, among the people of the world of Lord N'wrbb and Lady 'Nrrc'kth."

"And the name and purpose of this organization?"

"It is known—somewhat ironically, if I might add my comment—as the Universal Neighborhood Improvement Association. Its purpose is simply to resist the hegemonistic schemes of the others—equally of the Chaffri, the Ren, and the Gennine. Our enemies have agents as well. We have all encountered them, Major. Philo Goode, the Ransome couple, Father O'Hara—"

"But—a priest? A man of God? Whether one subscribes to Father O'Hara's faith or not, the fact that he has given his life to the service of the Divine—"

"Priest or not, Timothy F. X. O'Hara is still a man. Whether he joined the enemy voluntarily or was somehow hoodwinked or blackmailed or mesmerized into his role, still it is one he plays." Sergeant Smythe paused contemplatively. Then he said, "They can fuddle a man's mind, Major Folliot. Cast clouds upon the brain. I know whereof I speak, sah."

"Yes, Smythe. I recall your distress when you recalled the incidents of your trip to the burgeoning American metropolis of New Orleans. I am sorry."

" 'Nothing of it, sah. Perhaps Father O'Hara is more to be pitied than despised, but he is nevertheless an enemy. If we can win him back—that is, clear the pall from his mind and restore his loyalty to the human species and the respect of all intelligent beings—so much the better. If we cannot, we must fight him as we fight the Ren and the Chaffri and the Gennine."

"What, then, are we to do?"

"We'll get out of here, sah, for starters. If the Major will kindly wait a few ticks while I resume a safer identity . . ."

Smythe returned through the interconnecting door that led to Maurice Carstairs' office. He returned promptly in the guise of the nattily dressed, nearsighted Carstairs, squinting and blinking his weak eyes and blundering into furniture and doorways. He carried a gold-headed walking stick, using it almost as a blind man uses his cane.

"Mr. Singh, please—will you accompany Major Folliot and myself?"

"Of course, Mr. Carstairs," replied Sidi Bombay.

They left the offices of the *Illustrated Recorder and Dispatch* and climbed into a hansom that waited at the door. The driver peered down through the roof-trap and "Carstairs" gave him instructions.

"Can you trust a cabbie?" Clive inquired.

"He is one of us," Smythe answered.

"But if the enemy is capable of mesmerizing men—of planting devices for control in their very brains, or of abducting them and replacing them with simulacra—how can you know even that?"

"A good question, Major," Sidi Bombay interjected. "There are ways of knowing a natural being from a simulacrum, although they are less than certain and there is always an element of danger. Similarly, sir, when a man has been mesmerized, his behavior is often distinguishable from that of his true nature. But one always faces risks, and one must always take precautions. As you shall see, Major."

Clive bowed his head as the hansom pulled away from the kerb. He closed his eyes and pressed his forefinger and thumb against their lids. How to tell reality from illusion? Whom to trust? Were these two, Horace Smythe and Sidi Bombay, truly his companions of old, or were they illusions placed here to mislead him? If Smythe could pose as a mandarin, an Arab boy, a nearsighted publisher— could not an enemy pose as Smythe?

The hansom's wheels rumbled over cobbled streets.

Another question perplexed Clive. If it was George du Maurier's mental power, as augmented by Madame Mesmer's influence, that had drawn Clive across time and space to this London of 1896 . . . then how had Smythe and Sidi Bombay arrived here? They said nothing of having traveled across the years, but if they had lived continuously for these twenty-eight years, they should have aged, as had Clive's brother. And yet, neither seemed older than he had when last Clive had seen them in the Dungeon.

A shudder passed through Clive's body. There seemed no ready solution to his dilemma. He drew himself upright, dropped his hand, and looked around. The partly familiar, partly altered vista of London still surrounded him.

The hansom pulled to a halt in front of a building Clive had not seen since 1868—the gentleman's club where George du Maurier had brought him and Miss Leighton for a celebration following the premiere of *Cox and Box*, and where Clive had also last seen the senior Maurice Carstairs.

The front door of the club bore a black wreath.

"Carstairs" sent the cab on its way and the three men stood for a moment before the wreath. A small card, edged also in black, was affixed at its center. It read, GEORGE DU MAURIER, 1834-1896.

"Carstairs" rapped at the polished wood beside the wreath with his gold-headed walking stick. A liveried footman opened the door and bowed them inside, giving a series of startled glances, first at Horace Smythe, then at Sidi Bombay, and finally at Clive.

Sergeant Smythe peered nearsightedly at the footman. "Is that you, Browning?"

"Yes, sir."

"Is anything the matter, man?"

"No, sir. I just—I . . ."

"Out with it, man!"

"I could have sworn that you entered the club just a few minutes ago, sir. But that's impossible, for here you are." The footman managed a feeble smile.

"My associates and I will be using my private room for a short while. We are not to be disturbed."

Smythe stepped resolutely past the baffled footman, blundered off an overstuffed chair, grumbled at the staff for moving the furniture, collided with an elderly gentleman who tried frantically—but unsuccessfully—to avoid his pebble-visioned progress, and succeeded at last in leading the others to an inconspicuous corridor. This brought them to an even more inconspicuous room.

Bringing a key from his weskit, Smythe unlocked the door and ushered the others in. He locked the door behind them.

"No one is allowed in here," he explained. "No one, ever." As Clive looked around, Smythe said, "Dreadfully sorry about that encounter with the door-dragon. The real Carstairs must be in the building. This has never happened before—my fault, Major. Careless. No excuse for that."

"Spilled milk, Smythe. What now?"

"Now we change our identities, Major. I told you that we take precautions, and this is one such."

"Won't it appear odd, three persons entering this room and three others leaving?"

"We've a different way out, sah."

Minutes later three figures emerged from a florist's shop in a street not far from Carstairs' club. One was an officer of the Tsarist diplomatic service. The second appeared to be a laboring member of one of the darker races. The third was a jauntily costumed gentleman whose mustaches were waxed and twirled with self-indulgent care and whose right eye was magnified grotesquely by the thick lens of a monocle.

"Thus, in the fashion described so skillfully by the American author Mr. Poe, we hide ourselves from our enemies by making ourselves conspicuous." Horace Smythe nodded approvingly at the appearances of the others. "Come then, my friends. There's a marvelous game afoot!"

▪ CHAPTER 11 ▪
Neither Fang nor Claw nor Venomous Barb

The three ill-assorted figures—the Tsarist diplomat who was really a quartermaster sergeant, the unimposing workman who was really a master of intrigue and of esoteric studies, and the Continental dandy who was really the younger son of a Gloucestershire nobleman—cast eerie shadows in the lights of the strange instruments that covered a full wall of the room.

They had entered one of London's most splendid hostelries, made their way to a room kept in the name of Count Splitofsky, and descended by private elevator car to a chamber buried deep beneath the streets of the metropolis.

"This is a strangely timeless place," Sidi Bombay commented. "I find it peaceful to visit, it renews my soul. Here there is neither night nor day, neither summer nor winter. The illumination, the temperature, the degree of moisture here never vary. One can attune oneself to the infinite and the eternal."

"Good for the equippage, also," Smythe put in pragmatically. "This comes from a later time—p'raps Miss Annie would find herself at home here. Might even recognize some of the devices. The experts who installed this said that unchanging temperature and humidity would be best for all the gear."

"What about Annie?" Clive asked. "She is my own descendant, Smythe, as you learned when we encountered her in the Dungeon. Has she been hoodwinked by the enemy? Is she under a mesmeric spell?"

"When did you see Miss Annie last, Major?"

"Why, mere hours ago. She was at Tewkesbury Manor. She remained there when I came to London to see Mr. Carstairs. The real Mr. Carstairs, that is—Maurice Carstairs, senior."

"Quite understood, sah. I'm very sorry, sah. That could not have been Miss Annie. You were dealing with a simulacrum. Where did you first encounter her, sah, if I might inquire?"

"She appeared in a very peculiar sort of railway car, in a tunnel beneath a saloon where I had previously encountered Mr. Philo Goode. The publican in that saloon was . . . yourself, Sergeant Smythe."

"Yes, sah. As I mentioned, sah, there are simulacra to be dealt with. I assure the Major, I have no recollection of the incident he describes. Nor have I been under the controlling influence of the Ransomes and their mesmeric talents. My mind has been cleared. I worked long and hard with Sidi Bombay, and there is no longer the cobweb of mesmeric influence left in my cranium. I assure you of that, sah!"

Horace Smythe swept the hair from his brow to show a surgical scar, stark and white against the darker skin. "It took the skills of the ancient Egyptians to remove those devices from my brain, sah. It was a painful procedure and a risky one. But I am rid of them, and it was all worth the trouble to me, sah."

Sidi Bombay nodded his endorsement of Smythe's statement.

Clive put his head in his hands. "Oh, my God! And my brother and father—at Tewkesbury?"

Smythe exchanged a glance with Sidi Bombay. "One cannot be certain," the Indian replied, "but there is reason to believe that neither of those men was real. The Folliots are at the center of the struggle of Chaffri and Ren, Gennine and Neighbors."

"Neighbors?"

"A little joke, sah," Smythe said. "A taste for irony. The grand alliance that is forged to oppose the Chaffri, Ren, and Gennine, is known as the Universal Neighborhood Improvement Association. As I mentioned to the Major earlier, sah. Wherever you travel, sah, if you can locate an office of the association—its members are known simply as the Neighbors—you are in communication with our alliance."

"But Annabelle, Neville, the old Baron—if those are merely simulacra in Tewkesbury, where are the real persons? How can I find them?"

"That's a difficult problem, sah. You're sure you saw Miss Annie only in that underground railway, and then at Tewkesbury, afterward?"

"When I first emerged—Sergeant, Sidi Bombay—*is* this the ninth level of the Dungeon? Is Earth the ninth level?"

The Tsarist official and the Indian workingman exchanged glances. Sidi Bombay said, "You must try to understand, Clive Folliot, that the levels of the Dungeon are not simple things. Your progress through them—the progress of all of our party—was not accomplished as simply as one would descend from story to story in a tall building here in London. How did you reach London? Where were you last, in the Dungeon?"

"I—it's all so confusing." Clive clutched his head. "On the eighth level, everything seemed to be building to a climax. The Ren and Chaffri had shown their hands at last. On the other levels, they operated through agents and surrogates. But on the eighth level they were present in *propriae personae*. Then, almost miraculously I found myself stranded on the polar ice cap."

He paced the room, looking up at the great instrument panel that covered a wall. What was the purpose of the meters with their swinging pointers, the tiny lamps that flashed on and off in various colors, the panels upon which enigmatic messages flashed into and out of being, some of them in the English language, some in other languages which Clive at least recognized, still others in symbols so alien to his eye that he was able only to infer that they were language at all?

"There on the ice I saw Annie. You remember the Japanese marines we encountered in the Dungeon?"

"Indeed, sah!" Smythe responded.

"And surely you remember the flying machine—the aeroplane—in which Annie escaped from them, and with which she joined us at the castle of N'wrrb. Smythe, Sidi

Bombay—I saw Annie flying overhead at the pole, flying in that Japanese aeroplane. I waved to her and I'm sure she saw me. She waggled the wings of the aeroplane. I believe she intended to land and rescue me, only to disappear in the wink of an eye!"

The recollection brought a lump to his throat. He was convinced that the woman in the aeroplane was the *real* Annabelle Leigh. The woman in the subterranean car, the woman he had left at Tewkesbury Manor with a promise to return after visiting Carstairs in London—that woman was almost certainly a fraud. He tried to recall: Had he mentioned their polar encounter to her? Had she remembered it? Or had she feigned the recollection, permitting him to mislead himself in his eagerness to believe in her?

Where was the real Annabelle Leigh? Trapped in the Dungeon? Here on Earth, but stranded in the year 1868 while Clive and Horace Smythe and Sidi Bombay were in 1896, hardly a day older than they had been twenty-eight years before?

"Let's take this carefully, sah." Horace Hamilton Smythe had seated himself before a small panel of buttons and keys not unlike those used by the typewritists employed by newspapers and publishing firms. Clive had seen the like during his visit to the *Illustrated Recorder and Dispatch*.

"What do you intend to do, Smythe? This machine brings to mind those that Chang Guafe and I saw on the eighth level. Wondrous machines capable of storing amazing amounts of information, sorting through it and arranging it in many ways, then returning it to us upon request. Whole libraries and staffs of researchers concentrated like the Lord's Prayer engraved on the head of a pin!"

"Yes," Smythe said. "I know whereof the Major speaks. I know of such machines. And this here's the greatest of 'em all. Or, at least, it connects us to the greatest of 'em. Where the grand master machine is, I don't rightly know, sah. But what we've here is good enough for most jobs, and connects to the *real* big 'un if it's given a task it can't handle."

"And you're going to, ah, tell this machine my story? And ask it the meaning of my experiences?"

"Something like that, sah."

Even as he spoke, Horace Hamilton Smythe's dexterous hands had been flying over the face of the panel, tapping at keys, setting and resetting switches. The lights on the wall above him flared and flickered in bewildering patterns. The message board upon which Clive had seen so bewildering an array of languages carried on a dialogue of its own with Smythe's little panel.

"Perhaps the Major would be so good as to tell us what happened after the aeroplane disappeared." These words came from Sidi Bombay. Clive found himself wondering at the Indian's unfailing equanimity. When first Clive had met him, Sidi Bombay had been an ancient, wizened husk of a man. He had emerged from the horrors of the Dungeon a third his former age—young, virile, energetic. He had been dressed, in the time Clive had known him, as a humble trader, a morning-coated gentleman, a ragged workman. And yet he never lost his calm.

Clive recounted his experiences with Chang Guafe, describing the alien cyborg's disappearance beneath the Arctic waters. He described his encounter with the horrendous monster built by Dr. Frankenstein, the arrival of the space-train, the way that the two of them, Clive Folliot and the lumbering monster, had entered widely separated cars on the train. Horace Smythe's fingers flew over the keys and buttons. The message panel flashed a response, cryptic and unreadable to Clive but apparently meaningful to Smythe. The pseudo–Count Splitofsky said, "Chang Guafe survived that experience, Major, and is busy and well. What then, sah?"

"What then, Smythe? Is that all you have to say? 'Chang Guafe is busy and well.' Where is he, man? What is he doing? How did he escape from beneath the ice cap?"

"Easy, sah, easy," Horace Smythe said, attempting to calm Clive.

But Clive would not be soothed. "And how do you know where he is? I demand that you tell me, Sergeant Smythe, before we do anything else." When Smythe was slow to respond, Clive seized him by the lapels. "Tell me, man!"

Before Smythe responded, Clive felt the hand of Sidi

Bombay on his shoulder. "Calm yourself, Clive Folliot. There is nothing to be gained by treating one's friend as one's enemy."

Clive relaxed his grip. He was shaking. "You're right, Sidi Bombay. Sergeant Smythe, I apologize. I shouldn't have—have acted in such a manner. But if you know what became of Chang Guafe, you must tell me. At once."

"That's all right, Major Folliot." Horace Smythe, still garbed as the Tsarist Count Splitofsky, brushed his coat and adjusted his lapels. I can show the Major what became of Chang Guafe more clearly than I could ever explain it, sah. With the Major's permission, then . . ."

Unable to control his voice, Clive nodded.

"If the Major will take a seat, then." Smythe flicked a series of switches, adjusted a series of levers on the machine. The light in the room grew dim. Before Clive's amazed eyes a cloud of fog or smoky material arose and floated at eye level. Within it a scene slowly took form.

"Why—why it is myself! Myself and Chang Guafe and the Widow Shelley's monstrous creation. See us there, struggling across the ice floe. And see us, now, sailing before the Arctic zephyr. Sergeant Smythe, how can this be? What do I see?"

He plunged his hand into the fog—or tried to do so. It was no use, for the fog resisted, gradually, gently. He could shove his fingertips into it easily, but after the first few inches they felt a counterpressure, and the harder Clive pressed, the deeper into the fog he penetrated, the stronger the resistance became. After the first four or five inches, he found himself pressing with all his strength, perspiration breaking out on his brow, unable to reach any of the figures that he beheld.

He ended his efforts, withdrew his hand, slumped back in his chair.

"If you would merely observe, Clive Folliot," Sidi Bombay urged, "you would accomplish more than you would by attempting to intervene. It is the karma, after all, of those you behold. It is the will of heaven. One must not interfere."

"But—but it is I myself!"

"Indeed it is."

"Is this an image merely?"

"I think not, Clive Folliot," the Indian said.

"Nor do I, sah." Horace Smythe adjusted a knob, and the figures in the fog grew until they seemed the size of a child's dolls. "I believe we are actually seeing the Major, along with Chang Guafe and that other chap, the tall, pale one."

"You *believe*, Smythe?" Clive saw the space-train come to a rest on the arctic water. He saw himself and the Frankenstein monster clamber onto cars. He saw Chang Guafe slip beneath the surface of the frigid polar sea. "Can we do nothing to help him?" he exclaimed.

"We must not interfere, Clive Folliot." Sidi Bombay's voice was as calm as ever. "Nor could we. You saw what happened when you attempted to penetrate the fog."

"They don't know we're watching them. Are we actually seeing the past as it takes place, or is this an image merely?"

"Don't know as it matters, sah."

"The Major speculates upon matters of metaphysics." Sidi Bombay smiled.

"Can we see anything we want? Any scene in time or space?" Clive demanded.

" 'Tisn't easily done, sah. The controls of this thingama-bob are devilish hard to master. I can only tune in now and then. But I think I reached Chang Guafe because you was with him, sah. And now you're here. It all connects up somehow, sah."

"But you saw him before, you say?"

"Yes, sah. But you, sah, you're here now, ain't you?"

Clive nodded dumbly. Metaphysics indeed. It was all beyond him. "What's happening to Chang Guafe? Can you show me him?"

Without speaking, Horace Smythe operated the machine's controls. Water rushed upward, filling the volume of fog in the center of the room. Murk filled the space. A feeling of chill and moisture pervaded the room. Dark green forms wavered and silvery ones darted by like bullets. Clive realized that he was observing the bottom of the polar sea. A large shape, in part covered with a smooth, metallic carapace, crawled forward.

"It's Chang Guafe!" Clive exclaimed. "He's all right!"

Neither Horace Smythe nor Sidi Bombay spoke.

The phantom Chang Guafe crawled, crablike, along the bottom of the sea. Briefly the waters swirled and boiled, and by dropping down and peering up into the foggy area Clive could see the surface of the sea in an uproar, and the space-train above it, rising into the cold sky. Clive returned his attention to Chang Guafe.

The alien cyborg extruded a shovel-like scoop and lifted a gob of material from the sea-bed. With tiny tools that he extruded from his body, Chang Guage shaped the material into a tube and sent it rising to the surface of the sea. He sucked in air, inflating elastic sacs that appeared through openings in his carapace.

Gracefully, Chang Guafe rose to the surface. Again he changed his configuration, filling newly created fuel tanks with water. The water fed into Chang Guafe's body, reappeared as glittering particles through tubes that emerged beneath the cyborg's body.

Chang Guafe rose into the air, sped away from the Earth, and was lost to sight.

The fog grew as dim as if night were falling.

"That's all, sah."

"But where did he go, Smythe?"

"I don't know, sah. It 'pears as if the Major got too far away from Chang Guafe. Or Chang Guafe, from the Major, sah. Leastways, I can't hold the image past that point, sah."

"It is my guess," Sidi Bombay put in, "that Chang Guafe has gone in search of his people. Or perhaps he is headed elsewhere."

"And this is happening . . . now?" Clive inquired.

"This happened long ago."

"And where is Chang Guafe *now*—in 1896?"

The Indian shrugged. "Sergeant Smythe told you that Chang Guafe was well and busy, Clive Folliot. But that was in part surmise. I believe, also, that we will see him again, although I do not know when or where that will be."

Horace Smythe was manipulating the controls of the machinery, but the image in the fog faded, and he was not able to call it back. "What happened after that, sah?" he asked. "I mean, sah, after the Major climbed aboard the train, and the train rose into the sky. What then, sah?"

"And then, I found myself in London. In the home of my dying friend, George du Maurier. I had spoken with him, from the Dungeon. It was never clear to me whether we had truly communicated or whether it had been an illusion, a dream or mirage or hallucination. But it was no illusion—it was real."

"Mr. du Maurier is dead," Sidi Bombay said.

"He is now."

"Was he alone when you saw him? Was he conscious? Was he in command of his faculties?" Horace Smythe asked.

"He was not alone. He was attended by Madame Clarissa Mesmer, the granddaughter of the famous Anton Mesmer. He was conscious and fully coherent when I left him."

Horace Smythe and Sidi Bombay exchanged another glance. Smythe's fingers flew. Enigmatic words and symbols flashed across the message panel.

"Madame Mesmer is a very powerful woman, Major Folliot," Sidi Bombay said.

"Powerful?" Clive responded. "Do you refer to psychic power, or to human influence, Sidi Bombay?"

"Both, Major Folliot. And more."

"More, Sidi Bombay? Please elucidate."

"Her influence extends not merely to human agencies, Major Folliot. That is what I meant."

"Sidi Bombay, Sergeant Smythe . . . I fear that I have gotten into a situation that is far beyond my depth. At times I feel like a solitary adventurer, a Hercules or a Parsifal, facing monsters on the one hand and traitors on the other. Yet even that I can cope with. There was a time in my life when I should have cringed helplessly before these odds. Such is no longer the case. The Dungeon has changed me, strengthened me, altered me for the better."

He looked from Horace Hamilton Smythe to Sidi Bombay. "But at other times I feel like a piece on a chessboard," he continued, "moved about at the whims of others, a helpless pawn being played in a game I neither comprehend nor control."

"Chess is an ancient game," Sidi Bombay replied. "It was known in the Middle East and in my own country long before it reached Europe. We are, perhaps, all chessmen in the game of the gods. But we are not pawns. Sergeant Smythe I should take as a rook—powerful, straightforward, stalwart. As for myself—well, perhaps a bishop, cutting across the paths of others, striking at distant and unsuspecting targets, Major Folliot."

"And I? What chess-piece am I, do you think, Sidi Bombay?"

"You, sir? In my mind there is no question, sir. You are a knight. Your power is not so obvious, but then, sir, neither are your intentions. You seem to be moving straight ahead, only to strike to the side. Yet again, you move to the left or the right, then veer and plunge where your attack is unexpected. Or you retreat and at the last moment turn and slay your pursuer. You may never survive to become a baron, Major Folliot, but in the game of chess you are already a knight!"

Clive could not suppress a smile. He looked from Sidi Bombay to Horace Hamilton Smythe. "It was we three who entered the Dungeon together. You, Horace . . . and you, Sidi Bombay . . . and I. The rook, the bishop, and the knight—perhaps. But who is the king? Baron Tewkesbury? My brother, Neville? Baron Samedi? Father O'Hara? George du Maurier?"

"The king is dead, long live the king," Sidi Bombay intoned in a low, solemn voice.

Clive flashed him a look.

Sidi Bombay returned it but said no more.

"And who is the queen?" Clive resumed. "The Lady 'Nrrc'kth? My great-great-granddaughter Annabelle Leigh? Madame Mesmer? Lorena Ransome?"

Sidi Bombay spread his hands in silence.

"Time and again I have encountered chess sets in the Dungeon," Clive said. "In Green's house, for one. And in the strange room that was like a scene from the fantasies of Dr. Dodgson, for another. Chess sets, with real personages replacing the pieces. I appeal to you. You appear to know far more than I of our mutual situation. Share with me your information."

Sergeant Smythe said, "That we shall, sah. That we shall do." He took Clive's elbow and guided him to the seat that, in his guise as young Maurice Carstairs, he had just vacated. "If you'll sit yourself down right 'ere, sah, you shall have plenty of information. More, p'raps, than you'll enjoy!"

Clive fixed his companions with his gaze. "After this, my friends, I shall propose a further course of action."

"Yes, sah. As you say, sah."

"Sergeant, I shall thank you not to patronize me. We three entered the Dungeon together, there at the ruby heart within the Sudd. All that followed, all that befell us within the Dungeon, is the sequel of that event. I propose, therefore, that we three join—or rejoin—forces, and see this thing through to its end. *Now*, Sergeant Smythe and Sidi Bombay. *Now*, and without further delay or distraction. We have been through much, together and apart. We have suffered fang and claw and venomous barb. We have been imprisoned, have known privation and pain."

He pounded a fist into the palm of his other hand. "I propose that the three of us form a pact, that we swear a great vow, as blood brothers—yes, as blood brothers, despite the disparity in our station and the differences of our races—and see this through to its end!"

Without another word, the three men, a patrician Englishman, a hardy yeoman and professional soldier, and a dark-skinned Indian mystic, clasped one another's hands.

There was a moment of silence. Then Horace Hamilton Smythe winked his eye. "I was hopin' yer'd say somethin' like that, sah. Something exactly like that! Thank yer, sah! Thank yer! All very good, and it's time to get to work, then, sah!"

"Very well. Our first task shall be to reassemble the party of adventurers who have shared most of our experiences in the Dungeon."

"I thought it was just the three of us, sah. The Major and Sidi Bombay and meself, sah." Smythe's voice and the expression on his face betrayed a measure of disappointment.

"I understand your feelings, Sergeant Smythe," Clive said. "We three are more than associates, more than members of a business enterprise or a sporting team or a military unit. Yes, we are brothers! But we three cannot undertake this task without help."

"There's the Universal Neighborhood Improvement Association, sah."

"Indeed there is. And we shall act under their ensign, if you and Sidi Bombay so deem, Horace. But you must pardon me for feeling that we will do better if we but locate our own comrades. Those, at least, who still survive, and who are willing to join us in what must surely be the final confrontation between the champions of all that is just and decent and moral—and their sworn foes."

"Just who is it that the Major has in mind, sah?" Horace was looking more and more morose. "Surely we won't have to break up this team, I hope."

"Never." Clive shook his head. He saw the look of relief on Horace Smythe's face. Even the normally stolid and undemonstrative Sidi Bombay smiled and nodded.

"But look here, Horace, Sidi Bombay," Clive resumed. He pressed his thumb to one side of his nose, his forefinger to the other. Before his mind's eye there appeared images of uncounted adventures, unmeasured perils and privations in the Dungeon. And yet, all the suffering that he had undergone seemed, in retrospect, strangely sweet to him.

"But look," he repeated, "let me call to mind just a few. Horace, Sidi Bombay—is that marvelous mechanism not capable of tracking down a handful of individuals?"

"I do not know, Clive Folliot." The Indian looked doubtful. "You must tell me as much as you can, and I shall attempt to do as much as I can."

Clearly, Clive thought, it was Sidi Bombay who was the master of the machine.

"Chang Guafe you have already shown me."

Sidi Bombay nodded.

"And Annie, my darling Annabelle Leigh. If that was truly she, flying the aeroplane above the polar ice—but *not* truly she whom I left in Gloucestershire—then where is Annie now? And where is the aeroplane?"

The Indian held his palms outward in a strangely Western gesture. It was not necessary for him to say that he did not know the answers to Clive's queries.

"You do not know, but you can find out?"

The Indian frowned.

"Before you even try," Clive said, "let me complete the list. There is Shriek—"

"That bloody gigantic spider?" Horace Smythe's face reddened.

"Yes, Horace. A strange and alien being, but one who stood beside us through peril and privation. When last I saw her, the poor thing had been reduced to the size of an ordinary domestic arachnid. But where is she now? Can we bring her to us? And can we restore her to her proper stature?"

"That is as it may be," Sidi Bombay said. "We shall have to consider. But have you completed your list, Clive Folliot?"

Clive shook his head. "By no means, Sidi Bombay. There is Finnbogg—a dear, faithful creature and a staunch ally. He managed to return to his own world, did he not? There he would have been reunited with his own kind, but did he locate the littermates whom he so desperately sought? Has he made for himself a happy life, or does he yet bear the wounds of his suffering in the Dungeon? Ah, Sidi, I do miss Finnbogg. He was not the cleverest of fellows, to be sure, but there burned within his breast a flame of purity that we more sophisticated folk have long since lost." He paused before resuming. "And there is Tomàs—"

"Tomàs!" Horace Smythe practically exploded. "He showed no concern for us, Major, not even for you. And you told me that he was your blood relative, a Folliot!"

"Yes, Horace, that he is. Yet even the noblest house may, from time to time, spawn a rogue. Tomàs would be by no means the first such. And yet, Tomàs is not a thoroughgoing scoundrel. Good and evil war perpetually in the soul of every man. Why should a Folliot be an exception? And for well or for ill, it remains true that Tomàs is a Folliot."

"Even so, Major—even so! Why should we care for him, when he didn't care for us? Why, for all we know, he's just as likely to betray us again as he was when we first met him!"

"Everything you say is true, Horace. I cannot deny it. But still and all, he is of my blood—and he was our companion. I cannot see my way clear to simply abandoning Tomàs to whatever fate has befallen him. At least, not if there is anything we can do."

Sidi Bombay put in, "Is that the completion of your list, Clive Folliot?"

Clive stood with head bowed, as if he were studying the toes of his boots. He rubbed his chin between forefinger and thumb. "There is one other, my friends."

"Not the Lady 'Nrrc'kth, sah! I know how the Major felt, but the lady is dead, sah. We can't change that, sah."

"Not the Lady 'Nrrc'kth." Clive raised his eyes to his companions and lowered his hand to his side. "No, not she. I shall carry her image forever in my heart, my friends, but I know that I shall never see that beloved face, feel that precious touch again. Not in this world. Perhaps in another."

"Then who, sah?"

"Baron Samedi."

"That being of Hades?"

"We do not know that he is a being of Hades."

"But we saw him there!"

"As did he, us! Did you never hear of him during your sojourn to the city of New Orleans, Horace?"

"I—I'm not sure, sah. Should I have?"

"There is a cult there—at least we were lectured upon it, at Cambridge—called Hoodoo, or Voodoo, or Vodun. Imported to the Louisiana Territory with slaves from the island of Hayti. The cult is a combination of Christianity and animistic beliefs from the African region of Senegal. African gods and nature spirits, Christian figures, sacrifices and enchantments . . . it is a strange and wonderful religion."

"Yes, sah, I'm sure it is, sah. I'm sure that the Major's professors at Cambridge made it fascinating, sah. But what's it to do with me?"

"Baron Samedi is an important figure in the cult of Hoodoo. With his top hat and tails and his cigar—with his arrogant strutting and his cocky manner—he mocks death and all the powers of evil. He aided us in our escape from the nether regions—or from the level of the Dungeon that we took for them. I would be proud to have him at my side in the final confrontation with our enemies."

"And that's all, sah? There's no one else the Major wants?"

"Sergeant Smythe, do I detect a note of sarcasm in your tone?"

"Sarcasm, sah? In *my* tone? Sah, I'm just a straightforward farm lad wot's found a home in the army. Such things as sarcasm is beyond a simple soldier like me, Major."

"Very well, then. Let it go." Clive whirled toward the Indian. "Sidi Bombay, what do you think? You seem more than competent to operate these instruments. Is it possible to locate our former companions?"

"Perhaps, Clive Folliot."

"And to reach them? To communicate with them, to bring them here?"

"Perhaps, Clive Folliot. I will see what I can do. Perhaps you and Horace Smythe would care to leave me in solitude while I make the attempt."

Clive felt Horace's hand on his elbow. "Sidi can do it if anyone can, Major."

"But the space-train—"

"This would be another method altogether, Clive Folliot," Sidi Bombay said softly. He turned his back on the others and busied himself with the machinery.

"If Sidi wants ter be left alone, sah, I think we'd better leave him alone."

"What have you in mind, Horace?"

"I don't know, sah. P'raps a glass of ale. I know a pleasant pub not far from here."

· CHAPTER 12 ·
The Dandy and the Count

The Continental dandy and the bogus Tsarist count left the building via a cobbled alley. A pack of cats pawing through an accumulation of trash snarled in defiance, then gave way before the waved walking sticks of the two men.

"Will we need a hansom, Sergeant?" Clive asked as they reached the sidewalk.

"Count Splitofsky, if you please, sir."

Clive grinned. "Beg your pardon, your excellency! And you may call me—" he thought for a moment, "Monsieur Terremonde."

"Is a short walk only, M'sieur. Come, let us go."

Horace Hamilton Smythe—Count Splitofsky—slipped his arm through his companion's elbow and urged him from the mouth of the alley, into the bustle of a late London afternoon. As they stepped into the passing throng, a well-dressed couple drew back, casting hostile glances at them and commenting behind raised hands to each other.

Splitofsky guided Terremonde through the gray streets. A fog had already risen from the Thames, and the air was dark and chill. The feeble sun was a mere disk of milky pallor against the gray-brown sky. Drays, diligences, broughams, and hansoms filled the thoroughfare, their wooden fittings creaking and their iron tires clattering on the cobblestones.

At a busy intersection a harried bobby wearing the smart new tunic and copper helmet of the Metropolitan Police waved gloved hands frantically, trying to sort the onrushing traffic into some semblance of order. As Splitofsky and Terremonde strode past him, the bobby saluted smartly. Splitofsky and Terremonde, with almost military precision, returned the gesture by raising their walking sticks to the brims of their silk hats.

With startling suddenness the neighborhood changed its character. What had been a bustling district of neat offices and smart shops gave way to a grimy quarter filled with dosshouses, storage sheds, sewing lofts, and low dives. It was into one of these last that the Count Splitofsky guided Monsieur Terremonde.

"Are you sure?" Terremonde inquired. But before Splitofsky could reply, the other exclaimed, "I know this place! Why, this is the saloon where I was approached by the two women—where the publican was—"

"Don't say it!" Splitofsky hissed.

Clive—Terremonde—held his tongue.

The heavy door swung closed behind the two men. Terremonde stood gazing about himself while Splitofsky moved past him, toward the long wooden counter behind which an aproned publican slouched, elbows on the mahogany surface, engaged in conversation with a woman. She was one whom Terremonde had never seen before, but she was of a type with which he had of late become painfully familiar.

Splitofsky rapped his walking stick against the wooden railing. "Service, if you please, sir!" He spoke with a marked accent.

Folliot/Terremonde peered through an atmosphere composed of tobacco fumes, exudations of distilled alcohol, attar of roses, musk, stale perspiration, and London fog. The publican had looked up and was engaged in dialogue with Smythe/Splitofsky.

Could Terremonde believe his eyes? He rubbed them with gray-gloved knuckles. Using his walking stick as a pry and a prod, he managed to make his way through the tightly packed patrons of the saloon.

"Horace!"

The exclamation had no sooner passed Terremonde's lips when he realized that he had committed a potentially dangerous faux pas. The identities and loyalties of the denizens of the den were unknown to him, but after his

previous encounter with the two loose women, their ruffian associates, and the startling barkeep and "owner" of
the establishment, he feared that the very mention of
Count Splitofsky's true name might imperil the man.

But in the noise and bustle of the saloon, Terremonde's
word went unheeded.

Splitofsky's hand darted between two heavy types and
clutched Terremonde by the elbow, drawing him toward
the bar. Terremonde darted a look into Splitofsky's face,
then into the uncannily familiar face of the barkeep. "Who
are you, man?" Terremonde hissed.

"Smith, sir."

"That's Smith with an *eye* and no *ee*," Count Splitofsky
put in.

"That's right, milord." The barkeep tugged at his fore-
lock. "Matthew McAteer Smith."

"And who is the proprietor of this establishment?"

"That would be Mr. Smithson, milord. Mr. Oliver Oscar Smithson."

"And the woman with whom you were just speaking?"

Smith peered past Terremonde. "The lady with the
feather in her hair? That would be Miss Smithers, milord.
Miss Dorothy Daphne Smithers. And she is a lovely lass,
wouldn't you agree, milord, if I might venture an opinion."

Terremonde pressed his hand to his brow. His skin felt
clammy and there was a ringing in his ears. As if from a
distance he heard the bartender Smith speaking to Count
Splitofsky. "His lordship looks a bit peaked. Maybe we
should help him into the back room."

Splitofsky grunted assent.

Terremonde felt himself sliding, then a pair of strong
hands catching him under the arms. He didn't quite pass
out, but felt himself carried through the pressing crowd of
the saloon's patrons. Gaslight roared and wove, smoke
drifted through the miasmic atmosphere. He felt himself
laid on a couch, smelled the leather upholstery, tried to
focus his eyes on the wooden paneling overhead.

He found himself wondering what had become of his
silk hat and his polished walking stick. Faces peered down
at him. Voices buzzed and cloth rustled.

"You all right, sah?"

Clive pushed against the couch, struggling upright. Strong hands supported him. His head still spun, but he felt himself regaining strength. A glass was pressed to his lips. He swallowed a burning liquid, felt strength radiating from his belly even as the drink hit home. Brandy.

"I—I'm all right. I just—It was all too much for me." Clive raised a hand to his brow, and found that he was still wearing the gray gloves proper for an afternoon in the city. It must be evening now, and he still in daytime clothes!

"Horace?" He peered into the face nearest him. Was it that of the Count Splitofsky, or was it that of Horace Hamilton Smythe?

"Try to breath deeply, sah. You're looking better already, Major Folliot."

"I—I feel ashamed, Horace. To faint like a weak woman."

"It could happen to anyone, sah. As the Major says, sometimes it's all just too much. You'll be all right now, sah. Would the Major like another sip of restorative?"

Clive nodded, drank deeper, swallowed. "Thank you, Horace." His head was clear enough now to notice that his hat and stick had been brought along and placed on a nearby table. He looked from Horace Hamilton Smythe—yes, even in his identity of Count Splitofsky, there was no doubt in Clive's mind that the man was Horace Smythe—around at the others. The barkeep, the man who had been introduced as Matthew McAteer Smith. The woman, Dorothy Daphne Smithers. And the dignified individual looking on, surely that must be Oliver Oscar Smithson.

"You—you're all the same!" Clive heard his own voice exclaim.

"After a manner of speaking, sir, we are indeed." It was Smithson who spoke.

"But we have our differences, as well," said the woman Dorothy Daphne Smithers.

Clive looked at her more closely now. Her hair was long and lush, as black as jet and swept in graceful waves that set off her face to advantage. Her eyebrows were of the same shade, startling against a pale complexion made paler by the application of white powder. Her eyes were a deep and gorgeous blue, her features fine and graceful. Her figure, showcased as it was by the low-cut bodice and wasp-waist of her dark red gown, was lush.

Blinking with admiration, Clive smiled at her. "You do indeed, my dear. But still, Horace," this latter spoken to the Count Splitofsky, "who are these persons? What is this place? It was strange enough when I encountered Philo Goode in this very room—I think it was this very room. But I see only modified forms of your visage in every face I encounter. What is happening?"

"If I may answer, M'sieu Terremonde." The speaker was the impressive Oliver Oscar Smithson. He drew upon a black Cuban cheroot. His face was florid, set off by side whiskers that joined his graying mustache. His hair was thin, his belly not at all so. His brocaded weskit and finely tailored suiting marked him as a man of substance.

"Please," Clive replied.

"Welcome, Clive Folliot, to the Bathgate Chapter of the Universal Neighborhood Improvement Association. You have heard of us, I trust, sir."

"Heard of you?" Clive managed to climb to his feet. His knees were still wobbly but his dizziness was now past. He reached toward Dorothy Daphne Smithers. She handed him the brandy snifter. That was not what he wished to receive, but he took another sip of the liquor and set the snifter upon a low table. "Yes, I've heard of you, Mr. Smithson. Horace—Count Splitofsky—told me about the association. Horace and Sidi Bombay. That is not what I meant, sir. I mean, are you all relatives? Or are you simulacra, or those strange creatures that I am told are called *clones?*"

"Something like that," Smithson said.

"But not quite." That was Miss Smithers. Clive realized that her voice was as charming as her appearance. Cool, low, soft—yet with a suggestion of warmth, as if glowing embers had been banked against the time when they might be fanned back to passionate flame.

"Not quite? If you please, then . . ."

Miss Smithers exchanged glances with Smythe, Smith, and Smithson. "There are more worlds than you dream of, M'sieur Terremonde."

"I have learned much in the Dungeon, Miss Smithers."

"Of that I have no doubt, Monsieur. I have read your dispatches with enjoyment and admiration."

Clive felt himself coloring, yet feeling considerable pleasure at the recognition of his efforts. "Then you are aware of my adventures."

"Your adventures, Monsieur, have made you famous on more worlds than you can imagine. Those who know of them—of you—and of your companions . . . are widespread. You might walk down a street in Buenos Aires, in St. Petersburg, in Istanboul, or in Tokio, and barely one person in ten thousand would know of you. But yet there would be that one in ten thousand. And such is true not only in every great city of this planet, but also of Mars, of the worlds circling the great stars Procyon and Deneb, of planets circling suns so far from here that the very galaxies of which they are members are invisible to the unaided eye. Oh, yes, M'sieu Terremonde. Oh, yes. Wherever human foot treads—and indeed on worlds where no human being has ever set foot, but where the spark of awareness has blazed in forms more strange than any you have ever encountered—you are known."

"But about the Smiths," Count Splitofsky put in. "Would a word of explanation not be apt?"

"Indeed it would." Oliver Oscar Smithson, florid of face and fulsome of manner, took center stage.

"Each station of the U.N.I.A. is set up to serve a sector of some world. Except for those in more sparsely populated regions of the universe. There, a station may serve an entire planet—or many planets. And each such station, whenever possible, is staffed by persons of sanguinary connection. The association has long since learned that bonds of blood serve to reinforce bonds of political or other loyalties. Thus, this station is staffed by Smiths, and Smythes, and Smithsons, and Smithers. . . ."

"Our station in the American city of New York," Dorothy Daphne Smithers took over, "is staffed by Joneses. Joneses, Johns, Johnsons, Johansons, Jacksons."

"And our station at Marsport Central . . ." Matthew McAteer Smith added. The others turned to face him. "Well, the Martians' names are not easy for human tongues to pronounce."

"Are the Martians not themselves human?" Terremonde inquired.

Smith smiled. "Not—ah, not quite, M'sieur Terremonde."

"Ah, well—but then, I have made alliance in the past with creatures not of human form, nor of earthly origin. What form do these habitants of the red planet manifest?"

Smith shot an inquiring look at Smithson. The latter nodded an affirmative and the erstwhile publican struck a concealed stud worked into the woodwork of the wall. A section of solid walnut seemed to become transparent, as transparent as clear window glass. Terremonde found himself staring at a creature shaped something like a tropical jellyfish, floating high in the thin atmosphere of another world.

"As nearly as I can pronounce the station manager's name," Matthew McAteer Smith resumed, "it sounds something like this—" and he made a sound unlike any Terremonde had heard in his life, a cross between a rasp and a hiss and a dry, tortured rattling. "Every member of that station is related to the manager, and their names so indicate—although you will pardon me if I do not attempt to reproduce them for you."

Terremonde made a sound of acquiescence.

"And thus you see, sir, the importance of the Folliot family to the Universal Neighborhood Improvement Association." It was Count Splitofsky who spoke. "And perhaps," he added, "we would do well to make our way back to the place where our associate waits."

Terremonde blinked. "Yes. Yes, ah, let us do that."

"Are you well enough?" Splitofsky asked solicitously.

Terremonde indicated that he was. With the Russian at his side, he started for the door. Oliver Oscar Smithson and Matthew McAteer Smith offered their hands to each of the visitors. Dorothy Daphne Smithers did the same— to Splitofsky. Terremonde she treated differently, holding him in her arms and offering lush lips, breathlessly parted. Terremonde hesitated but a fraction of a second, then lowered his face to hers. The warmth of her reaction stirred him. He drew back. Some unspoken message passed between them.

He exhaled, released her. He wondered if he would

ever see her again—and if he did, what would be the result.

Oliver Oscar Smithson placed his hand on the elaborately worked brass door handle. "Before you go, my friends . . ."

Terremonde and Splitofsky halted.

". . . I must warn you. This building is located on an instability."

"Yes. That I know," Splitofsky said.

"When last I was here—" Terremonde began, but a look from Smith told him that there was no need to continue.

"I shall serve as M'sieur Terremonde's guide," Splitofsky said.

"Very well. Just . . . be careful, my friends. And Godspeed!" Smithson turned the metal handle and Clive Folliot and Horace Hamilton Smythe stepped through the portal of hell.

I've been here before, Clive thought. Flames leaped about him. Puffs of smoke erupted from miniature volcanoes that spread across a landscape unlike any on the Earth. The stench of sulfur stung his nostrils and the acrid atmosphere brought hot tears to his eyes. There was no visible sky. Instead, overhead, where leaping flames and roiling clouds of black vapor broke upon jagged points, a hellish inversion of the monstrous landscape that surrounded him loomed angrily, terrifyingly, threatening to fall and crush all that lay below it.

Somewhere in the distance a shriek rang out. Truly and literally, it was the despairing cry of the damned.

Clive Folliot felt a hand grasping his sleeve. He turned and looked into the face of Horace Hamilton Smythe.

"Say it ain't so, Major! Sure as me ma'am warned me, it's Satan's own realm and we're doomed. We'll cook for the devil's own dinner!"

The cosmopolitan manner of Count Splitofsky had fallen away, and though the man still wore the formal garb of the Tsarist diplomat, his manner was once again that of his true identity.

In like manner, M. Terremonde had become once again Clive Folliot, younger son of a country nobleman, major in the service of Her Majesty the Queen.

"It's hell, surely enough, Sergeant. But we are hardly damned! Get hold of yourself, man! You passed through the Dungeon; you know that Hell—*this* Hell, at any rate—is merely another level of the Dungeon."

"I remember, sah." Smythe was visibly calmer now. He released Clive's sleeve. "I'm sorry, sah."

"It's all right, Horace. I quite understand."

"I knew that this was a variable location, Major Folliot, but I never expected to find myself stepping from an Association office directly into Hades itself."

"Quite all right, Smythe. But now we've got to find our way out of here. You don't suppose Sidi Bombay has an eye on us, by any chance?"

"Don't think so, sah. He was going to try and locate our missing companions. Still, if we don't return . . ."

"All right. But we won't count on assistance from that quarter."

Their conversation was interrupted by a shriek as a devilish figure hurled a flaming trident at them. Clive dived to the right, Horace to the left. The trident whizzed between them, sizzling and crackling, leaving behind it a trail of noxious vapor.

Clive had landed on his hands and knees. Even as he scrambled to regain his feet, he spotted Horace in dire peril. The two had found themselves on a walkway of stone, hardly wider than a man is tall. When they had dived to avoid the flaming trident, Clive had landed at the edge of the walkway, but Horace, opposite him, had slipped from the edge of the path and was hanging by his finger-tips, scrabbling to retain his weakening grasp on the stone.

If he lost his grasp he would tumble into a pit of roaring flames.

Clive literally threw himself across the pathway, flying through the roiling, sulfur-laden air. He crashed to the edge of the walkway just as the fingers of Horace's left hand lost their purchase. Clive grabbed Horace's right hand.

"Hold on there, Horace! I've got you!"

Clive held on to Horace's right hand with both of his own.

Horace reached with his left and grasped Clive's wrist. "Help me! Major, help me!"

Clive tugged at Horace's arm, shoving backward with his elbows, dragging Horace back onto the walkway. "Don't worry, my friend. Don't panic."

He was already half the length of a forearm from the edge of the walkway. He could see the look of panic beginning to fade from Horace Smythe's face. Behind and beneath Smythe he could see the leaping flames and, amazingly, the fiendish forms that pranced and capered among them, howling their frustration at the loss of prey that they had thought their own.

"Shift your hand now! Grasp my shoulder, Horace!"

Smythe obeyed.

Clive now had one hand free. He braced it against the pathway, heaved himself to his knees, and simultaneously managed to pull Horace Smythe fully back over the edge. The two men clambered to their feet. Horace's face bore an expression of relief; Clive's, one of satisfaction.

In the pit behind Horace, a furious demon screeched his rage and hurled a trident at his departing prey. Clive shoved Horace aside—there was no time for a warning shout and the latter's reaction—and with reflexes speeded by long and arduous exposure to peril, snatched the trident from the air, even as it whizzed past them.

"Let us see what we have here." Clive studied the weapon. The shaft was as long as a man is tall; the tines as long as a sapper's carbine bayonet and as wickedly barbed as an Equatorian hunting spear. The weapon was made all of metal, and its heat pulsed through Clive's hands—but he did not yield it.

"Sergeant Smythe—can we return to the U.N.I.A. office?"

Horace turned in a circle. "I don't see how, sah. I don't see any doorway to take us back."

Clive nodded. "Nothing so surprising to that. We've encountered doorways before that seem to lead only one way and that disappear once you've stepped through them. Well then, there's only one thing to do—push on! We'll find our way out of this place and get on with our mission."

They set off down the pathway. There was nothing to either side but scenes of horror and torment. Flames shot upward, jets of noxious fumes assaulted their nostrils, the screams of the damned and the gleeful screeches of their tormentors tore at their eardrums.

The brightness of the flames and the blackness of the clouds of filthy smoke that arose from the pits obscured their vision, but now and then a vagrant current of foul air would part the flames and the rising fumes, and Clive and Horace could peer into the pits. The faces of the tormented tore at their heartstrings, their pleas for succor eloquent even in pantomime.

Clive stopped and leaned over the edge, the trident resting on its hilt, tines upraised.

"Can't stop, sah! Can't help them! We'd best move on!"

"But—I recognized a face! Those eyes, that hair! I cannot leave her to—"

"We can't help them, sah! And for all we know, those are either simulacra or illusions. We've encountered plenty of those, have we not, sah?"

A beautiful face peered up at Clive, appeal written in its eyes.

"She's on her knees, Horace! Look at her torment! We cannot—"

"We must, sah!" Horace was tugging at Clive's elbow, dragging him by main force from the tormented woman. Before they had taken half a dozen steps the flames roared up with renewed intensity. The woman disappeared.

"That was—"

"Never mind who it was, sah! Don't torment yourself, Major Folliot."

A huge batwinged form detached itself from the roof far overhead and swooped at Clive and Horace. Only the beating of its wings, the thump of their opening and folding, the hot rush of stinging sulfur fumes as it plummeted, warned the two men.

Clive turned his face upward, facing the apparition with new shock. "Tomàs!"

The thing pulled up half the height of a man above Clive and Horace. It had a hair-covered body that was an obscene parody of a human's trunk, but its legs were truncated and ended in feet like those of a great, ugly bird, in razor-sharp claws. Instead of arms it had wings like those of a bat, the rudimentary fingertips armed also with scythelike claws.

And its face—oh, its face was that of man.

"Tomàs!" Clive moaned a second time.

The thing swooped away and rose back toward the foul flame pits and hideous rookeries of the roof of Hades. It was as small as a calf, then as small as a duck, then it turned again and dived straight at the two men.

"Fight it, sah!" Horace Hamilton Smythe had broken his stunned paralysis and regained his voice. "It's going to kill us, sah—and I have no weapon!"

The monstrosity was diving toward them, driving itself to ever greater speed with its bat wings. Its form filled Clive with a mixture of horror and revulsion, its face was filled with demonic rage and an insane hatred, its eyes glared like living yellow-white coals.

And its voice—its voice screamed in a tone as loud and as piercing as the screeching brakes of a great steam locomotive: *"Die, Clive Folliot! Die and be damned here among the damned!"*

Clive ducked as the monster passed over him, and from the corner of his eye he could see Horace Hamilton Smythe do the same.

The monster pulled up and swooped away again, but not before raking the backs of both men with its talons. The claws ripped Clive's garments and tore at the skin of his back. He felt as though he had been scourged with two sets of white-hot barbs. He emitted an involuntary scream of pain, and heard Horace Hamilton Smythe echo that scream.

"It will come again, sah! It will come again! Fight it!"

"But it is Tomàs! He is my own kin! Horace, how can I—"

There was no time for the rest of Clive's question. The hideous being had flapped and stroked its way upward again, and now it dipped once more and plunged toward the walkway, its claws extended to rake and rip, its mouth open in a scream of rage half-human and half-demonic.

Clive sank to one knee, grasped the trident in both hands, and faced squarely upward into the eyes of the onrushing monstrosity. "Get down, Horace!" he shouted.

At the very moment that the creature's claws swept through the sulfurous air where Smythe's body had been, Smythe landed with a thud on the surface of the walkway. Tomàs—or the being with Tomàs' face and with the parody of his voice—swooped through steaming air, drove forward with another thrust of its powerful, leathery wings, then reared in midair and plunged razor-sharp claws straight at Clive Folliot's horrified face.

Clive launched himself forward and upward, the hot trident extended before him. With a jolt that ran up Clive's arms and rocked him onto his heels, batwinged monster and sharpened prongs met—and the monster was impaled on the trident.

Fuming, green-black ichor spurted from the monster's torso.

Clive dropped the trident.

The monster tumbled to the walkway and thudded onto its back, the shaft of the trident protruding from its fleshy torso.

Horrified, baffled, yet moved by the pathos of the wounded creature, Clive knelt at its side. "Tomàs? Tomàs? Is it truly you? Why did you—how—your own kind, Tomàs—"

He was halted by the pure hatred that blazed from the monster's eyes. "Better to die in my true form," the voice that was half Tomàs and half that of a screeching beast tore at Clive's ears. "Better to die in my true form than to live any longer as a putrid human, a corrupt Folliot!"

"But you were—" Clive got no further. The face that was that of Tomàs Folliot, the Portuguese sailor, writhed in its final rictus. The mouth pursed; Clive wondered if Tomàs was trying to whistle, but unstead Tomàs launched a gob of spittle. Only it was not spittle, it was the same ichor that still oozed from around the tines of the trident embedded in his torso. The fetid, slimy substance burned where it struck Clive's face, and he wiped it away with the cloth of his sleeve.

Tomàs' eyes glazed, his labored breathing ceased.

Clive felt Horace tugging him gently by the shoulders. "Come away, sah. Come away. He's gone." Clive allowed himself to be drawn to his feet. He watched as Horace placed a foot against Tomàs' corpse and pulled the trident from his body in the manner that Her Majesty's soldiers were trained to use when they retrieved bayonets from the bodies of enemy troops.

"Is there nothing I can do for him?" Clive murmured softly. "He was still of my blood."

"All we can do so, sah. Either leave him here, or . . ." Smythe gestured.

Clive hesitated for a moment, then nodded, breathing a silent prayer to whatever deity there might be, for the repose of whatever soul Tomàs might have had.

Horace Hamilton Smythe tipped the body over the edge of the walkway, using the toe of his boot to do so. The body tumbled into the flaming pit below and disappeared.

Clive Folliot tried not to hear the shrieks of glee that rose from the pit, nor to think too much about what they meant.

They proceeded along the walkway, Horace Smythe now carrying the trident that he had retrieved from Tomàs's body. How long they trudged, how many miles they covered, Clive and Horace could not gauge. The path that they walked changed in composition, now with a surface like marble, now like basalt. At one point it seemed to turn to metal, a gridwork of girders not unlike the structure of a railroad trestle. Beneath their feet stretched an abyss, and its bottom, lakes of molten sulfur.

Flames and clouds of foul gases rose from beneath the trestle. Clive turned his eyes upward. The hellish pit beneath his feet was duplicated above him, and he saw flocks of the hideous batwinged creatures clustered around pits and glowing mounds of sulfurous lava that rose like volcanoes from the hot rocks beneath their feet.

The creatures had human faces, and Clive saw the hate-filled visages of men and women he had fought on level after level of the Dungeon.

One of the batwinged creatures in particular caught Clive's attention. It was smaller than the others; for a moment Clive wondered if they bred as do humans, and if so, whether this was the child of such a process.

The creature locked eyes with Clive. Its face could have been that of an angel in some medieval painting, yet one filled with such pure malice as to send a shiver down Clive's spine despite the suffocating heat of his surroundings. Suddenly Clive recognized that scene before him. It was not the work of a medieval master, but of the fantasist Hieronymous Bosch.

The demon smiled and launched itself into the air. Its flock of companions followed—dozens of them, then scores, then hundreds. They did not head for Clive and Horace directly, but circled around them, cawing and shrieking in their horrid half-human voices.

"Let's hurry on, sah!" Horace urged. He increased his pace to a steady trot, heading for the far end of the trestle, but one of the demons landed squarely in the center of their path. Another followed, and another, until fully a hundred of the monstrosities blocked the trestle.

"Back, Horace—back the other way!" Clive and his companion whirled and started to retrace their steps, only to find their path blocked by another crowd of the demons.

Hopping like birds, flapping their great leathery wings like giant bats, flexing their talons in eagerness, the twin bands of demons closed upon Clive and Horace.

"It's the end, sah! I've that trident, and I'll take as many of them with me as I can. But still, sah—this is the end!"

Clive clasped Horace's hand in his own. "We'll go down fighting, Sergeant, if go down we must. But—"

He peered into the flaming pit that flanked the trestle. Craters smoked, sheets of flame flared upward, clouds of black, sickening smoke wafted around them. Screams of anguish and shrieks of glee rose to smite their ears.

And in a particularly dark and solid-looking cloud of smoke, a formally garbed human figure danced a jig, tipped his black stovepipe hat, and bowed satirically. From a pocket in his swallowtail morning coat, the newcomer drew a crooked stogie. He bit off its tip and spit it at the monster nearest to Clive and Horace. He placed the stogie between his teeth, leaned into a shaft of crackling flame, and drew it into life.

He blew a cloud of smoke from the stogie, into a crowd of batwinged monsters. Coughing and cringing, they drew away. He turned, drew on his stogie, and blew another cloud of smoke at the monsters menacing Clive and Horace from the other direction.

"Welcome, my friends," he smiled.

"Baron Samedi!"

"Major Folliot. Sergeant Smythe. A pleasure to welcome you to Hades."

"You saved our lives."

"A trifle. These demons are a nuisance. Not to be taken seriously."

"But one of them was my kinsman, the sailor Tomàs. I—I killed him."

"Regrettable."

"We have to get out of here, Baron. Can you get us back to London? Will you join us?"

"Join you? Oh, no, no, no! I'm much too busy. I have my duties here. I seldom visit your world—although I've had some interesting times in the island of Hayti. And there's a nice city called New Orleans that I visit on occasion."

"I think I know a bit of that, Your Grace." That was Horace Hamilton Smythe speaking.

"Indeed, colleague."

Clive said, "Colleague?"

"I believe that Baron Samedi works with the U.N.I.A."

"Correct, colleague. In Port-au-Prince. And in New Orleans. As I recall, Horace, our paths first crossed in New Orleans. You were in a bit of trouble there."

"Yes, I was, Your Grace."

"You're sure you won't come with us, Baron Samedi?" Clive was wondering, now, whether he had crossed paths with the U.N.I.A. himself, at different levels of the Dungeon. When things had looked hopeless, when he had thought himself lost, only to win through to surprising victories, had it been sheer luck, or sheer grit—or the concealed intervention of the Universal Neighborhood Improvement Association?

"*Non, mes amis,* I cannot accompany you. But you wish to leave Hades? Despite the salubrious climate, the colorful scenery, the active social life, and the presence of famous personages? Very well. You wish to return to London?"

"To see if Sidi Bombay has located Finnbogg—"

"Finnbogg?" Baron Samedi waved his cigar in the manner of a stage illusionist waving his magic wand.

Hell disappeared.

Clive Folliot found himself surrounded by blue trees. Overhead, filtering through the leafy canopy, in the center of a red sky, three green suns blazed downward.

· CHAPTER 13 ·
As an Alien in Eden

He whirled, looking for Horace Smythe, for the Baron
Samedi, for the monsters and demons who had surrounded
him until a split second ago. They were nowhere to be
seen.

The cries of the damned, the gleeful laughter of their
tormentors . . . were gone. Clive was surrounded by silence. The air was sweet, the only sound was the soft
rustle of a zephyr in the tall, friendly trees.

Somewhere a bird sang. Its call, a trilling, warbling
song, was so beautiful that it brought tears to Clive Folliot's
eyes. He raised his hands to brush away the tears, then
looked down to discover that he was newly garbed in a soft
outfit of green and brown.

He exclaimed aloud, voicing wonder at where he was.

No one answered.

There was no point in standing still. He sighted in on
the three green suns that blazed above the leafy canopy,
trying to determine a direction by which to orient himself.
He was not a tracker by any means. If he could only have
the skills of a Red Indian! But he had learned something of
geography at Cambridge, and some lore in Her Majesty's
service, and once satisfied he set out a steady pace.

As he strode along, he took stock of himself and his
clothing and possessions. His garments were made of sturdy
cloth, carefully tailored and excellently fitted. There were
no pockets in the tight-fitting shirt, the looser jacket, or
the trousers. He had neither weapon nor tool in his possession: obviously, then, he had been transported to this
place and left with only the proverbial clothes on his back.

But his boots were sturdy, the temperature was comfortable, and he himself was unharmed in any way. A fine escape from Hades!

The Baron Samedi was nowhere to be seen. He'd said that he could not—or would not—leave Hell with Clive and Horace Smythe.

Clive halted. Horace—where was he? The man had accompanied Clive to the establishment that housed the U.N.I.A's London station. Where was he now—still trapped in the realm of sulfur and brimstone? Or returned to the quarters where they had left Sidi Bombay?

There was no way for Clive to find out.

He continued his march, passing through clearings, crossing meadows, but always returning to the woods. This place—this world—might well be a paradise of its own sort, but Clive felt himself growing fatigued, and assaulted by hunger and thirst. He still had no idea where he was, whether this was yet another level of the Dungeon, an exotic realm upon the Earth, or a land of fantasy—even of illusion—into which Baron Samedi had cast him.

He came to a section where the forest was less dense, and where a stream bubbled clear and inviting over a bed of fine sand and small rocks. He halted, lowered himself to the strange, bluish grass, and studied the stream. It *looked* like pure water, but he knew nothing of the local environment, of the life and the materials of this place. For all he knew, the stream did not consist of water at all, but of some deadly chemical that would prove fatal should he imbibe a single sip.

But the Baron Samedi had been friendly. He had helped Clive and his companions on their first encounter in the Dungeon, and he had rescued Clive and Horace from the demons on the trestle in their recent and unexpected reunion. Clive would have to trust that Samedi had not sent him to his death.

He stretched out and plunged his face into the stream.

It was cold, pure, delicious! He drank, then splashed his face and hands.

He sat back on his heels, studying the sky. The three suns stretched away from him. He had no means of gauging their distance, but if he assumed they were all of the same size in actuality, he could infer that they stood in direct alignment. This world, this planet, was circling the nearest of the three—that was obvious. Then, depending on the time of year, the nature of the world's day and night would differ.

When the planet was at one end of its orbit, the three suns would appear in line across the sky by day, and would be hidden by the bulk of the planet by night. As the year progressed, the planet would pass between its own sun and that sun's two stellar companions, and true day would alternate with a ghostly false day as the two companion suns rose in what would otherwise be the planet's dark night.

A net descended over Clive's shoulders.

He tried to spring to his feet, but he was held down by the webwork of knotted cords. He twisted, seeking a look at his attacker, but he managed to obtain only a glimpse of pale hands and dark, ruddy cloth before a sack was placed over his head. He redoubled his struggles, then there was a stunning blow and everything was darkness.

He regained consciousness in a room that could have come out of a novel by Sir Walter Scott. Stone walls, vaulted ceilings, flaring torches, giant tapestries. He found himself facing a familiar visage. Raging, he hurled himself to his feet—or tried to, for he was held to a sturdy wooden chair by heavily knotted cords. And he was staring into a chillingly familiar visage.

"N'wrbb Crrd'fl"

"Indeed," the other hissed. "I thought I would never see you again, Clive Folliot. Our previous encounter was unpleasant enough for me."

The man was tall and slim. Even seated as he was, in a great stone seat more throne than chair, he towered above Clive. Now he stood and strode forward, leaning over his captive. His skin was as pale as an albino's. His hair was black with more than a suggestion of midnight green in it. His eyes burned with the brilliance of dark emeralds.

"You took the Lady 'Nrrc'kth from me, Folliot. And now she is . . ."

"Dead," Clive supplied. "Dead in the Dungeon. Lost to us both."

"Yes." N'wrbb Crrd'f nodded. He wore a silky mustache and a thin beard. In thought, he raised a long-fingered hand and slid bejeweled fingers the length of the beard. "Yes, she is dead. There is no way you can return her to me, but I will take some satisfaction from you instead."

He circled Clive's chair. Unable to rise or to use his hands, Clive could only follow his captor with his eyes. Finally N'wrbb Crrd'f stood before Clive once more. "Tell me, Folliot—how did you find me? How did you come to Djajj?"

"That's the name of this place?"

"It is. I thought you knew that."

Clive said nothing.

"I learned a wonderful expression from a fellow native of your world, Folliot. It is, *cat got your tongue?* I fear, I have no cat. But I have a wonderful kennel of dogs, Folliot. Very large, very hungry dogs. Do you like the beasts?"

Clive continued to study his captor. He would say nothing; instead of speaking, his mind raced. *Djajj*, yes, that was the world from which the beautiful 'Nrrc'kth had come to the Dungeon. She had been the captive and unwilling mistress of this N'wrbb Crrd'f. Clive had rescued her from her bondage, had fought and defeated Crrd'f. The Lady 'Nrrc'kth had joined Clive's band in their adventures, had become his own lady love—and had died in the Dungeon.

He had believed Crrd'f dead as well. Instead, here the man had returned to the world called Djajj, and Baron Samedi had sent Clive to that world! Why? Samedi had always been friendly—but he was also notoriously mischievous. And what merrier mischief than to send the unsuspecting Folliot to the world of Djajj!

Clive said, "What do you want, N'wrbb Crrd'f? You've got me at your mercy—at least for the moment! Are you going to do something about it, or are you just going to gloat?"

"Oh, I'm going to do something, my friend. You will not like what I do, but you will not suffer for long. Or from boredom!" The taller man's laughter was harsh.

Crrd'f stretched to his full height and paced once more around Folliot's seat. He paused again, hands clasped before his straggly beard. There was something about him that reminded Clive of a praying mantis. "I have something wonderful in mind for you, Folliot. But I don't want to dirty my hands. I'll have someone else help out."

He turned away and shouted, "Nvv'n! Nvv'n Yrr'll!"

There was a rustling, slithering sound, and from a doorway Clive saw a hideous parody of a man creep into the room. Was he unable to stand and walk like a normal human, or was it merely the fellow's manner that made him creep and twist forward like a snake? He was stocky, with shaggy unkempt hair that ran directly into a filthy, spade-shaped beard. Even across the stone chamber, Folliot could detect the stale odor of burnt weeds that clung to the man's ragged clothing of some pale shade that might once have been crimson.

"Master, master," the creature whined. It knelt before Crrd'f, fawning and cringing.

Unlike Folliot, Crrd'f carried a leather pouch slung by a strap over one shoulder. He opened the pouch and reached inside to draw a scrap of greasy, half-rotted flesh and throw it to the depraved wretch at his feet.

Nvv'n fell to his knees, scooped the disgusting scrap into his mouth, and swallowed noisily. A noisy eructation came from him. "Kind master! Good master!"

Crrd'f placed a heavily booted foot on Nvv'n's back and shoved him toward Folliot. "Put that in the shrinkage machine. And be quick—and I want you out of my sight, filth!"

Clive shouted questions and demands at Crrd'f but the latter had nothing to say. He merely stood, smiling cruelly, as the degenerate Nvv'n dragged Clive, chair and all, through a stone archway.

Folliot was astonished. This was another surprise on top of all the surprises he had already experienced. The chamber in which he found himself was tiled in white and fitted with tables and apparatuses such as he had seen only in the laboratories of natural philosophers at Cambridge.

What was this world of Djajj? It had seemed at first a virtual Eden wherein Clive was a lonely alien. Then he was captured by N'wrbb Crrd'f—or by the latter's unseen henchmen—and brought to a castle out of a past century.

And now . . . now he found himself in a modern laboratory. What had N'wrbb Crrd'f in mind?

The vile Nvv'n giggled and muttered to himself, half-intelligible words that told Clive nothing sensible or useful. Clive could see a strange apparatus on one laboratory table, a peculiar mechanism of glass retorts and metal parts, with a variety of oddly colored fluids and a pair of wires leading to something that he identified only distantly as a galvanic battery.

Nvv'n lifted the cover of a round, opaque container and scooped a handful of ground, greenish-brown strands from it. He packed these into a bowl connected to a thin, hollow tube. There was a flickering flame beneath one of the retorts; Nvv'n used this to draw fire into the bowl of earth-colored strands. He turned and blew a disgustingly odorous cloud at Folliot.

Clive turned his head away, clenched his lips shut, and strove mightily to avoid breathing in the disgusting smoke. But the bestial Nvv'n drew again at his makeshift pipe and sent cloud after cloud of noxious fumes at Clive.

At length, unable to hold his breath any longer, Clive inhaled a single wisp of the smoke. His head grew light, a roaring filled his ears, lights danced and spiraled before his eyes. He felt his stomach clench in an involuntary retching reflex, and all was once more black.

How long a time passed while he was unconscious, he could not tell. Strange dreams came and went, dreams in which the Lady 'Nrrc'kth was restored to him only to die again and again, dreams in which the Frankenstein monster grasped him by the throat and plunged his head time after time into ice-rimed brine, dreams in which detachments of Japanese marines equipped with buzzing aeroplanes attacked Mississippi River steamers.

He did not lapse into a normal slumber and then waken gradually. Instead, from the grips of a nightmare image in which a monstrous Philo Goode and Lorena Ransome batted him back and forth between them like a shuttlecock, he awoke into instant and crystal clarity.

"Being Clive!"

He looked and saw Shriek, the arachnoid alien who had shared so many of his adventures in the Dungeon, but whom he had not seen since his return to Earth and to the London of 1896. "Shriek!" he cried. He reached for the spidery creature and grasped one of its pincers between his hands, as he would have grasped the hand of a long-lost comrade.

Once he would not have reacted so to the alien. Once he would have recoiled in fear and revulsion. But his experiences in the Dungeon had taught Clive Folliot many lessons. Among them was the truth that the appearance of a creature had little to do with its inner nature.

Whereas the cruelly calculating N'wrbb and the disgusting degenerate Nvv'n both looked like men, they were at heart little more than vile beasts. While the spidery Shriek—as well as the half-mechanical Chang Guafe and the doglike Finnbogg—possessed the most admirable of human traits.

"Being Clive," Shriek grated again, "you live! I had abandoned hope for you, yet you live!"

"As do you, Shriek." Even in the dire situation that confronted him, Clive rejoiced. "Where are we now—and what have these beasts done to us?"

The arachnoid made that weird grating sound that passed for her as laughter. "Do I look any different to you, Being Clive, from the way I looked in the Dungeon?"

Folliot studied the arachnoid. He recalled, with a shudder that he hoped was not too visible, Shriek's expressed affection for him. He thought of the bizarre mating ritual of some spiders—perhaps of Shriek's kind—in which the female beheads and devours the male at the completion of their union. Shriek had shown her attraction to Clive, and he had managed as adeptly as he could to repel her advances. He managed to say, "You look just the same to me."

Shriek made her grating noise again. "And you, to me, Being! But look around you. Has anything changed?"

Clive realized that he was no longer in the laboratory. He had been returned to the chamber in which he had previously confronted N'wrbb Crrd'f. Only he stood on a wooden surface instead of the stone floor of the room. N'wrbb Crrd'f stood near his thronelike seat, smiling maliciously at Clive.

And there was something strange. Clive looked up at

the ceiling, and saw wooden beams and blazing cressets. Only they appeared to be hundreds of feet in the air. He looked at the walls, and they seemed as distant as the stone pilasters and stained-glass windows of a cathedral.

And N'wrbb Crrd'f . . .

N'wrbb Crrd'f strode ponderously toward Clive. Each step seemed to send shock waves through the air, each stride brought Crrd'f closer and made him appear larger and larger until he loomed over Folliot and Shriek like a titan.

He raised a fist the size of a boulder and brought it smashing down on the wooden surface. Clive managed to leap away just in time to avoid being crushed like a mouse beneath a mallet. The wood rebounded at the impact, throwing Clive into the air.

Shriek emitted a bloodcurdling cry and began snatching clusters of barblike hairs from her back. Folliot remembered her ability to alter the chemical content of her own glands and create substances that could produce many reactions in any victim who chanced to be stuck by the barbs.

Screaming at the top of her voice, Shriek hurled cluster after cluster of barbs at the giant hands of N'wrbb Crrd'f. Clive heard Crrd'f shout with pain and rage, saw him dance away, shaking the entire wooden surface with each ponderous step. But now Clive realized that the giant Crrd'f did not stand on the same level with himself and Shriek.

There was an edge to the wooden surface, and Clive ran to reach it. Half a dozen strides from the edge he realized that it was a platform raised many times the height of a man above the stone floor of the chamber. He approached the edge gingerly, careful of losing his footing and toppling from the edge. But before he could reach the edge of the platform he felt a terrible surge of pain. He was literally knocked backward and off his feet. He stood dizzily. Shriek was at his side.

"You understand now, Being Clive?"

"Has N'wrbb Crrd'f become a giant?"

"No, Being Clive. You and I are as mites."

Clive sunk to his haunches, holding his head in despair. "Is there no hope for us, then?"

"Who knows, Being Clive? I was already shrunken when I arrived here. But I have seen N'wrbb Crrd'f and his disgusting lackey Nvv'n shrink others. He throws them to his Finnboggi for sport."

"Finnboggi? He has Finnboggi here? Is *our* Finnbogg here, then?"

Shriek made a gesture that could almost have passed for a shrug. "If he is, he has been so beaten down mentally that he is as a dog. They all are as dogs. I have seen other victims of Crrd'f's treatment . . . some who regain their size, if they live long enough. I think you would regain your size, Being Folliot. I might even regain mine—if he does not shrink us again, and if his Finnboggi do not kill us first."

"They're bloodthirsty, then?"

"I don't know. More likely, playful. But their play—on your own Earth, Being Folliot, did you ever see two puppies playing tug-of-war with a strip of rawhide?"

Clive closed his eyes. "If only there were some way to—to reawaken the intelligence in Finnbogg. I know he is as smart as many a man I have known. But like a dog he is subject to control. When I first met him he was serving as a guardian, serving masters who held him in contempt. But with my friends, he was awakened to his own nature, and he served with us long and well. Now, he is reduced again, almost as if he were a victim of mesmerism."

"You have an idea?"

"All we can do is prepare ourselves. Our opportunity will come, my friend Shriek."

And it was not long before that opportunity came.

The despicable Nvv'n came first. Clive Folliot and Shriek had been kept on the wooden platform—Clive realized that it was nothing more than a tabletop—for days. Nvv'n came each day to throw them scraps of food and to offer them sips of water. Sometimes N'wrbb Crrd'f stood and watched; sometimes he stood close over them, taunting and laughing.

Shriek tore her hair and threw it at him, but N'wrbb Crrd'f dodged aside, laughing all the more. Shriek and Clive together tried to escape from their tabletop prison, but the zone of pain that surrounded it halted them. Even when they tried to hurl themselves through it, leaping from a distance half their own height, the force threw them back.

But today Nvv'n approached them wearing heavy gauntlets. He stood over the table, reached for them from above, and caught Clive first in one gloved hand. With crude skill he held Clive, bound him hand and foot, and dropped him helpless upon the stone floor. Briefly he repeated the exercise, this time making Shriek his victim.

N'wrbb Crrd'f sat in his thronelike chair, gloatingly overseeing the operation.

Now Nvv'n disappeared from the room. There was a sound of snuffling, of claws scratching on flagstone, of baying. Nvv'n reappeared, the leads of half a dozen slavering hounds grasped in his grimy fingers.

"Let the nice doggies go, Nvv'n," N'wrbb Crrd'f purred.

"Uh, yuh, yuh," Nvv'n slobbered. He unsnapped the leads from the collars of the hounds. With a chorus of howls and yelps, the half-dozen dogs, each of them ten times Clive's present height, charged forward.

"They aren't dogs!" Clive exclaimed. "Not real dogs. They're Finnboggi. They've lost their humanity—they've reverted!"

The nearest canine was almost upon Clive and Shriek. Clive twisted from side to side, desperately searching for a weapon—and not finding one. Even bound as he was, if he had a sword or a knife he might free himself and then try to stand off his gigantic attackers. But there was nothing—nothing! It would have to be his bare hands, then. Bare hands, and bound hands at that, against a pack of hounds as big as elephants.

But no—Shriek had weapons of her own! The clumsy-fingered Nvv'n had done a poor job on Shriek, and she was able to writhe and scramble until her claws were free of her bonds. She reached for clusters of quill-like hairs growing on her back. With pincerlike claws she hurled them at the leading hound. The hairs struck with unerring accuracy, planting themselves in the creature's soft, tender nose.

The hound sent up a yowl of pain and terror, screeching to a halt barely a yard from the two small creatures who had been slated for a cruel attack.

A second hound charged into the lead. Again Shriek pulled hairs from her back. Clive knew that the arachnoid alien could control the chemical secretions of her own body. She could choose the chemicals with which the tips of her barbed hairs would be coated, and thereby choose the reaction she would provoke in her enemies.

For a fleeting instant, Clive wondered how Shriek had been captured. More to the point, how she had been held captive, when she might have used her arsenal of emotion-inducing chemicals against the cruel Crrd'f and the drooling, subservient Nvv'n. Perhaps she had been captured unawares and held in a sealed chamber that prevented her from hurling her barbs. Perhaps . . . well, now was not the time to speculate. She *had* been captured, as had Clive, and now was their moment to die—or to escape!

Nvv'n was slobbering, wild-eyed with puzzlement and distress at the backfiring of his master's plan. The nearly mindless servant capered first to one side, then to the other. He made gestures with his hands, repetitive gestures that seemed at first to be meaningless, even mad. But Clive realized that he was in fact patting his clothing, looking around, searching for the pipe and ground material to which he was obviously addicted.

Poor Nvv'n, Clive thought. Double enslaved: to his master N'wrbb Crrd'f and to the foul stuff that he smoked in his pipe!

As for Crrd'f himself, the man was hopping about nearly as wildly as was his brainless lackey. First Crrd'f would yell at Nvv'n to bring the Finnboggi back to the attack, then he would bypass the slobbering dolt and urge on the dogs himself, slapping and shouting at them to attack. He backed away, ran from the room, returned in just seconds with a shortsword, and used it to poke the dogs' rumps, screaming at them to renew their attack.

And the Finnboggi, caught between Shriek's maddening barbs and Crrd'f's poniard, were yelping, cringing, tumbling upon themselves and one another.

What would Clive do to gain advantage of the situation? The tumbling hounds were indistinguishable from one another, but one of them, he hoped, was his own friend Finnbogg. If he could only do something to stop the mad tumbling, to get the attention of the hounds—especially of his friend!—he might yet turn the tables on the wicked Crdd'f and the buffoonish Nvv'n.

Finnbogg had loved songs, Folliot remembered. He'd loved singing. But Clive's mind went blank. Of all the hundreds of hymns, art songs, popular ditties, and soldier's marching tunes he'd ever known, not one could he summon up! Then he remembered. This whole mad adventure in the Dungeon had begun with a visit with his sweetheart to a music hall, as the guest of his friend du Maurier.

The play was *Cox and Box* by Sullivan and Burnand. And there was a tune that Clive had particularly liked, a ditty with lyrics that went around and around in the hearer's head. Yes! They were coming back to him!

In a tiny, piping voice he began to sing:

> *Not long ago, it was my fate,*
> *To captivate a widow*
> *At Ramsgate . . .*

And from one of the Finnboggi, astonishing in its canine yowling and yet clear in every syllable, the counterpoint:

> *I, 'tis odd to state,*
> *The same at Margate did, oh!*

And then Clive and six Finnboggi, in triumphant chorus and glorious harmony, concluded:

> *The happy day came near at length—*
> *We hoped it would be sunny;*
> *I found I needed all my strength*
> *To face the ceremony.*

Shriek had ceased throwing her barbed hairs.
The cruel N'wrbb had drawn back, nonplussed.
Even the slobbering Nvv'n stood, awestruck.
"Finnbogg!" Clive Folliot cried.
"Folliot!" The canine who had sung most vigorously of all that vigorous chorus leaped to the fore. In one pawlike

hand he scooped Clive up and held him before his face. "Clive Folliot, what happened to you!"

Before Clive could reply, Finnbogg looked around, an expression of canine bafflement on his face. "What happened to me? To all of my littermates—to my own mate and our pups?"

"Your littermate and pups?" Clive echoed.

"I wed, Folliot. Of course, you'd never have known. I found my mates, and I wed and sired six splendid pups on my lady-love. Three splendid males, as stout and active as their sire. Three splendid females, as fetching and affectionate as their dam. But—but after that, Folliot, more tragedy befell." He began to croon a mournful dirge, something that Clive recognized as "Addio, Mia Bella Napoli."

And even as Clive watched in amazement, the light of awareness and of recollection brightened in the eyes of all the Finnboggi. Hastily, Finnbogg placed Folliot on the floor near Shriek. Then, as if by plan, the six canines turned in their tracks. A sound unlike any ever before heard by Clive rose from six canine throats. It was an amalgam of grief and rage as six minds, six beings descended from a doglike ancestor but raised to human intelligence and sensitivity, regained the lost awareness of maltreatment meted out to them and their kind, to them and their loved ones.

And before Clive Folliot could so much as move, the Finnboggi had leaped upon N'wrbb Crrd'f. There were cries from the slender man, sobs and pleas for mercy. But there was no mercy.

What Crrd'f had done to the Finnboggi and their kin, Clive Folliot could not know. But what the Finnboggi did to N'wrbb Crrd'f was painful . . . and bloody . . . and final.

When it was over, when all that remained of N'wrbb Crrd'f lay still and steaming before the throne that Crrd'f had himself affected, Finnbogg—the original Finnbogg whom Folliot had met at the bridge on Q'oorna—came to Folliot.

"He made you little, eh?" Finnbogg sniffed at Folliot, then at Shriek. "Made you both little, eh?"

"I—I think Nvv'n was involved, too, old friend."

"Huh—Nvv'n. Nvv'n stupider as slug. Bad Nvv'n, but very stupid. Crrd'f smart. Bad, smart Crrd'f, hurt Finnboggi no more."

· CHAPTER 14 ·
"Your Dinner Had Grown Cold"

Clive Folliot blinked, shook his head, and gazed around him. The sounds of alien voices and distant places faded from his ears. Although no blinders had been placed before his eyes, the visions he had seen were similarly exotic. He had left this room in company of Horace Hamilton Smythe. With Horace he had visited the London headquarters of the Universal Neighborhood Improvement Association.

With Horace he had visited Hell—and brought about the demise of his rogue cousin, Tomàs—and very nearly perished—and been rescued by the Baron Samedi. He wondered, for a moment, what would become of the soul of a person who had already achieved Hell, and died there. That conundrum he would gladly leave to the theologians.

And from Hell he had been transported to the exotic world of Djajj, home of the green-haired villain he had first met so long ago in the Dungeon. How, he wondered, had he and Horace been transported back to this room? Had Sidi Bombay summoned them by means of some psychic energy?

Would he even have survived his latest trials, had he not previously been tempered in the Dungeon? Had he ever been able to stand up to his elder twin, Neville? Was he ready at last to meet that test?

Clive had grown in the Dungeon. The emotionally stunted and deprived younger brother had come into his own. Yes, he realized—he was ready to face whatever lay ahead.

Rising, Clive said, "Sidi Bombay, Horace Smythe—we have made a terrible mistake."

"Mistake, sah?"

"Yes, Sergeant. I share the blame for it. We all share the blame for it. But I, most of all—for my blood and my position call upon me to furnish leadership, and I have instead awaited the breezes and the buffets of fate to direct my course."

"What do you propose to do then, sah?"

"We have allowed ourselves to be manipulated by the Chaffri and by the Ren, by Father O'Hara and Philo Goode and N'wrbb Crrd'f and by my brother Neville Folliot. N'wrbb Crrd'f is no more—he came to a painful but not undeserved end. Still, my friends, we have suffered, and our companions and allies have suffered and some of them have died."

"I understand your feelings about the Lady 'Nrrc'kth, sah."

"Yes. I shall never forget that lady, and I shall not forgive myself for leading her into the situation that brought about her death. She is avenged, now, I suppose." He closed his eyes and conjured up for a fleeting moment a face of pale grace and tenderness, then banished it with a sigh. "And our other friends, Horace, Sidi," he resumed. "Faithful Finnbogg, Shriek, Chang Guafe. The Baron Samedi—a strange being, but with a noble heart at the last. They, too, I have seen. Horace—you were with me when I saw Baron Samedi."

"Aye, sah—that I was! And a welcome sight the fellow was, for all that he's an odd one! But for the Baron and his magical cheroot, you and I would have been meat for those winged demons, I'll take my oath on that, sah!"

Clive nodded. "And my own descendant, Annabelle Leigh. Where is she now? Horace Smythe, Sidi Bombay— where is she now?"

Before either could reply, Clive resumed. "We must take the initiative, my friends. We must not wait for the enemy to attack, for our friends and allies to cry out for our assistance. What we must do is strike to the heart of the problem. We must carry the attack to our foes."

He rose to his full height and shot a piercing look into

the faces of his companions. "Whatever weapons may be turned against us, we must not flinch! Neither fang nor claw nor venomous barb shall halt us!"

Sidi Bombay said, "What do you propose, then, Major Clive Folliot? And might I ask, Major—where have you been?"

Clive smiled. "I stepped out with Sergeant Smythe for a few moments of relaxation at a neighborhood pub. Would you not agree with me, Horace?"

"Yes, sah. But I might say, sah—we had a hellish time leaving the establishment."

The two Englishmen, one of noble birth and one of penurious farm stock, shared a hearty laugh.

Sidi Bombay looked on in puzzlement.

"But after we left the hot region, courtesy of Baron Samedi and his magical cheroot," Horace Smythe said, "I found myself back here, while you, sah, did not return for some time."

"Some time indeed," Sidi Bombay interjected in an annoyed tone. "In addition to the investigation in which I engaged myself during your absence, I also prepared a repast for the three of us, to be consumed upon your return. Your dinner had grown cold before your return, Clive Folliot. Where were you in the interim?"

"Indeed, sah!" Horace Smythe added. "Where were you for all that time?"

"You never were able to locate our lost companions, were you, Sidi Bombay?"

The Indian shook his head sadly. "I was not, Clive Folliot. I do not know whether the limitation lies within the mechanism at hand, or within my own poor intellect. Perhaps with unlimited time in which to work . . ."

"Perhaps my descendant Annabelle Leigh could solve the problem with one of her—now, what was the term she used? Yes! One of her drygoods schedules." He squeezed his eyes shut in concentration. "No, not drygoods schedules—*software programs*, that was the term she used. But she is not here either."

"We did see Baron Samedi," Horace Smythe said. "And the Major's distant cousin Tomàs. I think we shall never see Cousin Tomàs again—and good riddance say I. Begging the Major's forgiveness, sah."

"Losing a kinsman is never a happy event, Horace. But in this case, I cannot truthfully claim any great sense of bereavement."

"As for Baron Samedi," Smythe continued, "why, that gentleman says that he visits the Earth now and then. If any of us ever set foot upon the island of Hayti—a tropic paradise, I believe it to be, covered with lush rain forests from primeval times—we might encounter him there. Or even in the American city of New Orleans."

"At the moment Samedi waved his cheroot, Horace," Clive said, "do you recall your final thought before leaving Hades?"

"I thought of the London station of the U.N.I.A, Major. In fact, as I recall it, sah, I had quite a vivid mental image of the front door of the establishment."

"Indeed." Clive nodded. "And that was where you found yourself, I should think."

"Yes, sah."

"Whence you returned here directly?"

"I stepped back inside the pub for a moment, sah. In fact, I stayed for a while in hopes of Your Majorship's own return."

"Yes. I would imagine that you even partook of a sip of the establishment's wares. No, there's no need for excuses." He held up a hand, precluding a rush of explanation. "I did not return there, so in due course you returned here. Is that correct, Horace?"

"It is, sah."

Clive paced in a circle, the energy of concentrated thought translating itself to physical movement. "At the moment that Baron Samedi waved his cheroot, I was thinking of Finnbogg. And I found myself transported to the world where Finnbogg was at that very moment."

"His home world, Clive Folliot?" Sidi Bombay's interest had clearly been piqued.

"No, Sidi Bombay. He was on the planet Djajj—the original home of N'wrbb Crrd'f and the Lady 'Nrrc'kth. Finnbogg was there, and so also was our old friend Shriek. Both were prisoners of N'wrbb Crrd'f. By the time I left there, both were free—and the unspeakable crimes of N'wrbb Crrd'f had been avenged upon their perpetrator!"

"But how did you return here, Clive Folliot? And where are Shriek and Finnbogg now?"

Clive shrugged. "I cannot answer either question, Sidi Bombay, with assurance. Although I would guess—and only guess—that since I was returned to Earth, then Shriek and Finnbogg are now back upon their own respective planets. I cannot tell for certain."

There was a long silence in the room. The mechanisms that filled so much of it flickered and glowed in their own arcane rhythms. Outside, in the streets of modern London, Clive Folliot could imagine the sights and sounds and smells of a million men and women, horses and dogs and cats, steam railroads and iron-wheeled drays.

Victoria was yet monarch of the island realm and its far-flung empire. England was secure, her people prosperous and happy, and quite unworried about Chaffri or Ren or Gennine, traitors menacing her from within and invaders threatening her from without. England was powerful and serene.

Only those few who knew the secrets of the Dungeon knew how fragile was that power, how deceptive that serenity.

It would be easy for Clive Folliot to part with Sidi Bombay and Horace Hamilton Smythe. He could announce himself to British society as the long-lost African explorer, returned at last to his motherland. He would have to find a way to appear older than he did now, so that the discrepancy between his physical condition and his putative age might not arouse embarrassing questions. If the problems of reemergence grew too great, he could emigrate to Canada or Australia or some other of Her Majesty's distant possessions, and make a new life for himself.

But he would know all the while that England was in peril. Not merely England, but all of the Empire—all of the Earth—and even more! At any hour, at any moment, some agent of the Dungeon might strike. No—he could not escape his responsibility. He could not escape his opportunity.

"What lies behind all of our experiences in the Dungeon?" he asked his companions. And without waiting for a reply, he answered his own question: "The spiral of stars!"

Horace Smythe nodded. "You're right on that score, sah!"

"And if we were to travel to the heart of the spiral of stars—what do you think we would find there?"

"I don't know, sah," Smythe replied.

"It has never been done, Clive Folliot," Sidi Bombay added.

"I am not surprised to hear that," Clive said. "We have spent our energies in combat with henchmen. Divide and rule, that has been the policy of the enemy. And he has succeeded. He has set us at each other's throats, fighting, killing, imprisoning, and torturing one another. Every act of cruelty has created enmity and hatred and a desire for revenge. So it has ever been. Hittites against Egyptians, Hebrews against Philistines, Romans against Christians. The Spanish against the Incas—ah, there was one of the noblest of Man's endeavors, set upon, betrayed, and destroyed by greedy despoilers acting in the name of God! How many sins have been committed in the name of God!"

Clive shook his head. "Roundheads against Royalists here in England, the Union against the Confederacy in America. Wellington against Napoléon in our parents' day, Hannibal against Scipio in our ancestors', and doubtless there will be war, war, war in our descendants' day as well."

"So it has always been, Major. Ever since Cain slew Abel!"

"But why, Sergeant, *why*?"

"It's human nature, sah. Warfare and killing—it fits in with Mr. Darwin's theories of evolution. When nations battle, the strong and the clever survive. The weak and the stupid perish. It's cruel, sah, that I will admit, but it strengthens and purifies the breed."

"I cannot agree," Sidi Bombay interrupted.

"But I've seen you fight, Sidi! At my side, and at the risk of your own life for the savin' of mine! I'm grateful as an Englishman can be, Sidi, but your actions go against your words."

"I have fought when it was needful, my friend Horace, but such has not been my choice. And as for the notion that the weak and the stupid perish while the strong and the clever survive . . ." The Indian shook his head sadly.

"Well, what d'yer mean, Sidi?"

"Who goes to war, friend Horace. Betwixt two brothers—I make no reference to yourself and Neville Folliot, friend Clive—if one is powerful, courageous, active, whilst his sibling is a weakling and a coward, I ask you, Horace, which will go to war? Which is the more likely to die?"

"Well—but—but—" Smythe sputtered.

"The courageous brother will go to war, and in all likelihood he will lose his life. While the cowardly brother, remaining at home, will survive and marry and father children. Thus, according to your famous Monk Mendel and your Mr. Darwin as well, the race will grow weak and cowardly as the strong and the courageous are weeded out. Not the other way around, Horace. Oh, no, not the other way around."

Clive nodded in agreement. "What you suggest then, Sidi Bombay, is that war does not strengthen and purify the species, but serves rather to weaken and degrade it."

"Precisely, friend Clive."

"I won't quarrel," Horace Hamilton Smythe said. "You're a devilishly clever fellow, Sidi. Sometimes I think you missed your calling—you should have been a barrister!"

"Oh, no! As Dick the butcher said in your great Shakespeare's play, 'The first thing we do, let's kill all the lawyers.' No, a barrister I would not be, Horace."

"We digress!" Clive broke in. The others acted as if they were ashamed of themselves. "Intellectual discourse. Mr. Darwin, Monk Mendel, Shakespeare—all have their place, but I fear that London life has made you both soft and passive. You intellectualize, quarreling like a pair of Hebrews over their Talmud, when you should act!"

Horace, stung, returned, "An' what has it done for you, sah?"

"I have not lived a London life, my friends. Not these past years. It is life in the Dungeon that has shaped me.

That has made me hard, that has turned me, all against my will and my innate nature, into a man of action!"

He pounded fist into palm, stalking angrily.

"It is the Gennine who stand behind the Chaffri and the Ren alike. It is the Gennine, from all that we have been able to learn, who created the Dungeon. It is the Gennine, acting through Chaffri and Ren and doubtless through other forces and agents down through the ages, on the Earth and on Djajj and on the worlds of Chang Guafe and Finnbogg and Shrick and on what other worlds we know not and about which we can hardly even guess, who have fostered suffering and conquest and war."

He stood with his back to the others, gathering his thoughts. When he was ready, he turned once more to face them both.

"It is the Gennine who are responsible for the death of the Lady 'Nrrc'kth, who have worked unspeakable changes upon my brother and father, who have done I know not what to my own dearest great-great-granddaughter Annabelle."

Horace Hamilton Smythe and Sidi Bombay looked at each other. They exchanged low, grumbling words.

"It is the Gennine whom we must confront, my friends." Clive spoke with passion. "And their home, I believe, lies at the center of the spiraling stars. Somehow we must get there. If we must walk, Horace, Sidi, we will get there!"

▪ CHAPTER 15 ▪
By Cab to the Stars

"We can get there, Major, sah," Sergeant Smythe said. "And we won't have ter walk, neither."

"How, Sergeant?"

"The Major is familiar with the space-train, I know, sah."

"All too familiar. The monster created by Dr. Frankenstein is still aboard it, as far as I know. And we all saw it during its visit to the polar sea."

"Yes, sah, we did indeed. Well, that is as it may be, but there's more than one such train. There's a lot of 'em, connecting this and that point in the universe, sah. They don't just go everywhere, you see, sah. 'Tisn't like walkin' about in a clear field, you see. Even though the train don't use tracks like a steam railway, it's still a lot like one. It can only go on certain paths. There's obstacles and forces, like reefs and currents that stop a ship from goin' just anywhere."

"Yes, I understand, Sergeant Smythe."

"But there's also little cars that can run, well, like dinghies, y'see, Major. Small boats, as it were, that can go where a great ocean liner could never go."

"I believe I traveled in one such when I went to Tewkesbury."

"Like as not yer did, sah. They runs 'em, sometimes, on actual railway tracks. But that's just for convenience, sah. They can go pretty near anywhere. I reckon there's places the little cars can't go, either, but they can go a lot more places than the great trains can!"

"And they can travel through time as well as space?"

▪ 168 ▪

"Oh, yes, sah."

"There is a young man in Zurich, but recently arrived there from Pavia in order to attend the technical institute," Sidi Bombay put in. "Little more than a boy, Major, but a great mind already, whose thoughts will someday change the world. This boy believes that time and space are but aspects of the same essence. If we can travel in one, then why can we not travel in the other?"

"I've no quarrel with that—considering that I have come back to an England a quarter-century after leaving it, yet having lived but three or four years whilst away! Have we one of these little cars?"

"Sah—we have!"

They made their way from the hidden room, along a passageway and onto a platform similar to that beneath the saloon where Clive had previously seen Philo B. Goode and—seemingly—Horace Smythe.

"Is this corridor connected to others of its sort?" Clive asked.

"Yes, sah."

"The platform, the tracks where Annabelle and I boarded a car—whence we traveled to Tewkesbury?"

Again, Horace agreed.

"I don't understand, then. The Chaffri, the Ren, the organization that you men represent—"

"The Universal Neighborhood Improvement Association, Major Folliot," Sidi Bombay said.

"They all use the same tracks? The same system of transportation? And yet they are mortal foes?"

"Stranger things have happened, Major Folliot. Enemies who trade in wartime, rivals who conduct business at the same time that they strive for each other's destruction."

"If the Major will just climb aboard, sah." Smythe opened a door for Clive, in the side of a car similar to the one Clive had previously shared with Annabelle Leigh.

"Are we likely to be attacked?" Clive asked.

"Were you before, sah?"

Clive recounted the battle he and Annie had survived en route to Tewkesbury.

"They are everywhere," Sidi Bombay said.

"The Major is quite sure," Smythe queried, "quite sure

that the bodies of the soldiers faded from existence? They didn't remain behind, they weren't carried away by their comrades? They dissolved before the Major's eyes?"

"Precisely."

"And the survivors, sah—you say they climbed an invisible stairway and disappeared into the sky?"

"As nearly as their actions can be described, Sergeant Smythe, that is exactly what they did. I can assure you that the sight was an uncanny one—an uncanny one to my eye, even after all the strange events I experienced in the Dungeon!"

"Strange indeed. What do you make of it, Sidi?"

"I know of but one explanation. Ordolite ghosters. Does the Major know of ordolite ghosters?"

"A bit, Sidi Bombay. I learned of them on the eighth level of the Dungeon."

"Then you are aware, Major Folliot, that these ghosters are not precisely *ghosts* in the sense that our Earthly superstitions define ghosts. They are projections, phantom beings. They are simulacra of a sort, and yet not quite living simulacra. They are . . . material essences."

"So they are."

"Does the Major know the power needed to give ordolite ghosters their being?"

"The blood of a Folliot, willingly given."

"Yes. And which Folliot would willing give his blood to the Chaffri—or the Ren—for the creation of ordolite ghosters?"

"Willingly, Sidi Bombay, I would say that no Folliot would do that. Not even my brother Neville."

"Perhaps the word *willingly* is not precisely correct, Major. If a loved one were threatened, a Folliot or any man might yield voluntarily that which he would never give, under normal circumstances."

"Then you are suggesting that the troopers that Annabelle and I encountered were ordolite ghosters, powered by Folliot blood."

"When the blood is given, the donor dies. This is the way that ordolite machines work, Major. Not some of the blood, but *all* of it must be given. Still, once the donor has died, he may be restored. That is up to the operators—Chaffri or Ren."

"Still," Clive countered, "the secrets of life and death are matters not to be tampered with lightly. Once dead, if the Folliot is restored to life by mechanical means, is he truly alive? Can the divine spark be resummoned once it has departed, or is the Folliot restored merely to the appearance of life? Is he once again a man cast in the image of God, or is he what the inhabitants of the island of Hayti call a *zombie*?" Clive shuddered.

Sidi Bombay lifted his shoulders in a curiously arresting gesture. "Who can say, Clive Folliot? Unless one experiences this strange phenomenon, this death and restoration to life, how can one know? And further, this is the great paradox of the ordolite process. The blood, once given, can be used to power great numbers of ordolite ghosters."

"I supppose, then," Clive said, "the same Folliot might be impelled to yield up his blood and his life time after time. Whole armies of ordolite ghosters could be created."

"So they might, sah," Horace Smythe said. "So they might. And yet, if the sacrificed Folliot were restored as a zombie rather than a true man, might his blood be ruined for this use? Eh, Sidi Bombay?" He smiled, turning to the Indian. "Another nice conundrum for you, ain't it?"

Clive shuddered. He had delayed them long enough with his questioning. He climbed into the car, followed by Sidi Bombay and Horace Hamilton Smythe. Sergeant Smythe slid the transparent-paneled door shut. The three men were seated on a cushioned lounge. It was, Clive noted, almost identical to the one in the other car. He wondered if this lounge, too, held a cache of weapons.

Guided by the steady hand of Sidi Bombay, the car slid away from its platform and hissed softly into a black-walled tunnel. Specks of light flashed by, as small as atoms and as brilliant as flares. Illuminated patches moved past them in a blur, so rapidly and so puzzlingly that it was impossible to determine whether they were blobs of luminosity mere inches away or nebular formations of stars millions of miles from Earth.

The car swooped dizzyingly from side to side, and rose and dipped without warning, setting Clive's stomach into gyrations. Clive peered through the glasslike walls of the car, trying to discern features within the tunnel. From time to time it seemed that the track divided, and Clive could see passages leading off in incomprehensible directions.

Tunnels that led to . . . what? The mind faltered as it attempted to guess what cities of wonder or abysses of terror lay at the end of this passageway or that.

"Are we stil beneath London?" Clive inquired.

"Just a bit longer, sah," Horace Smythe called over his shoulder.

"And then, Sergeant Smythe?"

"We're doing what the Major said he wanted, sah. We're headed for the den of the Gennine."

But despite Horace Smythe's words, the car continued to plummet through tunnels as black as pitch, illuminated only periodically by luminous points and patches.

Once Clive caught a clear glimpse down a side tunnel and sprang upright with startlement. "Sergeant! Sidi Bombay! I could swear I saw a railroad tunnel, complete with London transportation cars and well-dressed travelers!"

"The Major is correct," Sidi Bombay announced laconically. "Not so very long ago, the London Underground was being constructed. I myself earned my shillings and pence by the sweat of my brow and the strength of my muscles, wielding a pickaxe in that enterprise," he added with a laugh.

"That project had barely begun when last I left the metropolis."

"And it is not finished yet, Clive Folliot."

"Did the workmen never break into this—this *other* network of tunnels—by error?"

"Several times."

"Then all of London must know of the Universal Neighborhood Improvement Association—and of the Chaffri and the Ren!"

"By no means, Major. We spoke before of bitterest enemies cooperating in what they find to be their mutual interest. So it is with this network of tunnels, and the concealment of these tunnels from the mundane world. Methods were used to . . . convince those who discovered our tunnels that they had accidentally penetrated ancient peat mines, burial barrows, or natural air pockets. They closed the passages and proceeded with their business. The few places where we can see into their tunnels, they cannot see into ours—or, if they do, they become convinced that they are seeing something altogether ordinary and workaday. They look, and they turn away uninterested, and they go about their business."

Clive shook his head. He peered through the forward panel of the car, over Sergeant Smythe's shoulder. Smythe, having abandoned the identity of Count Splitofsky, had resumed the costume of the nearsighted Maurice Carstairs the Younger. His walking stick lay on a cushioned seat at his side. His spectacles had been placed in a pocket of his frock coat, but he peered clear-eyed through the front of the car.

Looking ahead, Clive started. A shape! It looked vaguely human, suggestive of the armored warriors he and Annabelle had encountered near Tewkesbury. Clive began to sound the warning, but before he could utter more than half a syllable, the car had borne down upon the white form.

It shattered and splashed like a great oversized blob of sleet, spattering the angular sides of the car, flowing over the glass and past it.

Clive turned to peer behind the car. The form had regathered itself and was gesturing angrily after the car and its occupants. "That—what was that?"

"An ordolite ghoster, Major."

"It was unharmed by our impact upon it?"

"And we by its impact upon us."

"But Annabelle and I shot several of the armed troopers."

"You were using ordolite weapons, then, Major. You must have been. We've a stock of them in the car here!"

As if in response to a cue, Sidi Bombay lifted a cushioned seat and revealed a miniature arsenal. After passing weapons the size of carbines to Clive and Horace, he slung another such over his own shoulder.

Horace patted his weapon with one hand. "So much for universal peace and brotherhood, eh, Sidi?"

"War is an evil thing, Horace, and imperfect men commit evil deeds. I am neither proud nor eager to kill any being, but what one must do, one does. And one accepts the responsibility for one's acts."

A trio of luminous blobs appeared far ahead of the car.

"These . . . ordolite weapons . . . will work against the ghosters? The weapons will kill these creatures?" Clive asked.

"In effect they will, Major. Since the ghoster is not truly alive, of course, it is not exactly true to say that it is killed. But it is destroyed."

"And the ghosters have similar weapons, that will work against us—against solid, mortal, material beings?"

"Indeed. And since we are alive, we can truly be killed!"

"Then look ahead, Sidi Bombay!"

The three blobs—ordolite ghosters—were fleeing along the tunnel. Their speed was less than that of the car, and as a consequence the car was gradually overtaking them— but it was doing so at a snail-like pace. It seemed altogether possible that the car might strike them without shattering them as it had the previous ghoster.

Horace Hamilton Smythe pressed the car to its maximum speed.

The ghosters accelerated as well, using some principle of movement unknown to Clive. They had limbs and extremities, but they did not run along the tunnel floor so much as they floated above it. Floated and . . . *flowed*.

The car overtook them and the ghosters passed through its transparent forward panels.

Sidi Bombay had unslung his weapon and fired it at a ghoster. As had happened when Clive and Annabelle fought the troopers near Tewkesbury, no projectile sped from the ordolite weapon. Instead a beam of pure energy, pulsating and emitting light of a lurid, unnameable shade, shot from the muzzle of the weapon.

One of the ghosters faded from being.

Another of them was upon Clive. Rather than firing its weapon at him, the creation chose to envelope Clive, swarming over him and covering him like a thin layer of icy mist. It grew colder and more dense. Clive felt that he was simultaneously smothering and freezing.

Through the translucent ghoster he could see Horace Hamilton Smythe confronting the third visitant. Even as

Clive watched, both Horace and the ordolite creature struck gnarled studs on the stocks of their weapons and knifelike projections sprang bayonetlike from the tips of the weapons.

Before Clive's helpless eyes, Horace and the ghoster engaged in a deadly alternation of parry and thrust.

One lunged forward.

The other dodged inside, striking with the butt of his weapon.

The first whirled, lowering his head, butting at the other's face.

The second blocked the blow, brought his piece down stock-first to strike the other on the back of his skull.

Sidi Bombay stood watching, nearly as helpless as Clive.

Horace Smythe and the ordolite ghoster tumbled to the floor. Their impact shook the car and knocked them apart.

For a moment only, the ghoster was separated from Horace Hamilton Smythe. But in that moment Sidi Bombay brought his own ordolite carbine to bear, sending a bolt of glowing energy into the ghoster.

With a single grunt of pain and an audible sigh of despair, the ghoster faded from visibility.

Sidi Bombay reached for the disheveled Horace Hamilton Smythe, tugging him to his feet. The ghoster's carbine had faded along with its owner. Horace's lay harmless on the floor. Together, Sidi Bombay and Horace Smythe faced Clive Folliot.

Clive's field of vision was turning red. Through it he caught a last glimpse of the horror that marked the visages of his two sworn blood brothers. There was a ringing in Clive's ears, and he could feel himself beginning to lose consciousness.

He tumbled to the floor. He could see no more. But even through the rubbery clamminess of the ghoster he could feel the sharp blade of Horace Hamilton Smythe's ordolite bayonet.

At the risk of his flesh Clive seized the blade. It slid through the rubbery material of the ghoster and penetrated Clive's palm. He felt a moment of pain and then the hot pulsation of his own blood. He dropped the bayonet.

But it was as if his entire being were bathed in flame—a

flame that produced an agony unimaginable in all Clive's previous life, yet one that cleansed and purified and restored him. A scream filled his ears and he was unable to tell whether it was his own voice shouting in triumph or that of the despairing ordolite ghoster which had until this moment covered every inch of his being.

For a fraction of an instant he caught sight of himself in the glasslike wall of the car. He had staggered to his feet and now his reflection blazed at him like a human torch.

The ordolite ghoster was gone.

It was Clive's blood, he realized, that had destroyed the ghoster. Folliot blood, he remembered, was the powering principle of the ordolite ghoster machines—but it had to be blood willingly given. Blood taken without the consent of the donor was fatal to these strange, unliving creatures. It was Clive's blood that had destroyed the ghoster and saved his own life.

Clive leaned his head against the forward wall of the car. A shudder passed through his torso. With each gasped breath his body was regaining control.

"Will we encounter more of those?" he managed to ask his companions.

"We will encounter far worse than those," Sidi Bombay declaimed solemnly. "We will encounter creatures that will make the Major recall these ordolite ghosters with fondness."

Clive retrieved his carbine. He seated himself and began to study the weapon. It was a fascinating device, its stock smooth, and formed in a manner he had never before encountered. He held it to his shoulder and sighted along it. It was possessed of an aiming device such as he had never seen before. Even when he and Annie had faced the troopers near Tewkesbury, the battle had been so frantically fought and so quickly ended that he had lacked the time to examine his weapon.

And on this occasion, his scrutiny of the ordolite carbine was interrupted by the voice of Horace Hamilton Smythe.

"Better hold on, sah. We're about to leave the Earth."

Clive slung the carbine over his shoulder and clung with both hands to a nearby railing, preparing for the car to rise precipitously and plunge from the mouth of the tunnel, up into the sky.

Instead, with a stomach-sickening *whoosh*, it tipped forward. The tunnel in which they had been traveling took by far the steepest dip it had yet done. In less than a second it seemed that they were plunging straight toward the center of the Earth.

"Are we not headed for the spiral of stars?" Clive shouted at Horace.

"That we are, sah!" the sergeant hollered back over his shoulder.

"Then why are we headed downward instead of upward?"

"Things are not what they seem, Major!"

That was all Smythe had to say, and further questions from Clive brought no response from either him or Sidi Bombay.

Air screamed around the car, and the patches and points of light—nebular galaxies or luminous fungoids, blazing stars or glowing sparks—flashed past at dizzying speed.

Without warning the screaming ceased.

But the lights did not disappear.

Instead, a breathtaking panorama spread before Clive's eyes. He saw—or thought he saw—the sun itself, blazing and flaring in solitary majesty. But this was not the sun as seen at noonday, a ball of brilliant white against a field of sparkling blue. Nor was it the pallid disk of a watery English afternoon, nor the glorious orange flare of a midsummer's dawn.

This was the naked sun, a seething globe of white-hot gases standing against the blackness of the void. At first, Clive's eyes were unable to cope with its brilliance. Clive looked away, the afterimage of the sun still roiling, it seemed, against the insides of his eyelids.

Then he saw the worlds, and their moons, and the asteroidal worldlets and soaring comets, and the distant suns and nebulae in brilliant white and yellow and cream. And somehow he imagined that he could sense still more planets and suns and nebulae, black worlds and black stars whose radiance lay far outside the normal band of human vision, but whose reality he could not deny.

Perhaps Q'oorna was such a world, and perhaps he was gazing even now upon the Dungeon.

He scanned the sky for the telltale spiral of points of glimmering white. Somewhere, he knew, they glittered and whirled. Somehow, he knew, he had to go there.

▪ CHAPTER 16 ▪
Expedition from Earth

"Look ahead there, sah!"

It was the voice of Horace Hamilton Smythe, breaking in as it had done so many times upon Clive Folliot's reverie. The sergeant was pointing at a region of space ahead of the car and somewhat above it.

"Is it the world of the Gennine?"

"Not nearly, sah! It's the belt of asteroids, or planetoids to give 'em their proper name. Not little stars, they are, sah, but little worlds. Little worlds! Hundreds of 'em! Thousands!"

"I never knew such existed, Smythe! What distant star are we circling?"

"Our own star, sah. Our own! The asteroids circle the sun forever, fragments of a planet that may once have existed or that may never have come into being. No one knows the answer to that one, sah, but here they are nevertheless."

Sidi Bombay stepped past Clive and touched Horace Smythe on the shoulder. "Look thither, O brother. Thy lecture may impart knowledge more precious than pearl, but peril, not pearl, is our fate!"

He pointed, and both Horace and Clive gazed through the transparent roof of the car. Clive could feel his hand throbbing where the ordolite bayonet had punctured his skin. He was grateful for the semi-accident that had destroyed the enveloping ghoster and saved his own life, but he worried now that his wound would become infected. What strange effect might result from the cut he had incurred!

He peered at the wound. It was a small one, coinciding with the lifeline on the palm of his hand. It was no longer bleeding, nor had serious swelling developed. Still, he was not pleased with the color of the wound, nor with the throbbing, pulsing sensation that radiated up his arm from it.

"Sidi, Horace," he began, "does either of you know—"

But he got no further. A distant something glinted in the light of the even more distant sun. "What was that?" Clive gasped.

"Looks like a Ren ship!" Horace snapped back.

"Ren ship? You mean a space-train? Or a separate car like this one?"

"Not exactly, sah! Haven't time to explain! Sidi, man the mortar!"

To Clive's astonishment, Sidi Bombay could be seen once more opening the seat that revealed the little car's miniature arsenal. He removed a weapon with a tubular barrel and a heavy base-plate closely resembling the mortars with which Clive had become familiar while serving in Her Majestey's Horse Guards.

"Is that really a mortar?" Clive exclaimed.

Sidi Bombay said, "Of a sort, it is, Major Folliot."

"But you'll blow out the roof of our car if you fire it."

"The Major forgets that ordolite weapons fire bolts of pure energy, not material objects. The purpose of the mortar tube is to focus that energy so that it does no harm to our own car, but has its desired effect on that against which it is fired."

Clive bided his time, watching Sidi set up the mortar. It was obvious that he knew exactly what he was doing, and was an expert at his task. To offer assistance—interference! —would have been worse than useless.

Through the transparent wall of the car, Clive could see the Ren ship growing closer. It was unlike their own.

"It reminds me somehow of Chang Guafe!" Clive exclaimed, peering past Horace Hamilton Smythe.

"How's that, sah?"

"It looks like—like a combination of a machine and a living thing. Look, Horace! It has antennae and claws like crab's! It's changing, shifting its shape even as it approaches us!"

"Yes, sah! I'm familiar with Ren ships, sah!"

"You must have learned this during the years we were separated, Horace! And yet you appear no older than you did when last we saw each other on the eighth level!"

"You're right about that, sah!" was Smythe's laconic reply.

"But how can that be, Horace? Both my brother and my father have aged normally, as had my friend du Maurier, to the very brink of the grave."

"If I may explain, please," Sidi Bombay put in. "As one who has both aged and grown young, I have some understanding, perhaps." When neither Clive nor Horace demurred, Sidi Bombay continued. "Sergeant Smythe and I have lived our lives in spurts, one might say. Like a flat stone skipped across the face of a pond, Clive Folliot—am I expressing myself clearly enough?"

"I'm not sure that you are, Sidi Bombay. I'm not sure that I take your point."

"Well, you see, Clive Folliot, the stone may cross a pond a rod or more in width, while actually touching the surface of the water a few times, skipping onward each time. Thus Sergeant Smythe and I have skipped over the years, dropping in now and then to accomplish such tasks as were needed. You were away from the Earth for twenty-eight years—we have been away only for a few years at a time, but have spanned the same twenty-eight years all told."

Behind Clive there was a *thump* and a *whoosh*. He could detect a strange odor in the car, and inferred that it was an ordolite propellant substance.

Above the car a blob of energy arced through the black sky. Clive tried to follow its course. At first it was easy enough. The blob was a brilliant magenta in color, and it pulsed and glowed even as it flew away from their car.

The magenta blob writhed and turned visibly, as if it were a thing alive. Although it made no detectable sound, Clive had the impression that it was hissing like an angry panther. It swooped toward the Ren craft.

The Ren craft dodged to avoid the blob.

The magenta blob altered its course to pursue the craft.

The blob, sizzling and throwing off specks and fragments like a Guy Fawkes Day rocket, flew past the Ren ship.

The Ren ship, meanwhile, slid toward the car containing Clive and his companions. It flexed its external claws, opening and closing their pincers, showing their razor-sharp serrated edges.

Behind Clive, Sidi Bombay fired another round of ordolite ammunition from the mortar.

This time the ordolite ray coalesced into a blob of brilliant yellowish-green. The distinctive odor smote Clive's nostrils, and the sound each time the mortar was fired left Clive with a ringing in his ears. As he regained hearing he said, "They aren't firing back. Perhaps their intentions are peaceful."

Horace Hamilton Smythe growled. "Might be, might not be, sah. Take a look at that thing, eh, sah?" He pointed toward the Ren craft. It was impossible to tell whether the mixture of organism and mechanism was truly glaring hatefully at the transparent car. Perhaps the bulging, reflective features that looked like eyes were merely observation ports.

Perhaps not.

In any case, they gave the appearance of hate-filled, intelligent eyes.

"We are far beyond the Earth's atmosphere," Clive said. "Do you know where the Ren came from, Horace? Are they from another world circling our own sun, or are they from a more distant locale?"

"We don't know their home, sah! We—" Horace paused, pointing in horror at the Ren craft.

It had voided both rounds fired from the ordolite mortar. Now it was nearly upon the transparent car. It altered its position, upending itself so that its rearmost segment was exposed, moving toward the car.

It was shaped like the hindquarter of a scorpion—a curving, segmented organ with a barbed protuberance at its tip. Were the Ren ship truly a scorpion, the barb would have been coated with deadly venom. As it was . . . who could guess?

Horace threw the control lever of the car to the side, and the little craft dipped and swooped away from the scorpion-tail of the Ren.

Clive tumbled against a glass panel.

Sidi Bombay swung the morter away, so Clive would not collide with it. "Be careful, Clive Folliot! If we lose the services of our ordolite weapon, we are in peril even more grave than that which we already face!"

Through the glass panel, Clive could see the Ren's scorpion-tail twitch convulsively. A glowing blob detached itself from the barbed stinger and flew sizzling toward the car.

Horace Smythe jockeyed the controls, swinging the car through a series of evasive gyrations.

The luminescent blob—an angry, glowing orange—sped past. So close to the glass did its course carry it that Clive could make out individual sparks and tails of flame flickering across its surface. Again, while there was no audible sound, it seemed to Clive that the ordolite energy-blob hissed its hatred in some psychic manner as it sped past the car.

"What would happen if it struck us?" Clive asked. "Would it envelop our ship as the ordolite ghoster enveloped me in the tunnel?"

"It would do something worse than that, Clive Folliot. It could penetrate our car's wall as the rounds from our own mortar penetrate that wall. Once inside the car, it would disperse its evil, destructive energy into our bodies."

"Would it kill us?"

"Only if we were fortunate beyond belief. More likely it would—perhaps it is better not to say, Major Folliot."

"Tell me, damn it! Tell me, Sidi Bombay!"

"It would kill only our minds. Our wills. It would turn us into hopeless slaves of the Ren. We would obey them because we would lack the force to place our own choices above their commands. That is what the ordolite would do to us, Clive Folliot. To Sergeant Smythe and myself, at any rate."

"But not me? It wouldn't do that to me?"

"You are of the Folliot blood, Major. You might be exempt from its malign influence. There is no knowing without testing, and it seems foolish at this moment to make that test."

"I might not react to the ordolite at all?"

"Or you might be—you just might be, Major Folliot— the Master of the Ordolite!"

Before Clive could demand an explanation of that extraordinary term, the car in which the three adventurers were traveling was filled with a new light so brilliant that it dazzled the eyes. Clive threw a hand before his face. When he sensed that the flash of light had ended, he lowered his arm and opened his eyes again.

Afterimages danced dizzyingly. He blinked and caught a glimpse of Horace Hamilton Smythe struggling frantically with the car's controls. Facing about, he saw Sidi Bombay clutching the mortar tube. The car bucked violently. Clive grasped a handhold to keep from being thrown against one of his companions.

"What happened?"

Horace Smythe concentrated on the controls of the car, unspeaking.

Sidi Bombay said, "We're being attacked from the rear!"

Horace swung the car in a loop. As it swooped past the upended Ren ship, Clive caught sight of a being through one of the transparent domes that gave the Ren ship the appearance of a great face.

Then Horace had the car successfully turned and speeding in the opposite direction. Ahead of them a squadron of slim shapes appeared. They were gracefully formed, as artistically curved as oriental dancers. Their skins shone in metallic hues: the blue of a dragonfly's wings, the green of a hummingbird's breast, the red of newly shed blood.

Behind them flared the exhaust of rockets. Clive was stunned at the notion of using fireworks to propel great ships, but even as he recognized the nature of these craft, the logic of their means of propulsion became clear. One after another, they discharged what appeared to be concentrated bursts of energy.

Clive could not tell whether these were yet another form of ordolite weapon or some different device. Whatever the case, one of the newcomers scored a glancing blow upon the Ren ship. Clive saw the crumpling of metal plates and watched as the Ren ship reconfigured itself before his very eyes.

Another of the graceful metallic craft scored a hit on the Ren ship, this time to greater effect. The scorpionlike weapon of the Ren ship snapped at its base and tumbled through the blackness, swiftly disappearing.

Now the Ren ship sped forward, ignoring Clive and his companions in their transparent car. The Ren charged directly at the metal squadron. Blow after blow was struck against it, and the Ren ship did nothing to respond. It took each strike in turn, writhing and tumbling, sliding metal plates and organic components into place but struggling toward its foes nevertheless.

When it reached the metal squadron it spurted forward once again. Clive lost sight of it for a moment, but even as he strained his still-stinging eyes to see the ship, he realized that Horace Smythe and Sidi Bombay, also, had been gazing transfixed at the ongoing combat.

Sidi Bombay raised a dark hand and pointed a long finger. "Behold! The enemies, locked in final embrace!"

Clive followed Sidi's direction. Yes, the Ren ship had penetrated the metallic squadron's formation and had cleaved to a red-shining ship. More than ever, the Ren craft resembled Clive's erstwhile companion Chang Guafe. It was a living thing, and it clung and tore at the metal ship with great metal claws and saw-edged extrusions.

The other members of the metallic squadron swung or drifted in disorder. It was obvious to Clive that the ships—or their crews—were desperate to come to the aid of their comrade. Yet the energy-weapon that had temporarily blinded Clive earlier seemed to be all that was available to them. And they dared not fire upon the Ren for fear of hitting their own ruddy-skinned companion.

A circular saw blade was whirring against the skin of the metal ship. The red ship was larger than the Ren but appeared helpless to counter the attack. There were windows or glassed portholes on the scarlet ship. Clive could see movement within it, but could not discern the nature of the ship's crew.

At last the blade bit successfully through the skin of the scarlet ship. A gaping hole appeared as the Ren ship grasped the edges of the opening and tore at the ship, peeling away its skin like a hungry child tearing at the skin of an orange.

One of the occupants of the metallic ship pulled himself through the opening. For a moment Clive caught a glimpse of him. The crewman appeared to be human enough, wearing a helmet and baggy suit not unlike those used by deep-sea divers.

The Ren ship caught the baggy-suited crewman in a pair of pincers that resembled those of a shore-crab. For a fraction of a second Clive could see the man's mouth open to give out a scream of agony and terror. Although Clive could not hear the man, he imagined the sound.

Then the man was halved, snipped through the middle by the saw-edged pincers. Blood and viscera spurted from both halves of the body even as it tumbled away, trailing crimson gobbets.

Clive felt his gorge rising. His hand covered his mouth and he looked away for a moment, but almost involuntarily he turned back, transfixed by the scene of battle.

He had seen many sights of combat and bloodshed, had in fact participated in many, both in his first career as an officer of Her Majesty's Imperial Horse Guards and in his second as an adventurer in the Dungeon. But seldom had he witnessed such carnage, such horror as this. Perhaps the monster at the bridge in Q'oorna, on the first level of the Dungeon . . . or perhaps the cavern of the hideous sacs in which Sidi Bombay had been held prisoner and then rescued, rejuvenated . . . but even those scenes . . . he could not be certain.

The Ren ship—or being—reached through the rent in the metal craft's skin. It inched forward. It looked to Clive as if the Ren ship was trying to climb inside the metallic craft.

But the metallic ship's defenders must have beaten back the invasion, for the Ren ship pulled back its pincers, retreating before a counterattack that saw a squad of bulky-suited individuals clamber through that same rent, some of them clinging to the Ren ship's great claw and others pulling themselves forward in pursuit.

They were men, or at least they had the appearance of

diving-suited men, and they were connected to their own ship by what appeared to be hawsers. That was necessary, Clive realized, as the counterattacking troopers bounded from the skin of their ship.

The rest of the slim, metallic fleet filled the sky, circling the combatants but taking no other part in their struggle.

The troopers were armed with primitive weapons. Clive pressed his face to the transparent wall of the car, straining his eyes for the best possible view of the battle. The troopers were carrying—astonishingly, appallingly—axes.

No civilized man had fought with a battle-axe for three hundred years or more! But in Africa, Clive had seen men go into war armed only with spears. Had seen them bring down great murderous beasts with nothing more.

And in the Dungeon, at the castle of N'wrbb Crrd'f and the Lady 'Nrrc'kth, men had fought with halberds and daggers and swords. Clive had done so himself. Even upon his return to London in the year 1896, he had carried a saber. Its intended use had been purely ceremonial, yet he had carried it with him, and in dire circumstances he had been willing to use it.

The troopers were swarming over the Ren ship, chopping and prying with their axes. Clearly, they meant to get between the metal plates of the ship-creature, to attack the softer and more vulnerable organic components that the metal plates protected. They pried between the plates with their axes while the Ren ship shifted its shape, snapping at them with its pincers. Whatever smith had provided these axes, making possible the astounding tactics of these warriors, must surely have been one of the primitive geniuses of all time!

The Ren ship extruded a new scorpion-tail. It emerged from between metal plates, shining and dripping fluids. It enlarged before Clive's eyes, slowly flexing, then curling, then flexing again.

The Ren ship used its new tail as a prehensile instrument and a stinger all in one, snapping at its attackers. At his side, Clive heard a horrified gasp as the new tail struck a bulky-suited trooper. The trooper was impaled on the barbed tip of the tail. Clive saw him fling his limbs out in a powerful convulsion of agony and death.

Now the Ren ship flexed its tail in a snapping motion, pulling the trooper with it, cracking the hawser that attached the trooper to the metallic ship as an animal-trainer cracks a whip. The trooper was flung away from the ship, tumbling and dwindling into the distance. For a moment Clive caught a glimpse of the trooper's belly, where the Ren ship's tail had torn away a segment of the trooper's suit, leaving a hole the size of a dinner plate.

The Ren ship's barbed tail was covered with gore, and the opening in the trooper's suit showed black and red. Clive prayed silently that the trooper had died instantly when struck by the barbed tail, and did not have to suffer the agonies of this moment.

But for all the effectiveness of the Ren ship's attack, it was a battle of one against many, and every bulky-suited trooper who was rendered *hors de combat* by the Ren ship was replaced by two more, furiously wielding their axes.

Now fluids began to appear on the Ren ship, horrid ichor flowing from between its metal plates. It was not the red of blood, but a hideous purplish color that made Clive gag once again. The Ren ship moved more slowly, its jabs and slices exerted more in self-defense than in the interests of its attack on the metallic ship.

More and more troopers swarmed onto the back of the Ren ship. The being's scorpion-tail flailed and struck, smashing another trooper with its heavy, barbed tip. A pair of pincers snipped off the head of a trooper, and blood spurted from the collar of his suit. But it was clear that the tide of battle had turned.

The Ren ship loosened its grasp on the metal ship and pushed itself away. A squad of troopers could be seen hacking with axe-heads at the hawsers that held them to the ship. They curved away from their ship, clinging to the Ren, chopping at it with their axes.

Clive saw the transparent globes that seemed to be the Ren ship's eyes swing open. From one of them gore spurted. But from the other emerged something pure white that writhed and spun as it tumbled through the blackness.

Like a squid spurting through the ocean, the white thing squirmed and slithered through the blackness.

As it moved away from the Ren ship, it headed directly

toward the car containing Clive and Horace and Sidi Bombay.

As it approached the car it grew, and Clive was able to make out its shape in every horrid detail. Although it was as white as a field of fresh-fallen snow in the English countryside, it was identical in form to the black monster Clive and his companions had fought on the bridge at Q'oorna!

· CHAPTER 17 ·
Novum Araltum

The white creature was hardly larger than an English spaniel.

It whirled past the car, swung back, grasped with writhing tentacles, and plastered itself to the outside of the car. Through the transparent walls of the car, Clive could see that no feature of the hideous monstrosity of Q'oorna was missing from this pallid miniature.

As the white monster pressed its top against the flat panel of the car, Clive could see that this included even the human face on the top of its trunk. Where the black monster of Q'oorna bore the incredibly enlarged visage of Clive's brother Neville, a visage that cursed him even as the monster plummeted from the high basalt bridge, this white miniature bore another face equally familiar to Clive—and equally shocking!

It was the face of Annabella Leighton.

Clive's eyes bugged at the moment of recognition. He lunged across the car toward the white thing with Annabella's features. He pressed his own face against the cold, flat glass.

Yes, every feature, every line that marked Annabella was here. The softly flowing hair. The gently arched eyebrows. The eyes themselves, crying out with the depths of Annabella's love for Clive and the pain of his abandonment of her in her home in Plantagenet Court in London. The graceful, delicate shape of her nose and the generous fullness of her lips . . .

"Annabella!" Clive cried out.

He did not know whether the glass wall of the car would

carry his words to her, but he pressed his ear to the glass in hope that she would respond.

"Clive! My darling!"

Yes! It was Annabella's voice, thinned and strained by the thickness of the glass, yet unmistakably hers.

"Let me in! Oh, Clive, I beg you!"

"Sidi! Horace!" He turned to his companions. "It is Annabella! Help me! We must admit her to the car!"

"No, Clive Folliot. It is not Annabella."

"It is! How this monster has gotten her, I cannot even imagine, but it is she! I know it is she!"

"It's a Ren, sah! They can do that, sah!"

"No! Horace, you must remember the monster of the bridge. It had my brother's face. Now this one has captured Annabella. We must let her into our car. We must rescue her."

"It's all a trick, sah. It's just the Ren."

"I know, I know!" Clive turned away from the glass, forcing himself not to look at the face of his sweetheart. "I know of these monsters. But how can I—?" He could not continue.

"Please, Clive," Annabella's voice came again through the glass.

Beyond the white thing with Annabella's face, Clive could see the heavily suited troopers, those who had survived the battle between the red metallic ship and the Ren craft. They had launched themselves and were floating toward the transparent car. They held their battle axes at the ready.

"Oh, Clive, do not leave me to die! Please, Clive! In the name of our common love! Please! In the name of our common humanity!"

Clive grasped the handle that would unlatch the door of the car and permit Annabella to enter. He tugged at it, struggling to turn it.

Horace Hamilton Smythe grasped Clive's wrist in both his hands. He tugged Clive away from the door.

"Smythe, what are you doing? Release me! If you will do nothing to help me to rescue Miss Leighton, at least do not interfere with my own efforts!"

Horace Smythe grasped Clive by the shoulders and

shook him. "Get ahold of yourself, Major! You know that isn't Annabella. You know that very well, sah! You just said as much! You can't let her—it—in here. It can't be done, sah! We'd lose all our air, we should all die rather than one. But that doesn't matter, sah—that isn't Miss Leighton. I swear to you, sah, that isn't Miss Leighton!"

The troopers were close behind the white thing, axes raised.

"She will die!"

Like a man of two minds, Clive both knew that the monster was not Annabella, yet could not restrain himself from trying to save her. He very nearly succeeded in wrenching away from Smythe, but at the crucial moment, Sidi Bombay grasped Clive's other wrist. Together, the two men held him.

The first of the troopers was upon Annabella. She let go her hold on the glass of the car and pushed herself a few yards from it, ready to meet the trooper's attack.

The white thing was equipped with tentacles and claws and rows of fangs and venomous stingers, but instead of fighting the troopers, it merely waited for them.

At the first blow of an axe, the white thing bounded back toward the car. For a fleeting moment it regained its grasp on the car, pressed its trunk against the flatness. Again Clive found himself looking into the face of Annabella Leighton. "Good-bye, my darling," he heard the beloved voice whisper. "Even this, my love gives me the strength to forgive you, Clive. Even this."

With a maddened effort Clive broke free of Sidi Bombay and Horace Hamilton Smythe's grasp and lunged for the handle of the door. But even as he gripped the metal, a trooper was upon Annabella, his axe swinging.

The single blow split the white thing's trunk from top to bottom. Tentacles writhed, the mouth that Clive had loved opened and closed in a final scream of agony—a scream that was wholly silent—and gouts of ichor spouted from the two halves of the white thing.

The troopers continued to chop away at the pieces until the largest one remaining was smaller than the palm of a child's hand. Clive fell to his knees, convulsed by a dry retching as his empty stomach clenched and clenched again in horrified disgust.

"It wasn't Miss Leighton," Horace Hamilton Smythe told Clive again. "I didn't understand the Ren when we met that black giant on Q'oorna, Major, sah, or I'd have known that you was seein' yer brother's face and hearin' his voice. I saw another face, Major, back there on Q'oorna. When you saw yer brother, I saw me own ma'am. It was hard not doin' what she wanted."

"And I saw my own beloved child, Major Folliot," Sidi Bombay put in. "My child who had been taken by a tiger in the forest of Bengal—for whom I have never ceased to grieve, Major Folliot. The Ren have the power to summon from our minds the images of those whom we love. They use these images against us. But they are not real. They are deceptions, Major Folliot."

Clive wiped his watering eyes. "I know. I know that, Sidi, Horace. But still, seeing the beloved face, hearing the so-sweet voice—can you blame me, my friends, for for a moment of confusion? For a moment of madness?"

"No sah. No one could blame you, sah."

"But we must come to terms, Clive Folliot, with the challenge that we face." Sidi Bombay pointed one finger, as if at a stain that needed to be removed from a garment. "We must not allow that moment of madness to persist."

"And if I had opened the door to her—to it?"

"Chances are, sah, we'd simply have lost all our air. Likely we'd have been swept out of the car, and died. Or else remained here and suffocated. Small choice, eh?"

"What filthy beasts they are! I thought the Ren were human—in our encounters with them in the Dungeon, as suspect as their motives might have been, at least I thought they were human."

"They take many forms," Sidi Bombay said. "But the form in which we first saw the monster upon Q'oorna, and the form of this small white Ren, seem to be their natural shape. I do not understand the differences in their size and coloring, Clive Folliot. But they are the true Ren."

A full dozen troopers by now surrounded the car, some of them floating as gently as gulls caught in an updraft, others grasping at knobs and protruberant features on the outside of the car to steady themselves. Now and then, a trooper would peer curiously through the glass at Clive and Sidi and Horace, but for the most part they simply went about their business.

Their business was the attachment of tether-lines to the car.

Before long the car was hawsered to half a dozen metallic craft. The troopers had departed, returning without a word of communication to their own ships. The fleet began to move, and with it, Clive could feel the glass car moving as well.

"Where are they taking us?" he asked his companions.

"I'd guess they're taking us to their home world, sah," Horace answered.

"To . . . Aralt? I thought Aralt had been destroyed, Horace."

"Yes, sah. Din't know the Major was aware of that, sah."

"I learned it on the eighth level. There was a woman, a beautiful woman. Her name was Lena."

"I quite understand, sah."

"No you don't, Smythe. She was a Chaffri woman, and from her I learned that their home was a tiny world located in the sun's asteroid belt. You thought I was unaware of the existence of asteroids—planetoids—but Lena told me of them. She told me that the home of the Chaffri was Aralt—had been Aralt—but that Aralt no longer existed. It was destroyed."

"That is correct, sah. But the Chaffri are not a minor power. They most surely have an alternative headquarters. They will have moved their operations either to that headquarters, or to some lesser outpost. Those are surely Chaffri ships, and I'd wager all I've got that they're taking us to their base."

Clive slumped against the cushioned back of the plush, padded, dark-red seat. He covered his eyes with his hands. It might have been better, might have been better, he permitted himself to muse, if he'd succeeded in opening the panel, letting the air rush out of the car, letting himself die in the moment of his reunion with Annabella. Of course, it would have been an illusion. If Horace and

Sidi were right, if the white thing had been a Ren and if the Ren had the power to capture images out of their victims' minds and create convincing fancies of them . . . it might have been better to die.

"There it is, Sidi!"

Horace Smythe's voice interrupted Clive's reverie. Smythe stood at the now-useless controls of the car, pointing ahead. By looking around the car, Clive could see the metallic ships above and below, left and right of them. He could see the hawsers that connected the transparent car with the metallic ships, though the area behind each ship was distorted by the wavering pattern of its exhaust. The ships tugged gently, steadily.

Dead ahead of them lay a tiny disk, a perfect worldlet not significantly unlike the Earth, yet only a fraction of its size. Unsullied polar ice caps gleamed in the sunlight. Blue seas and green-forested continents could be seen through breaks in cotton-white clouds.

The metallic ships dropped toward the atmosphere of the miniature planet, guiding the little transparent car. The movement of the car from the point where the ships had attached their hawsers to its arrival at this planetoid had been a smooth and easy one.

But still Clive wondered at the nature and the intent of the Chaffri. The battle between the Chaffri ship and the Ren had been a classic confrontation suitable only in the conduct of implacable foes. The destruction of the white Ren was beyond Clive's comprehension. Representatives of a culture so advanced that it built craft to travel almost casually between the planets had then engaged in mortal combat armed only with axes. Clive had expected them at the very least to use ordolite energy weapons.

But axes?

They circled above a flat, grassy plain located on one of the islands that had to pass for continents on the planetoid. The passage of air created a screaming sound that shook the walls and vibrated the glass panels of the car, but they held.

The metallic ships dropped the hawsers, but they still surrounded the car and maneuvered it toward the plain.

"Can we escape, Smythe?" Clive asked.

"Not possible, sah. And besides, I thought the Major wanted to beard the lion in his den, so to speak, sah."

"The lion—the Gennine! But we have reached the headquarters—or at least a base—of the Chaffri, not the Gennine."

"Even so, sah. At any rate, sah, we couldn't get away even if we wished to. Those metallic ships have us outnumbered, outpowered, and outmaneuvered. This little car was never meant for serious combat. The ordolite mortar is a child's popgun compared to the armament of those metallic ships, Major Folliot, sah."

Clive pondered. "I suppose you're right, Smythe. Sidi Bombay, do you concur?"

"Without hesitation, Clive Folliot."

"Very well, then. Set her down, Smythe."

"Yes, sah. I've already commenced to obey, sah."

The transparent car spiraled downward. The grassy plain had been converted into something resembling a naval facility. Clive could see strips laid out that resembled docks, buildings that were the equivalent of pier facilities, and roads leading away from the area, disappearing into lush woods. He could only guess at their destinations.

The car touched down on rich grass and slid gently to a halt. Horace Hamilton Smythe methodically shut off its propulsive units and turned to unlatch the glass panels through which they had entered the car. He stood aside to permit Clive the privilege of being the first to step from the car.

All around them, Clive could see metallic craft coming in for their landings. Each of them was far larger than the glass car, could easily have dropped the car and a dozen more into its cargo hold, if the metal ships had cargo holds.

Red, gold, blue, green, silver, orange, bronze, one after another the sleek machines landed.

As each touched the earth and came to a halt, its ports opened and crew members poured forth.

But Clive and his companions were greeted by a party that emerged from a shed located near the woods.

The party consisted of men in splendid military garb, fancy uniforms of crimson and gold and blue and green that would have set to shame the fanciest dress uniforms of Her Majesty's military establishment.

The leader was a splendidly attired fellow whose gold-fringed shoulder boards swayed with his every step. His headgear resembled that of an admiral, and a tall plume rose from it to dip before the gentle breeze that coursed across the landing plain.

A sash that swept from shoulder to waist was covered with orders and decorations. A ceremonial shortsword clanked in its scabbard.

Clive peered at the man, trying to determine his rank, or even the branch of service of which he was an officer.

The man halted and saluted smartly. "In the name of the Chaffri, Clive Folliot, I welcome you and your companions to Novum Araltum. I am Muntor Eshverud."

Startled, Clive darted glances to Sidi Bombay and Horace Hamilton Smythe. They offered no suggestions. Muntor Eshverud—the name offered no clue as to the man's origins, nor did his speech, which was slightly accented but which Clive was baffled to place. Except—

Except that Eshverud used English, not the patois that Clive had learned was common in most regions of the Dungeon.

What could that mean?

Eshverud had lifted his spotlessly gloved hand in a military salute, and Clive returned the gesture uncomfortably.

"If the distinguished guests would be so kind as to accompany me to the field office." He gestured to the shed from which he had appeared. But—Clive blinked—was it a shed? The building was a bit larger than he'd thought at first, and its architecture was homey and attractive, rather different from the crude board construction he thought he'd seen.

He fell in beside Eshverud and noted that Horace Hamilton Smythe and Sidi Bombay similarly paired off with members of Eshverud's party. They set off at a brisk pace toward the building. Clive heard Horace Smythe anxiously questioning his companion about the care that their car would receive. The replies were reassuring. Sidi Bombay was engaged in dialogue, apparently on the subject of mess facilities and supplies.

"We observed your encounter with the Ren ship, Major

Folliot," Muntor Eshverud said. "You were fortunate that our patrol encountered you in time. Those are nasty things, those Ren craft. Nasty as the creatures that build and fly them!"

"You are at war with the Ren, sir? I did not quite catch your proper title."

"Muntor. My name is Eshverud. The other is my grade and position in Chaffri society."

"Very well, sir. And my prior question, if you please?"

"Yes. At war with the Ren. I suppose you might call it war. If a campaign of extermination is suitably termed a war."

"Extermination, sir? I have never heard of a war in which it was the acknowledged objective of one party to exterminate the other. Do you mean to annihilate the enemy to the last man, woman, and child?"

Eshverud smiled bitterly. His brow was massive, his whole face was broad. A thick mustache, perhaps blond in the Muntor's youth, now almost white with age, rose at its tips toward muttonchop whiskers.

"The last man, woman, and child, Major Folliot? A poignant phrase. Yes, I believe that the Ren would exterminate us to the last man, woman, and child. If they had the power to do so. Unless they chose to maintain a domesticated stock for food. They dine on the flesh of Chaffri, you know. Not often—there aren't enough of us to meet the demand. So we're considered a great delicacy among the Ren."

"I encountered a giant Ren when I first entered the Dungeon, Muntor Eshverud. In 1868, when I was in search of my brother."

Eshverud nodded. "They infest the Dungeon."

"The one we encountered—it had devoured humans and it displayed the countenance of my own brother. It cursed me in his voice!"

"The Ren have terrible powers of the mind. I do not doubt your story, Major—it is altogether credible. But I would suggest that the Ren plucked the image and the sound of your brother's voice from your own brain, and fed the information back to you in order to serve its own ends."

"I have come to believe that, yes, Muntor."

They were close to the shed. Now Clive realized that it was an inn, built in the Tudor style, half-timbered and covered with a roof of thick thatch. It had been full day when the glass car landed on the grassy field, but night fell swiftly on Novum Araltum, and the sky was already darkening. The sun was half hidden beneath the horizon, stars twinkled, and nearby asteroids wove a broad, glittering belt across the sky.

From a low chimney, a lazy stream of smoke rose slowly, and Clive could smell the familiar odor of burning peat.

The door of the inn was fitted with pebbled panes of amber-tinted glass. Lights from within gave the glass a warm, golden glow. Muntor Eshverud ushered Clive through the doorway into a world at once hauntingly familiar and disquietingly strange.

As an English gentleman he would not have frequented workingmen's pubs, yet he certainly knew what they were. There had been reason to visit them in the Dungeon, and he had encountered one, to his distress, upon his return to London.

Yet this establishment was not exactly a nineteenth-century pub. It had some of the feel of a country inn of an earlier and more wholesome age. He half-expected to see rural bumpkins, the hayseeds falling from their hair, raising tankards of ale and haunches of mutton. There was indeed a genial publican presiding over the proceedings, while serving wenches in daringly cut blouses and billowing skirts made their way skillfully among long common tables of broad, rough-hewn planks.

"Is this—pardon me, Muntor—" Clive addressed his companion, "is this the headquarters of an aerial base of the Chaffri? I fear that I do not understand, sir—although I will concede that it is a homey and pleasant place."

Eshverud smiled. He guided Clive by one elbow, maneuvering him through the crowded common room. He stopped at the bar and bent to speak with the publican. Even above the din of the room, filled as it was with drinking, eating, joking, singing, roistering Chaffri, Clive had no difficulty in making out the Muntor's words.

"Two everflowing tankards of your best, Jivach, for *Ma-*

jor Folliot and myself. A platter of good hot food. We'll be in a private dining room, the major and myself. And if I know my guest's tastes, Jivach, make it a point to send in your prettiest serving wench. And don't expect to see her back too quickly, Jivach."

And the man actually winked!

Clive let himself be steered into a private room where the furniture, although crudely hewn, was more than comfortable. Light came from an oil lamp, and the air smelled like England.

The two men sat on opposite sides of the wooden table. There were a million questions that Clive wanted to ask Eshverud. Questions about the Chaffri, about the Ren, about the Dungeon—and about the Gennine. There were so many questions, covering so immense a variety of topics, that Clive hardly knew where to begin.

But before the dialogue had gotten very far, there was a knock at the door and Muntor Eshverud called, "Come ahead, then!"

The door swung open, and the serving wench turned to shut it behind her even before she had set down her cargo. Clive caught but a fleeting glance of her, yet even in that instant he was utterly taken with her dark, glossy hair, her soft skin that glowed creamy and golden in the light of the oil lamp, the graceful figure and the generous bosom that swelled beneath the inadequate confines of her low and flimsy blouse.

He sat up with appreciation and waited for her to turn back toward him. She bent over her task, placing tankards of ale and platters of meat and rolls on the wooden table. As she did so, the material of her blouse billowed away from her warm bosom.

Clive blinked.

The serving wench straightened.

Their eyes met in startled recognition, and simultaneously they cried each other's names.

"Clive!"

"Annabella!"

· CHAPTER 18 ·
"Clive, My Darling Clive"

Without thinking, Clive rushed to Annabella—and she, to him. They embraced in a breathless rush of passion, their bodies pressed together like those of eager lovers, their mouths pressed to each other's as if each held for the other the ambrosia of life.

At last, for the moment sated, yet trembling, they managed to seat themselves. Still they remained, each with an arm around the other's shoulders, each holding the other's hand, each gazing into the other's eyes.

A chill ran through Clive at the thought that this Annabella was still another trick, a simulacrum or an illusion created to mislead him. But she was so warm, so real—the heightened beating of his heart, the tightening of his chest, the excited joy that he felt would not be denied. She had to be real! How had she come to Novum Araltum? How could this woman of nineteenth-century England be employed as a serving wench in an establishment on another world?

The questions would keep. She was Annabella!

"I expected never to see you again. Oh, my darling Annabella! I wanted to go to your home—to Plantagenet Court—but I knew you were no longer there. That in shame you had sailed away to America and settled there forever."

"I did that, Clive. I waited as long as I could for your return to England. I was . . . with child, Clive. Clive, with your child. With your daughter."

"Yes, yes Annabella. I know the whole story. I—"

"How do you know?"

"I was told by my great-great-granddaughter. *Our* great-great-granddaughter, my darling Annabella. Is it so strange to think that we have so remote a descendant? She is Annabelle Leigh, of the city of San Francisco in the United States of America. And she came to London in 1999, and from there was transported to the Dungeon."

"I have heard of the Dungeon, Clive."

"You were never there?"

"No, my darling. I never left Boston. Once I reached the New World, I determined that I would never turn back, never return to England. But I had no idea of the Dungeon. I lived my life, raised my daughter, taught her—" She blushed, the crimsoning of her skin visible not only on the softness of her cheeks but on the tenderness of her bosom.

"I know the law of your family. *Do as you will, take such lovers as you choose, bear a daughter, and teach her to do the same . . . and never, never marry.*"

"And my girls have kept that law—unto the year 1999, you say, Clive?"

"They have."

A smile crossed her face, a smile less soft than those Clive Folliot was accustomed to seeing on Annabella. "But how did you come here, to Novum Araltum? And . . . your age, Annabella. You appear little older than the tender maid I knew in Plantagenet Court."

"I would have waited for you in England, Clive, if I had been given any reason to expect your return."

"Did you never hear from me after I left? I wrote you letters—many of them."

"I never received them."

"I know. That was my shame. I wrote them only in my mind."

"I saw your dispatches in the *Illustrated Recorder and Dispatch*. Your reports and your sketches were excellent."

"I had hoped to collect them into a book."

"Your editors did so in your behalf, Clive. In both England and America you were an author of some fame. Alas, fame is fleeting, and after a few years you were forgotten. I fear that the readers of a later decade may never have heard of Clive Folliot. Still, scholars and collectors of volumes on exotic lands honor you."

"I was a famed author? My fame came and went, all unbeknownst to me, and I am now the pet of musty bibliophiles. Aye, so it ever was, I suppose." Clive shook his head, a wry smile upon his lips. His reports had been modest, his drawings crude and unpolished—at least in his own estimation. But apparently they were not so, in the judgment of others. Du Maurier's redactional services and Maurice Carstairs' promotional efforts must have done him better than ever he had guessed.

"And du Maurier?" he asked Annabella. "Did you ever hear from him?"

"He came to see me. He said that he had received emanations from you, from a distant and terrible realm. Clearly, that was the Dungeon, Clive."

"I visited him in London just days ago, Annabella. I saw him on his deathbed. He was attended by Clarissa Mesmer, the granddaughter of the famous—or infamous—Anton."

"George du Maurier was a good man, Clive. A visionary. A great soul who was born many years ahead of his time."

"And did any others come to see you?"

"Your father and brother."

"My *brother*! Neville came to see you?"

"He did."

"They came together to see me in Plantagenet Court. After a little while Neville sent the baron upon some errand, and then . . ." She turned away from him. As she did so, an errant tendril of dark hair fell across her bosom, drawing his attention to the tender valley of her breasts, where warm golden lamplight played.

"And then what?" Clive prompted.

She turned back but hid her face against his shoulder. "He told me that you were dead. He attempted to—to comfort me, Clive. He was so much like you, my darling, in every way. The curl of his hair, the features of his face, his hands, the very—the very smell of him, Clive."

"The monster!" Clive bounded to his feet. For the first time since Annabella's arrival, he thought of Muntor Eshverud. He looked for the Chaffri, but Eshverud had slipped from the room. Annabella had risen to her feet and now Clive placed his hands on her cheeks, peering deep into her eyes. "Did Neville . . . ?"

"Yes," she whispered. "I felt such confusion at the time, such weakness and despair. And afterward, Clive, such shame. That was the real reason I left England. I would have stayed and proudly borne your child. But after Neville . . . I could not stay."

"Are you sure that the child—?"

"It is your child, Clive. That I *know*! And the girls who descended from her, even unto Annabelle Leigh, are your descendants. All of them carry the Folliot blood. For better or for worse, Clive. I do not carry it, but all of our descendants do."

With a start, Clive realized that he was hungry. Through the entire trip in the glass car, the battle in space, and the landing on Novum Araltum, he had not eaten a bite. Now the smell of the hot food that Annabella had brought assaulted his nostrils. And with his hunger came a great thirst, and he lifted the tall tankard of ale and held it between himself and Annabella.

"We are together again, my darling girl. Together again!"

With their eyes they exchanged further thoughts. Annabella lifted the second tankard, and they toasted with elbows linked, then set to on the still-steaming haunch and rolls. Between mouthfulls of food and hearty draughts of ale they exchanged kisses and looks and caresses, and before the meal was over Clive felt himself yielding to old attractions, and found Annabella returning his attentions with the passion that had locked him to her in Plantagenet Court in long-ago London.

He slipped a hand into her bodice and she pressed against him, pressing her cheek against his and whispering in his ear daring syllables that he had not heard for months or years or a quarter-century.

The room was set up for private assignations, and thus they used it, Clive all forgetful of the Dungeon and its horrors and its perils. Forgetful of the sultry Lorena Ransome and the strangely colored Lady 'Nrrc'kth with her pale skin and green-tinted hair and eyes. Forgetful of the spider Shriek and the alien cyborg Chang Guafe and the faithful, doglike Finnbogg and the top-hatted Baron Samedi with his sardonic laughter and the lumbering Frankenstein monster. Forgetful of the Muntor Eshverud and of Clive's own companions Sidi Bombay and Horace Hamilton Smythe.

Happy and sated, with his arms around the soft shoulders of Annabella Leighton and her breath warm and soft on his own unclad chest, Clive slept. He was happy at last, happy save for something that nagged at a distant corner of his mind even as he slumbered in the soft golden lamplight.

The warm, pliant flesh was the hard carapace of an Egyptian scarab.

The deep, loving eyes were the faceted and glittering organs of an insect.

The strong yet gentle hands were chitinous claws.

The voluptuous torso that had so inflamed his passions was the segmented body of an—

Of an—

Clive wakened in terror, his being drenched in cold sweat. The lamp had burned the last of its oil. The room was plunged into darkness. Clive had no way of telling how much time had passed, but no sounds came from the tavern.

He pushed himself to his feet, clumsily pulling his clothing into a semblance of order, and staggered to the wall. There were a few errant rays of light, not so much illuminating the little room as suggesting the faint possibilities of illumination.

Clive staggered toward the source of the light. He collided with the wooden table and reached out to catch himself. His hand slid across a heavy platter now thick with congealing grease. A tall tankard, still half-full of strong ale, flew from the table and smashed upon the crude plank floor. Its contents splattered upward, spattering Clive's face and clothing like mud splashed from a London gutter.

He crashed against the wall and stared back at the place where he had lain with Annabella, straining his eyes to see her there. It had to have been a dream! He had been through too much. The rug had been pulled from beneath his reality once too often. That was it—that had to be it!

The lovely woman whose lush body he had so enjoyed could not be other than real. She could not!

The faint light did not permit him to see her clearly. "Annabella!"

She stirred—but her stirring carried to his ears the dry scrabbling sound of an exoskeleton. Clive could not believe that this was real.

"Annabella!" he repeated.

Again she stirred. He could see the vague, shadowy outline of her form rising.

He threw out his arms and one of his grease-coated hands collided with a closed shutter. He whirled and struggled frantically with the latches, and finally was able to pull back the wooden panels.

He had no time to appreciate the sight of the night sky above Novum Araltum. He turned back to the room and saw Annabella in a state of flustered dishabille. Her skirt was still pulled up around her waist and one sweet breast was exposed above her disarranged bodice.

"Clive!" Even through the semi-darkness of the room she conveyed the impression of a blush. She pulled up her blouse and arranged her skirt decorously. "Clive, I am embarrassed."

He gawked.

"It was unladylike of me, I know, Clive darling. But it had been so long, I missed you and longed for you so, my darling. You cannot imagine the times I dreamed of you— entertaining fantasies of you as I lay on my mattress— pretending that each tread on the stair, each voice of a passerby in the street, each clatter of carriage-wheel on cobblestone, was the sign of your return. Oh, my darling!"

She moved across the room toward him.

He recoiled.

"Clive! Please, Clive! Have I lost you? Did my appetites of the night disgust you? Am I branded now a licentious harlot? Oh, please, my darling Clive!"

He backed away from her, blinking his eyes in the semi-darkness. For a moment she would be his own dear Annabella, the warm woman whose scents still filled his nostrils, whose flavor still roused his taste buds. Then he would blink and behold a creature of horror and revulsion, something like a beetle and something like a mantis and something altogether alien that made his scalp crawl and his skin shrivel at the thought of what had transpired between them.

He bolted for the door. He pushed against it and found it unyielding. Then he hurled himself against it, unmindful of the pain that shot through him with each impact. Finally he grasped the handle and found that the door opened toward him, into the room.

He did not look back as he sprinted through the still night-shrouded inn, searching for an exit. He stumbled into the common room he had seen hours earlier. The tables had been cleared, the occupants had long departed. A great stone fireplace that had held a roaring log now contained warm embers from which rose a thin stream of gray smoke.

Behind him, Clive could hear Annabella's voice, breaking with sobs. "Clive, my darling, my love!" There was a shuddering intake of breath, as would be appropriate to a heart-shattered woman. "Come back to me, Clive! What have I done? Why have you left me?"

But the sound that accompanied that voice was not the sound of unshod feet. It was the horrid, dry scraping and rasping of the carapace of a giant insect!

Clive plunged through the wooden door, pounding onto a grassy area. Who were the Chaffri? In the Dungeon he had thought them human—had thought both the Chaffri and the Ren were human. But if the Ren were really the same species as the tentacled monsters he had encountered on Q'oorna and then in the sky above Novum Araltum, and if the Chaffri were in truth horrifying giant insects . . .

He was struck by another thought.

In the battle between the Ren and the Chaffri, the Chaffri had appeared to be human. He had not actually seen any of them, but their baggy costumes had betrayed a clearly human form. What could this mean?

Chaffri and Ren alike seemed to have the ability to pull images from the mind. Both of them could then fool their victims into seeing what the alien races wished them to see. It was a power not unlike the power to create simulacra and invest them with an imitation of life. This was the

power to mask themselves with illusions, and pass off their
own actions as those of others. A victim might see himself,
his brother, his lover—*anyone!*—when in fact he was in
the presence of an alien monster.

"Clive, come back!"

He heard the voice of his beloved, coming from behind
him. But he dared not turn, paralyzed equally by the fear
that he would see a gigantic mantislike creature and that
he would see Annabella—or the illusion of Annabella.

"Clive, please! Clive, last night was so wonderful! Oh
Clive, I need you! Come to me, please, my darling!"

He shuddered so violently that he almost fell. He ran
blindly from the inn. He knew that he was at the edge of
the grassy field where both his own transparent car and
the metallic ships of the Chaffri had landed. The sky was
ablaze with distant stars and nebulae and with the reflected light of the uncounted miniature worlds that made
up the asteroid belt.

He set off at a run, paralleling the edge of the woods
that surrounded the landing field. He could not hear
Annabella Leighton following, nor was there any indication of the presence of the Muntor Eshverud.

But ahead there loomed another low building not unlike
the inn that Clive had fled. Was it another inn, or was it a
structure of some wholly different sort, disguised by the
mental powers of the Chaffri to seem an inn? He wished
he could call upon George du Maurier to help him unravel
the puzzle. This was du Maurier's kind of conundrum.

For a moment he tried sending a mental call to du
Maurier. Then he remembered that du Maurier was dead.
Dead and gone, forever beyond recall or communication
from the living.

You are wrong, Clive Folliot.

He whirled. Where had the voice come from?

Don't look for me, Clive. You cannot see me.

"Du Maurier?"

Yes.

"Where are you?"

I am with your brother.

"With Neville?"

No. I am with your brother Esmond.

"But—Esmond was never born! Esmond spoke to me when I was in the Dungeon. Esmond was to have been the triplet brother of Neville and myself, and he died before birth."

That's right, brother.

"Esmond? Is it you?" Clive found himself swept by a rush of emotion unlike any he had felt in his life. "Are you my lost brother?"

I am.

"Where are you? Are you in Heaven? Does your soul reside with God?"

Heaven? God? What do I know of such things, brother Clive?

"But you are with du Maurier. He is dead. You must both be disembodied souls—the soul of the dead and the soul of the never-born."

Deep in Clive Folliot's mind there sounded the ghostly, psychic laughter of George du Maurier and Esmond Folliot. Then du Maurier's voice echoed once more, so that Clive could hear it but none other could. *There's no time to debate metaphysics, Folliot. You've got to get away from Novum Araltum. Rescue your friends if you can, but even if you cannot save them, you yourself must leave Novum Araltum.*

"Why, du Maurier? Leave Novum Araltum for where? Shall I return to Earth? To London? To Tewkesbury? To the Dungeon?"

None of these, Folliot. You yourself spoke of bearding the lion in his den. The lion is the Gennine, and you are the Master of the Ordolite. That must be the final battle in this monstrous war—and lecture me not on the virtues of peace. It takes two to make peace, only one to make war. When a warmaker and a peacemaker collide, the warmaker emerges covered with blood—the blood of his enemy!

Behind Clive he could hear a dry scraping, and a sweet voice crying out. "Beloved! Come back, my beloved!"

He raced through the night. The lights of distant stars and nearby asteroids cast a myriad of shadows on the grassy plain. Clive found himself studying them distractedly while he ran. He could hardly tell which was his own shadow, which that of a high clump of grass or a bush.

With a crash, he tumbled to the ground. He had tripped over something. He pushed himself to his hands and knees and stared in horror at the body of Muntor Eshverud.

The Muntor lay face-up, staring glassily at the star-ribboned sky. His eyes were wide and filled with horror. There was no apparent wound on his body, yet when Clive felt his chest there was neither heartbeat nor respiration, and when Clive felt his skin it was cold. Eshverud had been dead for hours—probably, Clive inferred, the Muntor had left the inn at the moment of Clive and Annabella's first ecstatic embrace. He must have been killed almost immediately.

And he was, to all discernible evidence, truly human.

Clive seized the body by one shoulder and a trouser leg and turned Eshverud onto his face. The cause of death was immediately apparent—his neck had been severed from the rear, so that only a flap of skin held his head in place. Something incredibly sharp and driven with overwhelming force had come within a hair's breadth of decapitating Eshverud.

There was a rustling behind Clive. He pushed himself to his knees and took a final look at Eshverud. The man's ceremonial shortsword still rested in its ornate scabbard. Clive grasped the sword, drew it from the scabbard, and ran once more. Behind him the sound of Annabella's cries grew faint and then ceased.

Clive halted, thunderstruck, when he found himself standing at the inn once again. Or was it the same inn? The architecture was similar but some subtle difference in the building's situation told Clive that it was not the same one he had left behind. He circled it, Muntor Eshverud's shortsword at the ready. He found a shuttered window and shoved carefully at the weathered wood.

The shutters had been left unbarred! Within the room Clive could see a few guttering candles, and in their orange-tinted light, a sight that sent horror coursing through him.

Horace Hamilton Smythe, erstwhile military man, mandarin, Arab boy, and Tsarist nobleman, now in his garb as a London scrivener, sat in a rough-hewn wooden chair. A beatific smile lighted his doughty face, and he was speaking with animation. Clive could make out only a portion of his words, but they were clearly a long, detailed recitation of his adventures in the Dungeon. From time to time he would speak in direct address, calling his listener "Mother," or "Ma'am."

The listener, sedulously sharpening serrated claws upon each other, was a giant insect that looked like a cross between a scarab and a gigantic wasp!

Even as Clive clambered through the window, the insect launched its attack on Horace Hamilton Smythe. The battle lasted mere seconds, but to Clive it might have been hours.

Clive crashed shoulder-first against the carapace of the insect, knocking it sideways mere fractions of an inch short of inflicting a horrendous wound on Horace Hamilton Smythe. The insect recovered its balance and came at Clive, striking out with razor-edged claws. Clive lunged at it, using the Muntor Eshverud's shortsword as if it were a dueling saber. The insect was as tall as Clive, and its claw-tipped limbs flicked at him with amazing speed.

Years of training by his father, Baron Tewkesbury, and his brother Neville, had given Clive a command of technique with the blade. On Earth he had never been a match for Neville, but years of adventuring in the Dungeon had hardened his muscles, quickened his reflexes, and given him the attitude needful to the fighting man whose every engagement can mean his life or his death.

A feint at the insect's face brought its claws up to protect glittering, faceted eyes. Like lightning, Clive dropped his point and lunged instead at the thin, muscular target that connected segments of the insect's thorax.

In the blink of an eye, Clive switched his tactics from those of a foil-wielding duelist to those of a broadsword-wielding yeoman. He flicked left with the honed edge of the sword, then right.

The insect fell to the floor, neatly severed in two.

To Clive's horror, both segments continued to twitch and to strike out at him.

Horace Hamilton Smythe stood by in a daze. Clive leaped over a razor-sharp claw as the insect continued to snap and swipe at him. He grasped Smythe's elbow and hustled him from the room.

· CHAPTER 19 ·
Prepare for the Final Onslaught!

Horace Hamilton Smythe stumbling at his side, Clive Folliot made his way back into the night. Novum Araltum's sky was still suffused with the ghostly glow of the asteroid belt, and in that light the two men staggered from the inn.

"She was—she was my—" Horace Hamilton Smythe stammered half-incoherently, permitting himself to be guided by the more determined Clive. Clive permitted himself to slow his pace and peer back at the building. There was no sign of pursuit.

Smythe was still muttering and mumbling.

Clive grasped him by the shoulders and shook him. "Sergeant Smythe! Come to order, man! You cannot permit yourself this kind of conduct!"

Slowly the light of reason grew in the Smythe's eyes. He raised a trembling hand and drew it across his face, then dropped the hand to his side and brought himself to a modified form of attention. "I'm sorry, Major, sah. I must have been— I thought I'd been freed of the Ransomes' mesmeric control, but I fear I was mistaken, sah."

Clive shook his head. "I don't think it was the Ransomes, Sergeant. They've enough evil to answer for, should we succeed in hauling them before the bar of justice . . . but I don't think they can be blamed for the evil that is taking place here on this world of Novum Araltum. I think the Chaffri are to blame for that!"

"But I could have sworn, Major, that I was back on the family farm, in the arms of my dear mother. She lived a horrid life, Major, a horrid life."

"I understand that, Horace."

"And here she was, restored to me, as pure and beloved as when I was a boy."

"Don't you see, Horace, what has happened? The Chaffri—they seem to be a race of giant, intelligent insects. A cross between a scarab and a mantis." Clive shuddered. "And they have an ability that permits them to reach into a victim's brain and draw from it whatever image most powerfully controls that victim."

"Then it wasn't my ma'am at all, Major?"

"It was a monstrous insect that would have slaughtered you as coldly and deliberately as a mantis slaughters an aphid! And as likely drained your vital fluids for its own delectation, into the bargain!"

"*Phaugh!*"

"Indeed, Sergeant Smythe. *Phaugh.* I couldn't have put it better myself."

"And you saw your own ma'am, too, Major Folliot?"

"No, Smythe. I saw . . . another. A woman who gave me her best, her tenderest, and most honest faith and service. And I gave her—well, never mind that. It was not she. It was merely another of these murdering Chaffri."

"You killed that one, too, did you, sah?"

"I escaped it, anyway."

Smythe turned, surveying the horizon. On this tiny world it lay close by, and the turnings of day and night were quick.

Clive followed Smythe's example. The first blush of morning was coming upon them. He could see the Chaffri's landing field, the warlike ships, and the complicated equipment used to fuel and service them. What should Clive's next move entail?

Horace Smythe interrupted the nobleman's musings. "Sah—Major Folliot, sah! What of Sidi Bombay?"

"Good heavens! The Chaffri must have him yet! Quick, Smythe, did you see any other building—other than the one where I found you?"

"I'm not sure, sah. I think there was another structure beyond yon stand of trees. I was in my childhood home, in our little cottage on the farm. There would have been a shed for the animals not far off, sah."

"Take me to it. At once!"

They ran there quickly. As they drew to a halt, Smythe pointed. "There it is, sah! I'd swear, it was just the shed we had in Sussex back in the twenties!"

"And to me it resembles a rustic inn, such as would stand in Devonshire in the sixties. But it's neither, Horace! It's one of the Chaffri's horrid nests, and poor Sidi Bombay is inside it, at this very moment falling victim to God knows what terrible fate."

"Do you see two doors to it, sah?"

The question went through Clive like a bolt of galvanic electricity. If he and Sergeant Smythe saw the building differently, could they coordinate their efforts to rescue Sidi Bombay? Or would they blunder about helplessly, each entrapped by his own set of illusions, neither capable of penetrating his true surroundings?

"I do see two doors, Horace! A main entrance to the inn, and another that must be the means of access to the kitchen."

"I'll take the one to our right, sah. You take the other. We'll find our way to poor Sidi—somehow."

"Stout man, Sergeant Smythe!" He clapped the other on the shoulder and set off, sword still in his hand, for the more distant of the two entrances to the building.

Even in the instant that Clive paused before plunging into the building, he was struck by the perfect imitation—or illusion—that the Chaffri had achieved. The walls were of timber and rough white plaster, the roof was thick rustic thatch, the windows fitted with diamond-paned glass. There was even the scent of the English countryside.

He shoved open the door and plunged into the common room of a typical Devonshire inn. The hearth, the rough tables and sturdy benches, the serving bar, even the wall decorations were chosen and arranged to perfection. But, Clive realized, they had not been chosen and arranged by the Chaffri themselves so much as they had been constructed by his own mind, functioning under the arcane compulsion of the Chaffri. Clive had summoned images from the half-remembered, half-idealized world of his young manhood as the cadet son of a country baron.

What reality lay behind the illusion of rustic woods and rough-hewn stone, he shuddered even to guess.

Clive had no time to stand and ponder. Sidi Bombay, for all he knew, lay in another room of the structure, in dire peril of his life. His mind might at this very moment be under the control of a mantislike Chaffri. The Hindu might be seeing a scene from the days of his youth, might imagine that he was in the village of his childhood, somewhere in the jungles of the Punjab or on the plains of Equatoria. Or he might be reliving a past experience that had involved him in the doings of the convoluted politics of the Indian subcontinent.

For an instant there flashed through Clive Folliot's own mind the horrifying thought that the mesmeric control and frightening responses of the otherwise stalwart Horace Hamilton Smythe might be the product of the same sinister powers of the Chaffri that he himself had experienced a few hours past.

Philo B. Coode . . . the self-styled Reverend Amos Ransome . . . the seductive Lorena Ransome, she of the shimmering black hair and dark liquid eyes and willowy figure so ill concealed beneath her seemingly modest but subtly provocative costumes. Were any of them what they seemed? Were any of them even humans? Or were these three nothing more than hideous chitin-covered monstrosities masquerading in human society?

And if Philo Goode and the Ransomes were hideous monsters making for themselves the most effective of all disguises—the disguise of their own victims' minds and memories—then who else might be monsters as well? Clive's brother Neville? His father, the Baron Tewkesbury? His closest friend, the recently deceased George du Maurier? Annabella Leighton and her descendant Annabelle Leigh, the dear, eccentric "User Annie" of the year 1999?

Clive shuddered.

A voice seemed to whisper from within his mind. *Hold fast*, it urged him. *Hold fast to your grip on reality, Clive Folliot!*

Clive looked around. "Is that you, du Maurier?"

It is I.

"But you're dead."

Again you point out the obvious, Folliot. Do not let yourself be distracted by such trivialities as death. Plot your course, my friend. Do what you must. Much rests upon your shoulders, Clive Folliot. The fate of millions. Whole worlds, Clive! Do not be distracted by trivialities!

Clive heard a popping and crackling.

He peered around the common room and saw embers still glowing in the great hearth, threads of smoke rising slowly from the glowing embers of a huge backlog that must never grow fully cold and dark.

Was it truly a log, or a simulacrum of a log?

He rushed through the opening that led to the private rooms of the inn. He thrust open the first of them and found nothing of interest within. The second room proved equally unrewarding.

The sound of heavy boots captured his attention and he saw Sergeant Smythe approaching from the opposite end of the inn, checking rooms just as Clive was, snorting and slamming doors in impatience and disappointment as he found each chamber untenanted.

"Sergeant!"

They had met at the center of the hallway. Two doors remained to be tried, one on either side of the passage. Without a word, each man reached to open the door on his right.

Clive heard a grunt of surprise from Sergeant Smythe, followed by a sound of impact, as of a blunt and heavy object connecting with a human cranium. But Clive had no time to go to Smythe's assistance. He had already shoved open the door of the room to his own right, and he stood thunderstruck by the sight it contained.

A thing as alien and terrible as any Clive had ever beheld towered above him, its gargantuan trunk and massive crown bent to avoid scraping the beamed ceiling of the room. Great masses of tentacles writhed and snapped about it, rows and clusters of them dripping a noisome gelatinous slime. Clawed appendages, suction rings, and pseudopods appeared and disappeared, twisting sickeningly. Clive's stomach heaved.

The thing tilted in an arc so that its top was pointed at

Clive. It was a circular membrane surrounded by waving, reaching tentacles.

The thing was one of the monsters that Clive had first encountered at the bridge of black obsidian on Q'oorna. That one had shown him the face of his brother Neville and had spoken to him in an obscene parody of Neville's voice.

This one showed him the face of . . . *Sidi Bombay*.

Clive was thunderstruck. But even as he stood gawking at the hideous sight, the face melted and ran like soft wax, reforming itself into the pale beauty of the Lady 'Nrrc'kth. The white skin, the emerald eyes, the shining, green-tinted hair were so real that Clive involuntarily raised his hand to touch the lady's cheek.

But 'Nrrc'kth was dead!

But George du Maurier was dead also, and yet du Maurier spoke to Clive and told him not to be distracted by the triviality of death!

" 'Nrrc'kth!" Clive cried out.

The emerald eyes pierced his own. The lips opened. A hideous roar emerged, not from the lips of the lady, but from the round membrane of a monster, that vibrated like the head of a drum.

Clive recoiled—but for a mere instant. He was armed with the sword he had taken from the Muntor Eshverud; and with a determination that the old Clive Folliot could never have exhibited, he lunged at the monster.

It snapped its trunk away from him and scuttered across the room with astonishing agility, propelling itself with its rows and clusters of tentacles.

"Enough, Clive Folliot! Enough!"

The voice was that of Sidi Bombay, and the words were followed by the distinctive laughter that Clive had so many times heard from the Indian.

Even as Clive stood, pop-eyed and open-mouthed, the monster began again to melt and reform itself in a manner not unlike that of the alien shape-changer Chang Guafe. It changed its form, its size, its coloration. It became a man, dark-skinned and nearly naked, garbed only in a white turban and spotless breechclout.

"Clive Folliot," Sidi Bombay said. He bowed extravagantly, giving the gesture a touch of irony that robbed it of all obsequy.

"The monster," Clive gasped, "the Chaffri! They're hideous things, Sidi Bombay, hideous great insect-things that can reach into our minds and steal the images of those we hold dear, and fool us into thinking that they're humans themselves!"

"I know that well, Clive Folliot."

"But—are you Sidi Bombay? Or are you one of them?"

"Here is the Chaffri who tried to work that deception on me, O Major." The African turned and with a graceful gesture indicated a rough cage. Where Sidi Bombay had obtained the cage, or how he himself had constructed it from scrap, Clive had no idea—nor any time to worry.

He took the few strides that brought him close to the cage. It was no larger than the carrying case that a lady would use to transport a pampered miniature spaniel on a country outing. It appeared to be constructed of ordinary wood, but the creature that it held made no effort to break its way free.

When Clive caught his first glimpse of the creature it resembled the Chaffri scarab-mantises with which he was already unpleasantly familiar. But even before he could catch a clear image of the thing, it changed. For a moment it was a miniature figure of the Lady 'Nrrc'kth, all pale skin and shimmering forest green hair and flashing emerald green eyes. And nude, utterly nude, its milk-white flesh the very image of cold yet voluptuous grace.

And then before Clive's eyes it turned to the image of his father, Baron Tewkesbury. But the baron as Clive had known him as a fierce and terrifying tyrant of middle years, not the pitiable husk of a man Clive had last seen in the library at their Devonshire estate.

Clive recoiled.

The baron raised a fist, and in a shrill voice began to berate him for treason to the House of Folliot.

And then he wavered again, and melted, and reformed into an image of a great hair-covered spider.

"Shriek!" For an instant Clive was filled with a pang of longing and yearned-for reunion with the alien arachnid who had been his companion on so many adventures in the Dungeon. But he had left Shriek, along with Finnbogg, on the planet Djajj. Could this be the alien?

But then the spidery Shriek changed again and was the nameless monster created by the cursed experimenter Frankenstein, the monster last seen by Clive climbing aboard a compartment of the space-train near Earth's polar ice cap.

"Enough!" Clive cried out. "Stop it! Reveal your true form!"

The monster shook its fists at him, then lowered them slowly to its sides. It wavered several more times, offering suggestions of Annabelle, of the tentacled monster once more, of Clive's brother Neville—or perhaps of Clive himself—before lapsing into the scarab-mantis configuration that Clive at last knew to be its true form.

"A lovely creature, is it not, Clive Folliot?" Sidi Bombay stood near Clive, smiling at him. He lifted the wooden cage in one dark-skinned hand and held it close to his face, smiling benignly at the creature within.

Clive saw the creature gesture helplessly at Sidi Bombay —once, then again—then relapse onto the wooden bottom of its prison.

"Is this the true Chaffri?" Clive asked.

"So it is, Clive Folliot. When we are fooled by it, a terrifying enemy. When we see through its deceptions, when we realize that it draws all its power over us from the recesses of our own minds—a piteous, helpless bug."

He placed the cage on the floor.

"But Sidi Bombay . . . when I arrived in this room, I saw one of the tentacled monsters that we now know are Ren. And it turned into *you*! Are you a Ren? Were you transformed?"

"No, Clive Folliot." Sidi Bombay shook his head. "I am nothing but a man, nor have I ever been other than a man. I can only guess that the Chaffri"—he nodded his head toward the insect in the cage—"plucked *that* image from your mind. Instead of creating the illusion that it was a Ren, it fooled you into thinking that I was one."

Clive leaped. "Sergeant Smythe!"

Sidi Bombay looked inquiringly at him.

"He is across the hall. He entered another room, Sidi

Bombay. Smythe and I were looking for you. We feared that you had been taken in by the trickery of these monsters."

"Hardly." Sidi Bombay smiled.

"But we must see what happened to Sergeant Smythe!"

With Sidi Bombay in his wake, the Indian stopping only to snatch up the wooden cage that held the now seemingly helpless Chaffri, Clive plunged from the room, crossed the hall in a hurried stride, and thrust open the door opposite.

Quartermaster Sergeant Horace Hamilton Smythe lay on his back. His eyes were closed, and blood dripped from the corner of his mouth.

Clive peeled back his eyelids. The man moaned and struggled. Clive helped him to a sitting position.

"What happened, Sergeant?"

"Uh . . . uhh," Smythe tried to speak.

Sidi Bombay placed the wooden cage on the floor and took Horace Hamilton Smythe's hands in one of his own. The other he placed gently on the sergeant's forehead. The Indian muttered a few words. Clive could not make sense of them. Sidi Bombay released Smythe's hand, then removed his palm from the sergeant's forehead.

Smythe blinked and looked at Clive Folliot and Sidi Bombay. He was clearly suffering still from the effects of shock, but his eyes were clear and his manner was lucid.

"I think someone hit me, sah," he said to Clive.

Clive could barely restrain a smile. "I believe so, Sergeant. Did you catch a look at your assailant?"

Smythe blinked with effort. "I'm sorry, sah. All I can remember is setting foot inside the room and—*crash*!—if the Major knows what I mean, sah. All the usual effects that the sensation-mongers speak of, sah. Rushing darkness, sparkling stars, and so forth, sah. Next thing I knew, there you were, sah. Your Majorship and Sidi Bombay."

The Indian was leaning from behind Clive, smiling reassuringly at Sergeant Smythe.

"Sidi Bombay!" Smythe exclaimed. "You're all right, my old friend."

"But of course, Horace."

"They didn't fool you, Sidi Bombay? The Chaffri didn't cast a glamour over your mind?"

"They tried," Sidi Bombay said. "I was not fooled by their childish prank, Horace."

Smythe grunted. "Me 'n Major Folliot was fooled for a bit. I wouldn't call that a childish prank, Sidi Bombay!"

"Someday you Europeans will catch up with the rest of the world, Horace. I pray only that you do not destroy it first!"

Clive asserted his leadership. "We'll leave such debate for a night's conversation over the campfire, men. For now, we've got to get away from this place and get on with business."

The others assented.

"Come along, then."

They exited the inn, Sidi Bombay carrying the wooden cage with the apparently subdued Chaffri in it.

Clive peered between the slats of the Chaffri's cage. "Are they really that size, Sidi Bombay? Hardly bigger than a housecat!"

"They are, Major Folliot."

"But their spacecraft—they seemed to be of a size to be manned by ordinary folk. People such as we. And even after I fought off the spell of the Chaffri that tried to destroy me—"

"I congratulate you on fighting off that spell, Clive Folliot." Sidi grinned. "Would you reveal to me how you did it?"

Clive reddened. "Perhaps later, Sidi Bombay. We have not the time for details now. Please to answer my question."

Sidi Bombay held up the Chaffri. It raged ineffectually against the bars. "They vary, Clive Folliot. They vary." He lowered the cage.

A bolt of vivid verdure flashed past them. Without a word, the three men flung themselves to the ground. Clive peered ahead. Full morning—or what passed for full morning on the planetoid Novum Araltum—had overtaken them. In the dim light Clive could make out the form that he recognized as that of the Muntor Eshverud, crouched some fifty yards away.

But Clive had seen Eshverud lying dead, his head very

nearly severed from his trunk. But if Eshverud's living
form had been an illusion, a glamour cast over Clive's
mind to conceal the Chaffri's true monstrous appearance
. . . if that had been the case to begin with, then the sight
of Eshverud dead might equally have been a deception.
But if . . . but if . . .

Clive squeezed his eyes shut, striving to clear his mind.
He opened his eyes again.

The Muntor had raised a rifle to his shoulder. In Novum
Araltum's morning light, Clive identified it as a Snider,
one of the Royal Army's breech-loading conversions based
on the old Enfield muzzle-loader. It was a weapon Clive
knew well. But instead of its normal ball ammunition, the
Muntor's Snider seemed to be firing the powerful ordolite
ray!

Muntor Eshverud loosed another ray that sizzled the
very air as it whipped past the three Earthmen. Then the
Chaffri was on his feet again, fleeing.

A single Chaffri spacecraft stood ready on the field, and
Eshverud leaped into it, slamming the metal port behind
himself.

Clive gave chase, Sidi Bombay and Horace Hamilton
Smythe following in his wake. But before they could reach
the craft, it had lifted from the field and flashed into
Novum Araltum's asteroid-sprinkled sky.

"Major, sah! I can see our own car! Let's get out of here,
sah!"

For a moment, Clive stood his ground, surveying the
situation. The Muntor Eshverud—presumably, one of the
scarab-mantis creatures himself, despite his astonishingly
persistent disguise as a human—had made good his escape.

Had not Clive seen Eshverud's nearly decapitated corpse
lying near the erstwhile inn? Another illusion, he mused
bitterly, another illusion on this planet of illusions. The
Chaffri must have plucked another image from Clive's own
brain and reflected it back to his sensorium so that he
perceived the corpse of a martyr when he actually beheld
a foul and definitely living monstrosity. The Chaffri must
have known that it was incapable of standing up to a man
such as Clive Folliot in honest combat, so had chosen to
hide behind a glamour and thus avoid the fight.

But even if Eshverud had escaped, the three Earthmen had still captured one of the Chaffri, and the three comrades were largely unharmed.

How many more of the enemy might surround them, what fate lay in store should they remain on Novum Araltum, could only be guessed.

But the three had left London on a mission to the home not of the Chaffri nor of the Ren, but of their common enemy, the mysterious and mighty Gennine. Why should they become bogged down here on Novum Araltum? There was little to be gained in this place!

"Right, Horace! Sidi Bombay, bring that Chaffri along—it may come in handy later on."

He set out, cutting the distance that separated him from the glass-walled car that had brought them here from Earth.

· CHAPTER 20 ·
"From Among Mine Enemies, Clive Folliot!"

The ship had apparently been left unmolested and unguarded. The entire aerodrome, in fact, seemed to be deserted, and Clive found himself wondering once again where the Chaffri had gone. Two he had killed, one Sidi Bombay had captured, and the Muntor Eshverud had made good his escape.

But there had been scores, perhaps hundreds of the Chaffri at this base. There must be thousands on Novum Araltum. Many thousands, perhaps. Where had everyone gone?

"Are we agreed, my friends? Do we resume our mission?"

Horace Hamilton Smythe and Sidi Bombay exchanged glances.

"You are our leader, Clive Folliot," the turbaned Sidi Bombay replied.

Horace Smythe merely nodded his assent.

Clive tried the door of the car in which they had traveled from Earth to Novum Araltum. It was not fastened. He opened it and climbed inside.

Horace Smythe followed Clive and busied himself with checking the car's controls, while Sidi Bombay circled the car examining its exterior, now scrambling across its top like a squirrel, now squirming beneath it like a ferret. Eventually he entered the car and sealed the door behind himself.

Sidi Bombay said, "Clive Folliot, the car seems unharmed."

"Everything's on the up-and-up," Horace Smythe put in.

Once again Clive Folliot felt the weight of leadership upon his shoulders. This was a position he had not sought, nor was it one that he wished to fill. But it had been thrust upon him. Were he a Fabian addressed by Malvolio, he could not have felt more heavily his responsibility.

Leadership was his—must he be burdened next with greatness?

"Have a seat, Major. It's a long journey we're undertaking, and there's no need to stand."

Even as Clive complied with Horace Smythe's suggestion, he closed his eyes and concentrated his mental powers, attempting to renew his contact with George du Maurier. For a fleeting moment he felt strange tendrils of thought and personality. He might be brushing du Maurier's psychic being, or perhaps that of his own unborn brother Esmond—or someone else. How many of his acquaintances were dead? Even the Lady 'Nrrc'kth resided now in that unknown realm that lay beyond the veil of death.

When he felt a brush of icelike cold yet feathery lightness, was his mind brushing against that of the lady of emerald and diamond?

Where, in the bewildering scheme of things, was God?

He felt the car shift beneath him, and opened his eyes. The car lifted from the surface of Novum Araltum, rocking and tilting like a wooden boat pulling away from a pier.

Beneath the car, the asteroid shrank with visible speed, the forests surrounding the aerodrome rapidly swallowing the tiny open patch from which the ship had risen. The few buildings that stood at the edges of the clearing were visible momentarily like the houses in a miniature Christmas display, and then they were gone.

Sidi Bombay had taken the controls of the car, and Clive sat watching the Indian. He stood barefoot and nearly naked, clad only in the white turban and breechclout he had worn when Clive and Horace found him at the inn. His dark skin, old and wizened when first Clive had encountered him in Equatoria and then stripped away and regrown as that of a young man amid the horrors of the Dungeon, glinted like fine onyx in the light of the distant sun and the still more distant stars.

Beside Sidi Bombay stood the wooden carrying case

that held the caged and helpless Chaffri. As Clive stared at the creature he let his mind summon up images of the men and women—and other beings!—he had faced in his adventures.

Amazingly, the Chaffri took on the form of each one as Clive thought of him or her. For a moment it was the oily and obsequious Tippu Tib, a slave trader whose enmity Clive had gained in Zanzibar so long ago. Then it became the ruthless and treacherous N'wrbb Crrd'f, the companion and self-proclaimed consort of the lost Lady 'Nrrc'kth— into whose clutches Clive had fallen on the planet Djajj.

Then for a moment Clive's thoughts settled upon the faithful, massive, doglike dwarf Finnbogg, also a former prisoner on Djajj. In that moment the captive Chaffri seemed to turn into Finnbogg. Finnbogg in miniature, Finnbogg reduced from the size of a good-sized pony to that of a housecat, but otherwise a perfect and living Finnbogg.

Sidi Bombay turned his head and looked, startled, at the Chaffri. He reached toward the case carefully, hesitantly.

Finnbogg sprang toward Sidi Bombay's extended fingers. The dwarf carried the half-organic, half-mechanical claw weapon that he had obtained at the battle with the Ren, that terrible battle atop the black, arching bridge on faraway Q'oorna. That claw, plus a set of murderous fangs as menacing as those of the underslung-jawed bulldog, were Finnbogg's armaments.

The Indian snatched his hand back from the Chaffri's cage in the nick of time.

Teeth and claw clashed against the wooden bars that held the Chaffri, and Finnbogg fell back against the floor of its cage, shifting from shape to shape to shape with a speed that defied the eye to follow or the mind to grasp.

"It was our friend Finnbogg," Sidi Bombay gasped.

"It never was, Sidi!" Horace Smythe demurred.

"You are right, Horace Smythe. It was I who saw through the illusions of the Chaffri on Novum Araltum—only to be taken in by this puny creature's flummery. A fool I am. The merest momentary relaxation of one's alertness, of one's mental barriers, and disaster awaits!"

"But it was I who was thinking of Finnbogg," Clive

half-apologized. "The creature must have been picking up my thoughts. But I thought that the images we saw of the Chaffri were mere illusions, and that only the one who provided the recollection upon which the illusion was based could see it."

Clive wondered how much time they had to pursue the question of the captive Chaffri—the use to which it might be put, the danger which it might present. "How long to reach our destination, Sidi Bombay?"

The Indian said, "We should reach our goal before long, Clive Folliot. The distance involved is very, very great. Far more of your English miles must be crossed than we three could count among us, but the car can cut across the distances rather than travel them. We will be there when we are only hours older than we were when we left Novum Araltum."

Clive turned from Sidi Bombay and Horace Hamilton Smythe. Outside the car's transparent walls, the darkness of the sky was pierced by the brilliance of uncounted remote stars, each blazing with its own frozen fire.

Feeling a hand on his shoulder, Clive turned to see Horace Hamilton Smythe. "It's a splendid sight, innit, sah?"

"You've been here before, Horace?"

"You were lost in the Dungeon a long time, sah. Sidi Bombay and I—and a good many others who have enlisted in the cause, sah—yes, Major, I've been here before."

Clive shook his head. "Understand, Sergeant Smythe, I was not in the Dungeon for the entire twenty-eight years. Far from it. The space-train that I boarded on Earth's polar region brought me across the years as well as the miles. It brought me and Henry Frankenstein's monster—and where is the monster now, I wish I knew. But you've been to many places, I suppose, Horace. Places unknown to me."

"Yes, sah. But I'm sure the Major has been to as many, and as strange."

"Perhaps, Horace. Perhaps."

Sidi Bombay reached to nudge Horace Smythe. The Indian pointed to an instrument mounted beneath the front window of the car. Smythe peered past Sidi Bombay and grunted his understanding. To Clive Folliot he said, "Best hold on tight, sah. This is the hard part."

Clive had no time to ask for clarification. Sidi Bombay pressed a lever, the ship lurched, and Clive Folliot found himself holding on for dear life.

It was like taking the famous coaster ride at Brighton. The car surged forward. Clive felt as if his intestines had been left behind. The distant stars, fixed though they were, seemed to move toward the car, accelerating by the moment. Their colors blurred and shifted as if every point of light in the firmament had been drenched in freshly shed blood.

The Chaffri behind its wooden bars launched itself into a paroxysm of terror and rage, racing around its cage, changing its form by the moment from beast to insect to indescribable monstrosity, screaming what might have been curses in a language resembling none that Clive Folliot had ever heard.

Then with a final surge and a jolt that produced an almost audible snap, the stars that surrounded the little glass car winked out of existence.

Clive felt as if he were floating, weightless, in the car. He held on to a brass rod, peering through the glass, trying to see what had happened. The car's mad acceleration had ceased, or at least it appeared to have done so. The star-scattered blackness that had surrounded the ship was no longer to be seen. Nothing was to be seen through the glass.

For all that Clive could perceive, the car might have been plunged into a sea of gray, featureless sludge. Above and below, ahead and behind, all were the same.

The Chaffri had collapsed on the bottom of its cage and lay there motionless—as far as Clive could perceive, lifeless. It had lost all form and had the appearance of a gray mass of undifferentiated protoplasm. As Clive watched, the blob stirred feebly. Apparently, all it could do was quiver.

"Is this all? Sidi Bombay, Horace, is this all?"

"No, Clive Folliot. Now we wait."

"For what? For how long?"

"Forever, Clive Folliot, and for no time at all."

Clive squinted into the gray nothingness. Forever and for no time at all—what did that mean? He looked at Sidi Bombay, looked at Horace Hamilton Smythe. Were they the vigorous specimens of young middle years with whom he had left Novum Araltum?

For a moment, Sidi Bombay appeared an infant.

For a breath, Horace Smythe appeared a feeble oldster.

Clive blinked.

No, it was Horace who was a child, bald and toothless, and Sidi Bombay who was an ancient, bald and toothless.

Clive raised his hand before his eyes. Was his skin smooth and chubby and unmarked, the hand of a baby? Was it papery dry and bloodless, the age-marked skin of a gaffer?

He blinked.

Outside the car the gray sludge was receding, organizing itself into a coherent form.

The grayness was flattening, hardening into a discernible surface. It extended in all directions, lying far beneath the car. Above the glass panes was blackness again, but this was not the star-sprinkled blackness that Clive Folliot had seen when the car was speeding away from Novum Araltum in vain hope of overtaking the Muntor Eshverud's Chaffri ship. This was an absolute and unbroken blackness, a blackness that might only be imagined by a collier trapped deep beneath the surface of the deepest coal pit in Wales.

Then slowly, so slowly and insidiously that Clive could not be certain of the moment it was first visible to him, there appeared high overhead the swirling, spinning, mesmeric pattern that he had seen so often before.

The spiral of stars!

Clive reached to grasp Horace Hamilton Smythe's sleeve.

"I see it, sah. No need to ask me if I do, Major."

"But what does it mean, Horace? We saw it in Equatoria, it was blazoned on the grip of that revolver you once carried, I saw it again at Earth's polar ice cap!"

From beyond Horace Smythe, Sidi Bombay said, "It is the Sign of the Ordolite, Clive Folliot. It is the home of the Gennine."

"Then it is our goal! Our goal at last!"

"It is indeed."

"Can the car carry us there?"

"It can, Clive Folliot."

"Then take us there, Sidi Bombay! Take us there, and our long struggle shall end in triumph at last!"

Clive caught Sidi Bombay and Horace Smythe exchanging glances again, but before he could demand an explanation, the world went spinning.

Clive's ears were smitten by a horrendous crash. Shards of shattered glass flew in every direction. Clive's clothing was shredded and his skin pierced or slashed in a hundred places. It was a miracle that neither he nor either of his companions was mortally wounded.

The car was spinning insanely, the gray surface and the black sky with its spiraling stars whirling vertiginously, first the plain above and the sky beneath the car, then the other way about.

Clive clutched at a metal bar but it came loose in his hand. As the car went end over end he tumbled with limbs akimbo. He felt himself collide with the bare flesh that must belong to Sidi Bombay. Metal rods and clumps of wooden furnishing and cloth upholstery torn loose by the impact tumbled and bounced crazily.

There was a shriek of triumph and Clive turned to see that the wooden cage that had held the Chaffri prisoner had been shattered, squashed flat by a piece of flying machinery. The Chaffri itself, reduced to little more than a puddle of grayish mud, formed its protoplasm into a perfect globe. It bounded once from a fragment of broken glass, assumed the form of a horrendous winged reptile, and launched itself from the car, flying through the unknown medium as fast as its flapping wings could carry it.

For a moment the car partially stabilized. Clive could see Sidi Bombay struggling frantically with what remained of the little craft's controls, and the machine responded—in part.

Sidi Bombay was unable to restore the car's level path, much less direct it upward again as he would need to do to reach the spiral of stars. But at least he managed to stop its dizzying tumble and achieve a precarious, wobbling descent toward the gray plain.

Long black lines became visible, dividing the plain into what seemed an endless pattern of parallel strips. Far beneath the car Clive could see the cause of the disastrous impact: it was the train that he had seen both in Q'oorna and at the Earth's pole—the train that traveled not along a pair of hand-laid tracks but through the labyrinthine maze of time and space.

The train had apparently descended from above the car. Perhaps deliberately, perhaps inadvertently, its engineer had rammed the glass car.

Now the train was descending ahead of the car. Folliot could see that the train was badly damaged, too. Not as badly damaged, to be sure, as was the car. But the crumpled metal and broken glass that could be seen on the train gave evidence that it had not emerged unscathed from its recent encounter.

"It's going to land beneath us," Clive cried out.

"Do you wish me to avoid it, Clive Folliot? I can bring us to rest some distance from it, and there we can make our plans."

Clive took quick assessment of the progress of the train and of their own. It would be less than a minute before they came to rest. "No, Sidi Bombay. We shall have to confront those rascals. We might as well do so at once."

Sidi Bombay cast a glance at Clive, behind his naked shoulder. "As you wish, Clive Folliot. You are our leader."

It was impossible for Clive to determine whether the Indian's speech contained a tincture of irony. He chose to remain silent.

"Best batten down, sah," the faithful Horace Hamilton Smythe reminded him. "This 'un may be a rough landing."

With Sidi Bombay still engaged at the controls, the other men cleared as much of the wreckage and debris as they could from the interior of the car. As he contemplated the remnants of the erstwhile Chaffri cage, Smythe sighed. "We almost had us one that time, di'n we, sah? We surely almost did!"

"Save the wreckage of the cage, Horace," Clive urged.

"But, why, sah?"

"I don't know. It may be useful."

The car bounced from the gray plain, bounded into the

air and struck again, slid in a skewing, curving course, and rocked to a halt. Clive peered at the already stationary space-train and calculated the distance between the craft as less than that of a cricket pitch.

Movement was visible among the cars of the train. Clive strained his eyes for a clear look at what was going on. To his horror and astonishment, black-and-green-armored troopers like those he had seen near his ancestral estate at Tewkesbury were clambering from several cars, and were setting up patrols the length of the train.

"Enemies again!"

"We can face 'em, sah!"

"But if the Ren are those tentacled monstrosities we encountered on Q'oorna and the Chaffri are these mantislike creatures . . ."

"They take many forms, Clive Folliot. That you must surely comprehend by now."

"Of course," Clive managed, "of course. But then—" He shook his head, unable to continue.

A squad of the troopers had left the train and were jogging along at a brisk, military double-time, headed for the remnants of the glass car.

"So much for the Universal Neighborhood Improvement Association," Clive managed. He climbed from the car, carefully avoiding the shards of shattered glass and broken metal. "Come along, men!"

"Ain't we goin' ter fight 'em, Major?"

"It would be hopeless, Sergeant. We'll talk to them and see what we can accomplish."

"But they'll take us prisoner, sah!" Horace's eyes registered the terror and distaste with which he viewed that prospect.

Clive did not answer, for he was standing near the crumpled and blackened prow of the ruined vehicle.

The squad of troopers trotted to within a dozen yards of Clive and halted in perfect unison. The commander of the squad, his visor pushed back to the top of his helmet to reveal a remarkably boyish and good-looking countenance, stood face-to-face with Clive.

Before Clive could speak a word, he was astonished to see the green-and-black-armored officer snap a smart salute, and say in a youthful and cultured voice, "My commander's apologies to Major Folliot and his companions for the unfortunate damage to their vehicle. Full compensation will of course be paid—and my commander invites the Major and his party to join us aboard the train."

While Clive pondered his answer, the officer reached up with green-gauntleted hands and began unscrewing the gleaming black-and-green helmet as if it were a part of a diving costume. The helmet removed and clutched beneath one elbow, the armor-clad commander shook out "his" long blond tresses.

The commander was a young woman—hardly more than a girl!

"I accept your commander's apologies and the invitation you convey as well," Clive responded. "But you have the advantage of me, Miss. You know my name and I do not know yours."

A winning smile creased the full lips that Clive no longer found boyish at all. "You do not recognize me?"

"I fear not."

"Well, I shall not tease you, Great-Uncle. I am your own flesh and blood, Clive Folliot. I am Anna Maria Folliot."

"Folliot!"

"Yes, Great-Uncle."

"But—but how—?"

"You are the younger brother of Sir Neville Folliot."

"I am that."

"Neville was my grandfather."

A frown creased Clive's brow. "How old are you, Anna Maria?"

"I am twenty."

"Then you were born in 1876."

The young woman's laughter tinkled like tiny silver bells sounding clearly through the crisp air of a winter morn in the English countryside. "You think so stolidly, Great-Uncle. Surely you must realize that time is neither so simple nor logic so straightforward as that."

Clive frowned. There was no end, no end to the surprises that the universe held. Every time he thought that he had found a simple and irrefutable truth, Nature proved him wrong. "I'm trying to calculate the year of your father's birth, Anna Maria. Your father, who would have been my nephew."

Anna Maria interrupted his thoughts. "He was born in 1858, Great-Uncle."

"But I never knew that Neville had married."

Again the beautiful girl laughed, and her laugh set Clive's blood rushing through his veins, his skin tingling in every limb. But no, this girl was his own flesh and blood! Once before he had come close to the unspeakable, before he had realized that Annabelle Leigh, his beloved User Annie, she of the incomprehensible speech and the irresistible manner, was his own direct descendant.

Anna Maria Folliot was *not* his direct descendant, but she was the granddaughter of his brother, and that knowledge forced Clive to abandon a certain line of thought that had barely opened to his contemplation.

"I don't mean to be discourteous, Great-Uncle, but we haven't the time to stand here and trace our family history. There's too much to do, too little time in which to do it. We can catch up on bloodlines and family gossip later on."

Clive looked at Sidi Bombay and at Horace Hamilton Smythe. Clearly, either of his companions was prepared to lift from his shoulders the responsibility for making such decisions as had to be made. There were earlier times in which they had taken the initiative, and there might be later ones in which they would do so again. But for now, Clive Folliot alone bore the responsibility of leadership. The responsibility of decision.

"Let's go!"

"You have no gear to remove from your car?" Anna Maria asked.

Clive shook his head.

The two Folliots, Clive in his London clothes of 1896 and Anna Maria in her gleaming armor, fell in side by side and began tramping toward the train. Clive cast a single glance over his shoulder. Behind them, Sidi Bombay and Sergeant Horace Hamilton Smythe were being marched by Anna Maria's armor-clad troopers. The relationship and manner of march could be interpreted as that of an honor guard—or that of troops policing prisoners of war.

Sidi Bombay had returned to the wreckage of the car and retrieved something. As Clive watched, he waved it once around his turbaned head, then placed it conspicuously in his breechclout. It was the cyberclaw which Sidi Bombay had obtained on Q'oorna, and which Clive had not seen since leaving that black planet. How Sidi Bombay managed still to have it, Clive thought, was merely one more of the endless mysteries of the Dungeon. But if Sidi Bombay felt that the cyberclaw might again be of use, Clive was pleased to see him carrying it.

At the train the party halted. Anna Maria took Clive's arm, separating him from his companions and herself from her command. At her encouragement, Clive climbed the steps to a seemingly undamaged car. Anna Maria followed close behind him.

She stood beside him, facing a splendidly uniformed man who sat behind an ornate desk.

"Grandfather," Anna Maria said to the older man, "Great-Uncle Clive is here at last."

Neville Folliot looked up from his desk and smiled at his younger brother. "So nice to see you again, Clive. Would you like a glass of brandy?"

• CHAPTER 21 •
"I Thought I Had Seen the Ultimate!"

Stunned, Clive stood gaping at his brother. He was unable to speak.

"Have you been deafened by some incident, Clive? Can you not hear me? I offered you a libation."

"What are you doing here, Neville? I saw you last at Tewkesbury. You and Father. And Annabelle Leigh, my great-great-granddaughter."

"But Clive, you have come to see me—not I, you. Why must I explain myself?" Neville's lip curled in a smile that was not unmixed with a sneer.

Clive's mind raced. Was this truly Neville—or a simulacrum? Or was he merely an illusion created by a Ren or a Chaffri? Clive had encountered all three. In fact, he had been told that the father and grandfather he had seen in Tewkesbury were false, as was Annabelle Leigh—the Annabelle Leigh who had accompanied him to the country manor. He stared at Neville, trying to determine whether or not he truly beheld his brother.

"What is the matter, little brother? Little Miss Minnie got your tongue?"

Little Miss Minnie! Yes, a variation on the expression, *cat got your tongue?* Little Miss Minnie had been Clive and Neville's childhood pet. Their love for the plump black and white feline was one of the few things upon which they had ever managed to agree. Both boys had adored the little cat, had doted on her, competing for her affection.

No simulacrum could know about Little Miss Minnie,

no clone would possess that information. As for an illusion, that was more difficult to determine. If Neville were really an alien, drawing the image and the very recollections from Clive's mind, then the emotionally charged memory of Little Miss Minnie would be a powerful tool for use in controlling him.

If only there were someone he could ask—someone to offer advice.

A ghostly voice whispered in Folliot's mind. *Clive, he is real.*

Du Maurier? Clive queried mentally.

No Clive. It is I, your brother Esmond.

Esmond? But how do I know . . . how can I trust . . .

There comes a time, my brother, when one must trust. One must! For you, that time has come, my brother. For you, that time is this very moment.

"It was your space-train that collided with the car in which my companions and I were traveling," Clive said to Neville.

"Oh, yes. I hope no one was badly hurt?"

"Through no agency of yours, Neville! It was sheer fortune that Sidi Bombay and Horace Smythe and I survived. I still—"

"You've made the acquaintance of your grandniece, I see."

"If you will be so kind as not to interrupt me, brother! We are working in the interest of all mankind. Of all mankind and more! The Gennine—"

"Please!" Neville held up his hand. "Please, little brother. I'm sorry I've upset you. I understand your being upset, of course. But—"

"What happened at Tewkesbury? What happened after I departed for London? Where is Annabelle? What of Father?"

Again, Neville interrupted by holding up a hand. In an odd moment of abstraction, Clive found himself concentrating on the intricate patterns worked into the cuff of Neville's sleeve. At first blush, the metallic threads were embroidered in a wholly abstract and even random pattern, but upon closer examination an orderly arrangement became visible. Buried within the swirls and streaks of the embroidery was the familiar spiral of stars.

"Please," Neville said, "seat yourself and be comfortable, little brother. We are not squabbling schoolboys any longer. At least, I hope we are not."

Fuming, Clive complied with Neville's request. The brothers locked eyes. Clive said, "I make no warrant to you, Neville. The stakes are far too high for me to bind myself to petty rules. But for the moment, at least— proceed."

Neville Folliot inclined his head. "Fair enough, brother Clive. Father is dead."

"Dead?"

"I spoke clearly, I believe."

"In what manner did he die? And when?"

"He was an old man when last we were together at Tewkesbury. The end came shortly after you took your leave. It was a peaceful end, Clive. In the midst of our ordinary rustic existence, Father slipped away quite quietly and peacefully. He was napping, and when it came time to waken him, the old man had simply ceased to live."

"Together at Tewkesbury? I do not recall such a meeting—unless you refer to an occasion in 1868 or earlier, Neville."

"I refer to our meeting less than twenty-four hours ago, little brother. Our meeting in the library at Folliot Manor."

"Was that truly you, Neville? I thought that was some surrogate of yours?"

"No, Clive. What gave you that idea?"

What had given him that idea, indeed? His conversation with Horace Smythe and Sidi Bombay. Had they, his two dearest companions, lied to him? Or had they been mistaken? Or was *Neville* the liar? Was his older brother lying *now*?

Esmond Folliot whispered in Clive's mind. *Trust him, brother. Now is the moment. You must trust him.*

"Never mind, Neville," Clive forced himself to say. "Never mind all that. It was you, then, at Tewkesbury. I trust you."

Clive dropped his head into his hands. Though he and

his father had been less than close, though the old baron had favored Neville over Clive and blamed Clive throughout his life for the death of his mother—a tragedy for which Clive was by no means culpable—still, he had been bound to the baron by the closest tie of blood, that of parent and offspring. The loss of his father affected him more powerfully than he had expected it ever would.

"I shall never see him again, then, Neville."

"Oh—you may!"

Clive raised his eyes to those of his brother. "What do you mean?" Perhaps, he conjectured, Neville, too, had been in communication with their never-born brother Esmond. Clive's own contacts with Esmond had been few and faint, more tantalizing than fulfilling. And yet . . . and yet . . . what an irony, if the disembodied soul of their never-born sibling should prove the great link that reunited the estranged brothers Folliot!

There were also Clive's contacts with George du Maurier. Those disembodied dialogues had commenced before du Maurier's death. Perhaps it was the forging of the mental bond with du Maurier while he still lived that permitted the more nearly complete exchange of thoughts to whatever realm it was that lay beyond the veil. . . .

"I mean," Neville Folliot said, "that to those who can travel through the web of time and space, all men are both dead and alive. Yes, both dead and alive. Father and Mother, you and I, your various sweethearts . . ."

Clive sputtered in protest at Neville's casual use of the term *sweethearts*.

Neville smiled. "Clive, you got a child upon Miss Leighton, then you abandoned her to go chasing off after . . . who was that strange creature with the death-white skin and the forest-green hair?"

"The Lady 'Nrrc'kth," Clive whispered. "She told me that she knew you, Neville."

A wistful smile brushed Neville's face, then departed. "That is true, brother Clive. The Lady 'Nrrc'kth and I were acquainted, and the pleasure was altogether mine."

Clive clenched his fists and his teeth, holding himself in check. When he was able once more to speak, he said, "The Lady 'Nrrc'kth was a finer woman than you are worthy to consort with, Neville. She was brought into this matter against her will, she served nobly and she died bravely in the struggle against the Chaffri and the Ren."

"Well, that is as it may be."

"And if I could return to the Dungeon, rescue her at the moment of her death, bring her to a safer place—would she truly live, Neville?"

"Alas, brother, she would not. That is the one immutable law of existence, both in the Dungeon and out of it. One lives one's life, one suffers one's death. We can visit the past and the future, to a degree we can change them. But the law of life and death is greater than our poor power to change."

"Then Father, too, is truly dead."

"Oh yes."

Clive raised his eyes once more to lock with his brother's. "And you are Baron Tewkesbury."

Neville smiled. There was a mockery of the self-effacement in his expression, and more than a hint of smugness. "I am, indeed."

"Shame to our house, Neville. That you should become Lord Folliot, you who are a traitor not merely to your sovereign but to your race, your world—a traitor to all free beings! Shame, Neville! I thought I had seen the ultimate in the venial and the traitorous, but you have exceeded anything I have seen before!"

Neville Folliot burst out laughing. "You are such a prig, Clive! And a hypocrite as well. You've confronted me over my little dalliances of long ago—".

"For which I paid the price!"

"—and I suppose you will condemn me for the union from which the lovely Anna Maria is descended."

"I do not know, Neville. Who is the girl's grandmother? Was Anna Maria's father conceived under honorable circumstances? Where is he? Who is he? Who is her mother? And where is your own spouse, brother Neville? You have much to answer for."

"Read me no sermons, Clive, and do not question me as if I were an erring schoolboy and you a master. You have begun to try my patience! I allow you your foolishness because you are my brother. And because you are fairly harmless. You border, occasionally, upon the amusing. But enough is enough. Now I shall have to decide what to do with you and your companions."

"What about my companions?"

"Oh, your country bumpkin and your dusky friend are safe enough. I've sent them off to work for their keep."

"Bumpkin! Dusky friend! Horace Smythe and Sidi Bombay are each a dozen times the man you are, Neville! If you knew the deeds of heroism they have performed—each of them, and many times, each of them!"

The heated exchange was interrupted by a series of thumps and cries from outside the train. Neville Folliot shoved himself from his seat and leaped to the side of the coach, where heavy drapes covered large windows. He shove aside the drapes, Clive Folliot at his elbow, their quarrel for the moment forgotten.

Outside the coach, the gray plain stretched endlessly in all directions. The black lines that Clive had seen from the aerial car—or that he had thought he had seen—were no longer visible. Perhaps they had been an illusion, after all.

Green-and-black-armored troopers were dashing from the coaches, forming into precisely aligned military units and trotting away.

Without a word, the two brothers headed for the exit. They clambered onto the gray plain. Clive bent for an instant to feel the surface. To the eye it appeared hard, solid, featureless. But to his hands it seemed to have no surface. He extended his fingertips, anticipating a substance like slate, but felt . . . nothing. There was no surface, no plane. Instead, Clive pressed his hand down, and at a certain point, it simply went no farther.

He straightened.

A mass of troopers had assembled, formed up in ranks and columns with a precision that would have made Her Majesty's Guards envious.

Standing before the troopers, her trim armor gleaming (and where, Clive asked himself, did the light come from?), stood Anna Maria Folliot. She held her helmet beneath her arm. Her hair swirled in a passing breeze, and Clive wondered where the wind came from.

For an instant he was immobilized by her beauty. She

had all the best characteristics of the Folliots—strong, solid bones, the complexion of the English countryside, softly shining tresses that flirted languorously with each zephyr. And she had another set of characteristics. If Neville was her grandfather, then three-fourths of her heritage were unknown to Clive.

Where had she traveled? What had transpired in her life? What had brought her to this strange locale, to the position of command and authority she clearly held?

Anna Maria faced about, looked questioningly at Neville, then nodded her acceptance of a set of instructions that he uttered so rapidly and cryptically that Clive was unable to comprehend their meaning. She turned away, toward the troopers, and issued a sharp command.

The troopers turned and moved off, trotting smartly toward the rear of the train.

Clive reached to touch his brother's arm, to demand an explanation of this newest turn of events. But Neville was himself moving away from Clive, trotting parallel to Anna Maria Folliot and the gleaming, armored troopers.

A mass of movement drew his attention and he sprinted forward, distancing the military unit. His brother was close behind.

The movement became clearer. It was a collection of bodies, all of them human, but garbed in a melange of styles ranging from the exotic and unfamiliar to that of urban civilization, from the ancient and primitive to the up-to-date, and, Clive suspected, beyond.

For a moment he was reminded of the polyglot corps he had faced when first he had sounded the huge gong in Q'oorna. Roman legionnaire, Apache warrior, Japanese Samurai, and European Zouave mixed indiscriminately. Some of the warriors, he discerned, were female—but that should have been no surprise, in view of his grand-niece's position of command under Neville.

And as the aggregation of arms and legs and torsoes writhed, a greater, darker mass rose from their center.

For an instant Clive thought it might be one of the monster Ren, replete with tentacles and suckers and claws, but this being was a monster of a very different sort.

It was clad in a black suit with tattered jacket and

ill-fitting trousers. Its skin was as pale as death—or as that of the Lady 'Nrrc'kth—but with the sickly palor of the grave rather than the exotic whiteness of that woman's icelike beauty.

Like a stag beleaguered by wolves, Henry Frankenstein's unnatural creation struggled to its feet. A spearman clad as in the days of Pharaonic Egypt clung to one arm, and a female individual wearing incandescent trousers and a blouse of what appeared to be writhing worms held to the other.

The monster spun, flinging its arms outward.

In a moment, his two attackers lost their grips on his black-clad arms and flew above the heads of their erstwhile comrades, crashing down onto persons unable to avoid the impact.

The monster roared. He lifted a foot. Another attacker, this one looking like an Aztec priest, clung to his leg. The monster uttered another cry of rage and swept his hand at the Aztec. The latter was dislodged, fell back to the gray earth, and was trampled, for his trouble, beneath the monster's massive boot.

Clive heard the crunch of human bones.

The monster turned as if seeking desperately for an avenue of escape. He locked eyes with Clive. The exchange lasted for only the briefest of moments, but in that fleeting instant Clive could read the monster's message.

Why had the soldiers attacked him to begin with? Clive wondered. But there was no time to resolve that question. The monster was an inhuman revenant, a being constructed blasphemously from the remnants of the grave. Clive's stomach twisted at the recollection of his encounter with the monster at Earth's polar cap. Clive had climbed aboard one coach of the train as it settled there amid the groaning ice. And the monster had boarded another.

Clive had found himself in London, in the last decade of the nineteenth century. Yet somehow the monster had wound up here—here in this strange, unworldly locale that was the nearest approach yet to the spiraling stars and the home of the Gennine.

The monster was struggling to extricate himself from the disorganized attack of his polyglot assailants. Beyond the clustered figures, Clive thought he could make out two more familiar forms, racing toward him. Yes, it was they! It was Sidi Bombay and Horace Hamilton Smythe!

The monster had recognized in Clive a familiar face. Though the dead-alive creation had expressed his hatred of Clive in their previous encounter, he was now struggling to make his way to Clive. He knew Clive, knew that he would remember him, and that he might be an ally, an ally of familiarity in the face of the alien and the hostile.

Flailing with his mighty arms, hurling attackers aside with every stride, the monster advanced. Clive was reminded of a mighty beast throwing aside ravening wolves. Who was the monster, who the assailant? To Clive's recollection, in Mrs. Shelley's novel and in the dramatizations that had brought her story to the playhouses of the world, the monster had been—at least initially—a creature of innocence. Called into being not by his own will but by that of the intemperate Dr. Frankenstein, the monster had been set upon by man and dog, had found in a blind hermit his single friend, only to be driven from the hermit's hovel by sighted men. Despised and rejected by all, even by his own creator, the monster had been abandoned to his fate, drifting to his inevitable death amid the polar ice floes.

But his death had not been inevitable!

Somehow the monster had found refuge in a cave of ice. Frozen there, he had remained for untold years, until released from his icy imprisonment by Clive and Chang Guafe. And now he was here!

Was he menace, or was he victim?

Had his rage at Clive been the pervasive instinct of a creature whose only desire was to rend and murder? Or was the monster simply reflecting the emotions that had been meted upon him?

Clive managed a feeble grin and the semblance of a welcoming, encouraging gesture.

The ghastly simulacrum of a smile on his cadaverous features, the monster lurched even more desperately toward Clive. He managed to break loose from his attackers, and then he covered the gray distance between himself and Clive Folliot with astonishing speed.

Even as the monster escaped his besiegers, Sidi Bombay and Horace Smythe were racing toward Clive. The three arrived simultaneously. Sidi Bombay and Horace Smythe could see that Clive and the monster were in some fashion acquainted, but they cautiously kept Clive between themselves and the giant being.

The brigade of armor-clad troopers under command of Anna Maria Folliot were tramping toward the quartet. In the opposite direction, the monster's ragtag erstwhile pursuers had formed into a disorganized band and were advancing again.

Behind them was the train. Ahead of them, an infinite and featureless gray expanse.

They could try to board the train, they could flee across the featureless plain, or they could stand and fight, caught between two parties of attackers.

And Clive could feel the eyes of his three companions upon him. They had turned to him for leadership—for decision!

Only for the barest fraction of a second, Clive Folliot squeezed his eyes shut and made a supreme mental effort. He felt as if he had left his body. He could look back and see himself and his three companions, the ragtag gang that had attacked the monster and the black-and-green-clad brigade commanded by Anna Maria, all of them frozen as if they were captured in a daguerreotype.

Nearby, Clive could see his brother Neville.

Neville alone, of the uncounted men and women before him, seemed unfrozen, aware of the situation, able to act. He raised a fist and shook it toward Clive. His mouth moved and words emerged.

But all in a strange, slow tempo, as if Neville were moving at half-time, quarter-time, one-eighth-time. Slower, slower, and still slower.

Clive found himself suffused in a blinding illumination.

George du Maurier said, *You are in command!*

Esmond Folliot said, *You are the Master of the Ordolite! Esmond!*

I tell you that you are the Master of the Ordolite!

What does that mean to you? Clive asked.

Go back!

You were never born. You never lived, Clive retorted. *What can you care?*

You must command!

I will not go, Esmond! Not until you answer my question.

Du Maurier—our schoolboy asserts himself.

Better that he does, du Maurier said. *Should a weakling rule?*

He has known sultans.

He has known Philo Goode, Esmond. He has known Timothy F. X. O'Hara!

And he has survived. What odds were quoted at the outset, du Maurier?

He has not merely survived. He has grown. He is nearly ready.

Hmm. Perhaps he is ready, then.

It is my fault, brother Clive. You were to have been firstborn. I tried to usurp your place and failed—

What do you mean? We know nothing of our lives before birth, Clive said silently.

You remember *nothing of them, you mean!*

What difference does it make? The succession of a rural barony, Esmond, really!

You do not understand, Clive! The next Baron Tewkesbury should have been the Master of the Ordolite! And that baron is rightfully you, Clive! But by my ambition, I denied myself life and I caused such disarray that Neville was born before you. Thus, he is now Baron Tewkesbury, while you are the rightful Master of the Ordolite! The two roles—that of the baron, and that of Master of the Ordolite, have been sundered. Go back and claim what is yours! Command in the name of your rightful authority! That is all that can save—

There was a crack as of nearby sheet lightning in an Equatorian thunderstorm, and Clive was standing surrounded by Sidi Bombay and Horace Hamilton Smythe and the Frankenstein monster.

He touched each of them, briefly, laying his palm upon the crown of their heads. To reach the monster's head, he had to stand on tippy-toe and reach as high as he could, but he succeeded.

All three moved. Their two bands of attackers remained frozen.

Neville Folliot, hatred and fear blazing in his eyes, continued to stride toward Clive, moving with terrible, slow deliberation. He had drawn a pistol and was raising it toward his brother.

Clive covered the distance separating himself and his brother before Neville could bring the weapon fully to bear. Clive placed his hand upon his brother's wrist. He exerted no pressure, made no effort to turn the pistol aside.

Instead, he said, "Neville, I am the Master of the Ordolite. I command you to lower your pistol."

With infinite slowness, Neville moved to comply. Desperation flashed from his eyes, his muscles twitched, sweat sprang from his brow. But with unerring certainty, he returned the weapon to its holster. He opened his mouth to speak, but his movements were so slow that Clive simply ignored them.

To his followers, Clive said, "I know what is to be done. Come with me."

He did not look back to see if they followed. The question did not enter into consideration. He set off at a trot, efficient and space-consuming but unhurried. He passed the band of armored troopers, slowed for a moment to contemplate his grandniece, Anna Maria, then shook his head regretfully. There was no time to learn to know her better.

Reaching the front of the train, he grasped a metal rod and hauled himself into the engine compartment. A normal crew was present—an engineer, a pilot, a plotter, a mechanician. They appeared unharmed but were as motionless as the warriors outside on the endless gray plain.

Clive turned to Sidi Bombay and the others. "Don't hurt them. But get them out of here."

"What—?"

"Obey."

As his aides removed the crewmen, Clive said, "We shall decouple this engine from the cars behind. We are going on!"

▪ CHAPTER 22 ▪
"The Gennine—Face to Face!"

The engine that pulled the space-train bore only a slight resemblance to the locomotives with which Clive was familiar.

"It looks like one of them bloody things that Missoor Verne writes about," Horace Smythe commented. "All pointy and smoothed off, like a bloomin' gigantic bullet."

"That doesn't matter," Clive said. "Just—can we run it?"

Smythe studied the controls, rubbing his chin and humming tunelessly the while. Clive's eyes darted toward Sidi Bombay. The Indian stood impassively; he, too, was watching Horace Smythe. Clive turned to look at Dr. Frankenstein's creation. The monster, like Sidi Bombay, was gazing at Horace Smythe in rapt concentration.

Unable to restrain his impatience, Clive peered from the cab. The enigmatic spiral of stars still hung in the blackness above the train.

Was the spiral revolving—or was Clive's distress causing him to imagine that it was? Were the stars burning suns uncounted millions of miles from the Earth and its own illuminating flame—or were they merely tiny points of light, no more than candles or miniature gas flames that hung tantalizingly just beyond human reach?

Clive knew that Annie had recovered the polished metallic machine she had obtained from the Japanese force at New Kwajalein Atoll. Could she now soar in it to those stars?

Back on the endless gray plain, Clive could see the two forces from which he and his companions had escaped. One party was still arrayed in precise alignment, clad in identical suits of gleaming armor; the other was as varied as the first was uniform, as disordered as the first was disciplined. And in either force, not a muscle moved.

Only the form of Clive's brother Neville moved. With agonizing slowness, Neville Folliot struggled toward the cab. His face was suffused with concentrated effort, his muscles bulged. His appearance was that of a man running through a vat of viscous fluid.

"Come along, then, Sergeant!" Clive could contain himself no longer. "Can you run this thing?"

Smythe turned from the complicated control panel. He frowned, then seemed to make an internal decision. "Yes, sah! I can do it, Major! I apologize for the delay, sah, but these controls are very strange to me. But I believe I can do it, sah. I'm willing to give it a go!"

"Fine, Sergeant Smythe!"

Sidi Bombay and the monster set about uncoupling the engine from the leading coach of the train.

Neville Folliot was nearing the platform.

Horace Smythe was working over the controls.

The engine vibrated.

Neville reached a hand toward the railing.

The coupler holding the engine to the rest of the train opened with a metallic clang.

The engine lurched forward.

Neville's fingers closed on the railing.

Sergeant Smythe pulled back on a lever.

The engine lifted from the featureless gray plain.

Although the engine was accelerating steadily, it had not yet achieved a great rate of speed. Far outside the window, silhouetted against the featureless sky like a black period on a sheet of gray foolscap, something was flying frantically toward the engine. As Clive stared, the point of blackness grew large. It took clear shape. It was a perfect miniature of the Lady 'Nrrc'kth.

Clive cried out, reaching for the beautiful creature.

"Stop, sah! Can't you see what it is?"

"It is the Lady 'Nrrc'kth, Horace!"

"No, sah! It's the Chaffri! It's concentrating all its force on you, sah! That's why I can see its true form! Don't let it in here again, sah!"

"Horace is right," Sidi Bombay called. "Keep it out, Clive Folliot!"

"No!" Clive shouted. "Even if you're right, it may be of use to us! Horace—see if you can get that cage back in order!"

In moments, Horace Smythe had jury-rigged the Chaffri's smashed cage, rebuilding it from its own smashed fragments. It was a makeshift job, but it looked sturdy enough, albeit untidy. Smythe stood aside, invisible from outside the engine.

Clive stood with his arms outstretched. "My darling! My Lady 'Nrrc'kth! You have returned to me!"

The Chaffri flew through the engine's window. Clive lunged aside as Horace Hamilton Smythe swooped upon the Chaffri, locking it once more in its cage.

Penned helplessly in its makeshift prison, the outwitted Chaffri went wild. In rapid sequence it assumed a dozen forms. Feathers, tentacles, scales, plates, fur chased one another across its skin. A series of piercing wails rose from it. Horrible fangs and claws scraped at the inside of its prison.

Finally it collapsed into a corner of its cage. It slithered, grew molten, puddled. With a twinge of guilt at his own gallows humor, Clive noted aloud that it looked like nothing more than a spoiled blancmange. It had only one discernible feature, a set of great teeth that it gnashed in frustration.

The engine accelerated, heaving forward and upward.

Outside the engine, Neville Folliot had finally drawn abreast of a window. The contrivance had lifted from the plain, but it moved at a height little greater than a tall man's thigh.

Clive bent and looked into his brother's face. Neville had managed to raise one arm painfully and grasp a metal railing on the side of the engine. But Clive realized instantly that Neville, unassisted, could not pull himself into the engine compartment. Left to his own devices, he would lose his grip and fall back onto the plain.

The engine was rising and accelerating ever more rapidly. Neville's feet had left the ground and he was clinging desperately to the side of the engine. Higher the engine moved, and faster.

Peering into the grayness, Clive estimated the distance the engine had now risen. If Neville fell from here he would surely die.

A hundred mixed emotions surged through Clive Folliot, a thousand memories flickered across the screen of his mind like images at a magic lantern show. Neville ragging and bullying him as a child. Neville leading him on a wild goose chase through East Africa. Neville appearing to rise from his casket and offer Clive the enigmatic journal that had led him to more grief in his journey through the Dungeon. Neville betraying Clive's trust time and again. Neville selling the Folliot honor

All Clive needed to do was permit Neville to fall and he might be rid of him forever. Other considerations aside, this event might leave Clive to inherit the title of Baron Tewkesbury. Neville had married and fathered a son, and that son had married and fathered a daughter, Anna Maria Folliot. Was Anna Maria's father still alive? If so, then with Neville's death the Tewkesbury title would devolve upon him; otherwise, upon Anna Maria. Clive had slipped to third place in the line of succession. But title or no, he could not cold-bloodedly permit his brother to die.

"This is not for your sake, Neville," Clive grunted under his breath. "This is for dear Little Miss Minnie!"

He reached his hand to his brother and drew him into the cab. He had every justification in the world to abandon Neville to his fate. But he could not do this.

The two brothers stood toe-to-toe. Each waited for the other to speak. At last Neville said, "Thank you, Clive."

With equal stiffness, Clive replied, "You are welcome, brother."

Neville surveyed the situation in the engine cab. He peered back at the gray plain where the remainder of the space-train still stood. He nodded as if he had been considering a difficult problem and had finally reached his conclusion. He looked closely at Horace Hamilton Smythe, nodded curtly to the man; then, at Sidi Bombay, and repeated the gesture, this time even more quickly and perfunctorily. At Frankenstein's monster he simply gazed, struck motionless as well as dumb.

The monster, hitherto as unmoving as a statue, opened

his eyes wide and raised a hand toward Neville. "Insect, do you wonder at the sight you behold? Know you not my origin and nature? As your puny race is to the God who made you, or whom you imagine to have made you, so is my kind to yours. My kind, of which I am the single representative, thanks to the wickedness of the very Man who built me and who then both created and destroyed the helpmate whose companionship was the sole beseechment of my prayer!"

Eyes fiery, the monster turned to Clive. "You, Clive Folliot, surprise me!"

"Do I?"

"I had thought ill of you, Clive Folliot."

"Indeed you must have! You tried to drown me by casting me from the boat crafted by Chang Guafe."

"I have a penchant for drownings, Clive Folliot. Try not my patience. Nonetheless, I have learned a good deal of your brother Neville Folliot, and it is clear to the judgment of any fair-minded observer that you have been harmed and offended by him. Even so, *in extremis*, when you could have consigned him to his doom simply by withholding from him your assistance—without taking positive action to his detriment, Clive Folliot—you granted that assistance. Tell me, Clive Folliot, why that was your act. I am puzzled. I had consigned you to the grade of mortal whose evil warrants no slightest consideration save to be crushed beneath the heel of an avenger as a helpless ant is squashed beneath a bumpkin's boot. I had considered you no more worthy of moral consideration than the gibbering, chittering thing that cowers in yon cage."

The monster paused and pointed dramatically at the Chaffri crouched against its bars, quivering and squealing softly and piteously.

Clive began to answer the monster, but before he could speak, the monster resumed his tirade. "You held the most violent of grudges, were the victim of the most heinous of affronts and provocations at the hands of your brother. And yet you have displayed a selfless consideration for his welfare and survival. Why, Clive Folliot, why? You are a member of the privileged and oppressing class of the most depraved and indulgent society on the face of the Earth, and even so, you perform an act of selfless charity. Do you even comprehend the motivation within your own breast that moved you to this act? Do you possess, after all, a moral sense worthy of my note? Tell me these things, Clive Folliot. Speak!"

Before the monster could catch his breath and resume still again, Clive managed to get his answer out. "I saved him for the sake of a little cat, Monster. That is the whole of it."

The monster drew a deep breath. But before he could launch another tirade, Neville laid a carefully manicured hand on Clive's wrist. "Does he always talk like that, brother?"

"Always, brother. For a while there, when he was trying to drown me, I thought it might be worth the experience to let him go ahead purely in order to escape his rantings."

Neville stared at his toes, obviously deep in thought. "Why *did* you save me, brother? Your answer to this exotic fellow may satisfy him, but I demand more of you. I did wrong you grievously, Clive. Have you forgiven me?"

"I have, Neville."

"But I have betrayed you more times than once."

Clive gave a bitter laugh. "Many more, indeed."

"And yet you forgive me again and again. Why, Clive? How many times will I wrong you, and how many will you forgive?"

"Seven times, Neville. Or seven times seven. Are we not so taught? The monster, poor soulless creature, may be motivated by revenge and consequently incapable of forgiveness. But our friend Sidi Bombay's philosophy is not so very different from that which is taught to us. And in the end, so Sidi has led me to understand, we determine our own fates. You will be saved or damned, my brother, by your own doing. Not by mine. I shall pray for you in either case."

"Pray for your enemies, Clive? Is that it?"

"I will pray for my brother. Enemy or friend, that is up to you, Neville. But my brother you are, will you or nil you."

Neville turned toward Horace Smythe. "Where are you headed, Sergeant?"

"There's only one place to go, sah. I'm certain that the Major knows it as well as I do."

"You are headed for the homeland of the Gennine!"

"Yes, sah!"

"Don't go there, Clive!" Neville Folliot grasped his brother's sleeve. The tables had been turned, the tyrant become supplicant. "Please, Clive!"

Neville turned from his brother, attempted to shove Horace Smythe from the engine's controls. Smythe resisted, and Clive pulled Neville away.

"What's the matter, older brother? Why are you so reluctant to visit the homeland of your masters?"

Neville sneered. "After so many years, Clive, you still maintain your invincible innocence! Very well—"

But before he could say another word, the engine was shrouded in absolute blackness and filled with a chill that penetrated to the very marrow of its occupants' bones.

"What—?"

The engine shuddered, but it seemed still to be moving forward. Clive peered outside. He could see nothing. Not the gray, distant plain below. Not the swirling spiral of stars above. The very air within the compartment seemed heavy, chill, and dark. The only light in the compartment was that emitted by the instruments before Horace Hamilton Smythe. They gave off an eerie glow, a pallid yellow that tinted everything into a monochromatic picture.

The cultured voice of Sidi Bombay said, "Major Folliot! Sergeant Smythe! Behold!" He pointed at the caged Chaffri. The others stared.

The Chaffri, which had previously subsided into a formless white puddle in the corner of its cage, now adopted a new form. It had grown arms and legs, and stood upright like a foot-tall mannequin. Its face was human, or more properly, demonic. Its nose was sharply pointed, its eyebrows arched. Its glossy black hair came to a widow's peak upon its forehead. A pair of perfectly formed horns grew from its forehead.

Its feet were cloven hoofs. It seemingly wore a scant, skin-tight costume, but as Clive strove to see it clearly in the yellow-tinged murk, he realized that it was not wearing tights at all. It was completely naked. It pranced and capered in its cage, and as it turned, Clive could see that it had a long, barb-tipped tail. In one fist it held a wicked-looking trident.

"Lor' 'elp us! What *is* it?" Horace Smythe gasped.

"We've already been through Hades in the Dungeon!" Clive exclaimed. "Not once, but twice."

"Aye." Horace nodded. "But I see no Baron Samedi to pull our chestnuts from the hearth this time, Major."

The caged creature had begun screaming at its captors, moving its free hand in a series of mystical-looking gestures and pointing its trident first at one, then at another.

"It's placing a curse on us!" Neville said.

The demon pointed an accusing finger as well as its trident at Neville. Its eyes glinted in the faint yellow light. Watching, Clive suspected that the demon would not have appeared yellow in a normal light.

Its incantation drew to a crescendo. A bolt of lurid-tinted lightning crackled from the centermost tine of its trident and spanned the distance from its cage to Neville Folliot.

Neville clutched himself where the bolt had struck. There was a peculiar scent in the air, discernible even in the dank, heavy atmosphere that filled the cabin. A wisp of smoke rose from a charred spot on Neville's gold-braided military tunic.

"You little bugger! You whippersnapper!" Neville slapped a hand on the wounded spot, rubbing vigorously. "I'll break you in two, you little fiend!"

He leaped toward the Chaffri's cage but Sidi Bombay stepped between him and the cage. "Please, Baron."

Mollified by the acknowledgment of his title, Neville drew up. The smoke had ceased to rise from his tunic, but when he took his hand away from the offended spot a circle of singed and blackened cloth remained.

"Why shouldn't I crush that little monster beneath my heel?" Neville demanded of Sidi Bombay.

"Because, Baron, he has told us something. His mind is tuned to the vibrations that surround us, and he has warned us of that which is to come. I had feared to take the Chaffri back into our company, but I see now that Clive Folliot was right to do so."

As if on cue, the engine lurched forward. The blackness that surrounded it and the dank, heavy atmosphere that filled it were gone. For a moment the compartment was filled with light, but before the travelers could take heart, the light assumed a reddish hue and a terrible howling and crashing filled the air.

"Oh, my lord!" Horace exclaimed.

A great roaring, rushing sound surrounded and penetrated the engine. Clive felt the floor shift beneath his feet. The cabin began to spin like a bullet emerging from a rifled gun barrel. Clive felt his weight increase as the centrifugal force pressed him down.

In the new light, the formerly yellow-tinted demon in its cage turned a dark, menacing red. Beyond the windows and doors of the cabin, Clive could see almost-human figures swirling and revolving along with the engine. Beyond them dancing flames and puffs of smoke made an unbroken background that surrounded the engine in all directions.

At first there were dozens of the demons flying around the engine, then Clive realized there were hundreds, thousands, countless hordes.

Like the transformed Chaffri in its prison, the demons were completely naked. And in their nakedness there was no mistaking the degree of perfection with which their anatomy mimicked that of humans. They were male and female.

A female demon approached the whirling cabin. She posed before a window, smiling invitingly and gesturing. Clive's eyes popped. She was not Annabella nor Annie nor the Lady 'Nrrc'kth. She was not Anna Maria Folliot, nor was she Clarissa Mesmer. But she possessed the female essence of each and every one of those women, and of the temptresses Clive had encountered in the saloon on his first night back in London, and of the women he had encountered on many levels of the Dungeon, and of those he had met in East Africa and in Zanzibar and aboard the ship *Empress Philippa* at the beginning of this whole incredible adventure.

She was every woman he had ever loved, every woman he had ever desired, every woman after whom he had ever lusted.

He stepped toward her.

She smiled at him. Her mouth was generous, her lips soft. Her eyes were huge and dark. They looked black until he peered into them deeply and realized that an ember glowed dark and red deep within each of them.

It was the color of Hell.

But Horace Smythe had been right, Clive thought. This was not the hell they had visited twice before, nor was there any Baron Samedi in this Hades to help them.

Clive Folliot was the leader of this party. He was the survivor of uncounted perils in his journey through the nine levels of the Dungeon. He was the Master of the Ordolite! That above all should have given him the strength and resolve that he needed to survive this moment of peril.

And yet, like a schoolboy desperate to have his first woman, he had clambered through the window and was about to launch himself at the female demon when he felt a huge, heavy hand grasp him by the ankle. He was drawn back bodily into the car.

He wanted desperately to join the female outside. He had to join her. In a moment of madness all recollection of Annabella Leighton, of the Lady 'Nrrc'kth, of Annabelle Leigh, and of Anna Maria Folliot were wiped from his brain. It was as if he had never known love, never known happiness in his life; the realization was strong upon him and he struggled to escape from the mighty grasp that restrained him, struggled to get to the one being in all of Creation capable of bringing him satisfaction.

"Insect! Hold still!"

The voice was enough to interrupt his obsession, to bring the focus of his eyes back within the car. He realized that he was in the clutches of the Frankenstein monster.

"Foolish creature! Think for a moment with your pitiful excuse for a brain! Use the feeble intelligence that the God in Whom you claim to believe provided you! What do you think you see outside this machine?"

"My love! The most desirable creature in the universe! Monster, let me go! Her face is the most beautiful I have ever gazed upon! Her breasts are of a beauty to make

Venus weep with envy! Her body is flesh that will melt beneath my hands! The honey of her loins—"

"Enough, fool!" The monster shook him until Clive Folliot's very teeth rattled. Holding him a foot off the floor at arm's length, the monster balled his fist and struck Clive in the face.

Stars danced around Clive's head. His ears rang.

"Now, weakling, look!"

The monster turned him like a helpless infant, so that he was facing out the window. For a moment the creature of demonic temptation was replaced by a male demon, rage written across his face, his trident raised as if to pierce and disembowel an enemy.

Clive Folliot blinked, shook his head like a dog emerging from a stream.

The demon was female again.

Then it was male once more.

"Know you not the tale of Incubus and Succubus, weakling?" the monster's voice ground mercilessly. "Do you wish to leave here and go with the demon?"

"No!" Clive cried. Then, "Yes!" He struggled but the monster's grip was like that of a hundred. "Let me go to it!"

"O man of India," the monster intoned, "but reach into some cabinet or chest of this machine and fetch for me a line."

Sidi Bombay complied.

Without releasing his grasp on Clive, the monster tied the line to his ankle and threw him bodily from across the compartment.

In a moment of astonishing clarity, Clive saw the car around him, the looks of amazement on the faces of Sidi Bombay and Horace Hamilton Smythe, the captive Chaffri prancing and gesturing in its cage.

As he flashed past his brother Neville, Clive saw Neville reach upward to pass him a sword.

Clive grasped the weapon's hilt. Then he was outside the car, surrounded by a raging inferno that singed his costume and raised a sweat on his brow but that somehow failed to harm him even as his hands and feet passed through dancing flames of orange and crimson.

The creature that confronted him was in its female form. The beauty of the temptress seemed greater than ever. She smiled and advanced toward Clive, arms outstretched.

He held the sword low at his side.

The female demon slid her arms against Clive's neck. She pressed her cheek to his, her lips to his. Did he gasp for breath, or did he part his lips in excitement? He felt her passion as if it were a tongue of pure flame piercing his lips and probing his mouth. The agony was unlike any he had ever experienced, ever imagined, and yet it was sweet beyond description. He found himself filled with a longing compared to which the most voluptuous of experience or of fantasy faded.

He felt her slide her hand from his neck to his shoulder, his arm, his hand. He felt—

He raised his other hand and smote himself a blow as powerful as he could manage. His head rang. The demon sprang away from him, tugging with a powerful arm at the sword his brother had given him. But Clive managed to retain his grasp on the weapon.

He blinked and stared at the demon.

It was male.

It thrust at him with its trident.

He was barely able to dodge aside. One tine of the weapon snagged his jacket and tore away a fragment of cloth.

The demon swept past him.

He turned to face it.

The demon recovered, raised its trident again, and charged toward him.

Again he was able to dodge aside, but only at the expense of a painful scratch that burned with a pain worse than the bite of a giant spider.

A third time the demon thrust its trident at Clive, but this time Clive was able to gather himself sufficiently to parry the trident with the sword his brother had given him.

The demon halted and grasped its trident in both hands, advancing like an infantryman with fixed bayonet.

The demon thrust, and Clive parried, then recovered.

Again the demon struck with its trident, forward and upward from below waist height. If the three tines embedded themselves in Clive's belly he knew that the demon could twist and pull, the barbs would hold in his flesh, and his entrails would be yanked from their cavity.

He lunged with his sword. It was shorter than the demon's trident, and Clive knew he was at a disadvantage.

He recovered, not having come anywhere near the demon in his lunge.

As the demon raised its trident to prepare for another attack on him, Clive stepped boldly forward. He was past the tip of the trident, and now the added length of his opponent's weapon was an impediment rather than an aid in the struggle.

He thrust at the demon.

The demon swung his trident in a clumsy attempt to parry. There was no contact with Clive's sword, but the shaft of the trident knocked against Clive's arm and torso, hurling him sideways. He regained his footing. For an instant, for the barest fraction of a second, there flickered across his brain the question of what he was standing on at all.

Clive saw that the demon had raised its trident in both hands and was launching a downward blow that would take him in the chest, but he hurled himself beneath the trident, striking upward with his sword, feeling it jolt against the heavier shaft of the trident, feeling the trident ride down the length of his sword and rebound off its basket.

The demon was disarmed.

It was defeated.

The flames around the engine flickered, guttered, disappeared.

Clive was floating some twenty feet from the engine, the long line that the Frankenstein monster had tied to his ankle all that held him in place. Far beneath the cabin he could see a universe of points and swirls of light, infinitely huge, infinitely distant, infinitely grand.

Above him, so close that he felt he could reach up and touch them, was a spiral of swirling stars.

▪ CHAPTER 23 ▪
Now and for All Eternity

He felt himself turning, floating and twisting gently. Something was tugging at his ankle. He looked to see what it was and recognized the engine, saw the monster in its window. He experienced a moment of insane hilarity, imagining the monster as an angler and himself as a mountain trout being reeled in to serve as a fisherman's breakfast. He would be gutted and boned and laid out in a pan of melted butter and broiled over a woodfire beside a country stream. It would all be so peaceful and pleasant—for the fisherman.

For the fish, another story.

Neville's sword was still in his—Clive Folliot's—hand, and as his boots thudded against the frame of the engine and he climbed carefully back into the car, he held the weapon toward his brother, hilt first. Neville took the sword from him and slipped it into its scabbard.

Clive knelt to undo the line attached to his ankle. The Frankenstein monster still held the other end, and methodically wound the line into a coil as Clive released it.

The engine lurched, then accelerated more smoothly, sliding effortlessly through the blackness toward the centermost of the spiraling stars. The spiral continued to revolve, but the engine had progressed so far that the outer stars in the constellation were visible more to the sides of the vehicle than above it.

Only the centermost star, its flames dazzlingly bright, lay directly overhead.

"Look, sah!"

Horace Hamilton Smythe's voice broke in on Clive's

train of thought, drawing his attention away from the tantalizing stars and back to the interior of the engine compartment. Smythe was pointing at the caged Chaffri.

Something strange had happened to the cage itself. Although its bars and slats had spaces between them, there must have been some force that held the prison inviolate, else the Chaffri could have flowed between the bars and regained its freedom when it was in its fluid state. Twice the Chaffri had been imprisoned in that same makeshift prison, and twice it had raged and scuttered, changing its form and its behavior repeatedly, unable to escape.

But now the prison itself seemed to be filled with water, and the Chaffri, responding to whatever influence had given it the form of a prancing devil, had since assumed a new shape. It had the upper half of a human and the lower half of a great, scaled fish.

Had it read Clive's musings of himself as a trout being reeled in by the Frankenstein monster, and in some exotic manner transformed itself in response to that imagery? But Clive had not been thinking of a hellish demon prior to the Chaffri's earlier transformation. . . .

With a shudder, the engine slowed again, coming very nearly to a complete halt. Again the exterior illumination of the swirling stars was extinguished, and the interior of the compartment was lighted only by the malign glare of the instrument panel.

And the Chaffri had assumed the form of the merman of legend. Fish-tailed, bearded, crowned; armed with a trident, but one of glittering gold, unlike the black weapon of Clive's former foe. The Chaffri had become the miniature of some pagan sea-deity—the Chaldean Oannes or the Philistine Dagon!

And through the murk, Clive could see a world of green currents, waving fronds, great aquatic creatures lazily swimming past the engine. He did not, however, see any mermen other than the miniature one into which the captive Chaffri had transformed itself.

But Neville Folliot must have seen something that Clive did not, for the elder brother uttered a glad cry. Raising his arms as if to embrace a long-lost beloved, he crossed the compartment in rapid strides and began to climb from it.

The monster, moving with surprising agility, seized Neville's leg and attached the line to it, just as he had to Clive's. "Don't let him go," Clive cried—but too late.

Neville Folliot plunged from the car.

Outside, in the sea-green milieu, Neville moved like a man swimming beneath the surface of the ocean. He seemed to be alone, and yet he reached and embraced an invisible lover.

Clive dashed to the window, grasped its sill, and leaned out. He plunged his face and torso into a tropical sea! Ahead of him he could see his brother, but his brother transformed into a merman himself! Neville's lower limbs had joined to form the hindmost section of a great fish, covered with scales, punctuated by graceful fins and terminating in a powerful flipper. He was wholly naked, and when his maneuvering gave Clive a fleeting glimpse of his face it seemed to have altered subtly into the face of a creature of the sea.

It was still Neville, but it was a Neville transformed.

And in Neville's arms was a creature of unsurpassed yet alien beauty. Her hair was long and waved gracefully in the currents. Her skin was white, her torso that of a perfectly formed woman of the most charming and voluptuous form. Her hips swelled gracefully into the hindsection of a great fish.

And even as Clive watched, the two forms embraced, moving sinuously, sensually, through the water.

Shocked, Clive drew back into the engine compartment.

He was perfectly dry. No drop of water adhered to his face or hair, no splash had soaked his garments. He spun and gaped at his companions, then turned back to the window. The scene had reverted to its former state. Neville was there, but he was fully human, swimming by drawing himself forward with his arms and thrusting with his legs. His sword in its scabbard hung from his waist.

Clive gasped, then leaned forward again. Again he felt himself plunge into water, its salt stinging his eyes. His reflex, learned in boyhood swimming lessons, drew shut his mouth and held the water from his nostrils.

He blinked and saw Neville once more as merman.

But this time he was not embracing a female of his kind, but dueling with a male! His sword was changed again into a trident, and through the blue-green waters Clive could see light glinting off the razor-sharp barbs of both combatants' weapons.

Neville struck a blow at his opponent, and Clive saw a greenish fluid flow languidly from the wound.

The merman thrust at Neville, but Neville dodged and plunged his trident into his enemy. The merman's trident flashed past Neville, missing him entirely but severing the line that held him to the engine with a single clean cut.

"Neville!" Clive cried. His mouth filled with brine, and he jerked involuntarily. He was back in the engine with Sidi Bombay and Horace Hamilton Smythe and the Frankenstein monster. "Neville!" he called again, hurling himself toward the window. Outside the engine he could see Neville as a man, turning and struggling in the blue-green fluid.

As Neville revolved, Clive could see his face. Agony distorted his features and a stream of bubbles rose from his lips. "I must help him! He's drowning!" Clive hurled himself toward the window but in an instant the light of brilliant stars filled the cabin.

The sea was gone.

"My brother! My brother!" Clive leaned from the engine, peering in all directions. Everything was as it had been before the engine's plunge into strange waters, save that the star directly overhead was closer than ever. Its rays bathed the engine, its coruscating colors casting strangely variegated shadows.

"We must go back! Neville will die!"

"Indeed, O Major." Sidi Bombay faced Clive solemnly. "Your brother is lost to you. To us all."

"Smythe, turn back! I command you!"

"I cannot, sah." Horace Smythe turned from the engine's controls. "There's no way I can take us back to the regions we passed through, sah."

"What do you mean, Smythe!"

Sidi Bombay placed himself between Clive Folliot and Horace Smythe. "He means, O Major, that we have passed through regions of the psyche. Hades, Poseidonis . . . there are many others. There is the icy wasteland populated by giant man-eating worms. There is the desert of storms. There is the Lake of Tantalus. There are Hells of every variety."

"Then let us return to that watery hell and rescue Neville!"

"It cannot be done, O Major. They are not places, nor can this engine bring you to them."

"You mean they are not real? But I experienced them— and this engine *did* bring us to them!"

"They are very real, O Major, but it was not the engine that brought us to them. It was the souls of the Folliots."

"Would I have truly died in the fiery Hell I visited? Can Neville still live in the watery one?"

"Folliots are tested, O Major, as other men and women are not. You passed your test, and are here with us still. Your brother, I regret, failed his."

"And died?" Clive looked up at Sidi Bombay with grief-filled eyes.

"Your friend du Maurier has taught you how little death means, Clive Folliot."

Clive balled his fist and struck it against his own thigh, a feeble release for the emotion he felt.

In his grinding, inhuman voice, the Frankenstein monster intoned, "Perhaps it was Neville Folliot who passed the test, little Clive—and you who failed."

Clive seized the tattered lapels of the monster's ill-fitting jacket and pulled himself to his fullest height. He still had to peer up into the monster's face. He attempted to read the expression that he saw in that corpselike visage, in the monster's great dark eyes. In their depths he saw only the tomb.

After a moment he released his grip on the black cloth and slumped back from the monster. "Perhaps you are right," he whispered. The words were bitter in his mouth.

With barely a whisper of metal on vegetation, the engine slid to a halt on the centermost sun of the spiral. Clive blinked. What had happened? The moment before, he had been conversing with Sidi Bombay and Horace Hamilton Smythe and the Frankenstein monster. The engine had been thrusting itself through the blackness toward the brilliant star.

And now, as if time had slipped a gear, the engine simply landed.

Clive said, "Sergeant Smythe?"

But before Smythe answered, the engine itself was gone. The metal shell, the power-plant, the glowing control panel, the chests of tools and equipment . . . were gone.

The miniature prison holding the captive Chaffri seemed to fade like mist dissolving in sunlight. The Chaffri itself hopped up and down, changing its appearance by the moment. It was an arachnoid alien like Shriek . . . a shape-changing cyborg like Chang Guafe . . . a creature of cold beauty like the Lady 'Nrrc'kth . . . a Japanese Imperial Marine . . . a canine-descended dwarf like Finnbogg. . . .

At the sight of the last, Clive was overcome by emotion. Of all his companions in his incredible trek, his perilous adventure—of all his fellows in peril and wonder—there was none more faithful than the loving, humorous, courageous doglike creature. Watching the chameleonic Chaffri cavort like a miniature Finnbogg, Clive could hear the gruff voice roaring out "Jeannie with the Light Brown Hair," "I Pagliacco," "The Little Brown Church," "Massa's in de Cold, Cold Ground," "Babylon Is Falling."

With a lump in his throat and a tear in his eye, Clive looked at his companions.

The Frankenstein monster slowly faded from sight, followed by Horace Hamilton Smythe and finally by Sidi Bombay. Even as the Indian disappeared, Clive thought that he perceived a smile on Sidi Bombay's face. A smile of understanding and acceptance.

Clive called their names, ran to the places where each of them had stood. There was no sign of their presence. He tried to reach them by the same psychic means that had brought him in touch with George du Maurier so many times, and with his unborn brother Esmond so few.

There was nothing.

Not the suggestion of an echo of a whisper.

Nothing.

Clive raised his face to survey his new surroundings.

• CHAPTER 24 •
"It Comes in the End to This!"

He had expected the surface of a star to be fiery hot. Though the stars appeared as tiny points of light, twinkling icy crystals, when seen from afar, still Clive had studied enough of natural philosophy to know that each distant star was a sun like the Earth's. A huge ball of burning, glowing gas. But this was not the case.

He found himself standing knee-deep in a mist that flowed to the random influence of unseen breezes. It was almost like being once more in the Sudd, the great Equatorian swamp through which he had traveled so long ago. There, with Horace Hamilton Smythe and Sidi Bombay, he had entered a gemlike boulder the size of a house, and found himself embarked upon his adventure in the Dungeon.

Now, although his boots remained dry and the footing they afforded seemed solid, the prospect was that of a mist-ridden bog.

Dead-gray trees lifted their boles and their skeletal, reaching limbs into the gray air. The smell was stale, like that of a centuries-desiccated tomb rather than a damp swamp. There was a remote sound suggestive of trickling water, but no apparent source.

If this was truly a star, then light should emanate from it, and in fact such was the case. A subtle glow was diffused through the drifting mist, a glow which appeared to come from the solid surface beneath the mist rather than from the vapor itself.

The sky was a darker gray, punctuated by the light of the other stars of the familiar spiral.

A low moaning startled Clive Folliot. He peered around in search of its source until he realized that it was merely the soft wind passing through the naked branches of the trees around him.

He tried calling the names of his erstwhile companions, but received in reply only faint echoes of his own voice, muffled by the mist that rose around him.

Should I walk, or should I remain here? he pondered. There was no apparent advantage to any one location as against another. The place in which he found himself might be as good—or as bad—as any to which he could walk.

But he decided that if he was to meet his fate in this strangely desolated locale, he would rather do so by traveling to meet that fate than by waiting passively for it to come to him.

There was no way of telling north from south, east from west. But he still did not wish to travel in circles, so he sighted on two trees and began walking from one to the other. Before reaching the second tree, he aligned himself with a third so as to maintain a straight line of progress. In this manner he traversed from tree to tree, moving steadily toward a goal unknown.

When he started walking, the land had seemed flat, although beneath the mist it was hard to tell unless he happened to step into a hole or inadvertently to kick a rise of earth. But now rises and dips in the landscape became more pronounced.

In some pockets, mist had accumulated to heights greater than Clive's. In other places, where the land rose, peaks erupted above the level of the mist.

The first pocket through which he walked contained an accumulation of mist far taller than Clive. As his chin dropped beneath the surface he gasped and clamped his mouth shut like a bather striding away from a sloping beach. He found that he could breathe the mist, and that he could see through it for a short distance. When he breathed it he found that it had a distinct flavor, not unpleasant, but one suggestive of untold antiquity.

Something swept past him in the mist. He couldn't tell what it was—a creature that dwelt in the eternal grayness of this place, to be sure. A bird or bat? Perhaps even some fishlike being that drew nourishment from the mist as fish did from water, and that swam through the attenuated medium as fish swam in the sea.

He continued on; something brushed against his leg. He reached to feel it, but whatever it was had fled at the first contact. He bent to see if he could determine the composition of the surface upon which he was walking, but the mist diffused his vision and the glow emanating from the ground dazzled his eyes when he leaned far over.

He walked on. There was no sense of fatigue, at least as yet, nor of hunger or thirst. He seemed to be trekking across a wasteland in which time as well as direction had lost their meaning.

He heard more sounds. Remote sounds, difficult to identify and impossible to locate. Something that might have been a whispered conversation, punctuated by titterings and hushing sounds. Something that might have been the growl of a large animal—or of an animal-like man.

The sound of running water, once more. A sound like that of a stream pouring over a cliff into a pool.

The ground rose, and before long he broke through the surface of the mist, and continued to climb and to climb until he realized that the ground itself had risen above the mist as well. It was of a distinct yellow color, with a surface more like smooth glass than of rock or soil, and it glowed from within, a glow that seemed to pulsate with a subtle, almost indistinguishable beat.

The gray tree trunks rose at irregular intervals from the yellow land. As Clive continued to climb he found that a stream flowed from higher on the hillside. After a while the land began to have a rougher, granular composition, closer to that of true earth. Rocks in the streambed bore coatings of yellowish lichen and slime; tiny bugs scuttled about, and small creatures swam in the water.

He lowered himself to his belly and tasted the stream. It was clean and he felt freshened and energized by the water.

He crossed the stream, letting it lap around the bottoms of his boots. He came to an opening in the hillside and without hesitation stepped into it. If some peril awaited, he would face that. He had grown at once more daring and more fatalistic; he had faced too many perils, gambled with his life too many times to be concerned with one more danger, one more risk.

A great machine whirred in the center of a cavernous room. A tiny man stepped from behind it, his hairless scalp shining pinkly in the diffuse light, his thick, rimless spectacles glinting. He was dressed entirely in white.

"Welcome to Gennine, Clive Folliot." He nodded in a friendly fashion.

"This is Gennine?"

"It is."

"And you are the mind behind all I have seen? The master of the Dungeon? Of the Chaffri and the Ren alike? It is you who have interfered with the lives of beings on a thousand worlds?"

The tiny man cackled. He could hardly have been taller than Clive's collarbone, and his voice and face indicated that he was very, very old.

"No, Clive Folliot. I am but a servant. A mechanician."

"Then tell me whom you serve!"

"Find out for yourself."

The old man gestured, and Clive saw that an archway beyond the great machine led on to a distant, cavernous gallery. Clive crossed the room of the machine, feeling a peculiar tug as he passed it, as if his whole being were somehow twisted in a direction he had never before imagined.

Through the archway he found himself face to face with a goliath who towered above Clive as Clive had towered above the wizened man who tended the machine.

The giant roared and swung a great club at Clive.

Clive stepped aside and the club struck the ground where he had stood a split-second before. "If you please," Clive murmured. He gestured at the giant and a bolt of blood-red energy leaped like a wavering thread of lightning from the tip of his finger to the giant.

The giant seemed bathed in electricity. His face bore a look not of pain but of startlement. He writhed, then collapsed to the ground, where he shriveled and shrank until there was only a pile of charred rags and the shattered remnants of a charred and splintered club where the giant had been.

Clive picked through the rags. There was no flesh or bone there. He rose and continued.

A centurion in Roman armor confronted him.

"Halt!" the centurion commanded.

"No," Clive responded softly. He repeated his gesture even as the Roman hefted a metal-tipped spear. The Roman glowed in the ruddy emanation for the count of a half-dozen heartbeats. Then he fell to the ground and shriveled until only armor and cloth and horsehair-crested helmet and shortsword and spear remained.

Clive confronted a Bwaka warrior from central Africa armed with an eccentrically shaped throwing knife.

A Frankish chief with a *francisca* flying axe.

A tribesman of Borneo with poisoned blowpipe.

A Naga with *dao* sword.

A German trooper with wheel-lock pistol.

A Maori with *toki* war-adz.

A fighting man with a Persian mace.

An Indian with a whirling flail.

A phalanx of Amazons.

He gestured and moved on.

A row of the writhing, tentacled beasts he had first encountered on Q'oorna. Ren.

A battalion of scarab-mantises. Chaffri.

Clive sighed, waved, moved on.

Another exit from the cavern and he stood on a cliff overlooking a desolate landscape of naked trees and drifting mist. He felt as if he had wandered into a purgatory— nay, a limbo—where he would face challenge after challenge, meet each in turn, triumph over every foe, and accomplish . . . nothing.

A mechanical voice grated in his ear. "You look disappointed, old friend."

He turned with a gasp. "Chang Guafe!"

The half-alien, half-mechanical being made the grating noise that passed for its laughter. "It pleases me to see you again, Clive Folliot."

"I was overjoyed to see you escape from beneath the

polar sea, Chang Guafe—but how did you get here? From distant Earth to this remote edge of the cosmos?"

"Easily enough when one can control one's configuration as I can, Clive Folliot. And you? And our companions?"

"Most are well," Clive said. "Some are dead."

"In time we all die," Chang Guafe replied. "Sooner or later—it's only a matter of sooner . . . or later."

"But we have reached the center of the spiral of stars," Clive said. "I thought that this would be the grand headquarters of the Gennine. I thought that after all our travail, once here we would confront our ultimate foe. We, or . . . I. For I did not expect to see you here, Chang Guafe. For all that you are a welcome sight."

"This is not the ultimate headquarters of the Gennine, Clive."

"Is it not the center of the spiral?"

"It is the nature of the spiral to change. Stars make their way from the edge to the center . . . from the center to the edge. No, my old friend. The center has yet to be reached."

"Can we get there?"

Chang Guafe gestured upward with a metallic appliance. "There is the home of the Master of the Gennine, Clive Folliot. And you are the Master of the Ordolite. You are known throughout the universe. Beings uncounted—races uncounted—are watching you."

"I did not ask for this. I did not want it."

"You did not ask to be born. The same thing, Folliot."

Clive nodded.

"Watch this." Chang Guafe began to change his shape. Extrusions and devices appeared on his carapacelike exterior skin. Plates scraped and gears whirled. An eyestalk taller than a man popped from between two rollers, swung in a circle above Chang Guafe, and pointed back so he could observe his own work from the outside.

"Now, Folliot. You can travel in style."

Chang Guafe had transformed himself into a sleek vehicle surmounted by a transparent canopy and cockpit into which Clive gingerly climbed.

"Hold on."

Chang Guafe launched himself into the air.

Clive felt a surge as Chang Guafe accelerated away from

the yellowish, mist-covered landscape. He peered back over his shoulder, wondering what ancient events had transpired on the star-world, who the aged man with the glittering spectacles could be. But there was no time to ponder.

A spectral figure loomed before them. It took Clive a moment to realize that the titanic being was of human form, so huge was it. It took him still longer to realize that despite its size—Chang Guafe and Clive could have fit into its fist like a toy—the figure was that of an infant in swaddling clothes.

"Turn aside! Turn aside, Chang Guafe!"

Instruments were extruded from the panel before Clive, as Chang Guafe adapted himself further to the role of aerial vehicle. The instruments were similar to those used by the pilot of a small boat, and Clive seized the steering device and swung away from the infant.

They confronted another gigantic figure. This time he adjusted his sight more quickly to it, and realized more quickly that it was a boy dressed in the fashion of his own childhood.

He swung away from it, tugging back at one control, swinging another to the side, guiding his host-craft above the boy, only to confront another giant figure, another youth, this one apparently of seventeen. Dark of hair, lanky of build, struggling manfully—Clive could not suppress a grin—to raise a straggly mustache.

Again and again Clive swerved, each time facing another figure, each older, each gigantic. A lad of nineteen years or so, dressed as for Cambridge. A bravo in his middle twenties, wearing the uniform of a lieutenant of Her Majesty's Horse Guards. A substantial figure in his thirties garbed in tropical pongee and pith helmet.

And others. One of forty-odd, putting on a small paunch, and one in his fifties, with graying hair and deeply lined face, and one in his sixties, bald of pate and sunken of eye.

They surrounded Clive, whichever way he swung the controls of his ship.

Clive undid a latch and swung back the glass canopy that covered his place. He climbed from the cockpit and closed the canopy behind him. The medium in which

Chang Guafe drifted was strange—it seemed as if Clive
were floating in it like a fly caught in a bowl of syrup; and
yet he was able to move freely, like a diver beneath the
sea.

As he watched, Chang Guafe reconfigured himself. "I
have done all that I can for you, Clive. You are the Master
of the Ordolite. It is now for you to triumph—or to fail."

A clawlike arm emerged from Chang Guafe. It made a
peculiarly human gesture, shaking hands with Clive Folliot.
Then it folded back into the alien cyborg. Panel after
panel folded, then turned, then folded again. Chang Guafe
became smaller and smaller until there was nothing left of
him but a metallic cube the size of a small dispatch case.
Then that folded in upon itself and, with a small popping
sound, disappeared altogether.

Uncounted giant figures stood pointing at Clive Folliot.
Pointing at him from above and beneath, from every side.
And every one of them was himself, as infant or as youth
or as wizened gaffer. Every one of them was himself.

"I am the Master of the Ordolite," he said to them
softly.

"You are that," they chorused.

He began to drift toward the star-world that was the
true center of the spiral.

His many other selves trailed behind him as if on single-
file parade.

CHAPTER 25

Master Versus Master

He stood on a glowing surface of pearl white, a surface that curved away and seemed to rise to a distant horizon. The appearance of this world was the same in whatever direction he faced. Left and right, above and below, there was nothing but glowing whiteness.

With a thought to find some feature or denizen of this world, he tried walking. A hundred yards or so in one direction. The only way he could measure distance was by counting paces, for there was neither object nor inhabitant by which to judge his location; the prospect at the end of his walk was identical to that at its inception.

"Are you here?" he called.

Surprisingly, his voice echoed. But there was no response. He searched his garment for an object with which to experiment, found a royal sovereign in his pocket, and threw it against the white surface that served here as earth. The glittering coin bounced back as high as his waist. He caught it with a sweep of his hand and returned it to his pocket.

He heard a distant buzzing sound, as of a single giant insect. Peering in all directions, hoping to locate the hornet or bee or whatever it was that had made the sound, he saw a distant speck against the featureless white sky. He squinted, shaded his eyes with one hand, strained to make out the speck.

It grew larger, accompanied by an increase in the loudness of the buzzing.

He recognized its shape—it was the Japanese machine which his descendant Annabelle Leigh had obtained at

New Kwajalein Atoll. Even though there was no discernible source of illumination in this world, light glinted from the Nakajima as it tilted and turned in its aerial course.

Clive waved eagerly, and felt his heart leap with joy as the Nakajima waggled its wings. Annie had seen him! She was headed toward him! Based on the apparent size of the Nakajima and the pace at which it was growing, he knew that it would take a fair while to arrive, but he was overjoyed nonetheless.

He heard his name called, and he whirled to find himself confronting a quartet of individuals.

There stood Amos Ransome, garbed in his dour clergyman's outfit of black frock-coat and white ecclesiastical collar. Beside him stood his sister or wife; her true identity had never been revealed. Lorena Ransome's hair was pulled back in a severe bun. Her dress was black, and covered her from neck to ground and from shoulder to wrist. But to Clive's astonishment, her face had been made up and painted like a hoyden's, with long, artificial eyelashes, unrealistic rosy spots on the cheeks, and lips the color of blood.

And the bodice of her dress had two circular cut-outs within which her tender skin was reddened with paint like that of an ancient Babylonian temple woman.

Framing Lorena Ransome on the side opposite Amos was Philo B. Goode, the bogus American mining magnate. He wore his broad-brimmed hat, stringlike cravat, brocaded waistcoat, wide-lapelled jacket, and intricately carved boots.

A cheroot protruded from the edge of Amos Ransome's mouth. A smirk marked his countenance. One side of his coat was drawn back and his hand rested on the butt of a silver-plated Colt navy revolver. Clive Folliot could not see the grip of the revolver, but in his heart he knew that it would be of black or midnight blue polished stone set with a spiral of diamonds representing the stars of the Gennine.

"Are you the Gennine?" Clive asked.

"Smile," Philo Goode replied, "when you call me that, pardner."

"Is this the end of the Dungeon?"

"It is, Clive Folliot. There is nowhere farther to go."

"This is the true center of the swirling stars? The home of the Gennine, the ultimate rulers of the Dungeon?"

"It is the home of the Gennine."

A roaring filled Clive's ears and points of light and darkness danced before his eyes. "You are merely people. I encountered you on the *Princess Philippa*. Penny ante gamblers, sharpers, petty cheats. You cannot be the rulers of the Dungeon."

"But we are." It was Lorena Ransome who had spoken. She slipped her hand from her companion's neck and advanced toward Clive. He stared, his eyes drawn, against his will, to her bodice. He had seen women naked and half naked on a half-dozen continents and on a dozen worlds, but never had he seen one who attracted and excited him as did Lorena Ransome.

"Stay back!"

"Clive."

"I resisted the fire-succubus!"

"An illusion. A figment of your own mind."

"I knew the Lady 'Nrrc'kth, the woman T'Nembi of Bagomoyo, females human and alien of world upon world."

"Then why fear me, Clive?" She slid her black-clad arms around his neck and pressed her lips against his own. Amos Ransome and Philo Goode dropped from his consciousness. He could think only of this woman, of Lorena Ransome. She had cast a spell upon Horace Hamilton Smythe, Clive knew, during Smythe's long-ago sojourn in wild America. Was she doing the same to him now?

He grew dizzy, felt himself falling into a state of vertigo. He could no longer identify the directions of up and down in this pearl-white world, could no longer discern the nearby from the distant. He could feel Lorena Ransome's long fingers beneath his garments, could not prevent his own hands from moving over her form.

"Good, Clive. Yes, Clive. Yes!"

A shrill voice was piping and a small weight leaped upon his back. He could feel tiny feet kicking at his neck and then a point of excruciating fire behind his ear.

Blinking and slapping at his neck, he leaped to his feet. A miniature Baron Samedi was prancing in circles, pointing at Clive with his omnipresent cigar. "Fool, fool, fool!" the baron shrilled. "Slave to your gonads! Goat! Behold your strumpet!"

Lorena Ransome stood scowling at Clive and at Baron Samedi. She was something hideous and terrible, something hardly human. It was as if the evil in human nature had been distilled and concentrated and reconstituted into a being of pure malignity.

Something furry collided with Clive's leg and he glanced downward to see that the miniature Samedi—apparently the Chaffri, the being that had somehow survived the dissolution of the space-train, reacting to some desperate subconscious thought of Clive's—had found its way here and had changed still again. It was now a miniature Finnbogg, massive in form and substance despite its diminutive stature, caninesque in its fidelity.

Lorena was the ultimate in evil, Lilith, the night monster of the Hebrew Book of Isaiah. She pointed a shriveled finger at Clive and screeched, "I'll get you, Clive Folliot!" She raised a second finger, pointed it crookedly at Finnbogg.

"You and your little dog, too!"

The Chaffri/Samedi/Finnbogg hurled itself at the far larger Lorena Ransome. Together they tumbled to the pearl-white ground, rolling over and over. Amos Ransome entered the fray, struggling to pull the tiny Finnbogg from Lorena. The man's curses, the woman's screeches, the canine's snarls blended to make a mad cacophony.

Clive watched, petrified.

A cold drop spattered off Clive's face. It was followed by others. He looked up and saw that somehow the featureless glowing sky had been occluded by a massive array of black, roiling clouds. Lightning flashed, thunder rolled, sheets and torrents of rain swept the pearl-white earth.

With a scream and a hiss, Lorena Ransome and her attacker dissolved before Clive's horrified eyes.

Philo B. Goode drew his nickel-plated navy Colt. "I'd planned a more elaborate end for you than this, Folliot. You are the Master of the Ordolite, don't you know?"

"I am he, Philo Goode. Consider the meaning of that, and conduct yourself accordingly."

"You survived more challenges than I thought you would.

More than I thought you *could*." He ground his teeth audibly, then gave himself a shake. "Sometimes the simplest means is the best." He raised the Colt and pointed it directly at Clive's face.

Clive thought of the Mandarin who had saved his life repeatedly. The Mandarin who seemed to possess supernormal, even supernatural, powers. The Mandarin who had proved to be none other than Clive's old friend and onetime batman Horace Hamilton Smythe.

He could see the tightness on Goode's face, the infinitesimal tightening of his finger on the Colt's trigger. Through some oddity of light and direction he caught a glimpse of the revolver's grip—polished stone of midnight blue picked with a spiral of glittering diamonds that swirled madly even as he stared, transfixed.

He could hear the soft click of the moving trigger, the slow explosion of the powder. A flare of red flame and gray smoke poured from the muzzle of the Colt, and from it emerged the solid lead ball, whirling as it flew across the space that separated Philo B. Goode from Clive Folliot.

The Master of the Ordolite slowed the passage of time until the bullet was barely moving. Clive smiled. So slowly that each muscular rearrangement was individually visible, Philo Goode reflected a grimace of bafflement and rage.

Clive parted his lips in an expression of benevolence, opened his teeth a fraction of an inch, closed them again upon the flying bullet. He permitted its velocity to spin him a full 360 degrees.

He faced Philo Goode once again and spat.

The bullet flew toward Goode, smashed his ribs, tore his heart to shreds. Blood spattered and rained on the still-wet ground. He toppled backward, the Colt flying from his hand.

Clive caught the whirling weapon and shoved it into his waistband. He faced the sole figure who remained with him: Timothy Francis Xavier O'Hara, priest.

"Ye did mightily well, lad." O'Hara nodded, his broad scalp showing pinkly against its thin fringe of white hair. "But what d'ye plan to do now? Ye don't think ye're goin' t' shoot me with that great cannon, do ye?" O'Hara pointed at the Colt.

Clive shook his head. "I didn't come here to shoot anyone, Father."

"Forget the Father business. I dumped that long ago!"

"What is this place?"

"The home of the Gennine."

"Who are the Gennine?"

"I am the last of the Gennine. We're an ancient race, Clive Folliot. Long, long ago we realized that we were dying out. We did everything we could to save ourselves—to no avail. So we created the Dungeon to amuse ourselves. To while away the time."

"It was all . . . for your *amusement*?"

"Yes."

"And now?"

"Now I'm all that's left—and I shall go, as well. You're the only one who reached this place, Clive. You should be proud. How many millions have entered the Dungeon— some who died fighting, some who settled down and made a new life for themselves there, some few who escaped and returned to their own worlds. Oh, very, very few of those. But there were some who did, yes."

He shook his gleaming head. "But now you've made it to the home of the Gennine."

"Are you human?"

"Eh?" O'Hara had raised his hand to his chin, dropped his gaze to his feet in abstracted concentration.

"I said, are you human? Or are you something else? I've seen shape-changers enough in this mad adventure."

O'Hara shook his head as if he could hardly comprehend the question. Somewhere the distant buzzing sound had grown louder, and Clive looked up to see the sun glinting on his great-great-granddaughter Annie's Nakajima 97. The aeroplane was close now, dipping toward the ground, its propeller whirling, its wheels reaching to touch the earth.

"I don't know, lad. Human, not human? What am I now?" He raised a hand to his eyes and looked at it. Clive thought the puzzlement in O'Hara's face was real. "I can't remember. I just can't remember. How was it that God made me?"

"God?" Clive exclaimed. "I thought you'd renounced your priesthood."

The Nakajima was closer, its engine's sound louder. How could O'Hara not hear it?

"I was a weak priest, Clive. Not God's fault. Mine. I wish I could hear a voice call me Father once more, and know that I was worthy of the name. That it was not a mockery or a rebuke to me. Oh, how I wish for that!"

A shudder wracked his body. "Not you, Folliot. Don't you call me Father again. You know me too well for that. The things I've done—the cruelties I've done—I and all the Gennine! Was I human at the outset? If only I could be forgiven. Not by God, but by one whom I've wronged. By one being who suffered at my hands." He studied his hands, holding them both before his eyes. Clive Folliot saw tears in those eyes.

"I forgive you," Clive said.

Timothy F. X. O'Hara smiled. "Thank you, Folliot. Thank you." He crumpled to the pearl-white ground and lay still.

Clive Folliot stood alone, staring into the sky. The spiral of stars, which had lured him and guided his destiny for so long, now revolved about him. He had become its center.

A chill ran down his spine and left him trembling. It was a chill provoked not by cold air, but by the reaction to his position. From the role of cadet son to a minor country house, he had risen above all others. The title of Baron Tewkesbury would pass through Neville's line rather than his own, but that was the most trivial of concerns.

He was more than a baron, more than an emperor. He was the Master of the Ordolite.

A soft wind caressed his cheek, whispered in his ear. Or perhaps it was a voice. Or a chorus of voices. Did he hear the disembodied tones of George du Maurier? Of his two brothers, one unborn and the second now gone across the shadowy line that separates the living from the dead? Did he hear the voice of the Lady 'Nrrc'kth, and that of her brother N'wrbb Crrd'f? Did he hear the voices of the women he had loved in his life, and of his other companions, allies and foes alike, in his quest through the Dungeon?

He thought he heard other voices, too—Father O'Hara and Madame Mesmer and spidery Shriek and Chang Guafe and gruff hearty Finnbogg. Tomàs Folliot and Baron Samedi and the Imperial Japanese Marines he had encountered at New Kwajalein: Lieutenant Takamura and Lieutenant Yamura, Sergeant Fushida and Private Onishi. The passengers and officers he had known aboard *Empress Philippa*, the partners in the sinister Ransome/Goode/O'Hara scheme and the officials of the Universal Neighborhood Improvement Association. The Sultan of Zanzibar and the men and women he had encountered during his time in Equatoria.

The gentle breeze became a raging cyclone, the whispering voice a roaring chorus of men and women, alien creatures and artificial monsters.

The Ren.

The Chaffri.

And the Gennine.

He was the Master of the Ordolite.

A single voice emerged from the cacophonous roar. "Clive, what will you do now?" It was the voice of George du Maurier. "You are the most powerful of men. Perhaps the most powerful being in the universe."

"I am not God," Clive said.

"Still . . ."

"I don't know, du Maurier. I have striven so long. Now that my strife is completed, may I not rest for a while? The Buddhists of India, upon reaching a certain age, renounce their belongings, their occupations, even their families. They shave their heads, don saffron robes, and wander the land, their only other possession a begging bowl from which to eat brown rice."

"Does that appeal to you, Folliot?"

"I knew a farmer once, du Maurier. A fine fellow. Perhaps, if I live many years, I might become like him."

"Then there are no more worlds to conquer, no more challenges to meet?"

"Glory has lost its charm, du Maurier."

"Are there then no more wrongs to right?"

Clive nodded. "Someday, perhaps. But for now, I am weary, my friend. Weary."

Du Maurier made no comment in parting. The chorus faded, the voices stilled.

But there was another sound, a faint buzzing that had grown louder and louder even as Clive Folliot turned to follow the course of the machine that was its source.

The Nakajima 97 touched its wheels to the glowing ground. The sound of its engine ceased as Annabelle Leigh cut the ignition. The aeroplane rolled to a stop.

Annie climbed from the cockpit and ran to Clive Folliot's side. She took his two hands in her own.

"I've come to take you home, Grandfather."

Clive looked into Annie's face and wept.

Selections
From the Sketchbook
of Major Clive Folliot

The following drawings are from Major Clive Folliot's private sketchbook, which was mysteriously left on the doorstep of *The London Illustrated Recorder and Dispatch,* the newspaper that provided financing for his expedition. There was no explanation accompanying the parcel, save for an enigmatic inscription in the hand of Major Folliot himself.

"Our revels," as the bard said, "now are ended." My friend Du Maurier's hand is no longer available to improve my poor efforts, but I have his model and his advice to guide me. Let these last portraits be my farewell to a great and dramatic phase of my life.

The fires of vengeance have burned themselves out. Was my adventure a success? I have achieved a glory beyond my dreams, but at the cost of dear Annabella, and of my own brother's life. More than anything else, I am weary now, and shall rest until I am needed again.

HERE IS THE GREAT LOOMING FIGURE OF BARON FRANKENSTE MONSTER, AS WE FOUND HIM IN THE ICE.

THE GREAT FLYING TRAIN CAME DOWN TO MELT OUR BOAT OF ICE — TO SAVE US OR TO DROWN US?

HAIL AND FAREWELL, OLD FRIEND.
GEORGE DU MAURIER AS I LAST SAW HIM.

PHILO GOODE, WHO NEVER
LIVED UP TO HIS NAME,
AND HIS HELLISH—
STAIRWAY INTO THE
BOWELS OF
LONDON.

TWO OF THE CHAFFRI SOLDIE
WHO ATTACKED ALONG
THE RAILWAY TO
TEWKESBURY.

MY FATHER - NO,
ANOTHER SIMULACRUM,
BUT THIS TIME, AT LEA:
THE MANOR WAS
AUTHENTIC.

CHANG GUAFE, AS
HE TRANSFORMED HIMSELF
IN THE SEA; BARON
SAMEDI. AIDES,
COMPANIONS, FRIENDS
WHOSE COMPANY
I WILL MISS.

ABOVE,

THE FIERY
DOOR FROM
PHILO GODDE'S OFFICE
AT THE PUBLIC HOUSE.

VEHICLES OF PASSAGE
THROUGH SPACE
AND TIME:
THE CAR
THAT
CARRIED SGT.
SMYTHE, SIDI BOMBAY,
AND MYSELF ...

... AND THE INSECTILE SHIPS OF THE REN.

AT THE CHAFFRI MILITARY
ENCAMPMENT, A BUILDING APPEARED,
THUS TO ME: SNARES AND DELUSIONS!

MY BELOVED
ANNABELLA, A
DISGUISE FOR ONE
OF THE CHAFFRI

FOR ONCE IN THIS ADVENTURE
A TRUE FACE — A CHAFFRI IN ITS CAGE

MY GRAND·NIECE —
A WOMAN SOLDIER!
ANNA MARIA·
FOLLIOT.

PERHAPS I SHALL NEVER
TRULY UNDERSTAND WHAT
MOVED MY BROTHER
NEVILLE, BUT I CAN
NOW, TOO LATE,
FORGIVE HIM.

THESE DEMONS TESTED
ME EN ROUTE TO THE
HOME OF THE
GENNINE.

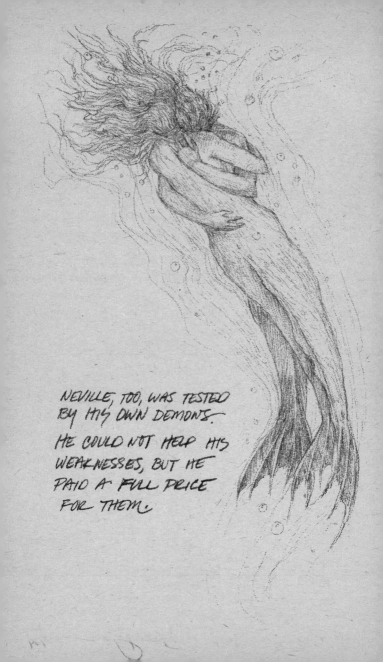

NEVILLE, TOO, WAS TESTED
BY HIS OWN DEMONS.

HE COULD NOT HELP HIS
WEAKNESSES, BUT HE
PAID A FULL PRICE
FOR THEM.

WHEN I NEEDED HIS AID ONE LAST TIME, CHANG GUAFE BECAME MY TRANSPORTATION.

AT LAST THE STORY ENDS. ALL MY TORMENTORS, ALL MY COMPANIONS ARE GONE, SAVE ONLY MY BELOVED DESCENDANT, ANNABELLE. GOOD RIDDANCE TO MY FOES, GOODBYE TO MY FRIENDS. LET US FIND SOME PEACE WHILE WE CAN.

Robert Gould 7/89